BABY DOLL
A NOVEL BY DIVINE G

Also by Divine G

Novels:

Money-Grip (Published by Q-Boro Books)

Money-Grip 2 (Published by Divine G Entertainment)

Enigma of Love (Published by Divine G Entertainment)

The Canarsie Connection (Published by Divine G Entertainment)

No Other Love (Published by Divine G Entertainment)

TGONG (Published by Divine G Entertainment)

Time Jack (Published by Divine G Entertainment)

Short Stories:

Averted Hearts (appearing in The Game, published by Triple Crown Publications)

Stage Plays:

Peak-Zone (appearing in Exiled Voices, Portals of Discovery, published by New England College Press)

Films:

Sing Sing (Co-writer of the A24 movie *Sing Sing*)

ISBN-10: 1-940765-43-9

ISBN-13: 978-1-940765-43-3

Draft2Digital Paperback Print Edition

First Paperback Published by Urban Books

Written by: Divine G

Edited by: Divine G

For information contact: Divine G Entertainment

Website: http://www.divinegentertainment.com

Email: divinegentertainment@gmail.com

Dedication

This novel is dedicated to the numerous family members, friends and associates who were very instrumental in helping me to get this novel written, edited and published. The list of supporters is so huge and extensive, I am very apprehensive about attempting to mention names, because from past experience, if anyone is inadvertently left out and feels he or she should have been mentioned, it creates a lot of bad feelings. So, this time, I am taking the safe road by sending out a universal dedication to all those who played a part in the success of this novel, without itemizing each individual name. If you were there, by my side, had my back, and was supportive, then you are the person I am referring to when I send out this dedication. This novel is dedicated to you for being there when times got extremely rough, rocky and raw. Once again, thanks for all the support, love and understanding.

CHAPTER 1

Breana "Baby Doll" Winbush swung at Nicole when she came rushing at her with a violent overhand right. Nicole's wild, uncoordinated swing just missed Baby Doll as she weaved the blow and caught Nicole just below the left eye with a straight right jab, causing a muttered shriek to escape from Nicole's lips.

Nicole was twice Baby Doll's size, but that didn't mean shit to Baby Doll, since she was used to these odds.

Nicole was furious now, especially since her five schoolmates and friends were standing on the sideline watching and rooting for her. Her bull-dagger features were growing manlier by the seconds.

Baby Doll saw the rage and embarrassment in Nicole's eyes; she was about to get real ghetto. The second Nicole rushed in again, Baby Doll blessed her with a two-piece.

Nicole's knees wobbled as she jumped away as though she had just touched a hot stove.

"Come on bitch!" Baby Doll said menacingly in a smooth and venomous tone. She saw Nicole trying to regain her bearings, and wondered should she rush in for the knock-out.

"You think I'm soft!?" Baby Doll's drop-dead gorgeous persona, along with her caramel complexion and chinky exotic eyes were now drenched with a viciousness that didn't fit her age.

She was sixteen years old, but from the way she danced around with her fists cocked, she looked more like a mixture of an Olympian boxer and a beauty pageant contestant. They say growing up in the hood had a remarkable way of epitomizing the saying "only the strong survive," and Baby Doll was a classic example of that fact.

The crowd of five schoolgirls looked on with jealous and envious eyes while rooting Nicole on. All of them were Nicole's friends, but Baby Doll didn't care. She wasn't unfamiliar with being picked on, while confronting totally uneven odds.

A crowd started to form as several other Canarsie High School students rushed over to watch the fight.

"Punch that bitch in her face, Nicole!" a teen with sleepy eyes shouted. "Beat her ass, girl."

"Fuck that conceited bitch up!" Nicole's best friend Jada shouted while clutching her schoolbooks close to her chest.

Nicole stood huffing and puffing with exhaustion and rage; her hesitancy was a clear indication that she was scared, and she was hoping nobody noticed.

Baby Doll saw Nicole was fronting by the look in her eyes, and was wasting her time, so she decided to end this bullshit, right here and now. She stepped toward Nicole while unleashing four swift, left jabs. Two of them hit their target: Nicole's nose. After implementing this setup maneuver, Baby Doll let loose a vicious overhand right to her jaw that took Nicole down to the pavement as if a rug was snatched from under her feet.

Staring down a Nicole clutching her jaw, Baby Doll said, "You better stay your big ass down, or—" Baby Doll saw Jada rushing at her and she turned to give her a piece of the action, but before she could turn completely around, she felt a hard blow to the back of her head.

Oh, so you bitches are gonna me! Baby Doll stumbled slightly from the sucker punch and started swinging savagely, not completely surprised the girls were now ganging up on her. In fact, she was kinda expecting this since it was obvious they were cowards and bullies, and just like cowards and bullies, they never did the "fair fight" thing.

Jada caught a fist to the nose, and like the coward she was, she quickly pulled back from the fight out of fear of messing up her hair or getting a permanent scar on her face. In an instant, she decided to wait for the others to get Baby Doll in a position where she didn't have to put in too much work.

As Baby Doll and the four remaining girls were going at it toe-to-toe, Nicole sprung to her feet and got back into the fight with a wicked kick to Baby Doll's stomach.

Baby Doll saw stars twirling before her eyes and felt the wind shot from her body; she instantly knew she was in serious trouble when her knees buckled. *My face! They're gonna mess up my face!* She covered her face as the blows rained down upon her head; she knew the sole reason they hated her was because of her beauty. Everybody hated her because she was utterly beautiful, and these ugly, no-boyfriend-getting bitches were just like all the rest. Even her mother and two sisters despised her because of the way she looked. To say she earned the name Baby Doll because she looked just like one would have been a gross understatement.

As Baby Doll weaved with her fists and arms shielding her face, looking like Muhammad Ali doing his infamous rope-pa-dope, she sensed her attackers were becoming even more enraged because they couldn't scratch and pound her face, and she was still able to get off punches despite the uneven odds.

Jada, however, was an expert at dirty fighting, and so she swung her leg in sweeping fashion and tripped Baby Doll.

Baby Doll fell hard to the concrete, allowing her forearms to cushion the fall and the terror gripped her because it was obvious they were going to stomp her out.

The moment she hit the pavement, the Nike sneakers, and soft and hard sole shoes started raining down upon her from all directions, aimed at all parts of her body, but Baby Doll protected her face, and prayed that someone would come to her rescue. When she realized she had no friends in this school, she held back the tears of rage, and rode the waves of this ass whipping like a true project trooper, vowing to get each one of these bitches back in the worse kind of way.

* * * *

Tera Smalls was behind the wheel of her cranberry red Ranger Rover Jeep with her uncle, Big Daddy Blue, in the passenger seat. Jodeci's "Stay" was blaring through the radio tuned to 98.7 Kiss FM, and Tera was tapping her foot to the beat. She was cruising down Rockaway Parkway, and it was obvious it was around three o'clock, since the high school students were moving about in droves. Despite her outwardly uppity mood, she was still upset that she had to drive her uncle to the club, since both of his cars were in the repair shop. As she was still contemplating how she was going to get Big Daddy to the club and get to her inventory meeting without being too late, she saw a huge crowd up ahead. Upon closer scrutiny, she saw it was a fight between a group of schoolgirls. The light turned red, and she brought the Jeep to a stop directly across from the commotion.

"Look at this foolishness," Big Daddy Blue said disgustedly as he watched the group of five teens trying to lay down a vicious beating on another teen. Images of the Rodney King beating and several similar vicious gang assaults at various prisons he was once housed at flashed across his mind. Just before they brought the girl down to the pavement, and started stomping her, he was able to see the victim's face, and as pretty as the young girl looked, and as hard looking as the attackers appeared, it was clear this was a case of young women's envious emotions gone wild. The sight turned his stomach upside down, and the urge to do something grew to an unbearable level. After a moment, he sighed and said, "Double park the car, Tera."

"Come on, Big Daddy," Tera shifted in her seat, realizing she was definitely going to be late now. "These young folks are crazy out here. It ain't like it was back in the day. They got guns, and don't mind using them, either. We need to mind our business."

"Just pull the damn car over," Big Daddy Blue demanded. "These children are our business. That's why the neighborhood is fucked-up the way it is; 'cause folks turning their backs when they supposed to be stepping up."

Tera sighed angrily, realizing it was futile to try to convince Big Daddy to look the other way once his mind was made up; she made a right turn when the traffic light turned green, and double-parked the Jeep.

Big Daddy Blue zipped out the vehicle with remarkable agility despite the fact he was fifty-nine with a head and face full of salt and pepper hair. The way he handled his medium built frame, the average person would've thought he was in his early forties. He yelled at the top of his lungs. "Hey, what's this!?"

Nicole and the others stopped on a dime, feet suspended in midair. One of the girls took off running, thinking it was the police; one more arrest and she was on her way to juvy. Jada scurried away, picked up her books from the ground and was about to run until see saw Tera approaching dressed in a sexy mini-skirt while styling the latest hood-oriented hair style and knew instantly that these people weren't cops.

Big Daddy Blue marched toward Baby Doll, who was curled up with her arms covering her head.

The girls who were stomping her moved out of Big Daddy's way with frantic haste as though a Mack truck was about to run them over. The bulk of the crowd of on-lookers started dispensing, realizing the fun was over.

Nicole spoke with an attitude, "Y'all need to mind y'all fuckin' business."

Big Daddy Blue ignored the comment as he kneeled and shook Baby Doll's shoulder. "You all right down there?"

She eased her arms down from her head; he saw she was indeed a pretty little dime piece and a half. Her infant, but regal facial features were super star model material if he ever saw one.

"It's all right. Come on, get up." Big Daddy rose to his feet.

"I don't know who the fuck y'all think y'all are," Nicole said in a real nasty manner. "Y'all rolling up like y'all running shit around this mu—"

"What you said!?" Tera stepped straight to Nicole and saw this big mouth, disrespectful chick needed an eye opener. She moved toward Nicole with a devious smile. "What if I slapped your disrespectful ass into next week!?"

Nicole stepped away, now scared out of her mind because it was obvious this woman had hood written all over her. *Wow, this lady ain't playin'!*

A male teen wearing baggy jeans, and a baseball cap turned backwards, was closely observing Big Daddy Blue and realized who he was. He inched over to Nicole and whispered in her ear. "Be easy, stupid! That's Big Daddy Blue! That nigga's a real O.G. He just came home from doing thirty years on lock down. He got mad shit in the smash; clubs and shit all over the place!"

Big Daddy Blue helped Baby Doll to her feet; he was about to go into one of his gang prevention lectures he'd utilized when he was a part of a prison youth outreach Program in an effort to talk some sense into these girls, but the moment this pretty little girl was fully onto her feet, she jetted toward the bigger girl.

In a flash, Baby Doll got off a vicious overhand right that dropped Nicole. It looked as though a rug was viciously snatched from under her feet by the way she rapidly collapsed to the pavement.

Big Daddy Blue didn't budge an inch as Tera went after Baby Doll and pulled her away immediately after she got off the blow.

The other girls were gearing up for another attack. Some of the boys made comments designed to instigate another round of fighting.

Sensing the situation was about to blow out of control, Big Daddy Blue went to Baby Doll, gently took her arm. "We'll give you a ride home, okay." He escorted her toward the Jeep.

Baby Doll didn't resist. It didn't take a scholar to see that she wasn't going to make it home on the bus without having to fight every step of the way. As she headed toward the Jeep, she scooped up her book bag, feeling good knowing she got the last hit in. That, according to her standards, made her the winner, even though they got the most hits in, and stomped the shit out of her.

Baby Doll got in the back seat while Tera got back behind the wheel and Big Daddy Blue in the passenger seat.

The Jeep sped away.

Baby Doll sat looking mean and ready to continue fighting if she had to. She decided to keep her guards up, since she knew that children her age were being kidnapped every day and that this could be a setup. She looked around to make sure the doors had a lock button that she could control and made a mental note that they did. Meanwhile, she heard the lady on the cell phone telling someone she was going to be late.

Big Daddy Blue turned in his seat and said, "What's your name?"

Baby Doll thought about the question, wondering should she give him her real name or her nickname. She stared into the old man's eyes, and she truly didn't feel scared or threatened. In fact, she felt a profound sense of security. She'd never had a father figure in her life, and realized if she could have one, she would probably want one that looked like this man. It was like his smile resonated a loving vibration. She decided to go with the nickname. "Baby Doll."

"That's a pretty name, Baby Doll," Big Daddy Blue said. "It fits you to a tee." After a moment, he probed further. "And where you live, Baby Doll? If you don't tell us, we can't drop you off."

"I live in Brownsville in Tilden Projects. You can drop me off right on Livonia Avenue near the 3 train, and I'll be alright from there. And what's y'all names?"

"I'm Tera," she said from behind the wheel, realizing she was going the wrong way and would have to take a hard right at the next turn. She turned on the Bobby Brown CD, her favorite R&B artist. The song, "Rock Wit Cha," seeped through the car's stereo system in a whisper-like fashion.

Big Daddy Blue faced front, and then said. "Well, they call me Big Daddy Blue." Before she could start asking why, he continued. "What's a pretty girl like you doing fighting in the middle of the streets?"

"'Cause I don't let jealous bitches fuck over me any ole way they want to." The energy within Baby Doll's words was as serious as a pissed-off pirate who'd just lost the map to his hidden treasure.

Tera nodded her head to that with a smile and said, "Sounds like my kinda girl. Full of spunk and feisty as hell. That means they was fuckin' with you and you showed them a thing or two."

Big Daddy Blue gave Tera a disappointed expression. He knew violence was a fact of urban life, but he also believed these young folk had to find better ways to deal with their differences. "So, what grade are you in, Baby Doll?"

"Tenth grade," she said, watching the people strutting along Rockaway Parkway, entering and exiting stores and other shops. Suddenly, the pessimistic component of her mind started coming to life. *Why did they stop to help me?* it wanted to know. They definitely didn't do it because they liked her. Nobody liked her.

Everybody hated her. And even all her friends were nothing but a bunch of fakes that only wanted to be with her when they could get something out of her. Definitely every nigga in the hood was out for some pussy, point blank and simple. Then, suddenly, a revelation dawned on her. *Yeah, that's what it is; this old ass nigga wants a piece of this young pussy, and this bourgeois chick is some kind of freak bitch or something, cause she's gonna help him.*

After tumbling this scenario around in her mind, she shot it down because the old man, didn't seem like a pervert. He was nothing like her mother's boyfriend Kevin, who was the ultimate pervert. But why did they help her? After toying with the question, she realized that maybe they really cared about her. She needed to search further, and so she put on her tactician hat and decided to start picking their brains. It couldn't hurt, since if they got crazy she could simply break out at a stoplight. "Why y'all stop to help me?"

Big Daddy Blue turned and faced Baby Doll. "I stopped because I think it's wrong to turn your back when someone is getting beat-up by a gang."

"But what if they was in the right? What if the person they ganged up on did some foul shit and was getting what they deserve? Would that still make it wrong?"

Big Daddy Blue smiled. He was impressed, since it was clear shorty was real sharp, and was trying to pick his brain. "Well, let's put this way. I'm from the old school, and we old-timers got a good eye for detecting coward moves. It don't take six people to stomp someone out, even if the person gettin' stomped out was in the wrong. Plus, I know how school kids are and how they got this way of dealing with pretty folks such as yourself."

Baby Doll lit up with something she couldn't describe. He understood her situation. She felt funny hearing those words indicating he knew they assaulted her because she was pretty. That bitch Nicole thought she was trying to mess with her ugly ass, bad breath boyfriend, Abar, and had stepped to her pointing her finger in her face, talking all this shit about she was going to fuck her up after school.

Baby Doll scanned Big Daddy's eyes and saw the sincerity in them were just as genuine as his words had sounded, and they didn't make her feel uncomfortable about her beautiful looks. After spending her entire life around folks that literally hated her because she was "pretty" and "cute", it was refreshing to finally come in contact with someone who wasn't out to hurt her because they were jealous of the way she looked.

Tera chimed in as she pulled the Jeep to a halt at a stoplight at the intersection of Rockaway and Linden Blvd. "To be honest with you Baby Doll, I wanted to keep going, but Big Daddy made me stop. But, after meeting you, I'm kinda glad we stopped. I like your style shorty. You got boss in your blood, girl, and all you gotta to do is get you a plan, stick with it, and you'll be a'ight."

She saw Big Daddy Blue's familiar smile of approval, and knew she scored a major point with him. She never fully understood why he was so fond of helping these badass kids in the hood, especially since he stayed getting stung by them. Just recently two of them tried to rob one of his clubs in East New York. She often suspected he was doing this with the kids because of all that time he did in prison and he was trying to make up for not being there for his own four children, who apparently grew up without a father. "You not only look like a fighter, Baby Doll, but also a winner. I can see it in your eyes, the way you walk and talk and think. And especially from the way you popped that big bitch in the mouth." She heard Baby Doll respond humorously to her comment, and she smiled. "Just don't waste or throw away your gifts like so many of the kids growing up in this place."

Baby Doll sat silently, allowing their words to churn inside her mind. She was blown away by their remarks. These people were acting like real friends, and they obviously liked her. They'd just met her, and already they showed her more love than she'd ever received from her entire family. Not only that, but she could also see they had big cheddar. By the way Big Daddy was dressed, he wasn't no bum ass dude, that's for sure. And this fancy-ass Jeep Tera was wheeling had to cost some major loot. But the most outstanding thing of all was . . . They were obviously feelin' her!

They said they loved a fighter!? Well, once they got to know her they were really gonna love her! This really started causing her nature to rise because she was certain they were going to go head over hills for her, since she was a master hood fighter by all standards.

She'd been fighting since the day she came out her mother's womb, and fighting was a thing she did better than anything else, since she was taught by some of the best; in fact, fighting came easy, since her sisters, her mom and her so-called friends made sure of that. It was time to go in deep. Find out more about them and see if she could use it to her advantage. "So what y'all do for a living?"

"I'm what you might call an entrepreneur," Big Daddy said, his voice deep with pride and confidence. "I work in the entertainment and retail businesses."

He's a businessman! That's why he's dressed like that. Baby Doll smiled as she spoke. "So you do stuff like Puff Daddy. You get people into the rap game!?"

Big Daddy turned and faced her, "Not that kind of businessman. I own the places where rappers perform. I own clubs and other businesses like clothing stores, stuff like that. You probably don't know much about clubs, but those are—"

"Why not?" Baby Doll said, almost offended. "I been to mad clubs before. I be sneaking in and everything."

Tera and Big Daddy laughed.

Tera said through her chuckles, "I'm also a businesswoman. I'm the manager of a Hair Salon, and a clothing store in Albee Square Mall. Big Daddy here is not only my uncle, but my boss as well."

She felt proud talking about what she did in light of the fact she came a very long way. She grew up much like Baby Doll, in the projects, poor with low self-esteem, battling against drugs, prostitution, and horrific abuses, even though her father and two uncles were the founders of one of the biggest drug organizations in Brooklyn and were eventually snatched away from the family when she was around seven years old and were sentenced to numerous decades in prison. Big Daddy was the only one who made it out alive.

Big Daddy faced front. "So what you wanna be when you grow up, Baby Doll?"

Baby Doll smiled because she sure did have a dream. She'd known what she wanted to be by the time she was old enough to comprehend the Jet, Ebony and Essence Magazines she enjoyed looking at. It wasn't like she was interested in any particular profession, like becoming a nurse, a lawyer, or scientist. She was more geared toward an outcome and would become anything as long as it could help her get to that outcome. She wanted to be rich! Filthy rich! Dirty rich! Ugly or beautifully rich! Rich! Rich! Rich!

A long time ago, she figured out that everybody who was somebody was rich. They had money, and everybody loved them. It went without saying that if she could become rich like those beautiful women in the magazines, she could stop everybody from hating her, envying her, stabbing her in the back, the rapes would stop, as well as the abuse, and people fucking her over for the dumbest shit imaginable. She had another dream, but she knew she couldn't share that one with anybody.

Baby Doll drew in a small breath of air and said with resounding energy, "I wanna be rich." She then recited Lil-Kim's adage to give her comment its proper emphasis. "Money, power and respect. Once you get the money, you get the power, and then you get the respect."

Tera smiled as she made the right turn onto Livonia Avenue and pulled the car to the curb. "Is this good enough?"

Baby Doll saw she was back in her old broken-down, beat-up hood, and said boringly. "Yeah, this is good right here."

Tera put the gear in park, turned and faced Baby Doll, and said, "After thirty seven years on this planet, and going through a divorce with two kids a little younger them you, I would say you sound like an old soul, Baby Doll." She smiled and then faced forward.

Baby Doll didn't want to leave and definitely wanted to see more of these people. She was about to give hints, but figured it was best to be herself and come straight out with it. "Hey, how can I keep in touch with y'all? I ain't never talk to peoples as nice as y'all before."

Big Daddy pulled his calling card from his inner breast pocket, turned and handed it to Baby Doll. "Here's, my card."

After Baby Doll took it, he stared deep into her eyes, and an onslaught of memories assaulted his mind. Besides the fact Baby Doll reminded him so much of his deceased daughter Amber, seeing her also made him remember how in prison he used to debate with other prisoners about how to solve the problems in the hood.

His position was always that most of the children were never offered an opportunity to better themselves, and unfortunately, most of the Black folks that could offer opportunities were too mentally and emotionally fucked-up to reach out and help those who were clearly deserving of an opportunity. There was no doubt in his mind this gorgeous little fighter was hungry and was sharp enough to become something in life. All she needed was an opportunity. In that moment, he decided to give her one and hoped she was smart enough to see it coming, and to utilize it for all it was worth.

"Listen here Baby Doll, how you feel about working after school? You ever had an after-school job before?"

"Yeah," she lied, since she knew where this was going, and wasn't about to say something to mess it up. "I even worked a summer youth job." This was the truth, but she had no intention of telling him she lost that job only after working two weeks, because she had a fight with her supervisor when he kept giving her hints about wanting to fuck her, even though she was only fourteen and he was in his mid-twenties. The lanky, nappy-headed Black man named Clarence Matthew had squeezed her ass and she busted him in the face with a beer bottle. Of course, he lied on her, claiming she attacked him for no reason, and since she wasn't into the snitching business she didn't tell on him; mainly because she knew he could go to jail, and putting people in jail was something she could never get with, especially after her mother made it clear that snitching was a cardinal sin even for the most pettiest of beefs. In the end, she was subsequently fired.

"So what kind a work is it gonna be?"

"It'll be something you'll find interesting," Big Daddy Blue assured her.

Baby Doll's enthralled mind stopped dead in its tracks. Her instincts were telling her to slow down as she remembered Big Daddy was a club owner, and clubs obviously had stripers. "I'm telling you right now, I ain't into showing my ass to a bunch of horny ass niggas, and shit, so if—"

"I look like that kind of person to you?" Big Daddy said smoothly. "What makes you think I'm stupid enough to jeopardize my business by allowing minors to work in one of my spots?" He saw Baby Doll flush with embarrassment. "Take it easy, Baby Doll,

I'm not trying to jerk you around. There are some good people in the world."

Baby Doll wanted to tell him to prove it, since every person she'd ever met had a hidden agenda, and she knew damn well Big Daddy Blue was no exception to the rule. Somehow, some way, he was getting something out of it for helping her.

Big Daddy continued. "Actually, I haven't figured out exactly where I might put you, but in few days, I'll figure it out."

There was a moment of silence.

"Here's what I need you to do," Big Daddy reached in his pocket, retrieved a huge web of money, peeled off a fifty dollar bill and handed to her. "This Saturday, get in a cab and come see me at that address any time after twelve noon. We'll talk and I'll fix you up with a good paying job. You cool with that?" He smiled.

"Yeah, I'm cool with that," Baby Doll said, mesmerized by the fact he gave her so much money just for a cab ride.

Tera spoke with a smile, "You take care, Baby Doll, and I'll be seeing you around. Be careful tomorrow; you got the last hit in, so that big bitch might want some get-back."

She dunked the money in her pocket, and said, "Then I guess I'll have to beat her ass some more." She got out the car as Tera laughed. She closed the door and waved as Tera pulled from the curb.

Baby Doll watched the Jeep fade away down Livonia Avenue, feeling as though she was being pulled into two different emotional directions. Furious because of the beat down, but utterly elated by the fact she could see a major payday hovering on the horizon. As she crossed the street, she knew Big Daddy's job offer was too good to be true. The song by Jermaine Jackson, "Tell me I'm not dreamin'," danced in her mind. Her mom played that song so damn much when she was a kid, every time something happened that was too good to be true that song had a way of popping into her mind.

As she approached her project building, 265 Livonia Avenue, Baby Doll was wondering if it would be a good idea to get her crazy-ass thuggish boyfriend, Ka-Born, to come up to her high school with a few of his homeys, so they could put the fear of God in Nicole, Jada and the rest of their coward-ass crew. One thing that was definite: she was not going to let them bitches get away with what they did to her, even if bringing Ka-Born up to the school might result in somebody seriously getting hurt. He had made it clear to her to never ask him to step to things that didn't call for bullets flying, because that was the only way he knew how to communicate. After considering the foul, dirty shit they did to her, stomping her out when it was a straight-up fair one, and Nicole was twice her size from the jump, she was willing to take it there.

CHAPTER 2

Baby Doll stood in front of the bathroom mirror half naked from the waist up with another mirror in her right hand, checking out the bruises, scraps, scars and other injuries scattered about her body. Her sculptured breasts with prickly nipples stood at attention and had pure youth resonating from them. They weren't outrageously huge, but they were surely much more than a mouth full, but her huge, shapely ass and a tiny waist were her strongest bodily features. Beyond the bathroom door, somewhere in the front of apartment # 5C, she could hear her older sister Tracy cursing out Jasmine (the baby of the family) for eating her hero sandwich she stashed in the refrigerator.

Baby Doll bumped into the cloth hamper as she moved to get a look at the bruise on her left side near the ribcage. She realized she hated this claustrophobic bathroom that matched the small three-bedroom apartment; the closeness of the sink to the bathtub looked like two wrestlers tussling on the canvas and bumping into things was standard practice. In fact, the entire room was no bigger than an oversized closet. As she examined the battle bruises on her shoulders, while struggling to block out the yelling match between her sisters, she was grateful she'd only received a few very minor scraps on her face.

"You better watch your fuckin' mouth!" Tracy screamed. It sounded like she then pushed Jasmine. "I'll slap the shit out your little fast ass!"

Jasmine shot back, "I didn't eat your stuff!" Her ten-year-old voice was squeaky and didn't match her age. She sounded at least five-years younger. "You buggin', Tracy! And you better not push me no more!"

Baby Doll wanted to go out there and tell the both of them to shut the fuck up, but she knew that would be like throwing cooking grease on a blazing fire, since she and Tracy were like archenemies. The deep-set hatred between them was mutual, but Tracy's extreme dislike stem from the fact she was insanely jealous of Baby Doll because of her looks, and she was still harboring animosity over the fact Ka-Born dropped her to get with Baby Doll. The craziest thing about it was that Tracy got caught cheatin' on Ka-Born and couldn't understand why he was shittin' on her. Vibing with her younger sister was Ka-Born's way of getting back at Tracy, and Baby Doll saw it as a golden opportunity. She had this trick-ass nigga splurging and showering her with gifts of all sorts, and she took advantage of every opportunity to fuck with Tracy's emotions, since Tracy had been fucking her over in the worse kind of ways ever since they were mere toddlers.

Some of the atrocious and unspeakable things Tracy did to her made it clear that they were not sisters even though they both came from the same woman's womb. No one could possibly call themselves a sister while standing by, enjoying herself and laughing as a perverted child molester raped her little sister. As though that wasn't foul enough, when Baby Doll tried to tell her mother about the vicious assault, Tracy had taken the side of the rapist, making her look like she was a liar. Her mother's boyfriend, Kevin Brown, apparently had this secret thing for young girls, and because Kevin was daggling a huge secret over her head, threatening to reveal this secret if Baby Doll refused to have sex with him, she was caught up in a vicious Catch-22 situation complete with never ending pain, suffering, and degradation. This, among other things, was the reason Baby Doll couldn't wait to get the hell out of this apartment, away from all these foul motherfuckers! Even their mom, Mildred, hated her, and the manner in which the jealousy often revealed itself made it very clear that it was because she was the finest looking woman in this whole twisted-ass family.

Looking at the rapidly formulating bluish mark on her chin, and the other one near her left temple, Baby Doll promised to tighten up her facial blocking game. The last thing she needed was to let one of these jealous hoes destroy her greatest asset, her beauty. The more she looked at the facial scars, the more she couldn't understand how them bitches slipped in a few hits to her face. She could've sworn she properly covered up.

Baby Doll moved the mirror in her hand while repositioning her body, and saw she had black and blue whelps all over her arms and her back. She pulled her pants down and saw a bruise on her right ass cheek and more on her legs. The more she looked at the bruises, the more her fury grew. There was no doubt, in the morning she was going to be sore and aching like there was no tomorrow. She stepped completely out of her pants, laid them on the hamper and opened the makeshift medicine cabinet just above the sink. She found the rubbing alcohol and the pack of cotton balls and began cleaning up her wounds. The alcohol caused a burning sensation that only served to lock her mind on getting them back. She was never the type to accept mistreatment lying down and was as vindictive as they came. Unfortunately for Nicole and her crew, they would learn this the hard way.

After finishing the alcohol rub-down, Baby Doll exited the bathroom, heading for the front door, planning to get the hell out of this mad house. Since her mind was filled with mixed thoughts of revenge as well as happiness, she felt the need to talk to someone. Jeanette was her ace rolling partner, and it was time to pay her a visit.

As Baby Doll approached Tracy, she saw her eyes lit up with hatred the second they landed on her. She geared up for another fighting match, and before Tracy could open her mouth, Baby Doll made an attempt to shut her down. "Don't look at me, 'cause I ain't have nothing to do with it."

Tracy hunched up her back like a cat as though she was about to pounce on Baby Doll. "Ain't nobody say shit to you, bitch." She knew Baby Doll couldn't have eaten her hero because she just walked in the door, but she was dying to find a reason to start some shit with her and this seemed like the perfect opportunity. "Since you so quick to put your two cent in this, it probably was you who ate my shit."

Baby Doll eased past Tracy and was heading for the door when she felt the violent push. She stopped and turned.

"Don't roll your eyes at me," Tracy said with her eyes brewing with malice. "Mommy ain't here to stop me from fuckin' you up, so you better keep it movin'."

Baby Doll wondered should she beat her ass again as she stared at Tracy with a serious screw face. The bruises from her earlier fight helped her to decide to take Tracy's advice and keep it moving, but not without getting Tracy back by rubbing a nerve the wrong way. "You's a freak for ass whippings, ain't you? No matter how many times I beat flames out your no-fightin' ass, you still keep coming back for more." As she unfastened the lock on the door, Baby Doll decided to hit her below the belt. "If you were that persistent with your men, you might be able to hold on to them, and stop them from riding my bra strap." She zipped out the door as Tracy started cursing and ranking like a lunatic.

Baby Doll decided to slide down to the corner bodega store on Livonia and Rockaway Avenue. As she strutted toward the store Baby Doll decided she was going purchase four forty ounces of Colt 45, a pack of Newports, two big bags of barbecue chips, two pounds of ground beef, a bag of hamburger buns, and two bags of French fries. She knew what Jeanette liked and figured since she had some extra dough, she might as well show some love to the only person who'd ever really showed her some love.

Baby Doll entered the store, waved to the Arab owner whose name she couldn't pronounce, even though he'd been working here for a month and change. The curly black-haired store owner usually would always smile at her in a flirtatious fashion, but today she saw he was cutting his eyes down one of the aisles. Baby Doll grabbed a red shopping basket and went to the freezer near the back of the store. As she opened the freezer door, Baby Doll saw what the owner was hyped up about; two little Black boys, one dark skin while the other was much lighter, both no more than ten years old, were roaming the candy section looking like they were about to shoplift. She shook her head disgustedly because the two kids were a dead giveaway; it turned her stomach to see little shorties stepping to their business on some real reckless shit.

Baby Doll looked the other way and saw the other owner of the store come from the back, pretending he was a shopper, while inconspicuously watching the boys. Baby Doll snatched up four bottles of Colt 45, placed them in the basket, vowing that she was going to mind her business. Basically, she was going to turn her back on the whole situation and let these tacky, sloppy little fools go on and jump out the window, but her heart was talking to her. Her heart was rock hard when dealing with most issues, but it became as soft as baby shit when it came to issues dealing with folks much younger than her. She saw both boys pick up a bag of Charms pops, look around suspiciously, cram the bags down the front of their pants, and kept pretending to be looking at items as they eased down the aisle. Baby Doll then she saw the owner rushing toward the boys about to make his bust for the day, and she rushed over as though her feet moved on their own volition.

Baby Doll said to the owner while waving her hand, "I got that. Be easy, be easy, man. Don't worry about it. I got them."

The owner said, "No, Baby Doll, me no want to hear it! They steal, they will go to jail!"

The boys frantically pulled the bags of pops from their pants as if they could somehow undo what they had just done by placing the items back on the nearby shelf. Their eyes were wide with genuine surprise, since they thought this dude was a customer.

"Come on, man," Baby Doll said to the owner, wishing she could remember this guy's name. But she was glad he remembered hers. "I got money, papa, and I'll pay for what they want." Baby Doll gave him a smile, and she knew she had him when she saw the blushing expression he gave her.

The owner then gave the boys a hard stare and said, "I no want to see you two in this store ever again."

After Baby Doll paid for items, she purchased and the pops the boys tried to steal, she and the boys exited the store. Baby Doll looked down at the boys with a motherly disappointed smirk, handed each one a bag of pops, and said, "What's your names?"

The light-skinned boy said, "Jabari."

The chocolate-brown-skinned kid said, "Jason."

"Where y'all from?"

Jabari said, "From projects right down there." He pointed.

Baby Doll knew he was referring to Brownsville Houses or Langston Hughes Projects. "Y'all ain't see that dude scoping y'all out like that? Y'all better tighten up y'all boosting game or y'all asses is going to jail, homie." She smiled at the two.

The boys laughed and skipped away.

"The least you can say is thank you," Baby Doll shouted at their backs.

Jabari shouted over his shoulder, "Thank you, Baby Doll."

Jason repeated, "Thank you, Baby Doll."

Baby Doll headed down Livonia Avenue, feeling good she did a good deed for the day, while noticing her bruises weren't as painful after what she had just done. She returned to her building but went up to the twelfth floor and knocked on apartment # 12B.

When Jeanette Morrison answered the door, Baby Doll saw her missing-tooth smile was resonating with happiness and it made her look like the ultimate alcoholic. Even the raggedy housecoat and the worn-out blue jeans she had on announced her substance abuse status. Her dark brown skin looked like crusty hard shoe leather, and her eyes glistened with a delirium that perfectly matched her deep, scratchy voice.

"Baby Doll!" Jeanette was truly glad to see her young homegirl. The sight of the bag brought on a case of anticipatory delight. "Come on in here, girl." She held the smile as Baby Doll entered, and when she heard the lovely sound of those beer bottles jangling inside the bag, she knew it was party time. "I see you came correct today, girl. Got some goodies, huh? Somebody must've hit you off some kinda lovely." As Baby Doll sat the bag on the rickety kitchen table that had thick gray construction tape holding one of the legs together, Jeanette's mouth started watering as Baby Doll reached inside the bag and pulled out a bottle of Colt 45. She hadn't had a good drink since yesterday and her body was aching for some alcohol.

As Baby Doll continued pulling the bottles of beer from the bag, she turned and saw Edna approach from the back section of the apartment. She had a light brown skin complexion, very rigid facial features, a short haircut, was dressed in faded blue jeans, and could've passed for a man, if it wasn't for the medium-sized titties protruding from the wife beater T-shirt she wore. Baby Doll could never understand what could make women become sexually attracted to other women, and if it wasn't for Jeanette's open-minded attitude and the true friendship she displayed toward her, Baby Doll would've never got into the habit of hanging out with a lesbian.

Edna saw Baby Doll and sighed jealously, struggling not to display her impatience with Baby Doll's habit of showing up any time she needed to burn Jeanette's ears out with a bunch of project drama, "What's up, Baby Doll." Her attitude changed instantly when she saw the four bottles of Colt 45. "Hey, I see we about to do this damn thing." She picked up a bottle, cracked it open, and took a swig.

Baby Doll saw Edna's response and was glad she brought something for a change. She pulled out the hamburger meat and said, "I hope you feel like cooking, 'cause I don't." Although Baby Doll was a superb cook and had cooked numerous meals in this apartment, today it wasn't happening because she had to kick it with Jeanette.

Jeanette smiled as she went for the hamburger meat, "Girl, you must've won the lotto, coming in here with a dinner and shit." She reached inside the bag, found the French fries, scooped up all the cookable items and headed for the stove a few feet away. She turned and examined Baby Doll's face, sensing something was wrong. She saw the scratch on her chin, and knew it was time to take a timeout. "Oh shit, Baby Doll, I see we gotta talk, don't we? Hey, Eddie, come on over here and fix up this meal. Me and Baby Doll gotta do some girl talk."

Edna burped rudely, sat the quart bottle down on the table, and jumped to the command as Baby Doll and Jeanette went into the living room. Baby Doll sat in the dingy, moth-eaten, dirty-gray armchair, while Jeanette sat in a stain-ridden beige sofa. Baby Doll leaned back comfortably and glanced up at the poster-like pictures plastered on the wall. There was about a dozen pictures of Black men and woman who were influential in the Black Power Movement of the late sixties and early seventies, and she could still remember the first time Jeanette told her about the great things Malcolm X, Huey P. Newton, Bobby Seale, Eldridge and Katherine Cleaver, Joanne Chesimard (Assata Shakur), George and Jonathan

Jackson, and Angela Davis had done to help change the way Black people were treated in this country back then.

Jeanette pulled a Newport from the pack and lit it up. "What happened to your face, Baby Doll? And what's up with the bag of goodies?"

"I got jumped by this bitch name Nicole and her peoples." Baby Doll said. "They from Bruekelene, and they think they run Canarsie High."

"Damn, how many of them was it?" Jeanette said in a motherly fashion.

"It was about five of 'em."

"If you need me go up there with you just say the word now. I can still throw down, you know. My knuckle game is still as wicked as it wanna be."

Baby Doll giggled inwardly, imagining Jeanette going up to the High and getting her feelings hurt. Jeanette was far too washed up to lock horns with one of them young hood rats. "Naw, I'm cool. I don't need you to hold me down with this. Them bitches are cowards. It took five of them to step to me, and believe it or not, I still did my thang. Plus, I was thinking about bringing Ka-Born up there with me and let him do him. He be talking all this thug shit about how he bust his gun, I'm a see if he's the real deal."

Jeanette vigorously shook her head no as she blew out the cigarette smoke. "I don't think that's a wise thing to do. He go up there shooting and shit, and the next thing you know, your ass'll be sittin' up in jail with a big ass bid hanging over your head. They got conspiracy charges, acting in concert, and all kinds of shit to get at folks that didn't even pull the trigger. You know how stupid these trigger-happy-ass niggas can get."

Baby Doll didn't want to admit it, but Jeanette was right. The last thing she needed was to be sitting up in jail because some dumb-ass nigga done went and killed somebody. But the thought of seeing them bitches lying in the gutter with some hot ones inside of them sounded real good. However, the reality was that if something did happen to them, she would definitely be the number one suspect. Half the school knew about their scuffle, and somebody was bound to talk if shit got funky.

For some odd reason this dilemma reminded her of her dream of getting the hell out of the hood. She hated this place with a passion, and her greatest fear was ending up like so many of the people around her: Trapped, ignorant, frustrated, uneducated, and filled with a hopelessness that could bring the most optimistic person to tears of despair. One of the forces that kept her going was the innate feeling that she was different from most of the teens around her; she wasn't a dummy and always believed she was destined for greatness.

Most of the time she felt like an adult trapped inside a teenage body. The way she saw the world around her was like she was viewing it through the eyes of someone else, and she felt comfortable hanging out with people almost twice her age and had been doing it that way for as far back as she could remember. When she was amongst girls her age, she literally felt like an oddball, since the things they talked about and the activities they engaged in were the most childish things that drove her crazy. Jeanette's words regarding Ka-Born doing something to get her caught up circulated through her mind, but despite the potential risks, she couldn't let Nicole and her crew get away without some type of punishment. "What I'm gonna do is get Ka-Born to come up there with me tomorrow and make sure I get a fair one with each and every one of them bitches. He ain't gotta get his hands dirty; all he gotta do is post up on the sideline and make sure nobody jumps in."

"Shit, I can do that for you," Jeanette said seriously as she flicked ashes in the ashtray. "I still say bringing Ka-Born up there ain't a good idea."

Ka-Born's most recent misadventure tugged at Jeanette's memory. "You know that fool shot some dude from Howard Projects the other night, and now the guy's peoples and Ka-Born are playing tit for tat. He shoots at them, then them fools shoot back at him." She shook her head in disgust. "I don't know what made you even dream of fucking with that crazy motherfucker. He ain't got shit going for himself, and he's gonna end up in prison or in the cemetery."

She looked at Baby Doll as she snuffed out the cigarette in the ashtray. "Just make sure you don't get caught in any crossfire, Baby Doll. Getting you sister back for shitin' on you can't be worth all the headaches of dealing with Ka-Born."

Baby Doll wanted to say, "You wanna bet," but instead she decided to drop the issue, "Now we can talk about the good news." She smiled as she leaned forward in her seat. "When I was fighting them bitches, this old-timer name Big Daddy Blue and his niece name—"

"Big Daddy Blue!?" Jeanette was definitely interested because this cat was big time back in the day. "You ain't talking about the one who did all that time and just got out?"

"I don't know if he just got out of jail, but I do know he got mad clubs and other businesses."

Jeanette smiled, "Yeah, that's him. He's into the club thing now. Yeah, that's him. You said you met him!? How the hell that happened?"

"I was fighting them bitches, and him and his niece Tera pulled up in a Jeep and broke up the fight. They gave me a ride home." She was about to mention the fifty dollars Big Daddy gave her but put the brakes on that with the quickness. Although Jeanette was considered her best friend, Baby Doll had learned many years ago to keep all her money matters strictly to herself. "And he offered me a job."

"A job!?" Jeanette instantly assumed Big Daddy wanted to throw Baby Doll's pretty little ass in a G-string and put her on stage. "Did he say what kinda job it is?"

She saw it in Jeanette's eyes; she was thinking exactly what she thought upon hearing his job offer. "No, but I told him straight up, I ain't into strippin'. He got some stores, and Tera works for him as a manager. The way he was kicking it, I don't think he's on some grimy shit."

Jeanette sighed while struggling not to say something to burst her bubble. Reflecting on Big Daddy Blue's reputation prior to him going to jail, she had to admit the man wasn't grimy, but he sure was ruthless. He'd probably sold as much drugs to the Black community as Nicky Barnes, and probably cracked as many heads as John Gotti. Her perception of Big Daddy Blue at that time was that he was the ultimate enemy of the people, and several times her Black Panther chapter tried to undermine Big Daddy's operation without even a smidgen of progress. But recently, she did get wind that he was nothing like he was back in the day.

Baby Doll noticed Jeanette was deep in thought, and wanted to know what she was thinking. "So what you think? You know I got's to get your view on this, girl."

"Hey, times are rough when it comes to finding jobs. With that maniac Bush in office, ain't no time to be thumbing your nose to a legit job. But I will tell you this. In my opinion, Big Daddy was a diehard hustler before he did that bid and might still be that same person. People that hustle at that level and intensity don't get that stuff totally out of their system, no matter how long they ass get put on ice. Of course, there's exceptions, but I don't know if Big Daddy's one of them. Despite what's said and done, I say go for it, girl. Just keep your eyes and ears open."

Baby Doll was glad she got Jeanette's blessing on this. With that all cleared up it was time to celebrate. "We better get us a hit of that Colt 45 before Edna dust it all off." She went to the kitchen, retrieved a bottle, two cups, and returned to the living room. Baby Doll cracked the lid, poured two cups, handed one to Jeanette, sat down, and sipped the malt liquor. "You mind if I holla at Ka-Born, and have him come here?"

Jeanette smiled. "Do you Baby Doll."

Baby Doll took another huge gulp and felt Jeanette's energy vibrating through the air. Her gestures indicated she didn't want Ka-Born in her apartment, and Baby Doll wanted to ease her concerns, since she had no intention of violating in that fashion. "Don't worry, Jeanette, when he comes, I'm breaking out. I know you ain't feelin' him, so I ain't gonna let him in your crib." She went to the kitchen and dialed his beeper number and hung up. She smiled because she used the emergency code and knew he would come rushing over thinking the shit was on.

Meanwhile, Ka-Born stood on the corner of Blake Avenue and Bristol Street looking at the emergency code on his beeper. His smooth dark chocolate complexion, his beaded eyes, and muscular built made him look like a displaced Zulu warrior. If it weren't for the baggy pants, the cream leather Timbs, and the expensive Sean John jacket he wore, with a diamond stubbed gold bracket dangling from his wrist, he could've passed for a handsome Congonese African. Standing next to him was his street team, Sinister and Ramsey. Ka-Born's heart started accelerating with excitement as he realized the emergency code number was coming from Baby Doll, his fine little trophy.

He snapped out of his semi-trance and started barking at his team. "Yo', son, I got some drama poppin' off in Tilden. My little shorty got a beef or some shit." He caressed the 9mm tucked in his waist. "Sinister, go get the ride, and tell Weasel to get on this corner until we get back." As he watched Sinister swagger down the block, Ka-Born smiled inwardly because he had been itching for some drama all day, and he was apparently getting his wishes.

CHAPTER 3

Tracy was looking out the kitchen window when she saw Ka-Born's sky blue Volvo come to a stop on Livonia Avenue. When she saw him getting out the ride, she frantically ran out the apartment on her way to the ground floor to intercept him. She knew he was going up there to see Baby Doll, and she'd been dying to confront him face to face to talk some sense in to him. She'd been blowing up in his beeper for the last two weeks, hoping he would call her back. She even had one of his peoples talk to him the other day, but he was still on some bullshit.

Tracy started pressing the elevator button with frantic energy. When it seemed like the elevator was taking too long, she bolted for the stairs. Five flights was nothing, and it was obvious she could intercept him before he made it to the elevator. She truly believed if she could just talk to him, plead with him, she could change his mind. She zipped down flights of stairs with the speed and urgency of a child on its way to the ice cream truck about to depart.

Tracy burst through the stairwell door, startling Ka-Born as he stood waiting for the elevator.

Ka-Born had his hand on his 9mm about to pull it, until he saw who it was. Instantly, a wave of furious rage coursed through his veins, and he wondered if he shot this bitch right here, could he get away with it. There were a few kids playing outside and tenants were coming and going, so shooting her was definitely out of the question.

When his eyes landed on her huge titties and then scrolled down to her shapely hips as his mind visualized her big bodacious ass, he felt his dick getting hard as the memories of how he used to wear that pussy out took center stage in his mind. She was nowhere near as fine as her younger sister, but she could put plenty of these other chicks out here to shame.

Tracy activated her puppy dog eyes and eased toward him with a sensuous voice. "Ka-Born, please listen to me, Boo. Before you go off on the deep end and start spazzin' out, please just listen to me."

Ka-Born was suddenly hit with an idea. It was an excellent way to get this cutthroat bitch back for shittin' on him like he was some bird-ass motherfucker. His dick was throbbing for some attention anyway, so it was only right he gave his man what he wanted. "I'll listen to you only on one condition."

There was a moment of silence.

Tracy saw it in his eyes; he was coming around! She smiled, "Whatever it is, I'll do it."

Ka-Born walked toward her, gently grabbed her arm and led her into the stairwell.

Meanwhile, Tracy felt her panties becoming moist because he was going to embrace her, kiss her, make up, and everything would be back to the way it used to be.

Ka-Born stepped into the stairwell as the smell of piss mixed with stale cigarette butts and beer assaulted his nose. *This was perfect*, he thought as he unzipped his pants, and pulled out nine inches of throbbing hot meat. "I need to know you're serious about getting back with me, and you know how much I love the way you do that thing, Tracy."

Tracy felt disrespected; she was about to flip out, but didn't want to take the chance of getting him mad. She hastily weighed her options, and realized at least he was talking to her, and promised to hear her out. Plus, he did say he was doing this to see if she was serious about getting back with him. She sighed and decided to go with the flow. "So if I do you right, we're gonna work this out between us, Ka-Born? You know I love you, Boo."

"Come on, Tracy," Ka-Born struggled not to blow up on her and didn't want to get her started with the talking. He gently grabbed her shoulder and navigated her to her knees and inserted his dick in her mouth.

As she sucked, slurped, and polished Ka-Born's rod, she couldn't help but notice he was manhandling her. Twice he damn near made her throw up when he rammed his dick down her throat. But each time he almost choked her, he immediately went back to his gentle bodily motions, which indicated to her that he didn't do it on purpose. She knew how men could get caught up in the moment when they were getting a head job, and so she quickly re-grouped and went with the flow.

Ka-Born was concentrating, making sure he didn't come too quick. He was going to make sure that when he did come, he would blast off in such a way that this bitch would never forget this event. He looked down and saw this foul, trifling bitch had the nerve to be acting like she was enjoying it. Then, he realized this was probably the same way she was acting when she was sucking Dondi's dick while she was supposed to be his girl.

As he recalled how mad peoples in the hood was laughing at him behind his back (and a few times in his face), and how some were saying Tracy did this as a way to deliberately start a war between him and Dondi, the anger started to mount and was making his dick get soft.

He aggressively shifted his thoughts to the situation at hand, and as a way to guarantee that his shit would stay hard, he closed his eyes imaging that it was Baby Doll that was hitting him off. Since he still hadn't tapped Baby Doll's thang yet, it didn't take much to get his imagination flared up, especially since Baby Doll was probably the badest bitch in the whole Tilden Projects, and probably the whole god damn Brownsville.

As Baby Doll's fine face skirted across his mind, Ka-Born sighed as his blood began to boil; his pumping motion increased two folds when he allowed Baby Doll's prefect breasts and her huge, round, shapely ass and small waist to pop into his mental picture.

He was seconds from reaching the point of no return. That exploding sensation was rapidly becoming uncontrollable, and with a gargantuan struggle Ka-Born slowed down his pace almost to a full stop. The nut eased back. It was time to lay this thing down the right way!

He pulled the 9mm from his waist and planted the barrel of the gun to Tracy's head. Looking down, he saw Tracy opened her eyes with the dick still in her mouth, and Ka-Born wished he had a picture of this wonderful sight. Her eyes were wide with terror, and with the dick in her mouth it made this cutthroat bitch look silly and pathetic.

"Did I tell you to stop!?" Ka-Born cocked the 9mm loudly. Then grabbed a handful of hair to make sure she didn't try to scramble away. Her fear was inspiring, and he resumed his pumping motion, this time making sure the tip of his dick touched her tonsils each time he thrust forward. "And if you bite it, you'll blow your motherfuckin' top off, bitch!" Ka-Born shouted and damn near scared her half to death. When he saw the tears streaming down her cheeks while she started trembling in fear, Ka-Born felt an intense resurgence of that exploding sensation. His pace increased as Tracy's choking and convulsing sounds took on a rhythmic tune in synch with his body movements.

Here it comes! Ka-Born's pounding motion increased as the heat in his groin reached a boiling temperature. He saw Tracy was about to throw up and just as his nut ignited, he cramped his dick all the way to its maximum capacity and held it in place while Tracy's forehead was glued to his stomach. He could feel her nose spewing warm air at the base of his stomach while his nuts were resting on her chin and his dick was spitting come down Tracy's throat. He noticed she was violently heaving as if she was about to vomit, but that only served to make the nut feel more pleasurable. Sighing in sheer ecstasy, Ka-Born realized this was the best nut he'd ever experienced as he pulled his nut dripping dick from her mouth and shoved her away.

"Don't spit it out!" Ka-Born yelled as Tracy started spitting. "Swallow it!" He took aim with venom surging through his veins. "Swallow every motherfuckin' drop!"

Suddenly, Ka-Born started laughing explosively when he saw Tracy struggling not to throw up while slurping down the nut. As he tucked his manhood back inside his pants, and zipped up his fly, he saw exactly why Tupac said getting revenge is the next best thing to pussy. Staring down into Tracy's eyes he saw something that made him wonder if he should start making plans to have this bitch murdered. It didn't take a mental giant to know there was nothing more dangerous than a jilted woman, who'd just been disrespected in the worse kind of way.

Tracy was devastated as she looked up into Ka-Born's eyes. *How could he shit on me like this!?* She loved this foul motherfucker, and this was the way he treated her when he knew she loved him. This shit was foul and fucked-up! And the only reason she cheated on his sorry ass in the first place was because he cheated on her. Her tears increased as it became clear in her mind that Ka-Born apparently hated her and didn't love her.

She struggled to her feet, fighting with every drop of energy not to look weaker and more vulnerable than she already appeared. The hot, slimy and salty aftertaste of the nut was turning her stomach.

By the way he was treating her it was obvious he never loved her! The urge to try to come up with another way to salvage their relationship was powerful, but by the way he just dissed her it was obvious what the outcome would be. Tracy saw as clear as day that he was getting his revenge, and based on the way he just treated her, she realized he was doing a damn good job of it. But she had a genuine knack for retaliating. In fact, revenge was something she'd mastered many years ago. As she stood staring at him, she vowed that she was going to get this nigga back if it killed her. She went into her victim's act to keep him off balance.

"Ka-Born, why are you doing this to me, baby. You know I love you, man." She wiped her tears as she started thinking of the best way to get him back. There was a wide selection to choose from, but she wanted one that would really tear him up from the inside out and would inflict serious physical pain. "You didn't have to go there. I told you, the only reason I fucked around with Dondi is because you went and fucked Donna, and you did it right in my fuckin' face." Her blood was boiling because it was obvious this nigga thought his shit didn't stink and that he had a right to do wrong and not have to deal with the consequences. But she would play along, rock his lowlife ass to sleep, and put it on him in a vicious way. *If he wants to play these foul games, then we can both play them together!* "Let's keep it real, Ka-Born, the least you could've done is put some shade on it."

Ka-Born wasn't trying to hear that shit, since the logical component in his mind indicated she was right. "I told you that bitch was sweatin' me, and I didn't fuck her!" He tucked his gun and headed for the door. "But you fucked Dondi, so you committed the ultimate violation. I didn't fuck her, so my situation is different." He lied.

He'd not only fucked Donna, but also tricked some major cash on her as well. Something he never did unless the chick was a super dime. Donna looked like a dime on the outside, but that pussy was as big, sloppy, and as smelly as a Stanley Avenue whore, and it was obvious Donna had been up and down, and around the town. After he sexed Donna out, he felt played, since he had jeopardized his relationship with Tracy to knock Donna's boots when her boots weren't even worth knocking.

"When you chose to flip, you killed our thing, Tracy." And with that he disappeared out of the stairwell, on his way upstairs to see Baby Doll.

Tracy pulled herself together and decided to use the stairs. As she climbed up the stairs, an excellent way to get revenge on Ka-Born entered her mind, and she smiled, realizing it could work. The excitement began to mount because if she could pull it off it was going to be one hell of a sight to see! She laughed inwardly as she picked up speed, not feeling too bad despite the utter disrespect she had just endured.

* * * *

Earlier, Baby Doll was looking out the hallway window as Ka-Born parked his car. Suddenly, she heard a door downstairs slam open, and someone racing down the stairs. Baby Doll shook her head, knowing who it was.

Tracy was always a cold-blooded sucker for guys with cars and fast money, and it disgusted her every time she saw Tracy degrading herself. Suddenly, Baby Doll's curiosity was activated. As she saw Ka-Born was almost at the entrance of the building she decided to be nosy. There was no doubt in her mind Tracy was going to confront him and engage him in a talk.

She tiptoed down the flight of stairs, heading for the ground floor. By the time she reached the third floor, she could hear Tracy and Ka-Born's voices. When she reached the flight of stairs leading down to the second floor, everything suddenly became silent, with the exception of Ka-Born sighing in pleasure. *I know she ain't go there*, Baby Doll thought as she became even more inquisitive.

She quietly moved to the second floor, peeked around the corner, stared down at the ground floor and saw Tracy on her knees sucking Ka-Born off.

As Baby Doll watched Ka-Born pumping inside of Tracy's mouth, she couldn't help but feel a wave of mixed emotions. She was elated and angry at seeing what was obviously a diss move. When she saw Ka-Born pull his gun and started talking to Tracy in a violent fashion, Baby Doll decided to head back up to the twelfth floor, since it was obvious the show was about to come to an end.

Tiptoeing back up the stairs, Baby Doll wondered if she was making a grave mistake by getting involved with Ka-Born on an intimate level. Jeanette and Edna's comments flowed through her mind, trying to convince her that she was playing a dangerous game by going out with Ka-Born. But when that voice in her head told her Ka-Born could help her get out of the hood, she swept those indecisive thoughts to the back of her mind. She had big plans for Ka-Born and had been working out the wrinkles ever since she not only decided to use Ka-Born as a way to fuck with Tracy's head but to also pimp this fool.

But had she known that Tracy's plan to get back at Ka-Born also included her, and it was an assault that was bound to get real ugly, she certainly would have altered her plans.

CHAPTER 4

Later that evening, Ka-Born pulled the Volvo to the curb in front of Baby Doll's project building. It was a quarter to eleven o'clock, and Baby Doll was in the passenger seat with a case of red eye from the weed she and Ka-Born had smoked earlier. A Nas CD was playing and Ka-Born was rocking to the hard-hitting rap song.

Earlier, after she saw Tracy suck Ka-Born off, she crept back up to the twelfth floor and waited for Ka-Born to get off the elevator. She kicked it with him briefly and they left the building. In the car she explained what happened at the High and how she got jumped. It took some serious convincing to make him agree to come with her to the school solely for the purpose of holding her down, without getting directly involved. Ka-Born took her to the game room over on Sutter Avenue and Hazel Street, and they blew two nickel bags of weed and then Baby Doll told him about the job that Big Daddy offered her. To her surprise, Ka-Born blew up, beefing about she didn't need a job, since he could provide her with money and anything else she wanted.

"My money is long; I got workers slinging my shit all over this motherfucker'! You ain't gotta work."

Upon hearing this, Baby Doll instantly started reevaluating her relationship with Ka-Born and saw she would have to shift the style of approach she used, and be easy with the information she shared with him.

As Ka-Born rattled on and on, beefing adamantly about her working for an ex-drug dealer-turned businessman, she realized she was going to have to get rid of Ka-Born and real soon, because he was bent on preventing her from doing anything that could help her grow and get out of her mother's crib. Plus, his violence was far more than just irritating; it was frightening.

Then he stated, "Yo, check it, Baby Doll. I don't know if your old trifling-ass sister told you, but I don't go away that easy. Once I decide something is mine, it's mine forever. I'm a real hard lover, and basically, you mine and only mine. Nobody can have you after me."

Baby Doll instantly caught a flashback of the woman in the building on the other side of the projects who was killed by her jealous boyfriend. With this circulating through her mind, she started second-guessing whether or not she made a terrible mistake when she decided to use Ka-Born to get back at Tracy, and to try to squeeze him for some money, and other things.

Baby Doll looked over at Ka-Born and decided to remind him about tomorrow since that discussion had occurred hours ago. She turned down the volume on the CD to just above a whisper. "I'm serious Ka-Born, I don't want you going up there tomorrow, and going crazy."

Ka-Born smiled as he spoke from behind the wheel, "I told you Baby Doll, I'ma do this the way you wanna flow. You said all you want me to do is hold you down. I got your back. You'll get a fair one with each and every one of them bitches. Now, if one of them niggas from Breukelene get involved then the sky's the limit, Boo."

Baby Doll looked at her watch, realizing her mother was going to be beefin' a mile a minute when she got upstairs. Her curfew was ten o'clock and as usual she got home a little later each night. She put her hand on the car door lever,

"I'm out" She was about to get out of the car, but Ka-Born grabbed her arm. She knew what he wanted.

Ka-Born slid over to her. "You know you can't break out without hittin' a nigga off with one of them wet ones."

Baby Doll sighed as she puckered up. This was the part she hated, but when groundwork was being laid it was obvious this was like causalities of war; you couldn't avoid them even if you wanted to. She reluctantly went with the kiss. It was sloppy, disgusting and totally uncoordinated. Ka-Born was in desperate need of a crash course in the proper way to tongue kiss a woman, and she wanted to give him some pointers, but his ego was way too delicate for that; nobody could tell him he wasn't the ultimate lover-man, and accepting constructive criticism was as foreign to him as truthful propaganda was to politicians.

Baby Doll broke away from the kiss when his hands started roaming; her juices started flowing and this wasn't the time to go there. She jetted out the car and six minutes later she was getting off the elevator. She went to the hallway window, waved to Ka-Born down below, and saw him pull off. She headed for the apartment.

As Baby Doll pulled her keys from her pocket, she could hear Marvin Gaye's voice whispering from underneath the door, and he was talking about "Mercy, mercy, me; things ain't what they used to be," which meant Mildred was up waiting for her, and apparently had company; probably that perverted motherfucker, Kevin. Baby Doll opened the door and entered the apartment.

Mildred was sitting on the sofa, with Kevin sitting in an armchair across from her. The two were talking with drinks in their hands and had both looked up when Baby Doll entered. Mildred's rough, but regal facial features became stern. She was a dark-skinned woman, a bit on the heavy side, and had a scar on her lower left chin that made her look more threatening than she really was. She was homely, but one could tell that she had once had a vicious body in her heydays.

Kevin, on the other hand, was a light-skinned Black man, slim, and could've passed for an R & B star if it wasn't for his skin blemishes, red-eyes and droopy features; all marks of a heavy drinker and weed smoker. However, his neatly trimmed goatee, and low-cut hair did do some justice, making him look much younger than thirty-nine years old.

Mildred rose to her feet while Kevin put on his best arrogant smirk.

Baby Doll was about to head straight for her room she shared with Jasmine, and she knew that wasn't going to work, but tried it anyway. She loved to pick her mother's nerves with carefully choreographed head games.

Mildred was furious now. "Girl, don't you walk away from me!"

Baby Doll stopped on a dime and folded her arms impatiently.

As Mildred stared at Baby Doll, a floodgate of memories opened up. The more this child grew, the more she looked and acted like her father, and that only made her anger that much more unbearable. Baby Doll's father, Patrick "Dubar" Johnson, was half Filipino and half African American, and was what they called back then, a flyguy. She had always known Dubar was way too fine to be with her, but at the time it was worth the headaches because she could at least say she was good enough to have one of the finest-looking men around. It boosted her self-esteem to be able to brag about Dubar to her friends and family. And back then just being able to say she had a child by the infamous Dubar was a victory, but ever since he walked out on her and vanished off the face of the planet, leaving her with a child to care for alone, she realized it really wasn't worth it. Unconsciously, she was taking it out on Baby Doll.

"Didn't I tell you ten o'clock is your curfew!?"

Baby Doll sighed, "I lost track of time. My watch broke. There was a shootout, and the police shut down a whole block." Her sarcasm was clear. "What do you want me to tell you, mom!? I'm late, and what does it matter to you anyway?"

Mildred moved toward Baby Doll with malice on her mind, but Kevin grabbed her by the arm. With his deep, raspy like voice, Kevin said, "Come on Mildred let the girl go about her business.

She's home, she's safe and that's all that matters." Kevin inconspicuously winked his eye at Baby Doll.

Mildred looked into Kevin's eyes, and realized this sort of open-minded logic was one of the reasons why she loved this man so much. He was one of the most sensitive men she'd ever been with.

Meanwhile, Baby Doll looked at the two with disgust. Shaking her head in partial disbelief mixed with admiration, she had to admit that Kevin was a true-blue player. He had Mildred wrapped literally around his finger, and he'd been doing this for years. She gave him money, fed him, and damn near worshipped the ground Kevin walked on. All he did was lay dick on her, freeload, get high, and meddle into family affairs. Not to mention he was the epitome of a pedophile.

As Baby Doll screwed up her face with vengeance, she allowed her mind to flashback to how Kevin had been playing her, forcing her to have sex with him when her mother was either asleep or not looking. The more she thought about the secret that Kevin had hanging over her head and was using on her every time he wanted to fuck her, threatening that if she said no, or told anybody about what he was doing to her, he would reveal this devastating secret, the more she wondered if Kevin would really reveal what happened several years ago.

But each time she went through this little mental aerobics game regarding this issue, she concluded that Kevin would reveal this secret, and he would destroy her with it without batting an eye. This was another reason she started dealing with Ka-Born, since it was obvious that the only way out of this Catch-22 situation was to have Kevin killed.

Baby Doll rolled her eyes and continued on her way to the bedroom. She entered and saw Jasmine was still up, laying in bed looking at TV. "What you still doing up, Jazz?"

Jasmine yawned and said, "This movie is good; I wanna see it all." Her drunk-looking eyes indicated she wasn't going to make it.

Baby Doll went to her schoolbooks laying on the desk, realizing there was no way she was going to be able to complete her homework assignments, but figured she would at least read the questions and write out a few bogus answers before going to bed. She glanced over at Jasmine, who was struggling to keep her eyes open. "Now you know you playin' yourself. Don't be crying in the morning talking about you tried. You better take your ass to sleep." Baby Doll smiled at Jasmine, who was probably the only one in the family who she had some patience for. Although Jasmine went against her whenever Tracy and Mildred started tag teaming her, she knew Jasmine was doing what any sane, younger sibling would do (go along with the mother and the oldest sister); she could never stay mad at Jasmine for long, especially since she and Jasmine shared rooms together, and Jasmine did try to show her some love when the others weren't looking.

Baby Doll flipped through the pages she was supposed to read, went to the end of the chapter and read the four questions she had to answer. She knew she had a remarkable ability to figure out things by a process called context clues (an elaborate form of guess-work), and she would be able to guess what the answers were.

After she wrote out the four perfunctory answers, she decided to call it a night. She turned off the TV, underdressed, got under the covers, and utilized her sleep-assistance tactic similar to counting sheep to help her enter dream state. Instead of counting imaginary sheep, she was counting each time she stomped Nicole's face into the pavement. Each stomp helped her enter dream state within minutes.

* * * *

The next morning, Baby Doll stood in front of her project building cursing Ka-Born out. He had promised her he would be there to drive her to school. She had told him to be here by a quarter to eight, and she had added fifteen minutes to that schedule to compensate for his usual lateness. But now she saw it was a quarter after eight and he still hadn't showed up. She had played herself once again, because he'd done this same thing before, and was doing it again. She sighed angrily since she was going to be late once again, and Mr. Dawson was going to blow his top because she promised him she wouldn't be late to class again. She looked at her watch and decided if Ka-Born wasn't here in three more minutes she was getting on the bus.

Three minutes came and went and she got on the bus along with two of her ex-friends who were also late for class. Raysheima and Michelle were quintessential jealous and petty-minded hood rats that hated anyone who looked better than them.

As the bus cruised down Rockaway Avenue, Baby Doll sat in the back of the bus, toying with the plastic makeshift knife stashed in her book bag. Since the school had metal detectors, there was no way she could get a real knife into the school, so she had to get creative.

She had contemplated bringing a real knife with her and stashing it in a hiding place near the school, but she remembered what happened to a student from Bayview projects who had done just that and got arrested when he went to retrieve the 9mm handgun. An undercover cop saw him stash his gun in a trash can behind the bagel shop (or maybe somebody snitched him out) and when he came to get it, they snatched him up. In any event, she was content with her plastic knife, since it had a vicious point on it and was sharp enough to cut her bed sheet with razor-like efficiency.

This time when them bitches come at me, I'm-a give them a buck fifty each! Baby Doll promised as the bus came to a stop at Riverdale

Avenue and she saw a group of people, including Darryl Edmond get on the bus. Baby Doll inched down in her seat, hoping he didn't see her.

Darryl Edmonds looked up and smiled when he saw Baby Doll in back of the bus. His soft, nerdy type features were unmistakable, and his Malcolm X-style glasses and outdated fade haircut only served to confirm this image. He weaved pass the straphangers and stood directly in front of Baby Doll.

"Breana, how you do?" Darryl said, smiling from ear to ear.

Baby Doll smiled back and wanted to scold him about using her government name, but instead she said, "Hey Darryl." She used to go out with Darryl when they were in public school. "What you doing on this bus? I thought you were going to Westinghouse?"

"I'm getting off at Hegaman," Daryl said with the smile plastered on his face. "I gotta transfer over to the B6 bus." He was still in love with Baby Doll, and his heart pounded as he gazed into her pretty eyes. "I gotta meet my class at the Brooklyn Library. We're doing a field trip assignment." He saw the scratch on her chin and hope she wasn't still fighting and carrying on. "I hope you're taking care of yourself."

"I'm doing good," Baby Doll said. "I see you still on top of your game." She enjoyed his company but disliked him as a boyfriend because he was simply too weak for her. She felt she needed a Lion, a king-of-the-Jungle kind of dude, not some kind of bird-ass dude that was scared of his own shadow and couldn't protect her from all the predators roaming the 'hood. She subconsciously knew Darryl was probably the best thing for her, but his weaknesses were just too much for her to bear. She softened her voice and said, "How's your mother doing?"

As Darryl went on and on about a bunch of mundane issues, Baby Doll's mind started wandering, thinking about how she was going to get busy with Nicole and her crew. She noticed just thinking about it made her nervous. No matter how many times she fought, just before the shit got funky her anxiety and nervousness got crazy. She called it healthy jitters, because the chemicals released always made her fight better. She recalled her science teacher called it adrenaline and had said it was the fight or flight chemical in the body. Mr. Harris sure didn't lie when he linked it to the activity of fighting, because she had whipped plenty ass once her heart started pounding, her sweat glands pumping sweat, and those chemicals poured into her bloodstream.

"Hey, you all right, Breana?" Darryl said when he noticed Baby Doll was daydreaming. "Look like you got some serious stuff on your mind."

"Sorry, Darryl. I do got a whole lot on my mind."

Darryl looked up and noticed his stop was coming up. "I'm out of here the next stop. Hey, Breana, I was wondering if we could—you know—ah, we used to have some good times to—"

"Sorry, Darryl," Baby Doll put on her sad face. "I got a man, and he's the real jealous type." She saw he was truly shattered. "But if things don't work out with us, I'll give you a call." She saw Darryl's eyes sprung open with delight and hope. She almost laughed in his face but held it back with a sincere struggle.

Darryl got off the bus waving and grinning like he was Mr. Lame himself.

Baby Doll cut her eyes at Raysheima and Michelle and saw they were amused by Darryl's antics. The urge to get up and pull their cards was very strong, but she didn't feel like playing the bully role right now, especially since they were straight cowards anyway and if she stepped to them, they would instantly bitch up and start copping a plea. In the past, she had stepped to them twice and all they did was deny whatever it was they had done and played stupid, so Baby Doll decided not to waste her energy on these insecure, petty-minded nobodies.

When the bus pulled up in front of the High, Baby Doll's heart was pounding as she got off the bus. What followed was indeed a surprise. As she approached the school entrance, several of the known class-cutters seemed to be smiling at her; even a few known enemies amongst this group didn't seem to have the usual malice written on their faces. This made Baby Doll even more nervous because it implied that someone had something in stored for her that would be crazy enough to satisfy all these enemies. Something told her to turn back, but her pride and ego were far too powerful for that to happen. She told herself that only cowards ran away from beefs, and a coward was something she definitely was not.

Baby Doll got past the metal detector without any problems and headed for math class. She barged into the classroom and Mr. Dawson gave her the look that said he would see her after class.

As she took her seat, she saw virtually the entire class was looking at her strangely. It couldn't be because she fought Nicole and her crew, she concluded, since the altercation they had yesterday wasn't the first time she had clashed with them, and after those fights, she'd never gotten a response like the one she was currently receiving. Something was definitely up. During the entire math class Baby Doll's mind couldn't focus on the class work as she tried to figure out why everyone seemed to be smiling and even giving her big-ups. The furthest thing from her mind was that they were showing her genuine love; such an act coming from these people was utterly impossible as far as Baby Doll was concerned, and so it never even crossed her mind.

In her next class the same thing happened, and now she was sure some serious shit was up in the air. And by the way things were unfolding, it was clear that, whatever it was, it was some real big shit. Since she didn't vibe with most of the people in this school, she couldn't just go up to them and ask, "What the fuck is happening?" Baby Doll hated that feeling, since it was like having a severe itch and not able to scratch it. It had the potential of driving a person insane! Although she had two half-ass friends from Bayview projects (Kaneisha and Dinasia), who were just as radical and disliked as she was, and had a lot of other things in common, they were nowhere in sight. She decided to rest her mind, because she would soon find out. She would clash with Nicole and her crew during lunch period, and it would be what it would be. If the shit was going to get funky on a whole new level, then so be it.

As Baby Doll moved to the next class, she couldn't stop her imagination from running wild. Images of Nicole and her crew shooting and killing her crossed her mind. Maybe they were going to use weapons to get at her. Baby Doll definitely feared death, but she also feared looking like a weak, punk-ass coward. She pushed these terrifying mental images to the back of her mind, refusing to allow them to get the best of her.

Then, finally, during lunch period, Baby Doll saw Nicole, Jada, Cookie, and the rest of the crew. Baby Doll and Nicole approached each other as though they were gunslingers about to engage in a duel. Baby Doll knew there wouldn't be any serious fighting inside the school; at least that's what she hoped, since they all agreed to settle beefs outside the school and off school grounds. But by the way things were going, that agreement was probably out the window.

When Baby Doll and Nicole were within a dozen feet from each other they stopped and stared at each other. Baby Doll, for the first time, saw that Nicole didn't have on her monster mug. In fact, she looked like she was scared to death. *What the hell is this?* Baby Doll wondered as Nicole eased closer to her with lowered eyes.

Nicole spoke with a humble voice, "Listen, Baby Doll, I'm sorry about that shit yesterday. I didn't know you was related to Big Daddy Blue! I mean—we—we didn't know—"

"Yo, Baby Doll," Jada rushed over to Nicole's side. "Please tell him it was a misunderstanding or something. We sorry about all the bullshit we put you through . . . ."

As Nicole and her crew rattled on and on about how sorry they were and how they didn't know Big Daddy Blue was related to her, Baby Doll was totally fucked-up by what was taking place right before her eyes. *This shit can't be happening*, she told herself. And the main question that bombarded her mind was why in the hell are they scared of Big Daddy Blue!? He had to be one big-time motherfucker, she confirmed and was now dying to get totally under his wing. But why hadn't she heard of him in the same way she heard of Fat Cat, Nicky Barnes, Papi, and the other well-known gangsters that everybody talked about and were basically urban street legends?

Then KRS-ONE's rap lyrics, which said, "Real bad boys move in silence", answered her mental question. The way Nicole and her crew were trembling and copping mad pleas, it was obvious Big Daddy Blue was up there with the real heavyweights, and she was elated by the fact she was about to start working for him. Nicole and her crew were street hood rats of the umpteenth degree with family members that were deep into the game, and if they were in fear of Big Daddy then that meant he was definitely the real deal.

Baby Doll rolled with the flow of this shocking experience like a champion. She didn't shit on any of them, although she wanted to, and didn't even ask how they come to the conclusion that Big Daddy was related to her. She simply went about her business while letting Nicole and the others think the beef was dead. But, in her heart, she vowed that this shit was far from over. All this did was give her the upper hand. They were going to put their guards down, and this would give her what she needed to even the score.

By the end of the day, she had forgot about the fact she had asked Ka-Born to hold her down, until she was exiting the school on her way to get on the bus and saw Ka-Born's Volvo parked across the street; she rushed over to him, and it took about two minutes for her to explain the situation to him.

"And you gonna let them bitches off that easy!?" Ka-Born said as he got out of the car. "Fuck around, they might be rocking your ass to sleep."

Baby Doll knew that was highly unlikely. The fear they displayed was far too sincere to be a trick, and instead of arguing with Ka-Born, she said, "Fuck them. It's dead for now. Let's get outta here." She saw Ka-Born looking at a dude named Jakwan from Breukelene, who just pulled up in a Cherokee Jeep and was a well-known supreme troublemaker. Baby Doll sighed, because the shit was about to get crazy.

Ka-Born rushed back into the Volvo and hastily started fumbling under the front passenger seat. He found his 9mm and tucked it in his waist. Ka-Born eased back out of the car.

"Come on, Ka-Born." Baby Doll said, almost pleading. "I asked you not to come here with that bullshit. You promised me you wasn't go—"

"This nigga hit up my man, AJ." He'd been trying to bump heads with this dude for months and was hoping he saw him up here today. *Yeah, nigga, we's gone do this dance today!* Ka-Born inwardly fumed as he watched Jakwan get out of the Jeep dripping in gold.

Baby Doll had to make a quick decision. She could either stay with Ka-Born and hope she didn't get caught up in the inevitable crossfire or get as far away as she could from this fool-ass nigga, and hear his mouth later, if he made it out of this situation unscathed.

It took Baby Doll about five seconds to make a choice.

CHAPTER 5

Big Daddy Blue sat at his maple oak desk in his elegant office over on Nostrand Avenue and Fulton Street, surfing through the files on his computer. The entire second floor of 535 Nostrand Avenue was owned by Big Daddy Blue and served as the headquarters for his business empire that consisted of three social clubs, a hair salon, and four retail-clothing stores throughout Brooklyn, all under his government name Gregory J. Williams. But what Big Daddy Blue prided himself on most was that he bought and owned each and every business property he possessed. If he didn't proceed from a standpoint of leasing with the option to buy, he wouldn't proceed at all. Indeed, he didn't have a whole lot of businesses, but unlike most businessmen he did own what he had and was therefore worth much more than the average cat doing business in the hood. He was reading last week's sales reports for the two East New York social clubs and wasn't very happy at what he was seeing. Sales were down, while costs were up, which in the business world was a fatal combination on a scale similar to that of full-blown AIDS mixed with active TB.

Suddenly, there was a knock on the door.

Big Daddy Blue looked up from the computer screen and said, "Come on in."

Preacher, a huge, baldheaded muscular Black man with a completely hairless face, entered. He was fifty-five years old (four years younger than Big Daddy) and didn't look a day over forty-five. His soft voice was totally inconsistent with the size of his body. "There's some young girl out here said you told her to come see you."

Big Daddy Blue squinted his eyes, trying to recall who he'd told to come see him.

Preacher saw Big Daddy didn't remember, so he offered him some helpful information. "She looks about fifteen or sixteen." Preacher's Mike Tyson-style voice went up two more notches. "She said you gave her this card and told her to come see you today about a job." He showed Big Daddy the calling card.

When Big Daddy saw the card, it instantly jogged his memory. Baby Doll's face popped inside his mind. She was that pretty little girl who lived in Tilden Projects. The one who was fighting that gang of girls by Canarsie High School and was doing a damn good job at it. He dubbed her the "tough little super dime," and he instantly remembered her name was Baby Doll, especially since that name fit her perfectly.

"Yeah, I know who she is. Send her in."

As Preacher exited the office, Big Daddy glanced over at the calendar and realized time was flying. It was about several days ago when he'd met Baby Doll, and already it was time to hook her up. Then, he suddenly realized he forgot to tell Helen over at the Pitkin Avenue store that he was sending another worker over there. He quickly activated the keys on the computer keyboard, searching for the monthly financial report to see if it was even feasible to add another worker to that team over on Pitkin, when there was a knock on the door. He hit the key to open the computer file and said, "Come on in."

Baby Doll opened the door, stuck her head in first, and then eased inside. She was dressed in a pair of black dress slacks with a matching jacket, and a white blouse underneath the jacket. In a fraction of a second, her eyes took in, all at once, everything inside this very expensive office.

There were gold-framed pictures all over the walls. The carpeting on the floor was crazy thick—it felt like she was walking on a pillow—and the furniture reminded her of the furniture in those movies where the actors were pretending to be the President of the United States. *Damn, Big Daddy is living large*, she heard that voice in her head say, as her eyes were wide with amazement.

Big Daddy smiled as he watched Baby Doll's mesmerized response. "If you stay on track, you can have something like this, or even more."

Baby Doll was jogged from her semi-trance. "Pardon me, Big Daddy. But this place is the shit—Sorry, I mean this place is real nice."

Big Daddy continued smiling, "Have a seat." He waited until she sat down and then said, "You want something to drink? Kool-Aid, juice, soda—"

"I'm cool," Baby Doll said. "I ate before I came here."

"So you like this office, huh?" He saw Baby Doll nod her head. "Yeah, I put a lot in this place to get it up to par." Big Daddy glanced over the office, feeling good and proud of himself, mainly in view of the fact he was able to get out of the joint and do so much legit business with groundbreaking speed. "So I see you came. That's good. To be honest with you, I thought you were going to catch cold feet." This was the honest-to-God truth, which was the reason he forgot he'd told her to come see him today. "So it's fair to say you're interested in working at one my places?"

"Yeah," Baby Doll said. "As long as it's something I can get with." She still had no idea what he wanted her to do and figured it would be wise not to lock into anything until she knew exactly what she was getting into. "So what you got for me?"

"What you know about clothing?"

Baby Doll thought about the question, and said, "I know about the basic stuff, I guess. Styles like Fubu, Armanti, Nortica, Enichi, and all that raw shit—excuse me, I mean raw stuff. You got a store where you sale stuff like that?"

"My stores carry some of those brand names, but we're more into stuff like Phat Farm, Rocawear, you know, the hardcore hip-hop gear."

Baby Doll was feeling that. She could already see her wardrobe was going to be the best in the hood. "So Tera works for you too?"

"You can say that." He saw the stats on the Pitkin Avenue store weren't doing well. "I helped her get started; she's stepping up." He didn't just help her get started; he actually laid out a red carpet for her. He loved his niece Tera but wondered about her sometimes.

"So where am I gonna work!? When do I start?"

"Not so fast, shorty. I gotta interview you first. There's some things I need to know before I hire you." He saw Baby Doll's smile turned into a frown. "Relax, Baby Doll, you got the job." He saw her smile returned, and it made him feel good. "I just need to go through the formalities. I definitely need to know your real name, address, date of birth; I need to see your working papers, social security number, your mother or father's signed approval—"

"I ain't got no father."

"Sorry to hear that. And I also need to know if you can work from four o'clock to seven o'clock?"

"Yeah, I can work them hours." She thought about the issue of getting her mother's approval to work after school and realized that was going to be an issue. Getting her Social Security number wasn't an issue. She gave Big Daddy her real name, dated of birth, address, and promised to produce her working papers, social security number, and her mother's written approval at a later date.

After Big Daddy finished typing the information into his computer, he said, "I got a place over on Pitkin Avenue. You know where that's at, right?"

"Yeah, it's not too far from where I live."

"If you want the job, you'll be working as an assistant stock clerk." He saw her eyebrows crunched up in confusion. "You'll basically be helping the manager of the store; her name is Helen. You'll be helping her organize the clothing that comes in, putting them on the shelves, stuff like that. I'll start you off with minimum wage, that's $4.75 an hour and you'll be eligible for a twenty-five cent raise every year."

"I'll take it," Baby Doll said with resounding force.

"There's a few rules we have, but the main one for our young workers is that we don't allow friends, boyfriends, and relatives to come hang out with you in the store . . ."

As Big Daddy ran down a series of rules and prohibitions to her, Baby Doll realized his use of the word "boyfriend" brought on a wave of reminders that told her Ka-Born was the type of boyfriend she had to be very careful with. His antics that day at the High confirmed that she had better hurry up and do whatever she intended to do with him and to keep it moving, or else she was going to whine up dead or in jail.

After Ka-Born snatched his gun from the car, and wouldn't listen to her pleas to be easy, before she could walk away Ka-Born made her get inside the car. He drove two blocks, double parked, ran back, and opened fire on Jakwan. He missed him but succeeding in riddling his Jeep with six bullets. Ka-Born then returned to the Volvo and zipped away, returning to Tilden Projects with his chest poked out like he did some real heroic shit. She wasn't no killer or a gunslinger, but she was wise enough to know that shooting at a dude didn't make him a killer, and by the way it unfolded, she sensed Ka-Born wasn't really trying to hit Jakwan. In other words, he was frontin', but she did give him some small props since even busting a gun in broad daylight took some degree of heart, even though it was a sloppy way of doing things.

The next day she returned to school, and assumed Jakwan would be looking for her. The way people ran their mouths she knew word had got back to Jakwan indicating that the dude who shot at him was seen with her, but she didn't see Jakwan, and was surprised everybody was still treating her like a sheer super star. It was amazing how knowing the right people, and being connected to someone who was busting their gun, could elicit so much respect.

Big Daddy Blue paused for a moment, and then said, "But my main rule for all the young folks who work for me is that you must be in school. You drop out, you lose your job. It's a non-negotiable rule. No school, no job."

Baby Doll wanted to let him know that particular rule didn't apply to her because she had already figured out that without education, she would never get out of the hood. She'd figured that out years ago just by reading magazines and watching TV. Once it clicked inside her head, she vowed that she would never play herself by doing dumb shit that guaranteed her stay in the hood or made her into a straight slave for life.

This was why she didn't get into the drug game, because most of the folks who got involved in that way of making money either got caught or ended up getting murdered over drug beefs. The money looked real good, but her sharp mind was able to see the long-range consequences, since it was the type of hustle that wouldn't pay off in the long run. She even discarded the whole boosting thing; it was like a game of snatching crumbs and was the type of work crackheads and other dope-fiends did to make a living.

She also had no intentions of following in the footsteps of her mom, aunts, or her grandmom, who were locked into doing home attendant stuff as though they were born to do that madness. Basically they were locked into a dead-end job that kept them in economic enslavement. None of them had an education; they barely made it pass high school, and it was plain to see that a lack of education was one of the main reasons for their state of affairs.

Baby Doll saw what time it was and came up with a way not to become a victim of all the insanity within the hood.

After the interview with Big Daddy, he rose to his feet and said, "So when can you have all that your paperwork?

"Maybe tomorrow." Baby Doll stood as well, looking into Big Daddy's hard brown eyes. She noticed he looked huger than he did the other day she met him. She wanted to pry into his life, find out why everybody was scare to death of him, but she knew self-control and patience was the best way to deal with her inquisitive mind.

"You feel like taking a ride over to the Pitkin Avenue store?" Big Daddy came from around his desk, not waiting for her to answer his question as he grabbed his coat. "Might as well introduce you to the team you'll be rolling with. Afterwards, I'll drop you off home." He headed for the door.

Baby Doll followed him out the office with excitement surging through her veins.

Ten minutes later, Baby Doll was in the back seat of a black Cadillac Jeep while Big Daddy was in the front passenger seat and Preacher was behind the wheel. She didn't know why, but she felt nervous. Normally when this sort of vibe started flaring up it was because her instincts were telling her something was wrong. But now she was confused because she didn't sense any danger coming from Big Daddy or Preacher, even though they were big and dangerous looking men. After a moment she attributed her nervous vibe to the fact she was in the presence of real gangsters. Genuine OGs! Although Big Daddy looked like a gangster, he damn sure didn't act like one. And her research definitely confirmed that he was one. She felt like talking, since it would ease her tension.

"Hey, Big Daddy," she said, and continued when she heard him mumble the comment huh um. "I heard people say you used to be a big time gangster. What's up with that?"

Big Daddy wasn't surprised by her remarks. He had always known he would never be able to completely get rid of the reputation he acquired years ago when he was dealing drugs. He cut his eyes at Preacher and saw he had a smile on his face; Big Daddy knew what Preacher was thinking because Preacher had warned him on several occasions that these young folks he was trying to reach out to weren't looking up to him for what he was doing now, but were praising him solely based on what he'd done in the past. This whole thug, street gangster, urban hoodlum, Ghetto gunslinging, drug dealing mentality was crippling the minds of the youth and was locking them into a vicious cycle of self-destruction.

Big Daddy was totally appalled when he saw how twisted this thing had the kids. He felt partially responsible for some of what was happening and promised to help undo some of the damage. But the harsh reality was that this thing seemed too far-gone to alter its course.

Despite this intense pessimism, it just seemed only right not to abandon the endeavor after spending years trying to get it off the ground. The plan from the start was to simply help those who he could help and be content with that.

"Yeah, Baby Doll, I did some things in the past I'm not proud of. All I ask is that you don't believe everything you hear. One day, when we get to know each other better, and you show and prove that you're about helping yourself to become a better person, I'll kick it with you."

That was cool with Baby Doll. He didn't spazz on her for being nosy, nor did he get all indignant like most other people would have done, so she concluded that his answer was sufficient.

Twenty minutes later, they pulled up in front a clothing store on Pitkin Avenue right off the corner of Grafton Street that had a huge sign above the entrance, which said, "URBAN-WORLD CLOTHING STORE."

Baby Doll got out of the car and followed Big Daddy into the store; Preacher was behind her. As Big Daddy started talking to a customer posted near the entrance of the store, Baby Doll stepped into the store. She had heard so much about this store, but had never gotten the opportunity to shop here. Her adrenaline was pumping because she was not only going to shop here but was going to be working in this place.

As her eyes swept over the interior, Baby Doll was in awe when she saw the place was as elegant as one of those major stores in Manhattan. There was beige wall-to-wall carpeting covering the floor with sleek racks of clothing scattered about the immediate area. There were signs indicating the various clothing sections, ranging from male to female, age ranges, adult and adolescence sections. This place was huge! She was surprised to see there was even a toddler's section.

In the back of the store she could see another section where a Jay-Z tune was coming from. But what caught her attention the most was the soothing smell of coconut mixed with some kind of raspberry-like incense that was coming from somewhere. All four walls were littered with huge posters of rappers and R & B groups and singers. Most of them she knew, and there were even some that she felt shouldn't have been up on these walls because she thought they were straight trash and didn't have a lick of lyrical skills, such Audio Two and Biz Markie. There were three customers admiring the clothing; one of them had a baby carriage. Baby Doll looked to her right and saw the cashier's counter with a slim redbone Black woman with a head full of gorgeous Shirley Temple curls and green eyes standing behind it. The smile on this woman's face was filled with sincerity.

Big Daddy approached and said, "Helen, I got another one for you."

Helen maintained her business smile as she came from behind the counter, but if she could speak her mind, she would've told Big Daddy to please stop trying to save the whole damn ghetto, since it was driving her crazy, but instead she said, "I think we can make room for another." Then she said to Baby Doll. "Hello, I'm Helen Daniels." She stuck out her neatly manicured hand.

Baby Doll smiled as she shook Helen's hand, "I'm Breana, but I prefer to be called Baby Doll."

"Baby Doll. My God that's a beautiful name, and it fits you perfectly."

Big Daddy cracked a momentary smile, and said, "You think you can get her rolling by tomorrow?"

"Hey, it's your store, Big Daddy. If tomorrow you want, tomorrow you get." Helen knew the routine, since just two months ago Big Daddy did the same thing when he hired Rayqwan and had brought him to the store a day before he was to start working. "I'll introduce you to your co-workers."

Helen led the way toward the back of the store. Baby Doll followed her while Big Daddy and Preacher went to a small room behind the counter.

When Baby Doll entered the back section of the store, she noticed the music was much louder and saw three teens about her age working diligently. There were two females and a dude. They all were dressed like Baby Doll— straight urban attire, baggy clothing and sneakers. The dude and one of the girls looked like they were cataloging clothes from cardboard boxes and placing the garments on nearby racks while the other girl was sitting at a cluttered desk typing on a computer. A few feet away, there were two huge pressing machines that looked like ironing boards with flip tops.

"Hey, listen up y'all," Helen said as she stopped in front of the deep-chocolate-complexion girl working alongside the male.

BABY DOLL

Baby Doll was on Helen's heels, and when she made eye contact with this girl, she could literally feel the hate resonating from her. "Ah, shit, here we go," Baby Doll mumbled under her breath and saw this mean-looking chick had some poorly kept weaves in her head and ex-crackhead lips that had pink scar tissue all over them.

She had stopped in mid-motion with a leather jacket in her hand and was staring at Baby Doll with a screw face as if she had killed her mother or something. Ug-Mug was the name Baby Doll instantly gave her, and when she made eye contact with the dude, she could feel the lust dripping from this Rikers Island-muscular built brother. He was light brown-skinned, had a real light goatee with a freshly trimmed Caesar haircut, and a crazy scar on his left chin that ran down the side of his neck, an apparent attempted murder mark, since it was smack dead on his jugular vein. He looked strong, ruthless and totally out of place, since he had "thug" written all over him.

Helen continued when she had their attention. "We got us another co-worker. I guess that's good news considering the fact it's gonna cut down on the amount of work." She really wanted to point out the fact that they would now have more time to sit around and do nothing, but she stayed focus. "Everyone, this is Breana, but she prefers to be called Baby Doll." She saw no one moved and she gave them the evil eye, and they perked up. "This is Sasha," she gestured to the girl Baby Doll had dubbed Ug-Mug. "Rayqwan." She nodded to the brother. "And over there is Angela."

Baby Doll saw Angela had a case of the smiles. Ever since she walked in to this storage room Angela had been smiling, and she didn't know if she should smile back or give her a hostile look. She'd always believed that people who smiled all the time were always scheming on something and used their smiling antics to keep people off balance.

Helen continued. "Listen, I want y'all to introduce yourselves, get to know each other. Baby Doll when you're finished, I'll be out here. When you're done, come and see me, so I can give you the rundown of all your responsibilities."

She was about to exit, but Rayqwan said, "Yo, Helen, tell Big Daddy I need to kick it with him before he breaks out."

"I'll let him know." Helen said then disappeared out of the storage room.

Baby Doll stood staring at the three as they stared at her. Baby Doll had already scoped out the situation, and made an assessment that Rayqwan was planning to get in her drawers, Sasha was as jealous as they came, and Angela was Sasha's flunky and would go wherever Sasha told her. The final determination was that this was going to be a drama-ridden experience that would test her patience. But she wanted this job real bad and would simply have to find a way to cope. She sighed loudly, and said, "Since I'm down with the team, I guess y'all can fill me in on the dos and the don'ts—"

"You ain't down with our team," Sasha said with attitude, as she resumed arranging the garments. "When you prove yourself that's when you—"

"Shut the fuck up, Sasha," Rayqwan said, "You don't speak for nobody around here. Check it, Baby Doll, all you gotta do is what you supposed to do and you be a'ight."

"Nigga, you one pathetic motherfucker, you know that," Sasha said as she tossed another leather jacket on the rack. "You trying to put on a show for this new bitch like she's gonna give you some—"

Rayqwan violently charged at Sasha as if he was about to knock her head off her shoulders, causing Sasha to damn near jump out of her skin and Baby Doll to almost burst out laughing.

"See!" Rayqwan said teasingly. "See! Look at you, a straight coward bitch! Flinchin' and bicthin' up like the coward you is. Say something else and see if I don't break yo' motherfuckin' jaw, ya crackhead bitch." Rayqwan winked at Baby Doll.

Angela saw what Rayqwan was doing and got up and got right up in Rayqwan's face, "You put your fuckin' hands on her and I'm gonna get involved. Don't front on me Rayqwan. That's my word to my mother you better not front on me cause she here."

Rayqwan's ego was rubbed the wrong way, and he shot back, catapulting the argument to the next level. A 50 Cent rap song masked their bickering.

Baby Doll was surprised by Angela's move because her looks were apparently very deceiving. She looked like the team follower but was actually the team leader. Baby Doll made a note to tighten up her personality reading skills, since she was way off mark with this one. After a moment she intervened into the argument. "Yo, check this y'all! Yo! Yo! Pardon me!"

Rayqwan, Sasha and Angela all stopped arguing and looked at Baby Doll with expressions that said, "What the fuck do you want!?"

Baby Doll continued, "Listen, y'all, ain't no sense in us getting all crazy up in here. We all working here, so we just oughta find a way to work with each other without all this drama. I'm sure we got enough of that shit out there on the street and at home. And I know when Big Daddy hooked us up he saw something in us for us to be here. The least we can do is not fight each other over straight bullshit."

Rayqwan, Sasha and Angela looked at Baby Doll, then at each other and with childish smiles they started nodding their heads in agreement.

Baby Doll pardoned herself and made her exit from the storage room. After Helen gave her a brief rundown of what to expect tomorrow after school, and five minutes later she was in the back seat of Big Daddy's ride on her way to Tilden projects.

During the ride it finally dawned on her—there was a good chance her mother might block her from taking this job. Mildred was a highly vindictive woman who never forgot anything and would probably deny her the job just to fuck with her head. The more Baby Doll thought about the possibility of her mom saying no and not signing the permission form she got from Helen, the more she realized she had a serious problem on her hand. It was time to lay down her ole get what she wanted routine and hoped she could convince Mildred that the extra money could help with the bills.

* * * *

That evening, by the time Mildred got home from work, Baby Doll had made sure the whole apartment was cleaned, and she had even prepared Mildred a beef stew and potatoes dinner. Tracy and Jasmine messed with her the whole time, trying to throw her off course with a whole lot of head games, but she was determined to get her mom to sign the permission form, and didn't care what they had to say about her.

The minute Mildred entered the apartment she saw what time it was. The apartment was cleaned spotless; it smelled like Pine-Sol mangled with the aroma of beef stew. Oh, yeah, somebody wanted something from her, and she wondered what the hell Tracy wanted now. She hung up her jacket in the closet and was glad she didn't have to cook tonight, since her feet were screaming for a break. She was hoping Kevin wasn't going to be late, because she needed a foot massage real bad. She sniffed the air and sighed. *Yeah, somebody wants something.*

As Mildred headed toward the kitchen, she cut her eyes into the living room and had to take another look. She smiled when she saw Baby Doll sitting on the sofa, pretending to be watching TV.

Now ain't this one hell of a surprise. Ol' hard-headed, foul-mouth, mother-hating, and disrespectful-ass Baby Doll wants something from her old momma. Well, it better be something in it for me, 'cause if not I don't wanna hear it. It was bad enough she had to bust her ass feeding and clothing these damn ungrateful-ass children, so there was no way she was going above and beyond anything more than the bare essentials. There wasn't any need in stalling this issue any longer, so she entered the living room, "So, what is it, Baby Doll?"

Baby Doll hated when she had to ask her mom for anything. Ever since she was a child, she avoided asking her mother for things, but unfortunately, she had to ask from time to time, and when she did, it was always turned into a major event. She sighed, "I found a job. This old-timer hooked me up to work at a clothing store over on Pitkin. It's a nice, clean place."

Mildred nodded her head. "So you figured if you butter me up by cleaning up the house and fixing dinner, I'll agree to let you work there? Why is that y'all bad-ass kids do what y'all supposed to do only when you want something!? Why can't y'all clean the house and fix dinner without all the—"

"Come on, momma," Baby Doll whined. "I just need you to sign this permission form." She pulled the form from her pocket and handed it to Mildred, but she brushed it away.

"Now you know damn well I ain't signing nothing until you explain to me everything about this job; how you got it, and who the hell is this old-timer?" She took a sit on the couch and folded her arms across her bulky breasts.

Baby Doll sat back down, and it took her about five minutes to tell her enough of the situation to give her a general idea what was going on. Obviously, she strategically left out anything she thought might provoke questions. When she finished, she saw Mildred staring at her without saying a word.

"Now, Baby Doll," Mildred said. "I know you got better sense to think I'm gonna let you work in that place." She saw Baby Doll about to lash out, but she held up her hand in stopping gesture. "You think I don't know who Big Daddy Blue is!? He's a god damn gangster, a pimp and all that—"

"Momma, he ain't into that no more! He's an honest businessman, who's trying to help kids get off the streets. There's three other kids my age working at his cloth store, and you can even go talk to them, and they'll tell you what time it is—"

"Big Daddy Blue got strip clubs, bars, and he was one of the biggest drug dealers in Brooklyn. No! Hell, no! You ain't working at no place owned by him. That clothing store is probably a front to cover up his other illegal dealings. Believe me, Baby Doll, I know how those niggas operate." She heard Big Daddy wasn't in the game anymore, nor was he dealing in any illegal activities, but she wanted to punish Baby Doll for all the hell she'd put her through, and for her disrespectful attitude she displayed toward her. Also, although she would never admit it outwardly, she was a bit jealous of Baby Doll. She knew that girl was going to make it, and for some strange, sick, sadistic reason, she didn't want her to. She would've been ashamed to even give the slightest hint of this warped aspiration, but it was how she felt.

Baby Doll saw the smirk on her mother's face. "This shit—this is crazy, Momma!" She sprung to her feet, about to go to her room, so she could curse, fuss and fume about this matter, but Mildred got up and cut her off.

With a pointed finger Mildred said, "And if you go behind my back and do it anyway, you will see how crazy I can really get."

Baby Doll stared into her mother's eyes, and wanted to tell her that she was a fuckin' hypocrite! Here she was acting like she was some kind of fuckin' saint, and she was the biggest weed smoker in the projects, and she used to sniff crazy blow back in the day.

On top of that she knew goddamn well Kevin was selling weed every now and then. She wanted to give her mom a serious piece of her mind, but she knew that would only complicate this thing even more than it was already twisted. She now had to salvage this situation as best as she could, and it was obvious that if she assaulted one of her mother's nerves right now it would not help.

Baby Doll eased by her mom, struggling not to break down in tears of hatred. Her fury was almost as blinding as the pain of knowing her mother would always try to undermine her and keep her down. Her regret that she even mentioned the job situation in the first place was even as twice as intense. She had really messed up this job thing because her intuition had warned her to do this job thing without getting her mom involved, and now she'd lost a major advantage.

As Baby Doll entered her bedroom, and slammed the door behind her, she was already formulating her next move as she sat on her bed, and every time the consequences of violating Mildred's direct order tried to enter her mind, she kicked them aside, despite knowing that they would be of a catastrophic nature.

CHAPTER 6

Tracy stood on the corner of Blake and Rockaway Avenues with her two homegirls, Yolanda and Nasty Nadine, looking like a bunch of thirsty chickenheads fiending for a quick trick. They were sharing a Newport cigarette, passing it around like it was a stick of hydro weed, and it was clear to any passerby that they were scheming on something, or someone. Just two days ago they had caught a lucky catch when they were hanging out near the Van Dyke Projects on the corner of Powell Street and Dumont Avenue, and a middle aged Black man pulled up in a green Cutlass Supreme, thinking Tracy and her crew were hookers, and offered them to take a ride and hang out with him. In accordance with their plan, they played hard to get, and with some probing the three got inside the car.

Nasty Nadine suggested they go hang out in East New York, and the man, thinking his dream of being able to fuck three pretty young things at the same time was finally coming true, complied with their every suggestion. By the time they got to New Lots Avenue near the factories off of Hegaman Avenue, Nasty Nadine was playing with the man's dick while he was driving, and once she saw the perfect spot she urged him to pull over.

Once the car was parked and the horny old man was rushing out of his pants, Yolanda placed a 007 switchblade to his neck, while Tracy took everything from his pockets, including his wallet and to her surprise a small .25 automatic. After they kicked him out of the car, they went joy riding, and blew the whole hundred and ten dollars on weed and beer. According to the driver's license and credit cards, Mr. Jonathan Minter, was their trick for that day. Now, they were back on the corners, lurking the streets once again for another trick that had a thing for young, naïve-looking project chicks that were poverty-ridden enough to fuck for a few crumbs.

As they moved down the street to the other corner, Tracy said, "I'm about tired of all this petty shit. We need to turn this thing up."

Nasty Nadine was chewing gum with excessive energy, and the lone curl that dangled in front of her left eye made her look deceptively innocent and child-like. She said to Tracy as her huge shapely hips swayed back and forth, "Oh, now that you got you a gat, you think you ready to step up your game, huh? Girl, you's a fake. You ain't no real gangster bitch."

Tracy wasn't in the mood for Nadine's humor. She had a plan that she wanted to get off, and since it involved getting at Ka-Born for shittin' on her and getting at Baby Doll for committing the ultimate disrespect and violation (going out with her ex-boyfriend) she didn't have any time for any of Nadine's bullshit. She knew Baby Doll had disobeyed their mom's explicit instructions and had went and got that job anyway, and would be rolling through this area in a few hours with her man. The urge to get Baby Doll in trouble by telling Mildred what she had done was strong, but she knew how much their mother hated snitchin'.

She even hated the smallest of tattle-telling, and sometimes it made even Tracy wonder if their mom wasn't wrapped too tight by the way she reacted when she thought someone was violating this cardinal rule. No other mother she knew got down the way Mildred did, and some mothers would spazz out on their children if they didn't share information with them when they felt that info was conducive to maintaining family law and order, but not Mildred.

Tracy spoke with venom in her voice, "Don't start that game-playin' shit with me, Nadine. I'm not fuckin' around with you right now."

Yolanda, with her raccoon eyes, and a light golden brown skin complexion with traces of acne, said as she pointed, "Ain't that

G-Boss right there." Her finger was aimed at the heavy-set thugster getting out of a red jeep who was dripping in ice and gold and was headed toward the nearby Bodega.

Tracy's head spun in the direction of Yolanda's pointed finger, and she saw it sure was G-Boss. She was surprised this crazy nigga from Ocean Hills had showed up. She had got word to him through her home-girl, Queenie, asking him to meet her at this store at around six o'clock, so she could propose an issue involving Ka-Born's drug activities with him. She looked at her watch, and it was five minutes to six. A wicked smile crept on Tracy's face as she moved toward G-Boss in trance-like fashion; she could already taste the sweet ecstasy of victory. When she saw Critter (probably one of the ugliest motherfuckers on the planet and was even more ruthless than he looked) sitting in the passenger seat of the Jeep, she felt woozy in the legs as her rag-tag team of sure-nuff hoochie mama's followed in her tracks. *Oh, yeah, goddamn it.* The fireworks were going be crazier than she had anticipated. *It's about to be on and poppin',* Tracy cheered inwardly.

* * * *

Baby Doll reached down, picked up the box of T-shirts and sat it on the long wooden table, and started pulling shirts from the box and laying them onto the table. Rayqwan was on the other side of the storage room mopping the floor, while Sasha and Angela were pressing Sean John pants so they could be placed on display in the showroom.

As Baby Doll unfolded the shirts while stacking them into a neat pile, her mind was still pondering her next move on how to handle the beef with her mom. She was glad she never told her mother the address of this store, and hoped even if she got up enough nerve to search the whole Pitkin Avenue, that she wouldn't blow up the spot if she happened to stumble upon her.

She started work three days ago, and when her mom approached her about coming home late, she told her that she had joined an after-school program in which she was a part of a spelling competition team. Sshe knew damn well Baby Doll was lying. Mildred was bitching a hundred miles a minute, but Baby Doll didn't care. She was going to work and that was it. If Mildred got crazy, Baby Doll would have to find a way to get around whatever she dished out. Baby Doll surmised that all this was just temporary, since she was going to get out of her mother's crib, somehow some way.

Baby Doll took the last pair of pants from the box and tossed it on the pile. She kicked the empty box to the side, pulled the next box to her, opened it, and resumed pulling and stacking the garments. She hoped her mother's forged signature on the permission document wouldn't be discovered, and most of all, that her mom didn't blow up the spot if this issue came to light. Jeanette helped her with this hurdle, and since she had once been an expert forger, she did her thing on that permission document. All it took was for Jeanette to look at Mildred's signature on an old telephone bill, and that was all she wrote.

Rayqwan approached Baby Doll and pulled her out of her daydream. "Yo, Baby Doll, you need a hand with that?" He didn't wait for her to answer as he started reaching in, grabbing pants. "I got some tickets to the Super Rap Fest. You wanna roll with me? Everybody who somebody gon' be there."

Baby Doll stopped in mid-motion. She was about to blow up on him, since he was a bold and disrespectful motherfucker. Rayqwan knew she had a man; he even saw Ka-Born picked her up from work twice, and it was obvious he was showing his grimy side. "You know I got a man, Rayqwan. How we gonna vibe with Ka-Born on me like a shadow?"

Rayqwan lit up with hope and took this as an indication that there were some possibilities here. She didn't say no, and that, by his standards, meant yes. Reading between the lines, this meant they could vibe on the DL, as long as they didn't get caught. "You ain't new to this thing, Baby Doll. Creeping is a way of the world. I can show you some tricks that'll tighten your game up and make you—"

"No disrespect, Rayqwan, but I don't hustle backwards." Baby Doll never once looked up from what she was doing.

Rayqwan was stuck for a moment. What the hell was she talking about!? "Hustlin' backwards!? What you tryin' to say!? I'm on some backward shit?"

Baby Doll stopped and locked eyes with Rayqwan with both hands propped impatiently on her hips. "Why would I creep with you, and you ain't even gotta a ride?" She was about to roll her head in Sheneneh fashion but kept it simple and clean. "Gettin' with you would like trading in a car for a bike. I can ride the iron horse by myself. Don't need much company with that type of transportation."

Rayqwan cracked an embarrassed smile, but he really wanted to dis the shit out of her, call her a conceited, shut-up bitch, even though she was technically right about his situation. He fought not to lash out, but his ego wouldn't let him wipe it on his chest. He wouldn't go crazy on her, but he would prevent his ego from being scarred. "But I bet you one thing, Baby Doll. That nigga ain't got no dick game like the one I can lay on that sweet, honey-glazed ass of yours." He threw her a kiss, hit her with another smile, and went back to what he was doing, vowing that he would stop playing games and get that ride he'd been planning to get, even if it was a borderline hooptie.

Baby Doll cracked a smile and continued stacking pants. She would've loved to take Rayqwan up on his offer, since she'd checked out his equipment downstairs and it looked like it was built to last. The thought of giving Rayqwan some play in order to squeeze him for some dough even crossed her mind, but it was obvious that if he was working here with her, his paper was way too weak for her. By the way he talked it was obvious he gave up the game, turned in his hustler's card, and was trying to avoid the lethal consequences of the street, especially since Big Daddy wouldn't tolerate it any other way while working in his place. Despite it all, she admired Rayqwan, but couldn't ride with him at the moment, since he was the kind of brother that wasn't in the equation of her current gameplan to escape from the hood; there was just too much shit she had to get right before she even thought about getting on a happy-go-lucky trip.

Baby Doll suddenly felt like someone was looking at her. When Baby Doll looked the other way, she saw both Sasha and Angela were apparently trying to eavesdrop on her and Rayqwan's conversation even though a Busta Rhyme rap song was in the background was obscuring their voices.

Sasha rolled her eyes so hard at Baby Doll, the hate vibrated the air in between them; Sasha then started whispering in Angela's ear, and it was obvious they were talking about her by the way Angela kept sneaking hate-laced peeks at her. When Angela rolled her eyes, Baby Doll knew it was time to start putting the finishing touches on her preemptive attack that would put them both in their rightful places. She would strike first, as usual, and would lay the business down properly, so that they understood that all that hating, jealous undermining, backstabbing bullshit was not going to be tolerated while she was working here.

* * * *

Big Daddy sat comfortably behind his desk with the phone clapped to his ear while leaning back in his cushioned swivel chair. "Mr.

Hudson, we been down this road before. Nothing has changed since the last time we communicated in regard to the Albee Square Mall store. I don't know what's so hard for you to understand. None of my business properties are for sale. I could care less what you're offering; my businesses serve a greater purpose." He listened intently to Mr. Ernest Hudson on the other end of the line while muttering, "Huh um," every so often.

Suddenly, Preacher entered, saw Big Daddy was on the phone, was about to leave, but Big Daddy waved for him to have a seat. Preacher obeyed.

Big Daddy sighed and said into the phone, "Mr. Hudson, I'll say it again. You will never get possession of my businesses because they're not for sale. Living or dead, you will never get them, so stop wasting your time. Now, what you should be talking about is how much you can contribute to my Youth Employment Program. Better yet, why don't you hire a few of these kids as a way of giving back to the community." He listened as he and Preacher made eye contact. After a moment, Big Daddy said, "Yeah, you're right, it can never hurt to try. I'm not upset by your actions, and I hope you understand where I'm coming from." There was a pause. "Yeah, okay, have a nice day." Big Daddy hung up the phone and sighed exhaustedly.

"That Ernest Hudson creep is acting up again, huh?" Preacher said as he saw Big Daddy nod his head and open up a file on his desk. "I see this chump don't take no for an answer. I came to let know that shipment of those Sean John jackets coming from Crown is not gonna happen. They ran into a problem with the manufacturer."

"Give that other distributor a call; the one in Jersey."

"International or Mastermade?"

"Go with International. That's a hot item, and it's going fast, so it's worth the extra shipping fees for overnight delivery."

"I'm on it," Preacher shot to his feet, and lumbered out of the office.

Big Daddy Blue leaned back in his seat and couldn't help but contemplate what Ernest Hudson was up to. Since Hudson was a multi-millionaire and had bet Big Daddy that he would get that Albee Square Mall store one day, Big Daddy wondered could he live up to his counter promise to Hudson that he could not get a single piece of his property, whether he was living or dead. Big Daddy was all too familiar with the extremes rich people would go to get what they wanted, and since Ernest Hudson was about as arrogant, vile, shrewd, and cut-throat as they came, he knew there was a need to put his guards up and keep them up.

* * * *

As Baby Doll exited Urban-World Clothing Store, heading for Ka-Born's ride, she could instantly feel the tension in the air. Ka-Born had his man Sinister in the backseat, and there was another car parked in back of K-Born's Volvo with Ramsey behind the wheel and Blade, another well-known gunman, sitting in the passenger seat.

Baby Doll immediately started telling herself that this was it. She was cutting Ka-Born loose, because it was obvious what was going on here. They were in the middle of another drug war, and she was in the middle of it because she was going out with this crazy motherfucker. But the more she insisted she was going to break up with him, the more the rational side of her mind was telling her she wasn't finished with him yet.

She forced herself to calm down and remembered the bigger picture, the larger objective of getting involved with Ka-Born in the first place. She sighed as she realized it was almost time to be put this main objective into activation.

In a few more months she would turn it up and get him to do the dirty deed. By then she was sure his heart would be so ensnared in their relationship, especially since she was about to give him a piece of this good thang, she was almost positive he would dance to the tune she played. She had it all laid out and knew she couldn't abandon the mission now.

Baby Doll got in the car with a golden smile, kissed Ka-Born on the cheek, and said to him as he started the car, "What is it now, Ka-Born? Who done fucked around and played theyself?"

Ka-Born didn't say a word as he pulled into the traffic, and she knew right then that this shit was beyond very serious. Whatever it was, it had Ka-Born in a real fucked-up mood, which was very unusual. He was like a class clown by nature and would take everything in stride as if life itself was nothing but one big game, even when the situation had life and death consequences. Baby Doll was about to probe further but decided to let him regulate the conversation.

By the time they pulled up in front of her project building, Baby Doll's nervousness and inquisitive mind was on the verge of panic. Ka-Born still hadn't told her what was up, but by the way he kept his burner laying in his lap, and from the way Sinister also had his weapon in the ready, it wasn't hard to tell that the drama was at its maximum volume.

As Ka-Born put the car's gear in park, Baby Doll wanted to ask him if she should she watch her back more than usual, since in this particular hood when it was on, that meant everything goes. Everybody was a potential target. Brothers, sisters, moms, cousins, the family pet, and especially girlfriends, were known to get blessed with the business.

Simply being connected to the person who was the subject of the drama could cost the most innocent person to get caught up in a web of sheer hell. Brownsville seemed to traditionally harbor some of the grimiest hustlers, ballers, dealers, and players. It was virtually a cultural thing in this area of Brooklyn to do the damn thing in the most unscrupulous of ways.It was as if the folks out there were striving to outdo each previous generation in griminess. Not surprisingly, as far back as the late sixties and earlier seventies when the Tomahawks and Jolly-Stompers gangs were running through that area, Brownville had won the title of being Brooklyn's most grimiest, hands down. Now, the general mentality was whoever could be the grimiest earned the Brownville Street title, and every person in the game seemed to inherently aspire to either gain or maintain the title.

Ka-Born started looking around the immediate area, as though bullets were about to start flying. Sinister was acting in a similarly tensed fashion. Ka-Born stopped and stared at Baby Doll.

Baby Doll stared back, and for some odd reason her heart started to pound because Ka-Born had that deadly look in his eyes. Baby Doll's mind took off on its own, imaging every fucked-up thing that could've gone wrong. Maybe somebody had got to Ka-Born and put some shit in the game.

They probably flipped Ka-Born, making him think I tried to set him up, or something. Maybe somebody lied and now Ka-Born was planning to kill me!

She slowed her terror-stricken mind down enough to think clearly. She instantly excluded the possibility of him killing her because if he was planning to do that he wouldn't do it right here in front of her building, especially since there were mad people on the street. Baby Doll sighed and said, "What's the matter, Ka-Born? You starting to make me nervous. I know this must be real crazy since you ain't say nothing to me."

"And you should be nervous," Ka-Born said, as he gave Sinister the head nod to get out the car, apparently because he wanted to talk privately with Baby Doll. After Sinister exited the car, and sat on the nearby bench a few yards away, Ka-Born said, "Listen, Baby Doll, you know I've been treating you real special." He smiled inwardly because he was sure he had her fine, sweet little ass where he wanted her. He knew she was one of those play-hard-to-get kind of bitches when it came to giving up that pussy. She knew by holding out for a crazy long time, it only made the desire to hit that thing that much stronger. The longer she waited, the more power it gave her, and the more control it put into her hands. Everybody knew Baby Doll was an extremely smart bitch, and nobody out there could say they were fucking that pussy. But after the little dance he had to do with G-Boss and them Ocean Hill cats, it looked like somebody had set him up because they apparently knew about his stash house. Ka-Born figured he might as well use this situation to speed up the process of him tapping Baby Doll's boots.

He sighed dramatically. "Check this out. I just had to bang out with some niggas from Ocean Hill. They hit up my little man Gizmo real bad, and I got this strange feeling that somebody close to me setup this whole shit."

Baby Doll looked at Ka-Born's hands to make sure he wasn't about to snuff her. "Ah, come on, Ka-Born, now you know damn well I don't get down like that—"

"No, I don't know." He lied. He knew it wasn't her. This setup had Tracy written all over it. "But what I do know is I been with you for about two months, chauffeuring you around like you the Queen Bee, and showering you with all type of high-class shit. And guess what?"

He grabbed his dick and jerk on it ever so slightly. "I still ain't get treated for doing right by you. Now, you know I got mad older brothers, and they in the game, and from what they tell me, when a broad is getting her shit greased, but you ain't getting your shit greased, then look both ways because a con is in play."

Baby Doll saw what this was about. This nigga was playing a fucking head game with her in order to get in her drawers. Scare her up a little, demand some pussy, and presto, he get his shit off.

"Ka-Born, you know I ain't like any of these bitches out here. You can't find one motherfucker out here who can say they dogged me out because that ain't who I am. Now, I told you, we gonna do this. I'll give you my most precious jewel, if you show me that you are down for me. If you down for me, then I'll be down for you on every level, no matter what it is."

"And you still think I'm not down for you!? Haven't I shown and prove that by now?"

Baby Doll knew he was right. He'd been treating her right as far as materialistic things and picking her up from work from time to time were concerned. He was late most of the time, and even completely failed to pick her up from certain places, but when compared to all the other utterly irresponsible fools running around this hood, Ka-Born did demonstrate himself to be slightly dependable, mainly because he was totally infatuated with getting into her pants. There was no doubt that once he got the pussy all that would probably disappear or at least slow down drastically. Baby Doll did some quick calculating and realized she would give it two more weeks and give him some.

"Okay, okay, I see what's up here. In two weeks, we'll make a big thing out of it. Hotels, Jacuzzi, the whole nine."

Ka-Born smiled inwardly. He could live with two weeks. Since he had about four other side bitches, it really didn't matter. But it was good a thing that he would finally be getting a chance to blaze those skins of Baby Doll. As much shit as he'd gone through to play in that thang-thang, he decided if it wasn't worth it he was going to get good and foul, and as crazy as a deranged hyena. He wanted strictly tight grippers, scrupulously hot and juicy skins, or it was going to be hell to pay.

After giving Ka-Born his ritualistic uncoordinated tongue kiss, she exited the car and went upstairs to her mother's apartment and tried to do some homework. Her mind was on the fact that someone had set up Ka-Born, and it was obvious that it had to be Tracy. For some odd reason, she felt a sense of concern for Tracy's safety. She hated her guts, but she didn't want to see her dead. Of course, during and immediately after one of their fights, Baby Doll was wishing death and eternal pain and suffering on her, but now that they weren't in the heat of battle, her inner heart was talking control. With a struggle she forced herself to get focused, because she knew Tracy would not only wish death on her but would actually facilitate that process.

Fuck that dumb bitch!

And with that she was back on track.

That night around eleven o'clock, Baby Doll and Jazz had a good talk about how it would feel to have their own crib. The talk lasted about ten minutes, and they got off a few good laughs. Baby Doll could never stay completely mad at Jazz for long, since she had that kind of personality that you couldn't stay mad with for long. Plus, Jazz was a survivor in every sense of the word, just like her big sister Baby Doll.

She was virtually the opposite of Tracy, who was the street tramp of the family, but was liked by Mildred, since she looked just like her mother. Jazz was sharp when it came to maneuvering into position and would go with wherever the strength was. She knew how to capitalize on any given situation; and when the drama was finished, she would secretly mend the relationship with Baby Doll. She was a master at playing both sides of the fence. It tickled Baby Doll's funny bone to see Jazz in action. It was, however, irritating at times, but Baby Doll learned how to go with it only because she saw a lot of herself in Jazz.

Baby Doll felt extremely tired and, as usual, was the last to go to sleep. Since Kevin was spending the night, Baby Doll knew it was wise to be on guard with him in the midst. Around one o'clock, she fell to sleep and was dreaming real hard. Her dreams were all over the place, and for some strange reason they were vivid and life-like. Sex was apparent on her mind because the moment she was in a deep sleep, she was in an exotic hotel with real flowers everywhere, and Egyptian-style wall coverings surrounding this unbelievably beautiful place. Ka-Born was dressed like King Tut and she was dress like Nefertiti.

Suddenly, they started caressing each other, kissing, hugging, and fondling each other in all the right places. Then they quickly undressed and resumed their sexual dance of foreplay. Ka-Born laid her down on a soft hassock and started tongue-kissing her downtown. It felt so unbelievably real. She was all into it, throwing that pussy, her body moving to a synchronized esoteric rhythm, toes curling, and sensuous moans of absolute pleasure. She even released a cup full of orgasmic juices and could hear Ka-Born slurping up her honey as if it was the best treat he'd ever tasted.

When she coked her legs wider so as it get into another round of this sexual ecstasy, she shifted her body and her dreamscape broke just enough for the real world to take control. She swirled up from the dream world and was surprised she was still experiencing the sexual pleasure from the dream. She looked down through sleep-ridden eyes, and saw someone's head in between her legs.

Kevin realized Baby Doll had awakened and rushed into a standing position with his dick at attention and his finger to his mouth as if to make the shush sound. He scrambled up to her and whispered into Baby Doll's ear, "Don't you make a noise. You know I will tell it if you make any noise. You want me to tell it?" He felt Baby Doll shake her head no. "That's good. Now, I want you to come into the living room, so we can have some fun. If we get caught, I'm gonna tell it all. And I mean all of it. So you better be real quiet, and you better not play no games. You hear me, Baby Doll?" After Baby Doll nodded, he tiptoed out of the room.

Baby Doll fought back the tears with every drop of energy she had. Twice she almost slipped, but she held onto the one image that kept her going. And that image was of Kevin in a coffin, stiff as a rock. She was hoping this wouldn't happened again. He'd slowed down raping her, and she was hoping maybe he had decided to stop all together. Deep down, though, she knew he would never stop.

As Baby Doll slid out of the bed and tipped toed toward the living room, she decided in that moment that she would have to alter her plan. It would have to be accelerated. Ka-Born would have to do the dirty deed sooner than she planned, because she was not going to take this anymore.

That's it. This shit is stopping right here and now.

Baby Doll entered the living room and lay down on the couch, and Kevin entered her with his condom-covered penis.

She realized she hated the way her body reacted even more than she despised Kevin. The mixed messages her mind had to endure were crazy! The beautiful feeling of being penetrated combined with the frustrating and infuriating sensation of knowing this was happening against her will made her more confused than an Alzheimer's patient on PCP. But one thing was definitely as clear as a summer day. Kevin had to die.

CHAPTER 7

Big Daddy Blue brought his white Cadillac Escalade to a stop in front of the two-car garage gate of his mini-mansion in Nassau County. He hit the open button on the remote control, and the gears in the garage buzzed to life, churning the garage door open.

The two-story house stood like a colonial masterpiece, with a picture-perfect white paint job, numerous neatly trimmed bushes, and a matching clean green lawn covering the entire perimeter. The in-ground pool in the back was nothing more than decoration and a symbol of success as far as Big Daddy Blue was concerned since he never used the damn thing, and neither did his current live in girlfriend Pamela Garrison. This million-dollar piece of real estate was Big Daddy's pride and joy; a representation of how far he'd come within just two years of his feet touching free land. With the exception of a few noisy neighbors, the neighborhood as a whole was excellent for folks trying to live the slow life, and to raise children. But ultimately what mattered the most to Big Daddy was that it was a decent enough place to call home sweet home. He was still paying a hefty mortgage and was on the verge of taking another one out on this house in light of the current financial turmoil his little empire was struggling to stay afloat.

As Big Daddy watched the gate grind upward into its compartment, he realized he was stressed out. It was the second Wednesday of the month, and that meant it was meeting night for this month of April. He'd promised Tera that he would leave this one night open for the two to discuss business, but as tired as he felt, he wished he could find a way to renege on that promise. But, pulling back wasn't something he was familiar with doing. Nothing he ever did called for pulling back; in fact, once he was involved, he was locked into the course of action to the end.

When the garage was fully open, he did a quick U-turn and backed the jeep into its parking space next to the brown BMW. He yawned explosively as he killed the engine, unfastened the seat beat and activated the close button on the remote.

As he opened the Jeep door, he saw Pamela standing by the door leading into the house. She was fifteen years younger than him, stood about five feet six inches, had smooth, silky skin like a baby's bottom, and possessed a regal type of beauty that announced pride, dignity, and self-respect. Even her walk was strong and filled with confidence. Pamela had come into his life and hung out with him religiously during the last five years of his incarceration. Upon his release he stayed true to form, since it was only right that he take her into his life as his other half and companion. Unfortunately, after getting to know her in a far more intimate fashion there wasn't a day that went by that he didn't ask himself why he was tying himself down with a woman who was money hungry and was still fascinated with dangerous men of the underworld. Indeed, she seemed to be interested only in his money and his past reputation as a gangster. But, she did take care of him at times, treating him literally like a king, and she was very obedient. And since he was sixty-one years old, he wasn't stupid or senile enough to start pushing people out of his life. He saw she had on those blue skintight sweatpants; the ones he'd always admired when she wore them.

Big Daddy got out of the Jeep and eased over toward Pamela, who had her arms extended for a hug and a kiss. His graceful walk totally concealed his actual age. Although he was an elderly person, he was well-preserved.

"My Big Bad Daddy is home." Pamela rushed into his arms and kissed him on the lips. She then wrapped her arm through his as the two entered the house.

Big Daddy sensed something was up by the smell of the dinner Pam had simmering on the stovetop. He watched Pam rush over to the bubbling pots on the stove. The mixed aroma of chicken parmesan, kidney bean soup, Rice-a-Roni, candied yams, and a few other scents he couldn't quite catch, was drawing a smile to his face because he knew Pamela was up to something.

"I see you laying down the mega meal tonight and it's just Wednesday." He saw her turn and blessed him with a gorgeous smile. If he was ten years younger, his nature would have risen by the sight of her body in those crazy-tight sweatpants, but in these years of his life, especially in the current state of mind he was in, it took way more than a big butt and a smile to get him into a pussy-whipped state of mind. "If it's money you after, it ain't gonna happen."

Pamela felt like a kid caught with her hand in the cookie jar. She was cold busted, but on top of that, all this cooking was a waste since he shot her down before she even buttered him up for the kill. "Big Daddy, you know I do you right without there being a quid pro quo for everything."

"Yeah, but when you start pulling out them candied yams of yours, I know to watch my wallet." He headed for the living room as Pamela giggled loudly. "Did Tera call and say she's gonna be late?" Big Daddy sat down in the armchair and began taking his shoes off.

"Naw, the only one called was Rachel." Pamela said as she stirred the bean soup. She scooped up a taste of the soup and checked it out. Grabbing the pepper she said, "I ain't trying to start anything, but I think Rachel wants you to help her out with her bills again. I heard it in her voice."

Big Daddy certainly didn't find that to be unusual. The only time any of his children felt the need to communicate with him was when they needed money from him. He'd long since stopped trying to find out what made them so desensitized to his reaction to their blatant display of ungratefulness and decided to focus on the future and his vow to leave a legacy that consisted of him taking part in that ultimate change. This was what led to his current crusade to help employ wayward youths in poverty-ridden communities.

He picked up the accounting textbook he'd been trying to read from cover to cover. Twenty minutes later, Big Daddy and Pamela were in the kitchen eating their dinner when Tera knocked on the door. Pamela got up to let her in.

Dressed in a forest green sleek woman's business suit jacket with a matching skirt that stopped just above her kneecaps, and was carrying a black leather briefcase, Tera entered the kitchen and saw Big Daddy putting the final blows on his meal.

"We couldn't wait for you," Big Daddy said with a mouthful of candied yams. "Pamela made her mega meal, so you know waiting to break bread with you wasn't going down."

"I already ate anyway," Tera said, heading for the study room. "I'm here for business, not to enjoy a mega meal." She then said to Pamela just before entering the study. "No disrespect intended, Pam."

"Hey, none taken." Pamela went to the table and started cleaning up as Big Daddy rose to his feet, wiped his mouth, and headed for the study room.

Big Daddy Blue and Tera dove straight into the business. The first topic was the level of profits her three businesses had made and the unlikely possibility of expansion.

Tera insisted that they should always be striving for expansion, and if anything came in the way of that goal, then it is something they should put on hold—at least until they got a firm foundation established.

Big Daddy Blue sighed impatiently because he knew where she was going with this. "Tera, tell me what are you trying to say. Put it on the table without all the sugarcoating."

"All right, Big Daddy, what I'm saying is that the way we are hiring all these kids is crippling us. You've dumped two of them on me just this month alone—"

"Dumped them on you?" Big Daddy shifted in his seat and caught himself before he blew up on his niece. "I made clear to you when I put you in charge of those two hair saloons of yours and the clothing shop that the mission was to try to give back to the community. Our way of giving back is to put some of those kids out there to work. Teach them about responsibility by letting them work for what they want, and make it clear to them that if they are willing to help themselves, than we will help them to help themselves. You agreed and I brought you on board. I'm getting the feeling that now that I put these businesses in your name, you trying to rene—"

"No, Big Daddy I'm not going there," Tera said quickly.

"How am I supposed to see this any other way? We promised to take this route, and we shouldn't abandon this course of action merely because there are some financial bumps in the road. Believe me, I'm aware of the financial problem we're in."

"I know what you're saying." Tera sighed, because she was hoping she could soften him up before hitting him with this head-banger piece of bad news. "But what you may not know is that it's worse than a crisis, and I'm sure we both know the numbers don't lie. That's what you always taught me. The numbers don't lie."

Big Daddy nodded his head because that's exactly what he'd always said. His heart rate increased as her comment registered clearly in his mind. *Worse than a crisis!?*

"Let's look at the numbers." Tera pulled her briefcase, opened the lid, pulled out the folder, and handed it to Big Daddy. "I took the liberty to get a professional and quite expensive assessment of our financial status now and in the future at the rate we're going."

Big Daddy Blue determined how many documents she was asking him to read, and who they were from. There were only seven of them and it was from Shearling Brothers, one of the best financial consultant agencies in the state. At least she was smart enough to get a legitimate opinion. He started reading, beginning with the first document. By the time he finished reading all seven of the documents the acid in his stomach was bubbling.

"Sorry I dropped it on you like this, but the facts are the facts, and we need to deal with them as they represent themselves to be."

Big Daddy hated to admit it, but Tera was right. This was worse than a crisis. As he allowed his mind to digest the information he had just read, he struggled to come up with a way around this financial disaster that was hovering on the horizons.

Maybe if I shifted a few things around, like—like—naw, forget that; that won't work. Maybe if I put a heavier strain of my clubs, find a new way of bringing in some under-the-table money that would come in by the barrel loads, and that way we could keep the clothing stores running at a reasonably effective level.

But what could he use to make that kind of money that didn't entail getting involved in any illegal activities? The more he thought about it, the more he realized there were none. The thought of firing any one of those kids was too much to bear. His heart literally ached at the thought of apparently not being able to hire any more of them. In light of what he'd read in those documents, the inability to do any further hiring was something that was written in stone as clear as the hieroglyphics stenciled on the walls of the pyramids. But he searched feverishly within the archives of his mind for a solution that would at least permit him to hold on to the teens he had working.

After about four minutes of pondering the situation while fighting not to delude himself into a false sense of reality, he had to bow down. If he continued to proceed in the manner he was currently taking the business, he would collapse it. This was a situation similar to a person trying to save a frantic drowning person who refuses to follow his instructions to stop thrashing. If this person were to continue to try to save this drowning person, he would subject himself to drowning since the drowning person would invariably kill them both. A wise person surely would not kill himself in an attempt to save a frantic person who was definitely going to kill himself and the person trying to save him. The sensible thing to do was to pull away, and unfortunately, Big Daddy realized he had no choice in the matter.

Big Daddy eased from his reverie with his stress levels increased tenfolds. "I see what you saying, Tera. I'm not feeling it. In fact, I'm hating it. But, I have to commend you for taking the company records and getting a second view. I guess I wanted to do that, but I was afraid of what I might find out, and was hoping that everything would work out in our favor. So what's your suggestion to this predicament?"

"It's only one thing we can do," Tera said. "We have to cut a few people loose. Cut all unnecessary spending, get out of this crisis, and most of all, implement a freeze on all hiring. As far as who to cut loose, I would stay last in, first out."

Big Daddy nodded his head. In the business world that was universally recognized as the fairest way to let people go. Last in, first out. He started counting off those he had to cut loose. There was the wild cat from Bushwick who he'd just hired two days ago; his name was T-Rock; then there was the girl from Bed-Stuy named Esther. When he got to Baby Doll, he sighed because he could see she had a lot of potential, and he sensed that this blow could throw her off course in a terrible way. She was hungry, a fighter, and a go-getter, and he knew all too well how many mistakes an ambitious, eager teen could make once their mind was made up to get what they wanted. He also was fully aware of how many fucked-up detours they could take in an effort to reach their dreams. He was probably one of the best knowers of this fact since his strong ambition was what caused him to get involved with the drug game many years ago. It cost him dearly. He recalled when he looked into Baby Doll's eyes and saw that spark that announced to the world that she was going to make it no matter what; the same spark of energy that Eldorado told him he had in his eyes over forty years ago when he decided he was going to be "rich"—the same goal Baby Doll said she was aspiring to accomplish.

He didn't want to let a single one of those needy kids go, but, like with the drowning person scenario, he had no choice.

* * * *

Baby Doll rushed out of her mom's apartment and hit the elevator button impatiently because Ka-Born was in the car waiting for her. She heard him blow the horn and wanted to yell out the window for him to hold his fuckin' horses. When the elevator stopped, Baby Doll pulled the door open and saw Mrs. Kirkland, the epitome of a fanatic church lady. She was wearing an old, beat-up lime-colored skirt with a match summer jacket, and the hat on her head looked like a bird's nest. Her cat-woman glasses and the cane only served to enhance her church lady persona. It was like she lived in her church outfit, since every time Baby Doll saw her she wore similar clothing.

"Hey, Mrs. Kirkland," Baby Doll said enthusiastically as she got on the elevator.

"Baby Doll," Mrs. Kirkland glowed with a smile. "How you doing, baby?" She truly liked Baby Doll since she was the most respectful child in the whole building, and probably the whole projects as far as she was concerned.

"I'm doing fine, Mrs. Kirkland," Baby Doll said as she hit the ground floor button and the inner elevator door slid close.

As the elevator churned downward, Mrs. Kirkland said, "What you been up to, Baby Doll?"

"I'm just trying to stay on top of my schoolwork," Baby Doll said, still smiling at Mrs. Kirkland.

"That sure should come easy for you, baby," Mrs. Kirkland wondered should she try it again, and instantly decided to go for it. "Have you changed your mind about coming down to the church with me? We sure could use a nice, respectful young lady like yourself in our congregation."

"I'm glad you feel that way about me, Mrs. Kirkland. Don't take it the wrong way, but I'm still not ready for the church. I—I got stuff that I want to do before—"

"I know, child," Mrs. Kirkland gently touched Baby Doll's shoulder to let her off the hook. "I didn't mean to put you on the spot like that, but as a servant of the Lord Jesus Christ, I'm obligated to try to bring the Lord's word to all his children, especially the ones who's always glowing with his grace."

The elevator stopped, the inner door slid open, and Baby Doll pushed the door open and held it as Mrs. Kirkland limped off the elevator with her cane in motion. Baby Doll again held the front door for Mrs. Kirkland. They talked as they moved slowly down the walkway heading toward Livonia Avenue.

"Baby Doll, I've told you this before, and I'm gon' keep saying it until you come around; child, you are unique. You ain't nothing like all these evil kids running around this place. Almost every kid I see and come in contact with is so disrespectful these days and ain't got a lick of morals either. Fighting and killing each other, and don't even respect their parents and old folks. I tell you, child, we are living in the last days, and everything in Revelations is coming to pass. But, somehow the Lord has touched you, baby, and bless you with a good heart. You belong in the church, Baby Doll. Your spirit is a pure as they come, and God has blessed you with the gift of goodness. Believe old Mrs. Kirkland when I tell you, you's a very special child, Baby Doll, and you never forget that."

"Thank you, Mrs. Kirkland." Baby Doll walked slowly alongside of Mrs. Kirkland, and still couldn't understand why the woman felt this way about her. She had often wondered if Mrs. Kirkland knew how foul-mouthed she could get, how she drank plenty of beer, how she smoked weed, how she could beat flames out of some of these so-called thug-ass dudes, and most of all, how she could be one of the most vindictive bitches in the hood when she wanted to, would she still feel the same way. Baby Doll enjoyed talking to Mrs. Kirkland when they met up like this because it confirmed for her that being nice, kind, and respectful to the elderly was the right thing to do. Baby Doll could never understand why teens taunted, teased, and disrespected old people, and Baby Doll had vowed she would never do it. She waved to Mrs. Kirkland and made the turn heading for Ka-Born's car, while Mrs. Kirkland headed toward Rockaway Avenue.

Twenty minutes later, Baby Doll sat staring at Ka-Born eating a Whopper. They were in a Burger-King over on Utica Avenue and Rutland Road, and Baby Doll was trying to find the right way to let Ka-Born know Kevin was raping her and she wanted him to kill him. She nibbled on the burger and fries in front of her and didn't even touch her milkshake. Her stomach had been twisted for the last two days, and she had ran through two bottles of Pepto-Bismol, with no results.

"I thought you said you had something real important to talk to me about?" Ka-Born said with a mouth full of food.

Baby Doll's tongue felt tied in a knot; she realized it wasn't an easy thing to ask someone to kill another person. She felt awkward and very self-conscious. If she put this in motion it would make her a murderer too, the voice in her head reminded her.

She felt herself gravitating toward changing her mind and forgetting about this whole thing, but Kevin's face and his smelly breath reentered her mind and galvanized her into action. She aggressively shook her head as if to say no and took a sip of his vanilla milkshake. She was going to do it, and that was it.

"Ka-Born, I hope what I'm going to tell you don't make you look at me differently." She paused as she stared into Ka-Born's eyes. The smacking sounds he made as he chewed his food were irritating. She continued, "I'm a rape victim."

Ka-Born stopped in mid-motion as he was about to bite into the Whopper. Did he hear her correctly? He sat his burger down. The thought of someone taking some pussy from a female who was his girlfriend was shoving him to a state of sheer savagery. "Somebody raped you!?" A rage began to boil in his stomach and made it difficult for him to breathe when he saw her head nod in agreement. "When did this happen!? You know who this motherfucker is? Where it happened at!?"

Baby Doll felt a surge of delight growing. He was visibly angry and that was good. "It's my mother's boyfriend, Kevin."

Ka-Born paused as his mind pulled the imagery into focus. "Hold up, you talking about wannabe, pretty boy, cornball-ass Kevin is raping you?" His voice rose almost to a shouting level, and Baby Doll gesture to him to quiet it down.

His first reaction was to start planning to let the bullets fly, but as he scanned his memory bank, trying to remember who this perverted motherfucker was related to, he slowed his roll to a slow crawl. When the circumstances started falling in place, he felt caught in a dilemma. But he saw Baby Doll staring at him with those gorgeous pleading eyes of hers, and it broke him down like a sawed-off double barrel shotgun.

She was asking for his help, and that was enough to catapult him into action. Plus, he could smoke Kevin in such a way that nobody would connect the killing to him. He was furious since he'd always hated perverted motherfuckers who fucked with young girls while also going out with the girl's mom's. That was greed at its best, and only a sick-minded motherfucker could stoop that low to rape a young girl that could technically be his daughter.

"How long he been raping you, Baby Doll?"

Baby Doll didn't want to tell him that these rapes had been going on ever since she was twelve years old, since it would make her look bad. How could she let this go on for this long? Her own mind screamed out. What would he think of her if she told him this? He would probably think she liked it because she never did anything major to stop the assaults from happening. After hearing this mental rationalization, she sensed he might shit on her, so she decided not let him know it was going on that long. She decided to decrease the number of years. "About a year. He's been raping me for a year. He told me if I tell anyone he would kill me."

"Yo, Baby Doll, you know this nigga gotta get it, right?" Ka-Born said as a sinister smirk crept upon his face.

"You motherfuckin' right he gotta get it." She knew it was time to lay groundwork to ensure that he didn't step to this faggot motherfucker talking. It was apparent if the two started talking Kevin would definitely put some major shit in the game. "All I'm saying is that you gotta step to him without all that talking shit, because he's a game tight motherfucker, and he got a gun. Don't step to him talking and get your wig pushed back."

"You ain't gotta worry about me," he said, looking around the restaurant. "So if I lay this nigga down, you know how to keep your motherfuckin' mouth shut?"

Baby Doll sighed impatiently. "Do I look like or ever been known to be one of those gossiping, big-mouth bitches that can't hold water?"

"I just want you to know that murder is no small crime." Ka-Born locked eyes with her as he picked up his burger. He saw she was serious by her screw-face expression. His dick got hard since pretty women in an angry state had a way of making them look more attractive to him.

After a moment Ka-Born said, "Conspiracy to commit murder is just as crazy as pulling the trigger. Loose ships don't just sink ships. They can destroy entire worlds."

CHAPTER 8

Tracy and her two homegirls sat on the project bench drinking malt liquor straight from a forty-ounce bottle. As usual, Nasty Nadine had that crazy curl dangling in front her of her left eye, and Yolanda's raccoon eyes looked puffier than usual. All three of them were sporting the newest hood style attire; baggy clothing by Baby Phat and Rocawear.

Tracy lifted the bottle up to her mouth and gulped the liquor down. She was still fuming over the fact G-Boss hadn't step to Ka-Born correctly. She fumed inwardly, brooding over the fact Gizmo got shot up instead of Ka-Born. She was even more infuriated by the fact that she was getting this vibe that Ka-Born thought she had something to do with them crashing their stash house; at least it looked that way. Two days after the shootout, she saw Ka-Born cruise by in his car and the snare on his face was one that said he wanted to kill her.

The expression was truly horrifying. Since she had dated Ka-Born for almost an entire year, she knew when he was really pissed off, and in this particular instance, she was certain of it. But the more she thought about how he dissed her, made her suck his dick and busted off in her mouth in a foul way with a gun to her head, made her sweep all the fear that was trying to develop right to the side, and keep formulating a plan that would work. Twice she thought about creeping up on him and shooting him with the .25 automatic they got from the herb they robbed. But that thought didn't last very long; she wasn't built for that kind of drama.

Plus, Ka-Born had cats all around him. In any event, if real live street thugs, gunslingers, and genuine gunmen couldn't get close enough to put his lights out, it went without saying that she, a merely nobody in the game, couldn't come close to pulling such a thing off.

Tracy looked up and saw Ka-Born's car cruise down Rockaway Avenue, and she could see Baby Doll in the passenger seat. The same fucking seat she used to occupy. The rage boiled inside of her, because this wasn't right!

Yolanda noticed Tracy was babysitting the brew a little too long. "Come on, pass that piece around. And what you staring at any way. Looking all mad and shit."

Nasty Nadine had peeped the fact that Ka-Born's car was what she had seen. "Tracy, you just oughta get that nigga off your mind. He's a foul motherfucker for even steppin' to your sister in the first place."

"What is you talking about!?" Tracy's nasty attitude was clear. "I ain't even thinking about no Ka-Born. That sucker-ass punk ain't worth the mental energy."

"Yeah, right," Nadine said. "Just a minute ago when his car slid by you had mad rocks in the jowls. You ain't gotta front on us. We fam, girl."

Yolanda handed Nadine the bottle and said, "As much as I stressed y'all when Supreme-Mind left me for that ho over in Van Dyke projects, even though he knew I was dick-whipped and sick out of my mind for his digging-my-back-out kind of loving, you know I ain't hatin' on you, girl."

Nadine laughed teasingly at Tracy and said, "Come on and cry some of them crocodile tears on this here shoulder of mine."

Yolanda and Nadine laughed, but Tracy cracked an insincere smile. She been so mentally wrapped up in getting Ka-Born and Baby Doll back for what they did, she'd forgotten how to laugh about anything related to them.

A moment later, Yolanda said, "But keeping it real, Tracy, you better be easy with that revenge shit you on, 'cause—"

"What you talking about!?" Tracy said defensively. "I ain't on no revenge—"

"That shit you did with G-Boss and them Ocean Hill niggas can could back to haunt you and us."

"She's right," Nadine added as a burp escaped from her lips. "You thinking people don't know you was talking to G-Boss just before them fouls tried to get at Ka-Born's and them tells me you playing yourself."

"You better be easy. I know that much." Yolanda took the bottle from Nadine. "'Cause if Ka-Born get wind you was talking to G-Boss just before they got on some bullshit, he's going to put the pieces together, and you know what's going down after that."

Tracy was about to hold on with desperation to the lie that she had nothing to do with the hit on Ka-Born's stash house, but she said nothing instead and took the bottle from Yolanda. She slammed down a swig of the malt liquor. She had to admit, Yolanda and Nadine were on point with their observations. *Damn, was I that sloppy!?* It wasn't hard to piece it all together when she really looked at it. She tried to remember who else saw her talking to G-Boss. It was obvious if people started talking, the word would touch Ka-Born's ears. After a moment, she was confident no one saw her besides her peeps. On the heels of this thought, a cloud of debilitating despair suddenly grabbed her when Ka-Born's hatred-laden face appeared inside her third eye. Her heart started violently pounding in her chest at the thought of what would happen if he found out what she'd done. That terror-stricken voice inside her head spoke to her, *Oh, God, he knows what you did! If he knows it's you that set him up, you know what he's gonna do to you! Would he actually kill me!?*

As if on cue, and right on the back of that thought, Tracy saw Sinister turn the corner, and his appearance answered her question in regard to what the consequences would be if Ka-Born found out. Tracy was momentarily paralyzed.

"Ah, shit!" Nadine hysterically scrambled into a panic-stricken flee upon seeing Sinister, since he had his hand tucked in his waist in gun-reaching fashion. She caused the others to instinctually follow her lead, but Sinister's gunslinger's rapid reach for the Desert Eagle was way too fast for them.

* * * *

Big Daddy Blue sat behind his desk in deep thought. Preacher sat across from him with one leg folded over the other. The question Preacher had just asked him was a very simple one, but like all simple things, it was filled with great complexity. It wasn't a yes or no answer, but one that required some elaboration. After what he found out from Tera the other night, he'd been racking his brains trying to find an alternative solution to the problem. He knew the first obvious response would be to cut back on all business activities until the situation was under control, but Big Daddy came too far, worked too hard, and taken too many risks to turn back now. He'd promised those teens that he'd never let them down as long as they never let themselves down, and that he would always be there for them. For him to bow to the pressures of a financial crisis was unacceptable, and he couldn't do it.

Big Daddy sighed, and said, "I'll answer that question after you tell me, in your honest opinion, do you think John Boy will result to gunplay if we can't pay on time?"

Preacher shook his head, because he didn't understand why Big Daddy was asking questions that he already knew the answers to. Although he could understand Big Daddy's selective realization, it seemed a waste of time to sit there dissecting a situation that had only two scenarios. "Well, let me say it this way. John Boy got mad respect for you. He came up under Big Smokey, so he's reachable on some issues, but with this I can say, he's gonna want that kind of money when it's due, or he's going to take it somewhere we don't want to go."

Preacher respected Big Daddy's noble and honorable mission to help some kids, but it just wasn't worth putting himself and all his loved ones in harm's way when some of those kids he was helping were utterly ungrateful and would probably stab him in the back the first chance they got. Proof of this fact recently occurred when two foul motherfuckers who were working in the East New York clothing store on Liberty Avenue had setup Big Daddy's Cleveland Street establishment. Lil Rah, and Big Earl found out that Big Daddy was the owner of this social club and had the joint robbed. Preacher had to hit the streets with the security team, Silverback, Starr, and Hakim, and find out who was behind it, retrieve the money, and dispense justice.

Upon finding out it was one of their own workers behind the hit, Preacher was surprised Big Daddy wasn't surprised. It seemed almost like he knew it would happen. Instead of breaking these cutthroat motherfuckers' legs or putting them in a body bag with a nice-fitting toe tag, Big Daddy unbelievably just sat them down, talked to them, and simply cut them off. Preacher was furious about that crazy-ass move for a whole week, and now he wanted to put everything they built in harm's way in order to avoid cutting a few of these bitch-ass, low life kids loose.

Fuck them! Preacher wanted to say, but he sighed and said, "I think you know that answer better than me, Big Daddy, being that you did some time with him in Attica. I wasn't there with y'all, but I heard how he was living then, and I know how he's living now. He's a gangster and a street thug for life. If you ask me, I say we take the money, if we can pay on time we pay. If not, I'll personally go toe-to-toe with him. Them drugs he's selling is what we should've been plotting on how to get out of the hood the minute we heard he got back in the game."

Big Daddy smiled. This was why he loved Preacher and had put him down with the program the minute he stepped foot from behind those prison walls. He was loyal, honest, determined, reliable, stubborn in a good kind of way, sharp with the academics, and was an intellectual bodyguard. He wasn't in the game anymore in the sense that he lived on the totally legal side, but he would always be a fence-straddler. He could be the best of both worlds, which was the reason why Big Daddy chose him as his right-hand man.

"I know three hundred grand is a lot of money, and we're gonna have to work the workers like government mules, but this thing with kids is something I gotta do, even if there are some risk involved. I know I said it a thousand times, but this is my calling, and I'm not going to fall short 'cause of an obstacle in the road."

Preacher shoved his huge bear-like body into a standing position. "I'll get right on it. I'll setup the pick-up and let you know the details." He exited the office.

Big Daddy leaned back in his executive style chair, imaging how hard and fast Tera was going to hit the ceiling once she found out what he had done. She had a right to be furious. He had to admit that it didn't make a lick of sense. In fact, the more he looked at it, the more evident it became that this was downright stupid.

But people also thought what he was doing in prison was stupid and look where it got him. With some stash money from his past exploits, he took every dime he had to his name, laid it smack dab on the table, and gambled it all. He bought one club, fixed it up, saved, worked, and saved, and bought another, fixed it up, saved, worked, and saved. Then, he bought a store front, turned it into a clothing store, fixed it up, saved, worked, and saved some more; he continued this process with a few other establishments, and before he knew it, he had a chain of businesses. After going through all this he was convinced that there wasn't anything he couldn't accomplish if he had his mind made up to do the damn thing. He was also convinced that if he could show this to the young folks in the hood, they would see this for themselves and would take their rightful place in society as great builders and producers.

The saying he used as a motivator suddenly came to the forefront of his thoughts. He sighed in satisfaction. Back when he was in prison, he would utilize various sayings and would use them as a tool for creating a perpetual flow of positive energy. The one he liked the most was the famous adage, "necessity is the mother of invention," and he realized it currently fitted this moment to a tee. If folks needed something bad enough, they would find a way. Big Daddy found a way to make this particular quote applicable to almost anything he got involved in, and right now it served its purpose.

But there was another saying that was struggling to shut down this favorite saying, and it always had a way of coming on the heels of it. It was probably even more famous than the first adage, and was started by some White guy named Murphy, which said, "What can go wrong, will go wrong." As much as Big Daddy wanted to believe otherwise, his gut instinct was promising him this big money bail-out tactic would end real bad.

CHAPTER 9

Ka-Born stood on the corner of Sutter Avenue and Mother Gaston Boulevard, in front of a grocery store owned by a bunch of Arabs, who pretended to like Black folks. Across the street he was watching Ramsey sell a bag of heroine to a skinny, bone-headed looking dopefiend woman dressed in dirty blue jeans. He was stressed and he knew his outer appearance showed it. He was waiting for Sinister to come back from the little investigation mission he sent him on. He had also told Blade to tell Kevin to meet him here on this corner.

Ka-Born looked to his right and saw Sinister walking briskly toward him; his hard be-bop walk was the most unique attribute Sinister possessed, and Ka-Born often warned him that it was a good/bad thing, because if hitters were hunting for him it wouldn't be hard to spot him a mile away from his unique and wild walk. With arms swinging in George Jefferson fashion, Sinister had a smile on his face and that told Ka-Born everything he needed to know without hearing Sinister utter a word. That bitch Tracy was the one who told G-Boss and his peeps the location of their stash house, and apparently was the root of Gizmo getting hit up.

Sinister pulled up alongside of Ka-Born and said, "You was right, dog. All I did was walk up to them stink bitches with the mad-grill face and acted like I was reaching for the heat, and they spread the fuck out like they had did some foul shit. If they didn't do nothing, they wouldn't have ran like that. Them bitches told on theyself, K"

Ka-Born nodded his head with an expression as emotionless as a catatonic mental patient; he was content he had quenched his suspicion. Now the plan would be simple; he would rock Tracy's ass to sleep by pulling back from her, make her think there was no beef, and when the time was right, he would lay her down to sleep—permanently, of course.

As dizzy, stupid, and gullible as she was, all he had to do was smile a few times at her silly ass and she'd think they were cool again.

But what really had Ka-Born under stress was the Baby Doll situation and the fact that she told him Kevin was raping her. He'd been doing some heavy thinking after she told him this, and also had to confirm who this bitch-ass pervert Kevin was related to. When he realized Blade was this pervert's nephew, he had to take another approach. Also, after some serious contemplating he realized that he was about to do something he saw as a clown move. He was going to act out on Kevin on some impulsive shit, and possibly hurt his homey, Blade in the process, so he decided to have a talk with Kevin first, on some man-to-man shit. Even if Kevin, lied he needed to look this chump in the eyes. In the past, he was always able to detect if a cat was lying by the look in their eyes, and he decided it couldn't hurt to see what time it was. Since he knew how foul some of these Brownsville chicks could get, he told himself that he couldn't simply rush into this thing with a blazing gun.

He was well aware of the several homicides that happened because a grimy, greasy bitch had lied on a dude for personal reasons, and Ka-Born just couldn't see himself being puppeteer in the same manner as those other weak-minded dudes allowed themselves to be pimped over a piece of pussy. Although he felt it in his gut that Baby Doll was telling the truth, her sharp way of thinking forced him to pause, because shrewd bitches were masters at getting even the most strong-willed brother to jump through a few hoops from time to time.

Sinister pulled Ka-Born out of his daydream when he said, "So we gonna hold off with them bitches?

"Yeap."

Sinister sighed. "If you ask me, this might make them more dangerous to us, since they might be thinking they gotta touch us before we touch them. If you would've saw how scared they was, you'd be ready to step straight to the business."

"All we gotta do is clean it up a little." Ka-Born looked at his watch, wondering why Kevin was late. He should've been here about five minutes ago. "A little later, I need you to run up on them on some joking-and-playing shit, and make them think they was trippin' and it's all good. As dumb as them bitches is, they'll go for it, believe me."

* * * *

Kevin moved down Blake Avenue on trembling legs. Ever since he'd gotten word from his crazy nephew Blade that Ka-Born wanted to kick it with him, he'd been damn near delirious with fright. He didn't have to be told that it had something to do with what he was doing to Baby Doll. That little bitch went and told on him. The minute he heard that Tracy and him were no longer dating each other and saw that Baby Doll was now dating this young fool, he'd suspected that she would try to get Ka-Born to do something to him. He'd met Ka-Born when Tracy was going out with him, and also knew Ka-Born hung out with his nephew, but he knew more of him from rumors that had a whole lot of truth to them. He was a typical project predator who terrorized the community and was well known for handling heat. They said he had no problem shooting people, and this rumor had Kevin scared literally out of his mind at the thought he had to talk to this crazy dude.

Kevin thought about not showing up, go on one of his ducking-and-hiding missions, but that would be suicide, and it would clearly be an admission of guilt. The rational component of his mind kept telling himself that the way to deal with this problem was to talk to him and twist this whole shit on Baby Doll's ass.

He didn't know how deep their relationship was, so he didn't know how far he could push Ka-Born into believing his story. Kevin looked at his hands and saw they were still trembling profusely. No good. He needed a drink before he talked to this dude. He saw the liquor store up ahead.

Kevin zipped inside the liquor store, bought a pint of Barcardi, and drank it straight up as he moved down the street constructing a story that he sincerely hoped would convince this crazy hoodlum that Baby Doll was trying to play him.

Five minutes later, he turned the corner and looked down Sutter Avenue. Ka-Born was standing next to that other crazy son of a bitch, Sinister. He shook loose of the jitters, poked his chest out, caught a flashback of how he used to move years ago, and put on the hardest face he could muster. Fear was a sure-nuff no-no. With the liquor flowing through the cells of his brain, Kevin moved toward them. He said what's up to his nephew and kept it moving toward Ka-Born. He saw Ka-Born whisper something to Sinister, and Sinister immediately broke out, heading down Sutter Avenue toward Rockaway. Is this good or bad? Kevin nervously asked himself. Even the liquor wasn't strong enough to stop his paranoid mind from overlooking that abrupt move. "What's up, Ka-Born. How you doing bro?" He stuck out his hand for a shake.

Ka-Born had on a crazy screw face. He looked at Kevin's extended hand and ignored it. "I ain't your homey, and ain't gon' front like we cool. We need to talk, you feel me?"

Kevin was certain now this was dealing with what he was doing to Baby Doll. It was time to win an academy award, especially since his life depended on it. "Yeah, my nephew Blade told me you wanted to talk to me. You sound a little upset? What's up? Everything a'right?"

"I know you know Baby Doll is my girl." Ka-Born stared at him for a moment and continued. "Listen, I'm gonna come right out and ask you, and if you lie, I'm gonna find out, and when I do, I'm gonna push your motherfuckin' wig back—"

"Wow, wow, young blood, you ain't gotta get all crazy like that." Kevin looked genuinely confused. "Tell me what's wrong."

Ka-Born locked eyes with him, searching for any signs of overwhelming fear. He propped his hand on the gun in his waist to get a reaction and was surprised when he didn't see it. He rode the silent wave for a few more seconds, not breaking the stare and said, "Is you doing something to Baby Doll you ain't supposed to be doing!?"

Kevin squinted his eyes in confusion. "Doing something to Baby Doll!? What are you talking about? Doing something like what?"

Ka-Born was confused now, because this cat looked like he didn't know what was going on. "Raping her, motherfucker! Are you raping her!?"

Kevin could've won ten Actors Guild Awards by the way he unveiled his utterly shocked expression. "Rape!? You said raped her!?" He shook his head. "Listen, young blood—"

"Don't call me young blood, nigga. You know my motherfuckin' name."

"Pardon me, Ka-Born. Baby Doll is trying to play you, man. She's a little fuckin' liar. Me and her had some words, and she told me she was gonna get at me, because I convinced her mother not to give her some money, and—and—me and Baby Doll has had fights ever since I been dealing with her moms. Me and her stay arguing."

He shook his head theatrically with a truly heartbroken expression. "I can't believe she went to this extreme to hurt me over a few bullshit arguments. I know she hates my guts, but this is crazy. I didn't do anything to that girl. She's young enough to be my daughter! She's only sixteen for crying out loud! Just look at how crazy that would be with a house full of girls. How the hell am I gonna rape that girl with all those women in that house? Go ask Tracy, and I bet she'll tell you Baby Doll is lying. As much as Tracy be running her mouth, did she ever tell you I was raping that girl? Now I know you was going out with Tracy not too long ago. Did she ever mention it to you?" He saw he had Ka-Born exactly where he wanted him, and now he was going to go for the knockout. "Listen, Ka-Born, I'm gonna share something with you, and I hope you don't get crazy. But Baby Doll came to me for some money a few weeks back and offered to have sex with me if I gave her two hundred dollars." He saw Ka-Born twisted up his face disbelievingly. "I'm serious, man. I told her I wasn't giving her shit, and if she ever approached me like that again I would tell her mother. I guess what's happening here is that she's trying to have you do something to me to prevent me from exposing her."

Ka-Born didn't know what to believe. Kevin sounded and looked like he was telling the truth. Plus, he didn't know Baby Doll long enough to put his totally "word is bond" on her integrity. The more he thought about how these females out here had a way of playing dudes, the more he realized Baby Doll might be trying to play him. He was glad he talked to Kevin first and heard his side of the story. "Listen, Kevin, this shit ain't over." He knew it was wise not to let this motherfucker think he pursued him even if there was the possibility that Baby Doll was lying. "I hear what you saying and all, but I'm going to keep looking into this shit, and if I find out you lied to me, you will be meeting my little friend." He lifted his Sean John jacket, revealing the Glock 9mm.

Kevin walked away feeling good because he sensed he wiggled himself into a victory. He was feeling even gladder that had put a puncher hole in the condom he used when he fucked Baby Doll last week. He was now hoping she was pregnant because that would set her little hot ass straight for going to Ka-Born. He was wondering if he could use that little secret he was holding over her head to fuck with her mind for flipping out and going to Ka-Born.

As he strutted down Sutter Avenue, pondering the situation, Kevin realized there was no need to approach Baby Doll. He felt a wave of contentment growing in the pitch of his stomach because when she found out her ass was pregnant, it would be like a punch from hell. Since he was sure the nuts he busted that night were the mother-load, he smiled with sheer delight.

CHAPTER 10

Baby Doll sat in class staring at the chalkboard that was filled from corner to corner with the class and homework assignments. Mister Duckworth, with his Bozo the Clown haircut and beaming blue eyes, was sitting with his head bowed at his desk reading while the entire class, with the exception of Baby Doll, was writing in their notebooks. Baby Doll hadn't felt this terrible and distressed in a while, and because her despair was mixed with a murderous rage and a debilitating physical sickness, it was truly a catastrophic moment for her. Everything was going wrong. She was waking up every morning sick as a dog, she missed her period, Ka-Born was acting crazy and didn't step to Kevin, her family was driving her crazy, her co-workers at the job were getting on her last nerve and she could even sense they were trying to fuck her around by blaming things on her.

This was the last month of school before summer vacation would begin and she had burned out all of her allotted absences. She wanted to take a week off and rest her overworked body, but if she took one more day off, she would be putting herself in danger of being left back. She was planning to go to the pharmacy today and purchase a pregnancy kit to find out if the reason she was sick was due to the thing she dreaded almost as much as death, and the way things were going she was almost certain the test was going to be positive.

Twice she almost broke down and cried. Four times she almost became insanely violent, feeling the urge to punch and stomp someone, anyone, everyone that came near her, looked at her wrong, or simple crossed her path. The blinding rage was trying to force its way from her body in the same fashion compressed water tries to escape a container with a hairline crack.

She turned and saw Nicole staring at her with genuinely concerned eyes. Ever since she found out about Big Daddy, she'd been trying hard to be her friend, but the residual anger circulating through Baby Doll's body at this very moment manifested itself in the form of a deep eye-rolling assault. To Baby Doll's surprise, Nicole didn't roll her eyes back and simply resumed writing down the assignments on the board.

Baby Doll didn't want to believe it, but the morning sickness and the missed period told her that she was pregnant. She didn't know how or why it happened, since the only person she had sex with was Kevin, and he had on a condom. Just the thought of being was a prospect she considered to be worse than death. She'd seen what happened to girls that got pregnant at a young age. They died slowly, their lives were cut short, they were trapped in a perpetual state of poverty, ignorance, and despair, they almost never bounced back from this blow, they dropped out of school, they got on welfare, they never got out of the hood, and definitely never became rich. Whenever she saw women with swelled bellies, the sight was instantly equated with guaranteed disaster, and from Baby Doll's current perspective she had no intentions of allowing that to happen to her. If she was pregnant, there was no doubt she would get an abortion, even if she had to perform the abortion herself.

"Did everyone finish writing this stuff down?" Mr. Duckworth said as he rose to his feet, pulling Baby Doll from her daydream. When the majority of the class answered affirmatively, he erased the board and began writing some more.

Baby Doll went back into her own little world. If she was pregnant, she couldn't go to her mother for any help; that much she was sure of. She would not make the same mistake she made when she went to her about the job. Mildred was a foul, evil bitch and would only make her suffer more, and would probably even make her have the baby just to guarantee that she would never become something greater than her. She would go talk to Jeanette and get her help.

The more she asked how she could be pregnant, the more she realized Kevin probably deliberately did something to cause this. She decided to step to him the first chance she got and to make him pay for this abortion. He should pay for what he did, especially since he was fucking her against her will.

A wave of hatred surged through her heart, and she wondered why Ka-Born was reneging on his promise. He was acting funny, and she could tell he wasn't going to do anything to Kevin. Maybe he was a cold coward at heart. Maybe he was getting on some bullshit because she didn't let him hit the skins yet. There were so many maybes popping into her head at once, she had to slow down her mind to a conspicuous crawl. Then, she suddenly remembered that Kevin was related to Blade, and she wondered if this was the reason he got cold feet.

After she got out of school, Baby Doll went straight to the pharmacy purchased the pregnancy test. As soon as she got to work, she went straight to the store bathroom and pissed on the strip. Lo and below, the damn thing turned blue. She sat on the toilet bowl, not totally surprised, but still wishing it didn't come back positive. She pulled her pants up and when into phase two of her plan.

When she got home from work at around seven-fifteen, she ate a quick snack and went up to Jeanette's crib to have a talk. Baby Doll sat with a cup of beer in her hand and Jeanette had one in hers. They talked in their usual home-girl fashion, but Jeanette had known instantly that something was tearing Baby Doll up from the inside out. She'd been like this for the past week and a half, but today it was at its worst.

"Baby Doll, what's the matter?" Jeanette said, hating to see her little friend all upset like this. "And I don't wanna hear that shit about it ain't nothing."

Baby Doll sighed loudly. She'd been planning to share this situation with Jeanette anyway, and now that she was certain she was pregnant, it was time to let it out the bag. "You ain't gonna believe this shit, but I'm pregnant."

"Pregnant!?" Jeanette literally scratched her head in confusion, because she knew Baby Doll was smarter than that. "How the fuck did that happen—I mean how did you get caught out there like that, Baby Doll?"

"I guess it was a defective condom or something. I don't know how this shit happened."

"Are you sure you're pregnant? You took one of those pregnancy tests?"

"Yeah. Ain't no doubt, I'm pregnant; got the morning sickness thing and I missed my period."

"So, who's the daddy?" She said teasingly with a smiled. "I guess it was Ka-Born since he was the only one sniffing around you."

Baby Doll nodded her head as a way to brush the question off. There was obviously no way she could tell her it was Kevin. There was no doubt Jeanette would step to Kevin on some beefin' and bitching shit.

But that wouldn't put that perverted motherfucker in a box and six feet under; it would only make matters worse, and certainly would not help her in the least.

Baby Doll took a huge gulp of her Colt 45 malt liquor and said, "I need you to go with me to get an abortion."

"Tell me the date, time, place and whatever else and I'll be there. I know how your foul-ass momma is, so you know I got your back, Baby Doll." Jeanette then took a long swallow of the beer as if to say, "I'll drink to that."

That evening around nine o'clock, the usual time Kevin arrived at the apartment from his job as a maintenance man work at the Transit Authority, Baby Doll stood in the hallway waiting for him to show up. This was an odd sight, and all the tenants returning home from work and from other places spoke to her with suspicion in their eyes. Baby Doll didn't care because she had to talk to Kevin out of her mother's sight or in her mother's apartment. She was a little tipsy from the malt liquor and felt like getting ghetto. When Kevin turned the corner, Baby Doll zoomed out of the building, stomping toward him. When she saw his arrogant smirk, she knew if she had a gun she would've shot him right there. He knew what he did, and he was fucking with her.

"We need to talk," Baby Doll grabbed him by the arm, and he snatched it away. "Motherfucker, we need to talk."

"Talk about what!?" Kevin shouted back, acting like he was going to continue on his way to the building.

Baby Doll got right up in his face with her finger damn near touching his nose. "We got talk about why the fuck am I pregnant, and you being the only motherfucker who fucked me, that's what the fuck we gotta talk about, nigga." She was seconds from snuffing him with a stiff right jab.

Kevin saw she was definitely going to make one hell of a scene. He could even smell the Colt 45 on her breath. His guts were growling, his head was throbbing, and he needed a shower. He inconspicuously scanned the immediate area, noticing a couple approaching the building were already staring at them, and decided it would be best to give in.

"Where you want to go?" He said it like an agitated little kid who couldn't get his way.

Baby Doll led the way and he reluctantly followed. They had cut through the projects, heading toward the far side. When they were near the project building on the corner of Dumont Avenue, she saw a bench and stood near it. The sun had set about a half hour ago, so it was very dark outside and there wasn't much traffic in this section of the projects. Baby Doll felt this was a good thing; the last thing she needed was for people to start talking about they saw her and Kevin on the street talking. She didn't waste no time telling him what was on her mind.

"I don't know what the fuck you did, but I'm pregnant, and since I ain't fuck nobody but your sorry ass, it's yours and you gonna pay for me to get rid of it."

"How the fuck I know you ain't been fucking somebody else? I know a cat like Ka-Born ain't gonna be with you without tapping that thang."

"Well, you best believe he ain't touch this yet." Baby Doll wanted to haul off and punch him so bad, she could literally taste it. "Listen, I ain't got time for all that other shit. I need at least two hundred dollars for an abortion—"

"You ain't getting two hundred dollars from me." Kevin said, and then folded his arms as if to place emphasis on his remark.

"You gonna help me get rid of this baby, or I'm gonna tell everybody what you been doing to me. I'll then have this baby, force you to get a blood test, and then what? Then everybody'll know you're a fuckin' child molester, you'll have my—"

"Are you threatening me!?"

"Call it whatever the fuck you want, but you ain't leaving me stuck with this problem, when you caused it—"

"You keep talking fly out your mouth, and I'll get to talking about what the fuck you did. You really think I won't tell what you did!?"

Baby Doll felt like she was slapped with a glove filled with reality. The thought of him revealing what happen that day she would never forget took the fight out of her as swiftly as a Mike Tyson overhand right. She was so worked up over the fact she was pregnant, and he caused it, she never anticipated him throwing this terrible secret in her face, especially at a time like this. There was no doubt if he started talking, her life would be over. She swallowed hard, forcing back the tears of despair and frustration. However, she knew if she bowed too quickly it would only entice him to go for the jugular, so she decided to stay the course she had initiated. "Listen, Kevin, I'm sick and tired of you throwing that fuckin' shit—"

"So, in other words, you don't give a fuck if I start talking about that shit you did!?"

Kevin saw Baby Doll was clearly defeated, and with those words he killed her attack. He had her little fine ass just where he wanted. His dick started pulsing into attention because if he wanted to fuck her right here on the street, he probably could have pressured her into it.

Instead, he decided to end this conversation and go on up to Mildred, so her attention-thirsty ass could treat him like a King. "I'm out of here." He started walking and shouted over his shoulder, not caring if anybody was listening. "That ain't my baby, so don't pester me with your bullshit problems."

Baby Doll watched him walk away as the tears welled up in her eyes, unable to hold them back any longer. Her knees got weak, and so she sat on the nearby bench and allowed the tears to flow freely. She welcomed the pain, because she felt it making her stronger, more bitter, more spiteful. She was changing, and sadly, it was all for the worse. The hate was becoming interwoven into her very cellular structure, and since nobody, with the exception of Jeanette and Big Daddy, had ever showed her any genuine love, she realized she hated everybody.

The good thing was that this negative energy was driving her to a place that she knew would enable her to deal with Kevin herself. She looked around at the project buildings and the people moving about the area as the moon was almost in its full position. Then, a thought came to her mind. With all the guns roaming around this hood, she could easily get her hands on one. She started recalling all the dudes who sold guns and was surprised she remembered their names; Bo-Pete, Face, Big Barkim, and Sinister were just the ones in her Project alone. There were other nearby projects such as Van Dyke Houses, Langston Hughes Apartments, Marcus Garvey Houses, Noble Drew Ali Plaza projects over on Hegaman Avenue, and the list could go on. Getting a gun wasn't going to be a major problem. She was saving up her money to buy a few things, and to start putting away for a crib of her own, but if she had to get rid of every dime to get Kevin permanently out of her life, she would do it without a moment's hesitation. As she felt a surge of happiness forming, the positive energy was instantly cut short when she realized she had to pay for the abortion first With that in mind, she cried even harder.

CHAPTER 11

In the month that followed, the events of June turned out to be a mixture of fortunate and unfortunate occurrences for everyone connected to Baby Doll. Big Daddy had done well with the money he borrowed, easily maintaining his youth workforce, and even managed to squeeze one more addition to his staff. Seventeen-year-old Tina McMillan was caught shoplifting food items from a supermarket while Big Daddy happened to be shopping.

After Big Daddy paid for what Tina tried to steal and talked the manager out of calling the police, he spoke with Tina and found out she was stealing in order to feed her infant child. It was impossible for Big Daddy not to take action after hearing this, and he immediately gave Tina a job at his store on Knickerbocker Avenue and Linden Street, even though he was far from out of the financial danger zone.

The biggest disappointment for the month of June had to be the violent altercation between Baby Doll and Sasha and Angela. Their eye-rolling rituals escalated into a shouting match, and before anyone knew it, Baby Doll invited them outside in the back of the Pitkin Avenue store. Sasha and Angela took Baby Doll up on her offer, double-teamed Baby Doll, and got the shock of their lives when they discovered that the two together couldn't handle her. Meanwhile, Rayqwan stood on the sideline instigating the matter and rooting for Baby Doll. When Helen was breaking up the fight, she got popped in the nose accidentally.

Upon receiving a phone call of the situation, Big Daddy rushed over, gathered the three girls, sat down with them, and talked with them for an entire two hours. When he was finished, even they had to admit that their dislike for each other was based on petty and minute things that were laughable when you really looked at the situation.

Although they shook hands and made up, Big Daddy sensed the tension between them was only temporarily put on hold.

As Big Daddy returned to his club over on Cleveland Street, he realized that the talk he had with the girls was more therapeutic for him. He felt brand-new and alive knowing he was being a father to these fatherless kids. Most of all, he was helping them, showing them the way to free themselves from a predicted future of self-inflicted pain, suffering and hardship, something he'd debated with other fellow prisoners many years ago, insisting that a person seriously into the business of helping could successfully change the behavior of the most hardened, wayward kid in the hood without being brought to the brink of economic and emotional ruin. So far he was a living example of that fact.

* * * *

Baby Doll and Ka-Born were clashing like the Titans in one of those Greek Myths. Baby Doll worked on Ka-Born daily, trying to get him to do something to Kevin, and every time she tried to find out the reason he didn't want to do anything, he simply told her that he was still conducting his own investigation. Through a series of carefully coordinated questioning, Baby Doll had put the pieces together that Ka-Born had approached Kevin, who had apparently put some major shit in the game.

Kevin had even slowed down his sexual assaults on Baby Doll, which could only mean he was afraid of stirring up too much tension. When she was going out with this guy the same age as her named Ray-Ray, Kevin was on her almost once a week. Now that she had a genuine thug for a boyfriend, he was apparently proceeding with caution, especially since Ka-Born had stepped to him.

Baby Doll and Ka-Born's biggest clashes occurred when Ka-Born wanted to have sex with her and she made clear that she would give him some only when he stepped to Kevin. Ka-Born was furious and threw it up in her face that she promised to give him some in two weeks and that she had went over the deadline by a whole week.

Baby Doll threw up in his face that he broke his promise by not stepping to Kevin. Surprisingly, Ka-Born held onto the cat-and-mouse game, even though Baby Doll gave clear hints that she was on the verge of breaking up with him. If Ka-Born hadn't worked so hard and invested so much time and money on getting into Baby Doll's pants, he would have simply gave up on her. His four side bitches were all excellent bed buddies, so he figured he could wait it out for as long as Baby Doll wanted to play the game. But he was certain about one thing: Once she agreed to be his girl, she couldn't leave until he said so.

By the middle of the month, Baby Doll did get around to buying herself a gun from Big Barkim, but couldn't get up enough nerve to shot Kevin with it. Sitting in her room one late night with the gun in her hand, she thought about all the consequences if she got caught. The thought of going to prison and never pulling herself out of the hood and becoming rich was more terrifying than death itself. During this deep contemplation, she also discovered that the way to kill someone and get away with it didn't entail the use of a gun, mainly because a gun attracted too much attention.

The ear-shattering bang would tell everyone what happened, and even if a person fled the scene, there was a damn good chance someone would see that person. For the first time, she wondered why folks resulted to the use of loud-ass guns to get rid of folks instead of using things like a knife, poisons, attacks made to look like accidents; quiet ways that didn't blow up the spot.

As she pondered ways to get Kevin out of her life, she realized there was more than one way to step to Kevin, and she started working overtime constructing a plan that would rid her of the person she could literally say she hated.

By the end of the month of June, Tracy was still plotting and scheming on how to get back at Ka-Born and Baby Doll. She was still hesitant about the incident with Sinister, even though he approached her afterwards, claiming he was just joking and playing. She didn't trust Sinister for anything in the world, and damn sure had no intentions of going to a party with him in the Bronx.

Tracy still couldn't believe Sinister asked her to go uptown to a house party just weeks after he scared her silly. Tracy had sworn up and down to Nadine and Yolanda that it was a setup, which prevented the two from going without her. If they knew what was going on behind their backs, it would have been easy to say Tracy was gifted with ESP, since she was correct in her intuition. Ka-Born was arranging a shootout where Tracy and her motley mob would just happen to get caught in the crossfire.

When Tracy didn't go for the ruse, Ka-Born wasn't the least upset. He was unusually taking his time while keeping his eyes on his watch and the calendar. It certainly didn't matter how much time it took, since Tracy wasn't going anywhere anytime soon. It was just a matter of time before he would cash her check, eat her dog food, arrange a one-way ticket to Hell's highway, and any other catch phase synonymous with pushing her wig back.

* * * *

When the hot, scorching month of August ushered its way in, Baby Doll still hadn't figured out a way to deal with Kevin. Nor had she wiggled her way from Ka-Born's now pestering pursuant, which had almost reached a level of stalking. It was the first Saturday of the month, and Baby Doll sat on the bench in front of their project building with Jeanette and Edna, drinking ice cold Heinekens while watching the kids having a water fight that consisted of fragile balloons and spray guns.

Jeanette was dressed in red shorts with a matching tank top and couldn't seem to stop smiling with her missing tooth for all to see. "Baby Doll, we should go to the beach next week."

"Shit, just say the word," Baby Doll said, dressed in white shorts that made her behind look bigger than usual. "We should make plans for this weekend if you ask me." Her matching white tee shirt revealed all her shapely curves, and twice she almost caused an accident as she crossed the street. Even her toes peeking through her sandals were beautiful enough to have a scrumptious flair to them.

"Coney Island might be a good idea. We can turn this thing into a big event." There were almost no words to describe the physical beauty that resonated from her during these blistering hot summer months when a limited amount of clothing was worn. Baby Doll sat her bottle of Heineken down next to her and leaned back on the bench.

Suddenly, a little, brown-skinned boy who lived two buildings away ran up to Baby Doll with a lovely smile on his face and started talking to her. "Hey, pretty lady," The little boy who looked no more than five years old said. "Can I have a kiss?"

Baby Doll laughed and Jeanette and Edna joined in.

"Ain't you a little too young to be flirting with girls four times your age?" Baby Doll said, realizing that he was so adorable. She touched his little shoulders and he touched her hands with his tiny mitts.

The little boy jumped into Baby Doll's lap and kissed her on the cheek. He then scooted out of her lap, ran back to the other children, and resumed playing.

"Damn, Baby Doll," Edna said, "You got the whole projects jocking you for some rhythm. Even the littlest of the shorties want a piece that thang of yours." She saw it sparked some laughter from both Jeanette and Baby Doll. "Shit, I might as well put my bid in before I fuck around and miss—"

"Naw, Eddie," Baby Doll said seriously. "I ain't playing when I said I'm strictly dickly. I love y'all like family, but I don't play them lesbian games."

"Not only that," Jeanette said to Edna with the bottle held near her mouth, about to drink. "you keep talking about cheatin' on me and your ass is gonna find all yo' shit sitting out on the sidewalk." Jeanette was laughing outwardly, but inwardly she was dead-ass serious. She took her drink and savored the taste of the beer.

After a moment Edna brought her laughter to a stop and said, "I know one thing for sure, Baby Doll. If you don't do something with that crazy-ass Ka-Born, you might find yourself in a real fucked-up situation."

She'd heard some rumors on the street, but didn't want to start spewing them around, so as to not give them any credence. But because she liked Baby Doll and saw her as family, especially since Jeanette embraced her as family, she felt it was only right that she pull her coat to what Ka-Born was up to.

"I heard this foul-ass dude is talking about doing something to you and your sister, Tracy. I didn't catch all the details, but knowing that trigger-happy Negro, I can say with confidence, it's got something to do with violence."

Jeanette chimed right in. "It might be wise to just cut his ass loose totally and get away from him, Baby Doll. Tagging him along like that can end up real bad. This fool's emotions and ego is all tied up in this thing now, and you know how shit can get when an ignorant, dumb-ass fool's emotions get all scarred up. Being that you let him get a taste of that good stuff, this situation could get real ugly if yo' shit got him open."

Baby Doll sighed, already knowing where they were going with this because she also heard the rumors already. The real deal was that Ka-Born was getting real upset, almost desperate, because she wouldn't give him some pussy, and he felt that she had played him. "I got wind of that bullshit he's talking. And you right, I do gotta do something about Ka-Born." She saw Jeanette's concerned, motherly expression. "Be easy, Jeanette, I know what I'm doing. When I cut him loose he'll go about his business and won't take it there." She took another swig of the beer, and that little voice in her head told her that she knew damn well it wasn't going to go down that simple.

CHAPTER 12

Tracy sat on the hood of a blue Toyota that was parked on Powell Street near Blake Avenue on the outskirts of the Van Dyke Projects, sucking on a blunt. Nasty Nadine and Yolanda stood in front of her dressed in expensive summer wear. It was ten-thirty, and they were enjoying the hot August night. Earlier the temperature had reached a staggering 106 degrees, and the late-night cool-off was well appreciated.

Tracy sucked the marijuana smoke into her lungs, held it as she passed the blunt to Yolanda, and wondered where was she going to get some more money. She let the smoke out slowly. She had just spent her last five dollars on the bag of weed and the Philly cigar. Dondi wasn't going to give her any more money; his blow connection just got knocked and he couldn't re-up. From the way he was talking, he might not be able to re-up for another week, since he had to start back dealing with a supplier over in East New York.

The thought of cracking on her mom for some paper crossed her mind, but she definitely didn't want to hear her mouth about her not having a job, even though she was eighteen years old, and was a tenth-grade dropout. Boy, did her mom know how to hang on to shit, and every chance she got to throw shit in her face, she took full advantage.

She'd been tearing up the house looking for Baby Doll's stash to steal, but still hadn't found it. There was no doubt Baby Doll was saving money, because she always talk about getting her own place. Baby Doll wasn't wasting money on clothes and other things, so it went without saying that she had to have a stash, and Tracy had full intentions of finding it.

She saw Yolanda was hogging the blunt and said, "What the fuck you doing, bitch!? That shit better get back to me; that's it for tonight. When I go to crash tonight, my head gots to be right!"

"Word up," Nadine snatched the blunt from Yolanda's hand. She sucked on the blunt and stopped when she noticed Yolanda had slobbered in the tip. "Damn, Yolanda, why you can't smoke without drooling over the fuckin' blunt?" She wiped some of the saliva off and smoked.

Suddenly, Tracy saw a set of car headlights slowly approaching. She slid off the hood of the car to get on point. In this hood, slow-moving vehicles was always an indication that drama was afoot, and any thinking person knew it was proper protocol to keep their eyes open, and their feet ready to roll. When the gray Ford Taurus came to a stop with the passenger window open, Tracy saw a dark-skinned Black man smiling. He was cleaned-shaven, with a short Afro, and could have passed for an African tourist.

"Hello, young ladies," Rudeboy said. His Jamaican accent was very thick and filled with benevolence. "You are looking so lovely on this beautiful night. How would you like to have a good time with me?" He showed them a handful of money.

Tracy saw the money and almost rushed to the car, but quickly maintained her composure. She saw Nasty Nadine and Yolanda giving her the eye to activate their innocent, naïve-urban-airhead broad routine. Tracy caressed the small waist pouch that matched her yellow short outfit to make sure the .25 automatic was there; the mere activity of touching it gave her a strong sense of reassurance and confidence. She unleashed the loveliest smile she could throw at this horny old man, and the routine was in full swing. "I don't know if we can do that mister. We ain't no prostitutes."

"I no mean to disrespect you," Rudeboy insisted innocently. "I just was looking to have some fun with some pretty ladies."

Nasty Nadine moved up to the passenger window. "So where we going if we agree?"

"I have a wonderful place on Foster Avenue," Rudeboy said, now realizing that his homies were right about these chickheads; they were thirsty. "I'll take you there, and bring you back when we're—"

"What do you mean by having fun?" Yolanda said rhetorically. Her skepticism was so powerful it almost fooled the others. "We don't normally just go jumping in cars and hanging out with complete strangers."

"Okay, okay," Rudeboy said. "I'll give you two hundred dollars each to have safe sex with me." He showed them the huge web of money. "I even got lots of condoms. See." He showed them the two boxes of Trojan condoms.

Tracy and her crew saw the money, thought about the two-hundred-dollar offer and were momentarily stuck, their hearts racing with anticipation, a blinding craving, and especially greed.

Tracy pulled the two to the side and whispered to them, "This is easy money. Let's go for it."

"I don't know, Tracy." Yolanda said, not understanding why she felt nervous and scared about this whole thing. "It just don't feel right—"

"Fuck that; we gettin' this lame ass nigga," Nasty Nadine said. "He ain't no different from the others. We'll get him to a nice, secluded place, get the drop on him, and y'all know what time it is."

With innocent smiles on their faces, the three of them agreed to hang out and got inside the car. In accordance with standard procedure, Nasty Nadine sat in the passenger seat, while Tracy sat in the back of the man, and Yolanda sat next to her.

As the Ford Taurus pulled off, about two blocks away Ka-Born started the black rental car, turned on the headlights, and followed the Ford. He said to Sinister in the passenger seat, "Check out the area and make sure you remember who saw them get in the car."

Through the tinted windows, they saw that the only person on the street was T-Bone and his girl Lynn. They were standing near the building talking intently. Ka-Born and Sinister couldn't see if anyone was looking out their windows, but it was all good anyway, since the Ford Taurus was stolen and couldn't be linked to any of them once their dead bodies were discovered.

* * * *

At about the moment Rudeboy pulled up in the car and propositioned Tracy and her crew, Big Daddy sat in the VIP booth in his Cleveland Street club. Mariah Carey was blowing softly sung lyrics through the surround sound jukebox speakers that were position all over the club, even in the floor in some areas. Nursing a Vodka and tonic, Big Daddy Blue examined the ten customers at the bar, the two couples on the dance floor, and the four groups occupying the three booths on the other side of the club. For a Thursday night, this was a decent crowd, not the best he'd seen, but enough to keep the place afloat. Actually, business had been good at this particular spot, unlike his club in Bushwick over on Evergreen Street.

Tonight was the night he was supposed to meet John Boy here so that they could talk about some kind of proposal John Boy wanted to present to him. Big Daddy took a sip of the drink, sat it down, and hoped John Boy wasn't trying to pull him back into the drug game. He'd made it clear to the world that he'd never take that route ever again.

Now that he saw the legit world was far less complicated than he thought, he was now able to sleep at night without wondering whether or not the next day would be that day when some other gangster would roll up on him and blow his brains out. Not only that, the drug business was indeed the root of so much destruction that he wanted to get physical with all the drug dealers currently roaming the hood, but he knew that would only result in him engaging in self-destruction.

The drug problem was so deeply ingrained in the hood that an attempt to remove it completely would be like trying to remove a malignant cancer from a sick patient that has already begun to deteriorate—once a doctor started cutting and removing, the process never stopped until the patient had nothing else to cut out, and eventually died. It was a harsh analogy, but the reality unfolding before his eyes made it an unmistakable one.

Suddenly, Big Daddy saw John Boy and two of his associates enter the club with Preacher in tow. John Boy had a baby face with a goatee, and a head full of long, salt and pepper-colored dreadlocks. He was about forty-five years old with a muscular physique and could easily pass for thirty-five. He wore hip-hop attire, with baggy jeans and oversized clothing. Big Daddy could never understand why he was trying to fit in with the kids, since it indicated that he refused to grow up. Big Daddy rose to his feet so that John Boy could see him.

John Boy saw Big Daddy and moved toward him. "Big Daddy Blue!" He gave Big Daddy a handshake and a hood-style hug.

"John Boy" Big Daddy said, as he sat back down and John Boy sat on his right hand side. The two associates of John Boy went to the bar to flirt with the women who were unaccompanied by a male companion, and to have drinks. Preacher stood by the entrance talking to the two bodyguards, Starr and Silverback.

John Boy sighed and said, "About that money you borrowed; the reason I returned the portion you tried to pay back is because I want to take that money and invest it in a business, and I figured you can help me get the project off the ground, Big Daddy."

Big Daddy locked eyes with John Boy. The Stare was unemotional, but inside Big Daddy's mind, there was a hurricane of emotions. "Listen, John Boy, we been down this road before. I'm not getting back into the game, and I—"

"This ain't got nothing to do with you getting back in the game! I heard you loud and clear back then; I respect your position. You know you my nigga, Big Daddy—"

"Don't call me nigga, John Boy. You know that word don't sit right with me, and I told you a hundred times. I don't like that word used around me."

"Sorry, man," John Boy threw up both hands in surrender. "I'm not trying to disrespect you when I call you the N word. It's used as a term of endearment. Everybody use that word nowadays to show love. Even White folks use it to express love for one another."

"If they understood how many Black folks were murdered, maimed and mutilated with that word being shouted at them, they might not be so willing to throw that word around as a term of endearment."

John Boy saw a major academic debate about to materialize, and so he brought the conversation back on track. "As I said, I'm not asking you to get back in the game. Even when I approached you back then, I was only trying to find a connect, and now that I got one, I don't need to ride you about any hook-ups. I got this idea, you see. I want to open a few clubs, start trying to broaden my horizons a little. With this rap thing blowing the fuck up the way it is, it's only right I start diversifying—"

"You gonna give up them drugs?" Big Daddy said, "You know that shit is killing us. Them drugs are destroying all Black communities. You give up the drugs, I'll roll with you."

There was a moment of intense, uncomfortable silence. John Boy gave him his answer through the act of silence.

Big Daddy continued, "Just 'cause you loaned me some money don't mean my views and morals have changed. I told you John Boy, when you let go of the drugs, I'll ride with you on any project. But I won't compromise my morals, principles, and integrity when I know it's hurting—"

"But you'll take my drug money and use it to get yourself out of a bind. What's the motherfuckin' difference? You used my money when you knew it came from drugs. I ain't trying to judge you, Big Daddy, but what you just did showed me that if your situation get bad enough you will flip back to your—"

"As long as I'm paying you back, that's all that matters!" Big Daddy almost shouted, and instantly caught himself. He sighed, feeling his anger growing beyond his means to control it. He had known this was going to happen. He knew he would regret borrowing that money, and he was now wishing he could take it back. From the moment that money touched his hands, his conscious had been killing him because technically John Boy was right. If he had completely extracted that underworld bullshit out of his system, he never would have gotten back in bed with John Boy, even if it was just a bullshit loan, and it was for the kids.

He sighed as he forced his anger to get back onto its leash. Although Big Daddy regretted he'd made this bad decision, he wasn't into the business of allowing community destroyers to pressure him into helping them to further destroy the community.

"We ain't gotta turn this into something it ain't gotta be, John Boy. Now, I'm getting old and I ain't what I used to be with a lot of things. But with age comes integrity, and I ain't afraid to say I'm walking the straight and narrow when it comes to the law. But you best believe ain't no pussy here. A coward I never was, and a coward I will never be. If backed in a corner, you of all people know I will come out spreading some hot ones."

He didn't like engaging this sort of talk, but he knew folks involved in the world from which John Boy lived needed reminders every so often and seemed to only understand the universal language; unfortunately, it was the language of violence.

"You steppin' to me like this when I told you where I stand when it comes to them fuckin' drugs tells me that you think I'm a sucker, or you think I'm getting soft enough to let you run over me. To make this thing real simple and sweet, I'm not helping you build more drug houses disguised as strip clubs and dance halls, and all that other shit. I'm against the drugs, and you know that. I don't rock your boat even though I know you dealing that shit all over the hood, 'cause I know selling drugs for some people is all they know, and for some it's about putting food on the table. It's fucked up some folks think they gotta use other folks' misery to pull themselves out of a situation. When people sell drugs they're missing the bigger picture, but some people gotta figure things out on their own, and some may never figure it out."

Big Daddy took a long swig of the drink, noticing John Boy had a crooked smile that reminded him of some of the younger prisoners he used to bark on for almost getting themselves killed over an unpaid gaming or drug debt, forcing Big Daddy to have to come to their rescue. "All I've ever asked is that you stay away from what I'm doing. Let me do what I'm doing to help, and I'll let you do what you doing to make your living." He paused for several seconds, allowing his words to sink in before continuing. "I don't think that's much to ask for."

John Boy was speechless, but not surprised in the least. He couldn't say anything because his people warned him, and he was hoping it wouldn't have to come to this. He rose to his feet. "Well, Big Daddy Blue, I was hoping we could make some big moves together, but I guess I thought wrong. Excuse me for misreading the signals. My deepest apology." His sarcasm was crystal clear. "So

BABY DOLL

that means I'll be receiving my three hundred grand by the end of next week. Every dime." He turned and headed for the bar to gather his crew.

Big Daddy took another sip of his drink and realized the tone of John Boy's final remarks was filled with an emotion that was foretelling. As he watched John Boy and his crew exit the club, he realized John Boy wasn't going to get "every dime" and by the way he said it, Big Daddy knew it was time to start gearing up the troops. Turning down John Boy's request for assistance despite the fact he'd bailed Big Daddy out of a difficult situation was a guaranteed beef that would test him to see if he was serious about still having the ability to let some hot ones fly, or if he was selling wolf tickets.

* * * *

Rudeboy was breathing hard from the wonderful penis massage Nasty Nadine was laying on him. Her soft, caressing hand wrapped around his dick was making him want to pull the car over and slide up inside this fine little hood rat. As they talked and giggled with youthfulness, he felt deeply saddened by the fact they would be dead very shortly.

Yolanda was almost on the brinks of biting her nails; something was wrong, and she didn't know why she was feeling this way before. They had done this particular thing on several occasions, but she never felt this way. She didn't believe in ESP, but what she was feeling was telling her there was a need to reevaluate that position. She kept looking in back of them and couldn't figure out if the headlights were from the same car or a difference one. Her heart was pounding. An image of her lying in a coffin flashed before her eyes. She moaned as if she were in pain. She saw the groan got Tracy's attention. Then, she realized she was probably tripping from the weed. Maybe they got hold of some bad weed that was sprayed with some kind of chemical. She forced herself to calm down.

Tracy was becoming extremely anxious with every minute that passed. She was about to pull the gun and force the man to pull over, since Nadine was taking way too long to set it off. She examined the late-night streets and saw they were still cruising pass a residential district on Ditmas Avenue. Their plan was always to force the car to pull over in a secluded commercial area where there were no eyes to see what was going on. Looking ahead, she realized the factory-laden area was rapidly approaching.

A few minutes later, Nadine saw the factories. It was time. She pulled her hand away from Rudeboy's dick.

"Hey, Rudeboy, this looks like a perfect place for us to get busy. Let's get off a quickie before we get to your house."

Tracy was on her heels, "Yeah, come on, pull the car over. Give me one of those condoms. I want you to do me first."

Rudeboy was tempted, but he knew Ka-Born and Sinister were following him, and he agreed not to make any stops. "I like your energy, but I'd prefer to wait until we get to my home. It's better to do it in a bed, in a nice clean environment." He smiled at Nadine, hoping she continued massaging his wood.

Tracy, Yolanda and Nadine all had panic-stricken expressions. Tracy and Yolanda looked at each other as if to say "What next? What do we do now!?" This never happened before, and surprisingly, they never planned for it, because every time they told the herb to pull over to get some of this pussy, they obeyed.

Tracy wondered if it would be wise to pull the gun, put it to Rudeboy's head, and force him to pull over. As the factories zipped by, she knew she'd better do something in a hurry. She pulled the gun from her pouch and got her mind ready to go with the flow.

Nasty Nadine was confused and didn't even realize that her facial expression had sheer terror written all over it.

Rudeboy noticed their silence and knew they were up to something because apparently things didn't go as planned. He smiled because he could hear them thinking.

Yolanda was second from losing it totally. The faster her heart pounded, the faster her delirium grew. The thought of death galvanized her. Sensing that Rudeboy was up to something, she shouted, "Pull the fuckin' car over!"

Rudeboy and everyone else in the car were startled clean out of their seats.

Yolanda started rambling, "Nigga, pull this fuckin' car over and let me the fuck out!" She grabbed the gun from Tracy and aimed it at Rudeboy's head. "I said pull this motherfuckin' car over, nigga, or I'll blow your top off!" Yolanda was crying now; her intuition was telling her they were in danger, but she didn't know why and refused to believe this gut instinct was due to the weed.

Rudeboy was far from scared. He'd had guns pulled on him by professional killers and had wiggled his way out of point-blank range gun confrontations. These bitches were nobody but a bunch of silly-ass hood rats, and he had a job to do and planned on doing it. He said politely, "Listen, you guys, there's no need for all of this violence." He turned his head to get a better look at the gun Yolanda was pointing at him. Upon noticing it was a .25 automatic he smiled, but was a bit concerned by Yolanda's wide-eyed, hysterical looking facial expression. "Please, you must relax. I will pay you very well; I'll even give you extra. I just want to have some fun—"

BLAAM!

The loud blast that followed after Yolanda pulled the trigger not only scared her and the others into a state of terror, but when the blood and chucks of brain matter was sprayed every which a way and splattered in their faces while the car went into a savage spin, they were traumatized with something much stronger than shock and were catapulted into a nightmarish dream world.

* * * *

Ka-Born was startled when he saw the gun flash ignited inside the car as the Ford Taurus pivoted violently to the right, and crashed into a parked car, and continued tearing forward, totaling two other parked cars before coming to a stop.

Ka-Born brought the car to a screeching stop about several cars from the Ford, tied the head scarf over his face in train robber fashion, and was out of the car with his 9mm in his hand, running toward the wreck. He couldn't believe this shit was happening, and it was obvious one of those hood rats was carrying a heater and had apparently shot Rudeboy. As he rushed over to the car, he saw Sinister was directly behind him with a train robber scarf covering his face and his ratchet ready to roar.

Ka-Born saw people in the nearby tenement buildings were already turning on lights and peering out of windows.

When Ka-Born approahed, he started firing into the car without a second's pause, and Sinister did the same. After pumping over a dozen rounds into the vehicle, Ka-Born and Sinister fled back to the black rental car. Ka-Born and Sinister jumped inside the car, and Ka-Born did a U-turn and sped away.

After making a couple of turns, Ka-Born forced himself to lighten up on the gas pedal, so as to not attract any attention. He was trembling with anger as he cruised down Linden Boulevard, heading toward Brownsville. His mind was cluttered with a thousand different issues. He flashed back to the moment he started pumping bullets into the car and had seen Tracy look up into his eyes just before he fired the first shot. He now realized that the way she locked eyes with him gave off a vibe that she knew it was him behind the mask. But it didn't matter, he surmised, because he saw at least two of his bullets tear into her. Then the issue of Rudeboy slid into his thought process.

As if Sinister was reading his mind, he spoke with a serious attitude right on the heels of this thought. "How the fuck are we gonna explain this shit to Knotty Rob!?"

Sinister saw a full-fledge war on the horizon. The thought of banging out with Knotty Rob's crew even scared Sinister's crazy ass, since Knotty Rob had a team three times the size of theirs and could outgun them even on their worse day.

CHAPTER 13

Baby Doll stood in the middle section of the store, punching price tags on to the sleeves of each of the woman's summer blouses hanging from the circular rack. Rayqwan was four aisles away doing the same thing, but to children summer outfits. The Naughty by Nature oldie but goodie rap tune "OPP" was pumping softly through the store's audio system and was struggling to saturate the atmosphere with an uppity mood floating in the atmosphere.

Baby Doll saw Helen was ringing up the items of a short, stocky Black woman who was styling an old busted-ass weave that was literally falling apart. Baby Doll welcomed the sight because for the first time in two weeks, she felt the urge to laugh. Ever since Tracy was shot twice, once in the upper chest, and the other in the stomach sixteen days ago, Baby Doll was on edge and was scared. The fact that Ka-Born was also acting very strange, and had even stopped engaging in their little cat-and-mouse, merry-go-round game didn't help ease her mind much, because it implied that the rumors may have been correct.

The word touching some people's ears was that Ka-Born was responsible for, or may have even personally shot Tracy. Although Tracy swore on her hospital bed that it was men wearing masks, Baby Doll knew the code of the street mandated that her statement could not be one other than the one she'd gaven. Just yesterday Sinister was shot and killed while standing on the corner of Sutter Avenue and Amboy Street, and Baby Doll instantly started wondering if it had something to do with Tracy's shooting.

As Baby Doll saw Rayqwan approaching her, she realized she was still feeling a little guilty because she hadn't gone to Kings County Hospital to visit Tracy and Nadine. She couldn't seem to let go of the fact that Tracy was her unmitigated enemy. Tracy never even put any cut on the fact that she hated Baby Doll, and it was clear to all that if Baby Dill was lying in that hospital bed loaded with bullets, Tracy would not be there by her side.

Years ago Baby Doll decided to do unto others as others would do onto her. She heard one of her schoolmates in Junior High School utter this quote, claiming it came from the Bible, and upon closely examining this thought-provoking quote, it made so much sense to Baby Doll that she incorporated it into the way she dealt with situations like the one at hand.

"You all right, Baby Doll?" Rayqwan said, noticing she was daydreaming. He started helping her with the chore. "I don't know why you don't go on and take that leave of absence Helen offered you?"

Baby Doll wanted to tell him that the leave of absence wasn't with full pay, and that even a loss of half a pay would put her in a messed-up situation. "I'm cool, Rayqwan. People getting shot in the hood ain't nothing new." She also wanted to tell him that now that her mother knew she was working and had gotten the job without her permission, her punishment was that she had to buy her own school clothes, pay a portion of the rent, and help with the food bill, or leave the apartment.

As a result, her money was extraordinarily tight, and instead she said, "Tracy'll be all right. The doctors said her gunshots wounds could have been fatal if they were inches in either direction. Now, Nadine, that's a different story. They said she's permanently paralyzed from the neck down. They said a bullet severed her spinal cord." Baby Doll wanted to go see Nadine, since she never let Tracy piss in her ear with a lot of bullshit, but going to see Nadine without visiting Tracy would look real crazy. To avoid the drama all together, she decided not to visit any of them, not even to view Yolanda's body at Unity's Funeral Home, nor did she attend the funeral services that took place last week. It wasn't that she didn't care, but it was mainly because she was coping with her own problems. The biggest of the problems had to be Ka-Born. Lately he'd been driving around just staring at her without saying a word. Now she was wondering if she did the right thing by telling Ka-Born it was over and to stop coming to see her.

As Baby Doll punched the tags on the garments, a chill crept through her whole body as the image of Ka-Born laughing when she told him she was breaking up with him re-entered her mind. Then he had said, "You can't leave until I say so. I don't let a chick use me on her terms. Right now, I'm not ready to let you go." The bone-chilling calmness of this statement said he wasn't going to let her go and was now about to do something real crazy.

Suddenly, the door swung open and Ka-Born entered the store. He was pissy drunk and was rambling. "Baby Doll, where the fuck you at, girl. Come on over here with yo' fine-ass self!"

The lady with the twisted weave rushed further into the store, thinking bullets were about to start flying. The three other customers took cover, also suspecting bullets were about to fly. Since this was a store that catered to the hip-hop world, they assumed the rap lyrics about busting guns, gats, and heaters would apply in this situation. Helen immediately got on her cell phone. Sasha and Angela were peeking out from the storage room with smug smiles, enjoying the festivities.

Ka-Born continued shouting while on wobbly legs. "You's my woman, bitch! Baby Doll, come on out here, girl. We gotta do some serious talking." He staggered about and was scanning the interior of the store. Then he turned to Helen, who was activating the dials, text messaging Big Daddy. "Hey, Helen, where the fuck is my girl? You know Baby Doll's my girl. Where she at!?" He saw Helen was speechless. "Oh, so I see what time it is; you frontin' on a nigga too, huh?"

Helen saw the woman with the crazy weave on her cell phone and raced toward her; she snatched the woman's phone from her hand. "Don't call the police! We handle our own business around here. This ain't nothing but a bullshit boyfriend-girlfriend beef." She saw the other customers put their phones back in their pockets upon hearing Helen's statement. Helen saw Ka-Born smiling at her, since he also heard the comment and wanted to let this fool know that she didn't do it for him.

"Now, that's keeping it real, god damn it!" Ka-Born said, and almost stumbled backwards, but quickly caught himself. "We don't be snitchin' up this mufucka! Po-po don't got shit to go with this."

The thought of the police brought on a wave of reminders. He could still see the police cars surrounding the area where Sinister got gunned down. They killed his ace partner, and he knew who did it, but didn't have enough guns or able-bodied thugs to avenge his death. But that was going to change soon.

Knotty Rob was going to pay for this shit. Even if Ka-Born had to lay low for five years, he was going to make him feel his wrath!

Baby Doll had crouched behind the rack the moment she saw Ka-Born enter the store. When she saw he was drunk, didn't have a gun in his hand, and was apparently talking like she was still his girlfriend, she relaxed some as she peeked over the clothes rack at his every move. She saw Rayqwan stood staring at Ka-Born with pure hatred in his eyes. Baby Doll hoped Rayqwan didn't try to step to Ka-Born while he was in this state, because she didn't want to see him get hurt or killed on account of her.

Meanwhile, Helen was calling Big Daddy. To be safe, she text messaged him with the following statement: *777 BIG PROBLEM AT PITKIN AVENUE STORE! BABY DOLL'S BOYFRIEND ENTERED STORE. HE MAY HAVE A GUN!*

"Baby Doll, get your ass out here, girl, so we can make things right again!" Ka-Born shouted and propped his hand on the 9mm tucked in his waist. "You know them motherfuckers killed my man Sinister!? They did him dirty." He stopped as if the thought had shattered his world, and he started struggling to hold back the tears. "They did him dirty, Baby Doll."

Then, suddenly, he looked around at the people in the store and when his eyes landed on Rayqwan, he saw him staring at him with a vicious screw face filled with hatred. Ka-Born detected the arrogant smirk on Rayqwan's face and realized that look felt like an assault on his manhood, and especially to his thuggery. "Oh, so you still hatin', huh, bitch-ass nigga?" He pulled the gun as he moved toward Rayqwan.

The people in the store, including Helen, literally got down to the floor.

Baby Doll realized she had to do something. No longer could she stay put and hope this situation would somehow fix itself. She rushed from behind the clothes rack. "Naw, naw, Ka-Born, don't even go there. That's my word to my mutha, don't even do it like this." She got right up in his face, blocking his path. She was surprised Rayqwan didn't move a muscle and was still staring at Ka-Born with the most fearless frown one could imagine.

* * * *

Big Daddy rushed out of his Evergreen Street club with Preacher in front of him. They both jumped in the Escalade as though they were detectives on their way to an emergency call. From behind the wheel Preacher pulled the jeep onto the street and was zooming down Bushwick Avenue within seconds.

Big Daddy was on his cell phone talking in an urgent, but calm fashion, "Yo, Silverback, listen up, bro, I need you to bring a few of the brothers over to the Pitkin Avenue store. We got a major problem."

On the other end, Silverback said, "Possible gunplay, or what!?"

"Yeah, it's possible. Come correct and meet me there as soon as possible." He disconnected the phone and put it in his pocket.

"I think it's time we step to this kid on a whole different level," Preacher said. "He's got to be on some serious drugs, or he need a crash course in the rules of respect for even thinking he can go there with some shit like this."

Big Daddy said nothing as he watched the hot August streets and the people strolling about their business. He knew Baby Doll's boyfriend was one of those lost causes who was dangerous to everyone that crossed his path. He'd bidded with so many of these types of individuals, he could now spot them twenty miles away. The day Baby Doll introduced him to Ka-Born, he saw it, but held his tongue. An attempt to interfere could have caused unnecessary friction between him and Baby Doll and, in any event, would have been a waste of words because he was certain Baby Doll wouldn't last long with him. He even sensed that Baby Doll was dealing with him for some unspecified reason that had nothing to do with love or physical attraction; maybe because of his access to fast money or the thrill of being with a thug. Whatever it was, it wasn't for love, that much was for sure.

Big Daddy cleared his throat and responded to Preacher without taking his eyes off the scenery. "We gonna step to this kid, but not on some roughneck shit."

Preacher gritted his teeth, because he was sick and tired of Big Daddy and his delusional tactics of trying to kill these conniving kids with kindness. But instead of starting an argument that would go nowhere real fast, Preacher just said in his usual fashion, "Hey, you know how I do it. It's your call, Big Daddy."

* * * *

Baby Doll tried to pull Ka-Born to the side, but he knocked her hand away.

147

"We can talk right here," Ka-Born said, with venom is his voice. The alcohol had him now believing that Baby Doll was the root of all this shit. Had he not dealt with her, Tracy wouldn't have gotten all crazy on him and he wouldn't have had to smoke her dumb ass. And to top it off, he didn't even touch the skins. His rage began to boil, and the urge to break Baby Doll's ass up was growing stronger by the minutes. He shouted in her face, with his pointer finger touching her nose. "Fuck these nosy motherfuckas. You think you all that 'cause you got this bullshit job!?"

"Ka-Born, you need to go home and sleep it off," Baby Doll felt a wave of embarrassment forming, because all eyes were on her and everybody was now in her business. "Put the gun away, Ka-Born, please." She saw him theatrically tucked the weapon in his waist, and she could almost hear the people in the store sigh with relief. "You coming all up in here like this ain't the way you supposed to do this—"

"So how the fuck am I supposed to do it!?" His anger was growing. "I told you; you don't set the rules for when you can leave, I do. What is it? You on some shit 'cause I ain't step to that nigga Kevin!?" He saw this really got under her skin and decided to go in harder. Ka-Born was going to make her ass feel it. "How the fuck I look like putting some hot ones in his ass when you fuckin' that nigga for cheddar? Yeah, I stepped to him and he told me you fuckin' and suckin' for peanuts, bitch—"

Baby Doll tried to push him, but Ka-Born swatted her arms away. She was sizzling with rage. This punk motherfucker was putting her on blast in front of her co-workers, and she wasn't going to stand for it. When Ka-Born was about to continue his verbal assault, Baby Doll took a swing at him. The blow nipped Ka-Born's chin.

"Oh, so you think you man, huh?" Ka-Born said and was about to knuckle up.

"What's the deal here!?" Big Daddy stepped through the door with Preacher and Silverback in tow.

Silverback had a gun concealed behind his leg out of the customers view. Preacher went straight up to Ka-Born and manhandled him into a dopefiend headlock while Silverback disarmed him.

"Yo' motherucka!" Ka-Born tried to fight the intrusion but was more scared than he was upset. "Yo, get off me, man. Get the fuck off me!" He struggled against Preacher's massive body weight without much luck of breaking free.

Big Daddy gave Preacher a head nod, and Preacher shoved Ka-Born away.

Preacher gave Ka-Born a look that literally could have ignited a keg of gunpowder. Not surprisingly, Ka-Born slowed his role drastically and immediately.

Big Daddy knew he had to quickly get this matter under control, and the best way to do that was to get Baby Doll and Ka-Born out of the store. He said to Baby Doll and Ka-Born, "I need to talk to you two outside." Big Daddy turned and headed for the door.

Baby Doll and Ka-Born followed. Preacher came along, while Silverback went to the back room behind the cashier's counter. The customers were so upset by all the commotion that they immediately left the store as Helen apologized profusely for the inconvenience.

Outside, Big Daddy gave Starr a signal indicating everything was cool. Starr was sitting in the passenger seat of a Brown Buick Regal with Hakim behind the wheel.

Big Daddy waited for Baby Doll and Ka-Born to catch up to him, and said, "Let's take a little walk." He started walking as Baby Doll got on his left while Ka-Born got on his right. Preacher was trailing them with his eyes riveted on Ka-Born. As they moved down Pitkin Avenue at a leisurely pace, Big Daddy said, "You all right, Baby Doll?"

"I'm okay," She felt like this was all her fault, and was hoping Big Daddy didn't fire her for causing this.

Big Daddy looked over at Ka-Born, and said, "I see you been drinking, and I guess that explains why you would put your hands on a female and come up in my place of business with a gun, and totally disrespecting me?"

Ka-Born was momentarily wordless. His high was gradually fading and now he started realizing he played himself. "Yo', listen, Big Daddy Blue, I ain't mean no disrespect to you, man. It's just that I got mad shit on my mind, man. My homey just got murdered, and shit, my peeps is flipping on a nigga, and Baby Doll here know I'm feelin' her and she shittin' on a nigga like—"

"Why you gotta use that word, nigga so much?" Big Daddy had promised himself that he wouldn't get on these young folks too much about the use of that word, but he saw Ka-Born was gearing up to OD on it. He couldn't take it anymore and decided to set some ground rules. "I know y'all young folks don't mean any harm when you use that word, but it tears me apart when I hear it. Please, brother, if you can be easy with that word in my presence, I would greatly appreciate it." He concentrated to keep his tone very respectful. "Can you do that for me, please?"

Ka-Born was surprised by the humble tone of the infamous Big Daddy Blue. Talking like that, he didn't sound like a gangster. He sounded like a cold-blooded bitch or something, not like the thug, Super OG he'd heard so many war stories about. The alcohol was about to make him do something stupid, but his common sense took control and made him not jump to conclusions that could cost him his life. "No doubt, no doubt, Big Daddy, I'm feelin' that. I'll try to go easy on that word around you."

"Now, I guess we can take this from the top," Big Daddy said, "I obviously want to know what was so serious that you had to come up in my store like that?"

Baby Doll got nervous because she just knew Ka-Born was going to tell it all. He was drunk and furious, and that meant he was going to continue shitting on her. The last thing she wanted was for Big Daddy to know that she was trying to have Kevin killed. She spoke quickly, "This is something me and Ka-Born can work out on our own."

"With him waving a gun around, you and I both know that ain't gonna cut it. Today, we're getting to the bottom of all this nonsense, because if you get hurt in anyway way, I'm coming to see this young man, and I ain't coming to pat him on the back either."

"So, what you trying to say?" Ka-Born's tone wasn't as respectful as it should have been, but he wasn't the type to take threats in a calm fashion. "The way you coming out the side of your mouth, sound like you—"

"It sounds like I'm telling you this," Big Daddy stopped abruptly, causing Baby Doll and Ka-Born to do the same. He faced Ka-Born and said, "I'm gonna put some mufuckin' fire to your ass if you keep talking to me like I'm your bitch!" He stared at Ka-Born as Preacher came up behind him. He hated this part of the process of forcing these little wanna be thugs to listen. Unfortunately, they respected only one thing, and that was people who didn't play no games.

Ka-Born looked around and saw he was on East New York Avenue, and there wasn't a lot of people walking about. Since he didn't have his gun, he felt weak and vulnerable. "You right, you right. My bad." He saw Baby Doll was enjoying this and now he felt like a wounded animal with no way to escape. His ego told him he still had to come out swinging but had to do it in a smart way. He held his head up defiantly.

"What caused all this, Baby Doll?" Big Daddy said as he resumed walking. Everyone followed along in their previous places.

Baby Doll sighed, realizing there was no way around it. "I told him I didn't want to be bother with him anymore, and he told me I can't leave until he says so. He's been following me around and everything, and then he came to the store all drunk and everything."

Ka-Born was furious because he saw where this was going. Big Daddy was going to cut him off from seeing her. "Yeah, but tell him why you cutting me off? Yeah, tell him you on some shit with me because I won't shot your mother's boyfriend, Kevin, because you told me he was raping you. And you full of shit because I step to the nig—I mean the dude and he said you was lying on him because you wanted money from him and had even offered him some pussy for some money. Yeah, you talking. Now talk about that there, Baby Doll."

Baby Doll felt naked, and the size of a thumbtack. The cat was out the bag, and there was no pulling it back. She wanted to say something but couldn't. She felt dirty and soiled like a tramp, even though Kevin forced her to have sex with him and he was lying on her.

Big Daddy was beyond furious. *So, Baby Doll was being abused by her mom's boyfriend.* The blinding fury that was rapidly forming was making it difficult to conceal his emotional reaction to this information. Now it all made sense; she went out with this young thug to get him to stop Kevin from raping her. Or maybe there was something else going on here that he needed to explore. But first he had to redirect this whole situation. "Ka-Born, you don't have to belittle her."

"Fuck her, she's a tramp!" Ka-Born shot back. "All I ever did for this girl is treat her good; she took all my money, had me driving her around all over the fuckin' place, to school, to work and all that shit, and I treated her like a motherfuckin' queen. Even after I did all that for her, she ain't never did a motherfuckin' thing for me, not even gave me a piece of pussy! Nothing! She never—"

"How old are you, Ka-Born?" Big Daddy knew the perfect way to shut this fool up. "I know you driving a nice ride and all, and I'm assuming you got a license."

Ka-Born didn't detect where this was going and blurred out a response "I'm eighteen, and yeah, I got a license. A legit one at that." He said proudly.

"You talking about she ain't give you no pussy?" Big Daddy said smoothly. "Do you know how old Baby Doll is? In fact, I know you know how old she is, being that you used to deal with her older sister."

Ka-Born saw it, but it was too late. Technically he was too old for her in the eyes of the law. He'd thought about this before, but he'd been rolling with her without anybody saying anything, not even their mother, it felt like it was all good. He felt a decisive defeat inching its way into the picture and wasn't going to let it go down just like that. "She's sixteen and I'm eighteen; a bullshit two-year difference. She was with it, and so was I. And, anyway, what is it to you? You ain't her real father."

"When she's working in one of my places, you best believe she's one of my children. Yeah, and one of my real children at that. The minute she steps foot in my store, she becomes my daughter, and she will be treated as one of mine."

"Man, all I knew is she owe me for all the shit I done spent on her." He said to Baby Doll. "You gon' pay me for all the cheddar I been giving you, and all the while you was playing me, pimping me like I was some kind of clown-ass dude—"

"You must've been a clown, you let me do it," Baby Doll fire back. "I didn't get with you to play you, and you know it."

"Yeah, you got with me to get revenge on Tracy," Ka-Born said, his anger about to burst at the seams. "If that don't say you's a foul mother—"

"Okay, okay," Big Daddy saw it was time to stop this, realizing it was probably best to kill this whole thing. It wasn't going anywhere, and he now sensed there was no way to neutralize their beef, other than to keep them away from each other. "This is the way this is going down. Baby Doll, do you still wanna go out with him?"

"No, I told him I don't want to be bothered."

"You heard her, Ka-Born?" Big Daddy looked into his eyes and saw what he didn't want to see. "She don't wanna deal with you anymore, and that means you gotta leave her alone." He saw his heartbroken reaction, and knew it was time to make sure he understood what would happen if he got stupid. "Now, listen here, I been in the game for years, and I will tell you this, if something happens to Baby Doll, you can best believe you will be the first on my hit list. I got a lot of ears and eyes on these here streets, and it's not much that jumps off that I don't know about or have the means to find out."

He wanted to add that he knew of his involvement with Tracy's situation, but Baby Doll didn't need to hear this. "Make no mistakes, you will find out how I got to be who I am, if she even comes down with a scratch caused by you. This is not a threat, it's a guarantee." He allowed this warning to soak in and then he stepped closer to Ka-Born. "It ain't all that serious. It'll be fine as long as you respect the rules."

Realizing Ka-Born's ego was probably scarred he decided to balance the blows. Now it was time to show some love even though he felt this wild, wannabe gangster didn't desire it. It was universal law that when you broke someone down, you had to build up the individual simultaneously to prevent the person from becoming bitter and unreachable, and thus, very dangerous. "There's hundreds of women out here dying to get with a sharp, handsome brother such as yourself." He cracked a smile, hoping it would help, but he saw that it didn't. "Hey, if you need me to give you a hand with finding—"

"I'm cool, Big Daddy," Ka-Born poked out his chest and then locked eyes with Baby Doll. "I'm-a pull back, you know what I'm saying? On the strength of a real OG such as you, I ain't got much of a choice but to pull back."

Baby Doll saw the utter hate and devastation in his eyes, and knew she succeeded in earning herself a lifelong enemy that would hunt for any way to sting her. But if Baby Doll could have read Ka-Born's mind, she would have known that he had plans for her that called for action that was far worse than what he had done to Tracy. Ka-Born's wicked, trifling mind was churning with an insidious fervor that oozed with a hatred that resonated the air between them. Because of the genuine smile plastered on his face, Big Daddy missed it while Baby Doll instantly underestimated it.

CHAPTER 14

Big Daddy Blue made it his business to make sure that each and every kid within his youth employment program saw that their summers went out with a bang. He vowed, and lived up to this promise, that no one would return to school not feeling the summer was something worth talking about. One way of fulfilling this task occurred when Big Daddy rented four charter buses and took all twenty-five teens who worked for him, along with one friend each, to Bear Mountain in upstate New York, all-expense paid. Although the young folks had the time of their lives, Big Daddy seemed to be having a greater time. He was choked up with tears of happiness by the fact he was finally doing something he'd dreamed about for years.

Just before Labor Day, he upped the stakes. He rented another fleet of buses for the same kids and took them to Six Flags Great Adventures Amusement Park. By the time the kids were back in school, already wishing the school year was over before it even got started, Big Daddy was once again back in an economic crisis as a result of the splurging he had done on the children in order to leave an impression on them that he hoped would keep them from deviating away from the proper path.

A month later, when he went back to the drawing board to find a way to get from under the financial turmoil, he started re-experiencing doubt about this endeavor to help poverty-stricken children from the hood. He again wondered if all the benevolence was even worth all the headaches and heartaches. At times it was clear that the very people he was trying to help were undermining him in the worst kind a ways. It wasn't all of the kids, but it was enough of them to make him pause.

Tina, the girl who was caught stealing, and he had saved her from being arrested and then turned around gave her a job, continued stealing and was now stealing from him. It was evident she was a kleptomaniac and needed professional help. When she refused to attend a behavior modification program that Big Daddy went out his way to put in motion, he was forced to let her go.

There was also the situation involving Sasha and Angela. In their obsession to get revenge on Baby Doll, they were stealing, lying, and conspiring, and had walked themselves right into a situation where Big Daddy was forced to let them go. Then there were other incidents where Big Daddy had to let four additional kids go when they would not change their behavior and continued cutting class, getting high, selling drugs on the DL, gang banging, dropping out of school, committing crimes of all calibers, and in general engaging in highly destructive activities that violated all of his rules for maintaining employment with him, even though he was going out of his way to help them get beyond all these obstacles, and distractions.

Cutting these kids loose was probably the most painful experience of his life, and each time he let them go, he heard Preacher state loud and clear: "See, I told you so." But these ordeals weren't enough to stop Big Daddy from moving forward with his program, and the saying, "a few bad apples don't spoil the whole bunch" definitely applied.

Eager to demonstrate to his youth employees that when they did the right thing they would be rewarded, Big Daddy found the best example from his teen workforce and moved that person up the ladder.

It was a toss-up between Donna Campbell and Breana "Baby Doll" Winbush. Some would probably say the system he used to decide who won the salesclerk position in Tera's Downtown Boutique store in Albee Square Mall was a bit unorthodox, but when one owned a chain of businesses they were apparently afforded the luxury of making their own rules to some extent.

Baby Doll won because she possessed the right blend of attributes that were prefect for the job; she had street and book smarts, was disciplined, respectful, trustworthy, loyal, followed instructions well, and most of all, because Big Daddy knew she was struggling with a family situation far worse than Donna. The day he decided to give Baby Doll the award, he realized there were a series of unanswered questions concerning her situation.

Although he never told anyone, after hearing Ka-Born say that Baby Doll's mom's boyfriend was raping her, and that Baby Doll wanted him knocked off, he couldn't turn a blind eye. He did his own investigation into this chump Kevin, found out where he worked, how long he'd been dealing with Mildred, and discovered that he didn't like this creep, even though he didn't find a smoking gun of him abusing Baby Doll. He had a secret letter delivered to Kevin at his job that said:

"WE KNOW WHAT YOU'RE DOING TO BABY DOLL!! IF YOU EVER DO IT AGAIN, YOU WILL DIE. WE ARE WATCHING YOU CLOSELY!"

He had also had someone watching Kevin after he read the letter, and his nervous response was enough confirmation for Big Daddy to conclude that this child molester was doing something to Baby Doll. In any event, before he gave Baby Doll the new position, he figured it couldn't hurt to pry a little into that issue.

On a dreary day in the month of November, Big Daddy had instructed Helen to send Baby Doll over in a cab to his Fulton Street office the moment she arrived at work. When Baby Doll entered the office and took a seat in front of his executive style desk, Big Daddy saw she was visibly nervous.

"So, what's up, Big Daddy?" Baby Doll said, concealing her nervousness with a peppy smile. "What I done did now? If it's about that soda I spilled on them shirts, I told Helen I'll pay for the damage—"

"Relax, Baby Doll, this has nothing to do with them shirts. I called you over because we need to talk. I've been thinking about a lot of things." He leaned back comfortably in his cushioned chair. "There's been some stuff that's been on my mind, and I figured it's time to come right out and ask you. I know you remember that time when you broke up with Ka-Born, and we walked and talked." He paused and continued when he saw Baby Doll nod her head. "Okay, now, I know you remember when Ka-Born said your mother's boyfriend was brothering you?"

Baby Doll felt frozen with surprise. She was momentarily speechless because she honestly didn't know how far she should go with this. A vibe told her this was an opportunity, while another vibe was telling her to be easy. Upon hearing this, it reminded her of the fact that Kevin hadn't touched her for months and was acting like he was totally scared of her. She'd attributed his response to the fact that Ka-Born and him had words, and that he was being precautious so as not to stir up a beef with Ka-Born. But, upon hearing Big Daddy's inquiry about that matter, she was now wondering if he had his hands in this. Even though Kevin stopped raping her, she still wanted him dead and wondered if she could play on Big Daddy to get him to put that perverted bastard in a nice, lonely grave. After a moment Baby Doll said, "Yeah, I remember that. So what about it?"

"Listen, Baby Doll, you know I treat you just like you my very own daughter. You agree with that?"

"Yeah, you treat me real good all the time."

"And haven't I always keep my promises and always was willing to help you when you needed help?"

"Yes, you do, Big Daddy. You never broke a promise with me ever since I known you. And you help me all the time. You kinda rough on making me stay on top of my grades and everything, but I know it's all good. How you say it, tough love?" She smiled, because he was definitely about to go there.

"With all that said, Baby Doll, you know how I am about telling the truth." He paused. "I'm gonna come right out and ask. Did Kevin ever do anything to you that was inappropriate?" He saw her squint her eyes as if she was confused, and so he put it to her in its most unadulterated form. "Did he ever rape you, Baby Doll?"

Baby Doll saw he'd just dropped the million-dollar question on her. She stared into Big Daddy's big brown eyes and wondered what would he do to Kevin if she said yes. It didn't take long to conclude that he wasn't going to kill Kevin; that was for sure. He would give Kevin a scare of his life, maybe even have some of his boys beat him down. But, from what she learned of Big Daddy, he was no longer a killer. He'd told her about himself, how he built himself up while in prison, got an education in business management through a correspondence course, helped create a prison outreach youth program while incarcerated, had a huge treasure buried in an abandon garage dump in a Brooklyn landfill, how he retrieved that money upon his release from prison, how he built an empire with that money, and how he vowed he would never do anything to go back to prison.

As these facts circulated through her brain cells, the reality became clear. No, he wasn't going to kill Kevin, and therefore there was no need to create a situation that would allow Kevin to get off easy. Because she didn't want to lie to Big Daddy, she simply left the whole issue hanging in the air.

"Big Daddy, please, I really don't wanna talk about that. And please don't make me talk about it. And for my mother's sake, please leave it alone." She generated a misty-eyed look to make it look good and she saw she had Big Daddy where she wanted.

"Yeah, you right. I'm sorry I brought it up. I don't know what got into me, Baby Doll." He got his answer, and it was as clear as day that she was telling him that she was being raped by Kevin but didn't want to outright snitch on him. "The actual reason I called you here, Baby Doll, is because I wanted to let you know that I'm promoting you."

Baby Doll's eyes sprung open with sheer delight. "You promoting me!?" She didn't know where this promotion would lead her, but she knew enough about the word *promotion* to know it meant more money.

"Yes, I'm moving you over to the store with Tera. You'll be working as a floor clerk. You've be selling clothing and getting a commission, which means in addition to the weekly wages, you'll get a percentage of the items you sell. In other words, the more clothing you sell, the more money you can make."

Baby Doll was smiling from ear to ear, and since she was hungry for that beautiful, mean green, she knew this was where she wanted to be. "Thank you, Big Daddy."

"You put the work in. You earned it and therefore you deserve it. Don't thank me, thank yourself."

As Baby Doll struggled to get into the rhythm of being an eleventh grade student earning a decent salary as a boutique sales clerk, she had thought she had mastered the art of dealing with a house full of jealous females, but had found out that the saying that said sometimes family could be a greater enemy to ones well-being than an outsider could ever be had a whole lot of truth to it. Everybody hated the fact that she had money, wasn't mismanaging it, and wasn't going to allow a bunch of money thirsty family members to fuck that money up.

Not surprisingly, Tracy's utter hatred for Baby Doll grew tenfold. Once Tracy's feet touched ground outside of the hospital, she had embarked on a holy crusade to turn Baby Doll's life into something far more disastrous than a living hell. To Baby Doll's utter surprise, Tracy didn't have no shame in the great lengths she would go to in order to attack her; stealing, cheating, lying, and manipulating were only a few of the things she subjected Baby Doll to. Tracy even went so far as to use the Church as an avenue of attack; she started going to Church every Sunday, talking biblical gibberish, as though being shot had driven her insane, and had dubbed Baby Doll a sinner who needed Jesus in her life. When Tracy started back dating Ka-Born, Baby Doll knew for certain she had went plumb crazy.

Even more surprising, Ka-Born did more than just fall off. After he lost his homey Ramsey, and then his older brother Sha-Sha, to the almighty gun, initiated by the most catastrophic element to the Black community, drugs, Ka-Born had fallen into a rut, and literally couldn't get out of it. His heavy drinking escalated into excessive weed smoking, which paved the pathway to uncontrollable coke sniffing and then to experimental use of heron. Once big horse got a hold of him, he was done, and the only thing left to do with him was to put the folk in him.

Not surprisingly, one of the reasons he got back with Tracy was because he needed a female companion that wanted him, now that he'd fallen completely from grace. Most of the hood rats didn't want him anymore, especially since he lost his ride, was no longer a baller, had become the typical street-corner bum, and a shameless beggar. He also needed a get-high partner, and Tracy was that perfect person for the position.

Baby Doll's desire to get out of her mother's apartment grew in an exponential fashion. If it wasn't for Baby Doll's determined will to become someone greater than her mom and other female family members, she would not have bowed to her mother's madness. Mildred made it clear that she suspected that Baby Doll was responsible for Tracy being shot by unknown assailants, who had never been apprehended, and that was the blow that almost broke the camel's back. The argument that ensued was one that could have caused Baby Doll to leave home for good, but there was nowhere besides Jeanette's crib she could go, and she couldn't imagine going to that extreme.

By the time the winter rolled in, Baby Doll, Jeanette, and Edna were into club hopping. After seven episodes, Baby Doll saw this activity was a waste of money and full of unwarranted drama, since all it could do was delay her from getting her own crib.

She also had aspirations to go to college and had spoken to her guidance counselor Mrs. Carmine about what she should start doing to get ready for college. Although she still had no idea what she wanted to major in, she was sure that she wanted to be around money, so she insisted she wanted to go to college for business administration. In the end, Mrs. Carmine gave her some brochures and told her to return in a few months for further discussion. Because her mom had no money saved up for her college education, nor did she have any money saved up for that purpose, she was forced to learn about government grants and bank loans.

When the New Years rolled in, Baby Doll felt like she was on top of the world. She saved up almost two grand, despite having to give her mother money, and she predicted that by the time the school year was over she would be well on her way to getting her own apartment. She dreamed about having her own apartment almost every night. If she dreamed, it was guaranteed that before the dream was over she would somehow pop up inside her own apartment with a huge muscle-bound brother with a dick as big as a horse and could last for hours.

Then, on her Birthday, Big Daddy gave her a gift she would never forget. This particular April 7th would be engrained on her mind because she had always wanted a car, and had given hints of this fact to Big Daddy. It felt good to know that he was paying attention to her. He paid for Baby Doll to go to driving school, and within two weeks she was able to drive. She took the driver's test to get her learners permit and passed. She just knew Big Daddy was going to get her a car, since it didn't make sense to know how to drive and not have a car to show off what she learnt. When the Month of May rolled in with no car appearing on her doorstep, she had stopped waiting and started making plans to get her own car after she moved out, which would hopefully be any day now. She was so close to having enough money, she went and talked to Jeanette, and she agreed to sign the lease when the time came.

On the third Friday of June, right after she received her report card that indicated she was promoted to the twelfth grade, and after she cashed her check, Baby Doll went to add some money to her stash. She sensed something was wrong by the way Jasmine was laying on her bed, looking at TV with a nervous expression.

When Baby Doll opened the closet and saw the Samsonite suitcase locks were broken open and all her money was gone, she literally stood staring at the empty container with her mouth hung open and her mind locked so tight with disbelief, it could have made the locks on Fort Knox look like child's play. Slowly kneeling down to her knees, she allowed her tears to flow as she checked the suitcase anyway to make sure this was actually happening and was not a dream. The suitcase was stripped of every single dime, and this was not a dream. All the months of heavy sacrifices swirled inside her memory bank, the missed lunch breaks, the boring weekends without going to parties, the abstaining from drinking beer, and the penny pinching on all levels, just to save money for her escape from this crib, started driving her mind into a state of delirium. It was all gone, and she still found it hard to believe.

Baby Doll rose to her feet in a catatonic state, and she literally had blood in her eyes. Red was swirling about her vision, and the only thing on her mind was murder. She didn't even have to ask herself (or Jasmine) who did it because it had Tracy written all over it. She heard the TV in the living room was on, and had seen Tracy watching the TV as she walked by. Now that she thought about it, she did remember seeing that silly-ass smirk on her face as if to say, wait until you see what I did to your shit, bitch. She also recalled that her eyes were blistering red from the drugs she had apparently consumed with the money she stole from her. In Mildred's room, she heard the TV and knew her and old sorry-ass Kevin were in there doing whatever they did when the door was closed.

Baby Doll quickly changed her clothing, putting on her brown sweat suit, because when she put the blows on Tracy she was going to put it on her the right way this time.

This was officially the straw that broke the camel's back, and Tracy was going to find out that she played herself in the worse kind of way, and if she had to beat every motherfucker's ass in this house, she was going to get back every dime of her four thousand dollars or she was going hospitalize Tracy's dope fiend ass permanently. She hoped Nadine wouldn't mind a paraplegic partner because she was going to make sure she broke this bitch's neck and that she would be sitting in a wheelchair next to Nadine if she didn't get her money back.

When she was dressed, she stomped into the living room, and as she approached, Tracy jumped up to her feet, ready to fight. Before Tracy got out a word Baby Doll caught her with a devastating overhand right. Tracy crumbed down upon the sofa as if her legs were transformed into spaghetti. Baby Doll commenced of beating, pounding, pulverizing Tracy's face.

As Baby Doll beat her mercilessly, she talked to Tracy as she blessed her face with bone-breaking punches, "Didn't—I tell you—to leave my—shit—" Tracy tried to break free and swing back, but the attempt was futile. "I want every—dime of my shit back—right this—motherfuckin' minute—and now—I gotta—show your dumb ass—that I ain't fucking—around with you—"

Finally, Tracy was able to unleash a bloodcurdling scream that could have awakened the entire Tilden projects.

Mildred jumped out of bed, frantically flung her house robe on and bolted out the room with Kevin behind her. She followed the screams of Tracy, thinking that Ka-Born was beating on her daughter again. When she turned the corner and saw Baby Doll beating Tracy like she stole something, she raced over and punched Baby Doll in the side of her head, knocking her off Tracy.

Baby Doll stumbled to the side and tripped over the coffee table. She landed hard on the floor and went into a blind fit of rage. Without thinking, as the years of frustration, rage, mistreatment, and abuse finally came to ahead, Baby Doll sprung onto her feet, charged at Mildred and punched her right in the mouth, causing Mildred to fall on top of Tracy, who was lying on the sofa curled up into a fetal position, her face covered in blood.

When Mildred realized what just happened, she became furious and tried to jump back up and continue the fight, but Baby Doll followed up with another blow to Mildred's face, and the blow was so bone-shattering that it took all the fight out of Mildred. She also saw in Baby Doll's eyes that she was in the zone, and the expression was one that said if she was pushed any further, she would take it somewhere that might result in someone losing their life. Mildred was filled with fury, but she knew she had to bow down at the moment.

Breathing like a wild rabid beast that had just ran ten miles, with her fist squeezed so tight, the skin on her knuckles were flaming red, Baby Doll woke up from their maniacal trance. Looking at her mom and Tracy with blood all over them, she suddenly realized what she had just done. Mildred was holding her mouth blood streaming through the cracks of her fingers, her wild eyes about to spring from their sockets. The look on her mother's face told Baby Doll that she fucked up beyond comprehension. That look also told her that she had finally committed the ultimate violation that could result in only one consequence.

Mildred shook some senses back into her punch-drunk mind by shaking her head. She saw Baby Doll was out of the zone. Mildred rose to her feet in a calm fashion and said, "Pack your shit! You don't live here anymore!"

CHAPTER 15

Big Daddy Blue was staring out the window of his club on Evergreen Street at the construction team down the street on the corner of Wilson Avenue. The construction workers were renovating an establishment that was going to be the beginning of the end of his stay here in Bushwick. If this was twenty-five years ago, this blatant display of aggression would've been grounds for an all-out war, complete with covert strikes, and maybe even a few carefully coordinated contract hits on major players involved in this outright disrespect. Big Daddy was seething with an anger that was making him feel dizzy. He wondered if all this stress mixed with rage was flaring up his high blood pressure and made a mental note to go get a check-up before the week was out.

Preacher came over to Big Daddy and massaged his shoulder, and said, "The ball is in your hands now. John Boy is sending a clear message that he don't respect us anymore. Like I said, I'm with whatever you decide." He knew this was the correct thing to say, but in reality, he knew if Big Daddy refused to fight this time, he would find it very difficult to continue working with this operation. "There's only two options here, Big Daddy. We—"

"I know what the options are, Preacher. You don't have to keep reminding me." Big Daddy stared at the huge neon light sign being hoisted into its position over the front entrance of the new establishment. The sign read, "John Boy's Lounge and Social Club." He sighed because he'd been planning to get himself one of those high-tech signs once he got a good financial flow going. Big Daddy pulled himself from the window and found a sit at a nearby booth. He had to make a decision; that much was for sure. He thought after he paid John Boy his three grand, he would wipe the beef they had on his chest and keep it moving.

Merely because Big Daddy didn't help him start up a bunch of undercover drug spots, John Boy was now setting up shop next to him with the intention of undermining his ability to make money out here in Bushwick.

Big Daddy waved to Preacher to sit across from him. He knew Preacher wanted to take it to the streets. Do it according to the so-called code of the street, which basically said that when folks got out of line, the transgressee had to confront the transgressor with acts of senseless violence. Big Daddy wanted to take it there, but in the long run, logic dictated that both parties would come out losing. He watched Preacher take the seat and said. "I know where you want to go with this, Preacher. I'm feelin' you, I understand where you coming from, and I'm grateful that I got a brother like you on my team." He let that hang in the air for a moment. "But banging out with John Boy over this ain't worth it, no matter how you look at it. I will admit this much, he's way out of line, but when we take ourselves out of the street world, this is perfectly all right, since this is a free world with a free market according to the rules of business."

"Yeah, we know all that, but this ain't got shit to do with business, Big Daddy. What this chump is doing is trying to stop us from eating. He knows we're struggling to keep our heads above water and trying to keep it clean. John Boy had over a dozen other places he could have set up shop, but he chose this location solely to get back at you. And, to top it off, he knows how much you despise them drugs, and now just to mash it in your face, he's going to load up the neighborhood with so much drugs, by the end of next year this place'll be run down, and flooded with dope-fiends everywhere. He'll steal all our business, and before the years is out, our doors will close permanently. If we strike right now, hit this chump hard, heavy, and let him know we're willing to take—"

"No, we can't do that," Big Daddy Blue said. "If we bang out with him, bodies will drop, it'll be tit-for-tat. Since I'm not into playing games, if we bang, we will play strictly for keeps, the bloodshed will be crazy, the police will get involved, they'll make arrests, and I will die before I go back to prison. For me to go toe to toe with John Boy I will be committing suicide even if we do succeed in running him out of this area. It's a losing battle ether way it goes, and the wise thing to do is to simply—"

"That's bullshit!" Preacher said, surprising even himself at the level of aggression in his voice. "I can hit this motherfucker in such a way that he'll never be able to bounce back. There's always a way to get rid of a cutthroat fool like John Boy, who's a threat to the Black community."

Big Daddy realized he was just struck with an issue that he'd been searching for an answer for. He also felt it was time to get Preacher back on track, since he was allowing his frustration to cloud his judgment. "Yeah, you right. There's always a way for Black folk to kill each other. I've asked this question maybe a thousand times if I asked once. Why is it that we Black folks find it so easy to kill each other? Do you know we spend more time fucking each other over, plotting and scheming to tear each other down, and will actual kill any Black person at the mere thought of seeing that Black person about to pull himself out of the grit and grime. It's the strangest shit I have ever seen, and if we could learn to work together, we could help each other out of our collective misery, but most of us would prefer to live in an utter hell before they would work together."

"Crabs in the barrel," Preacher said, realizing this particular topic, as usual, had Big Daddy deeply depressed. "We of all people know the solution, and what we're doing is a part of the solution, but let's keep it real. We can't sit around all caught up in this Black love talk while we got folks trying to kill us and whoever else that cross their path. Sure, we're dealing with a lot of self-hatred issues, and we shouldn't contribute to it by being so quick to bring the noise to another Black man, but let's face it. Some folks are so far gone, there is no talking to them. They're here to rape, rob and exploit other Black folk at all costs and will murder anyone that gets in their way. Even you know the only way to deal with a diseased mind with that level of toxicity is to deal with him on the level he can understand."

"You might be right," Big Daddy Blue said, "but it's just so sad that most of us just don't see that if we spent as much energy as we waste on concocting ways to fuck each other over, and dedicated the same amount of time and energy to fix our collective problems as a people, we wouldn't be in the pitiful state we're in. Socially, economically, and politically we tend to be our own worst enemy, because we too dam busy fuckin' each other over."

He sighed and realized he needed a drink. He got up and went to the bar, talking while he fixed his drink. "That's why I started this youth employment program. It's a way of doing something about the problem, instead of sitting around bitchin' and complainin'. I know you know this, Preacher, but we need to look at all this before we dive into a decision of going to war. While in prison, I realized that there is no way you can change people once they're set in their ways. When I was working with those inmate organizations, I used to bring in young brothers, and tried to groom them to become leaders of the organization, you know, help them learn about running an organization. And, man, let me tell you something. That was probably the most stressful, and disappointing experience in my life."

He shook his head in disbelief. "These young fools were undermining me, stabbing me in the back, plotting and scheming to knock me out of my position as the President, and all I ever did for them was show them mad love, and tried to give them something that could've helped them to be better people. Yeah, of course, I was hard on them most of the time, but running an organization requires that people take things seriously. Unfortunately, our inability as a people to take things like business seriously is one of the reasons we're in the state of affairs we're in." He went back to the booth with his drink, sat down, and sipped on the drink. "You know they got this Black woman professor who calls it Post Traumatic Slave Syndrome. And the way she be dropping it, the sister got this thing down to an art."

"Big Daddy, you're preaching to the choir, man. And by the way, that sister's name Joy Leary." Preacher sat all the way up in his seat. "I know what time it is with you, Big Daddy. And if I didn't believe in what you're doing with the kids and these businesses, I wouldn't be here by your side. I could go back to the hustling world and take my chances getting rich, but I do believe we can make a difference by doing legit things. But, unfortunately, this issue with John Boy is one of those situations where, if we bow and bend to his bullshit, we'll be empowering him and even enabling him, and most of all, we'll be letting the community down because we're in a position to stop this fool from doing what he's about to do, but we're about to do what ninety-nine point nine percent of us always do."

He didn't have to say what that was, because they'd talked about it so much, it was literally engrained inside his long-term memory cells. Most Black folks simply looked the other way, or either ran away and hid from the problems plaguing their own communities.

In almost all Black communities, those able and in a position to stop a problem before it gained momentum would usually sit right on their asses and do nothing, and then when the problem started to consuming them, they would then sit around once again, and cry, complain, blame, point fingers, and again, sit and do nothing.

"Preacher, do you think we got enough manpower to do a dance with a fully armed drug dealer, who's equipped to go to war with other drug dealers at a moment's notice?"

Preacher smiled broadly. "I'll say one name. Sweet Charlie." He saw Big Daddy had apparently forgotten about him. "We've had Brother Charlie on standby so long, he's going crazy with boredom."

Big Daddy was jolted into a state of realization upon hearing the name Sweet Charlie. He nodded his head, realizing there was a way to do this thing without blowing it out of proportion. Sweet Charlie was a world-class contract killer who was so good at what he did, his name was even known in other countries all over the world. Besides the fact he was an ex-CIA agent who got kicked out of the agency for having difficulty obeying the rules, he also was extraordinarily rich, well connected with almost all top underworld organizations, and most of all, he was real cool with Big Daddy and Preacher. One of the big mysteries about Sweet Charlie was that nobody knew where he got his money from, but most people automatically assumed that his riches were intricately connected to what he did best, and that was kill people.

Big Daddy Blue sighed; he didn't like what he was feeling as his approach toward this problem was rapidly changing. And in light of the consequences of running from this problem, common sense was pissing in his ear, telling him that he had to re-construct his ideas and approaches toward handling things.

He hated to admit it, but he was getting soft, too soft to be in this sort of business he was currently in. Clubs were still a part of a world that catered to the underworld, and basically had its own rules that worked in conjunction with the rules of the street. There were many times he contemplated giving up the few clubs he had and to convert all these establishments into other less headache-oriented businesses, and now he was going to seriously consider giving them up.

He looked up and saw Preacher had a smile plastered on his face, and he knew he had to stop letting his fantasy of one day seeing Black folk loving each other come in the way of him dealing with situations that called for a particular course of action. It was obvious to all that there was no way to save everybody; some folks would have to die in order for others to live. It was a hard pill to swallow, but how the young hip hoppers say it, "It is what it is!"

Preacher cleared his throat, realizing that the very mention of the name Sweet Charlie was enough to make Big Daddy see that there was a way to deal with John Boy without destroying everything they built, or putting themselves in harm's way. He decided to put the clincher on this issue. "Make the call, and you know Sweet Charlie will roll with us. You and I both know he don't do half-ass work, so it's a guarantee it won't come back to haunt us."

Big Daddy nodded his head as he saw that the use of Sweet Charlie was probably the only option.

* * * *

Baby Doll sat in the cushiony lounge chair, waiting for a customer to enter the store, so that she could cater to this person.

Wilma, a fellow co-worker, who was a short, stocky, dark chocolate-complexioned woman in her mid-twenties, was currently showing a fat Hispanic woman a silk blouse. In the background, Bobby Brown's greatest hits CD was once again dominating the store airwaves; he was currently singing about "his prerogative," and Baby Doll noticed Bobby Brown songs no longer excited her like they once did. This was due to the fact Tera was running the CD in the ground and would catch an attitude if anyone even hinted at changing the CD.

Baby Doll was daydreaming; she never thought she could experience so much stress and still be able to do all the things she was doing. Working, going to school, living with Jeanette and Edna, preparing for graduation, finding a college, getting a college loan, acquiring a grant were more than enough to drive her mad, but also dealing with living so close to her family was probably the worst of it all.

Tera came from the back of the store and saw Baby Doll daydreaming. "Hey, girl, it ain't that serious." She retrieved the small box from the counter and was on her way back to the other section of the store, when she remembered the message she had to convey. "Big Daddy said he's coming to talk to you. He said he got your message, it's just that he's been dealing with some things." She saw Baby Doll's sad face and sat down next to her in the empty chair. "Damn, girl, you been depressed for two weeks. Don't you think it's time to get over it? Wipe it one your chest, brush yourself off, and keep it moving. Ever since your mom kicked you out, you been looking all crazy and shit."

She smiled hoping the humor would make her laugh, but saw it wasn't working. "All right, check this out. I'll lend you some money to help you get that apartment you been working on. The most I can stand right now is five hundred dollars; it isn't much, but I'm sure every little bit can help. I know you're gonna ask Big Daddy for some money, but I need to tell you that Big Daddy is going through some major financial problems. He's even thinking about closing down two of his clubs. He's been fighting to keep his youth employment program alive, but it's killing him. He said he'd rather close down an establishment that could generate a source of income before he cut you guys off." She shook her head to signify that even she didn't see the logic in it all. She sighed as she rose to her feet. "But I guess he's living his dream, and that's all that matters. If you need that loan let me know." Tera walked away.

Baby Doll was elated by the offer, but it still didn't alter her bad mood. Five hundred dollars was literally a drop in the bucket. Although two weeks had gone by since she was kicked out of her mother's apartment, she still couldn't understand how her mother sided with Tracy even when she knew Tracy stole her money. Four thousand dollars was a very serious amount of money that the average person from the projects would kill for, and yet her mom was acting like she was wrong for feeling and reacting the way she did once she discovered her money was stolen. Yeah, she knew she had committed the ultimate sin when she struck her mom, but her mother knew at the time she wasn't in her right state of mind, and Mildred had hit her first, and did it in such a way that the malice was clear. Baby Doll was almost certain if somebody had stolen four thousand dollars of her mom's hard-earned money, she would've done more than just popped a parent in the mouth.

About twenty minutes later, a customer entered, and Baby Doll catered to her every whim. The slim, high-yellow woman was wearing a tight dress with high heels and had apparently gone berserk with the perfume. The woman had on so much of the snuff, it started making Baby Doll sick, but she handled the situation like a pro. It often amazed Baby Doll at how she could mask her stress once she was in salesclerk mode. She sold the woman a nice set of pants and made a five-dollars commission off the sale.

When Big Daddy arrived, Baby Doll got in his car that was parked right out front of the boutique store. Although Tera forewarned her that Big Daddy was dealing with a money situation, she just had to ask anyway and felt a little self-conscious about it, but she was totally sick and tired of staying with Jeanette and Edna. She enjoyed having them as friend, but living with them was not a good idea. She knew this would happen, but because she had nowhere else to go, there wasn't anything else to do other than simply deal with it.

Baby Doll said to Big Daddy, "I know my timing is probably way off, but I could really use an advance. I'm willing to agree to have some of my money taken from each check, but I can't deal with Jeanette and her girl Edna." She never told Big Daddy, Jeanette and Edna were gay, since she didn't want him assuming she was also gay because she hung out with gay people. "I gotta get out of that apartment. I just can't take it anymore."

Big Daddy could feel her pain, and his heart went out for her. He couldn't tell her no, that much was for certain, and he wasn't in a position to give her everything she wanted, so he decided to meet her halfway. "I'll give you two grand. That's enough to get you started, and then we can work something out once you get in an apartment."

Baby Doll was elated with joy; she scooted over and kissed Big Daddy on the cheek. She saw it made him feel good. Now, it was time to butter him up even more, and let him know that she was grateful. "I ever tell you that I only met my father twice?" She saw he was listening intently. "The minute I saw him, it was like I was looking at myself, but in a man's version. I was about seven years old. I was so happy, and I thought he would be just as happy." She paused in deep thought. Her pain was very clear. "I can still remember that day. It was like one of the biggest events of my life, seeing my daddy."

She shook her head dreamingly. "But after that I came to the conclusion I didn't have a father. He was never there for me, he didn't give a shit about me, he never came to my rescue when I was being ganged up on by my family, when people was trying to bully me. Even when—" She caught herself; she was about to mention the rapes, but remembered she never told Big Daddy what time it was. She played it off and continued, "But you know what, Big

Daddy. That day I met you and looked into your eyes, I said to myself if I could have a father, it would be you. I had just met you and I knew there was something about you that I loved. And if I didn't say it before, I'm saying it now. You have been a father to me, and I love you for that, Big Daddy."

There was an intense moment of silence.

Big Daddy felt all choked up, because he was on cloud nine. She was the first of the kids he'd been helping to express a deep thanks that was filled with sincerity. Of course, there were those that thanked him profusely, but their gestures were phony. What he'd just heard made what he did more than worth it. He'd always known Baby Doll was special, and the level of maturity she just displayed was a clear indication that she was going places.

"Baby Doll, thank you for that." He was about to go into the fact that he saw her and some of the other kids he been helping as his daughters and sons more than his actual children, since they didn't care a damn thing about him, and only communicated with him when they needed money or other favors, but instead he looked at his watch with the intention of cutting their meeting short. "I'll get that money to you by tomorrow morning. Tell Tera to call me tonight."

Baby Doll got out the car and watched Big Daddy drive away. She was feeling more than good; she was feeling brand-new!

* * * *

Within two weeks, Baby Doll stepped foot in her very own apartment located on St. John Street and Buffalo Avenue in Crown Heights, Brooklyn. It was a one-bedroom apartment on the second floor (Apt #2D), very small, but it was hers and that's all that mattered. She had a party the following weekend and invited

Jeanette, Edna, Tera, Wilma, and her male next-door neighbor named Karl Lockhart, a construction worker who was in his late twenties, and was basically trying to get with Baby Doll. The party was a success, and Tera detected Edna was a bulldagger (a she/he), but she didn't blow it up the way Baby Doll thought she would.

About a week after moving into the apartment, Baby Doll was on her way to the supermarket and saw a group of little kids brutally taunting and teasing a little boy and girl because the two didn't have any money to buy any ice cream from the ice cream truck that had just pulled away. The two kids held their heads up high and took the abuse like true hood troopers. Baby Doll wanted to mind her business and keep it moving, but something inside of her just wouldn't allow it.

Baby Doll gave in to the temptation and bought the two kids two pints of ice cream each, and it made her feel real good when she watched the two kids flaunting and showing off their ice cream to the other teasing kids, especially since the taunting kids had eaten all of their ice cream and the tables had turned on them.

Baby Doll worked full-time during the summer break and made sure she took advantage of any opportunity to work overtime. Saving, penny-pinching, conning Karl out of his money, and saving some more became so much of a part of Baby Doll's life that by the end of the summer, she had pulled herself once again out of financial strife and back into a stable economic flow. When she started back to school as a twelfth grader, she was the badiest, most elegant, sleekest dresser in the whole school, and rightfully so, since she was a salesclerk in a boutique store, and got first dibs on all the latest styles at half price; it was only right she would be the flyest dresser in her school. She was wearing gear that the other girls didn't even know about until months later, and the jealousy and envy was unstoppable, despite the fact they thought she was related to Big Daddy Blue.

* * * *

Meanwhile, Big Daddy was experiencing some technical difficulties. His and Preacher's endeavor to get Sweet Charlie to assist them in dealing with John Boy was in activation, but it wasn't going as smoothly as they would have preferred. Sweet Charlie agreed to do the hit on John Boy. The plan was simple. Charlie would stir up a beef John Boy had with another drug crew in Bedstuy controlled by a dealer named Country. After Charlie would drop one of Country's main runners and then make it look like it came from John Boy, Charlie would then step in and lay John Boy down.

This was designed to make it look like Big Daddy had nothing to do with the hit once it went down, and it was believed that with John Boy out of the picture, his Bushwick club would be shut down without much drama. In fact, to throw John Boy off, Big Daddy and Preacher visited John Boy at his club, congratulated him, and assured him that there were no hard feelings about what he'd done when he set up shop right across from him. Not surprisingly, John Boy was full of himself, since his place was the talk of the town, and was swallowing up all of Big Daddy's business. Big Daddy bit down on his tongue and had kept it moving, feeling the urge to bring the noise to John Boy in an aggressive manner, but Preacher immediately kept him on track because it was just a matter of time before John Boy would get what was coming to him.

The plan was working very well, until the day the hit on Country's main runner, Skelow, was about to go down. An hour just before the silenced bullets were about to explode, John Boy got arrested for possession of a kilo of cocaine and a firearm as he was entering his Bushwick club. It was apparent the arrest was due to a snitch that had a beef with John Boy and had known his schedule. The minute the arrest went down, the streets started talking, and because Big Daddy was hurting real bad financially, the haters were quick to start throwing shit in the game. With the help of a few mean-spirited rumors, the first response almost everybody had was that someone from Big Daddy's camp had done the snitching. The rationale was that Big Daddy's workers knew their jobs were on the line, they were intimidated by the way John Boy was flexing his muscle, and they were scared to bring the drama in accordance with street protocol. As a result, they were the ones that went to the police.

Needless to say, whether or not Big Daddy Blue and Preacher felt the best way to deal with this situation was to avoid engaging in senseless acts of deadly violence, it really didn't matter what they wanted, because John Boy's people weren't into the non-violent approach, and these young, trigger-happy, wild-heads definitely had no respect for old timers that used to be world-class gangsters.

CHAPTER 16

Baby Doll wiggled her hips in a rhythmic fashion to Karl's gentle thrusting motions. He was inside of her and was handling her in a way that proved to Baby Doll that Kevin was solely out to hurt her on all levels. Baby Doll wanted screamed in ecstasy as Karl's manhood eased in and out of her as her legs were cocked high in the air. She came once and was hoping Karl could last for another nut. Although she was enjoying herself immensely, it was evident Karl was enjoying this sexual encounter even more than her, since she made him wait two months before she laid down with him. She had learnt many years ago that the longer she made men wait to get a piece of the pussy, the more leverage it gave her. As long as they were chasing a carrot on a stick, she could dig real deep into their pockets and come up with a jackpot every time. Now, she hoped Karl didn't flip out now that he got a hit of the skins. In the hood hit-and-runs were about as common as pissy stairwells in project buildings; you couldn't avoid them even if you wanted to. Also, after spending years watching how dudes ran through Tracy, and how she'd drop her drawers if a dude merely gave her the time of day, she knew she would never follow in those footsteps.

Baby Doll saw Karl was about to blast off; his pipe got as hard as cobalt steel, while his pumping motion became urgent as if a fire were erupting in his groin. Baby Doll immediately stopped him from pumping, squeezing her grippers real tight. With her arms wrapped tightly around Karl with her muscles clamped on Karl's manhood, she decided she wasn't finished yet; every time Karl tried to resume the sexual dance, she whispered sensuously in his ear, "Be easy, boo. Let's make it last." Karl was breathing like a mad man in her ear, and it was exciting her.

After a moment, Baby Doll got on her knees with her picture-perfect ass pointed at Karl, and he obliged her as he slid inside of her doggystyle. Baby Doll was oohing and ahhing as Karl went fast to slow then from slow to fast. He was swirling around, poking inside of her with jerking thrusts, and every time Karl was about to explode, he stopped while Baby Doll activate her grippers. After a moment the doggy dance began again.

Ten minutes later, Karl laid Baby Doll on her back in the missionary sex position and began the standard routine. In and out, slow and easy, swirl it around, making sure each hit connects with her clitoris, and then take it from the top. Five minutes into this pleasure-provoking procedure, there was no stopping Karl from coming. The point of no return had taken control of his biological workings, and the fire couldn't be extinguished. With her legs propped on Karl's arms, Baby Doll saw this was it, and so she squeezed her vagina muscles with all her might, noticing it was making her ejaculate right along with Karl. The feeling was mind-bogglingly pleasurable, she instantly noticed, and knew she was hooked from here on in. As their juices flowed in unison, Baby Doll and Karl hollered with pleasure, sounding like a cacophony of exotic music that was soothing not only to the ear, but moreso to the soul.

In the months that followed, Baby Doll had to work over time to check herself because she was turning into a sex fiend, and was literally wearing Karl out. When she noticed Karl was getting a little tight with the money, she was slapped out of her dick-whipped trance and immediately started cutting back. The pussy party was officially over, since Baby Doll would never give up that almighty dollar for a good piece of dick, no matter how excellent it was. Some females may beg to differ, but for Baby Doll money was what made life worth living. By the time she was ready to graduate from high school, she had Karl back on his leash, and she was back in charge.

Baby Doll also befriended a woman named Ruth Wallace who lived on the first floor of the apartment building she lived. Ruth was Mrs. Kirkland's identical twin in that they both were advent churchwomen, they were elderly, and to Baby Doll's surprise, they both felt a good vibe pulsating from her, insisting that Baby Doll was meant to be in the church.

Why are all these church folks gravitating toward me like this? She had asked herself immediately after receiving Ruth's remarks. She still couldn't see how or why they felt she was made for the church. She figured these ladies had to be bugging and didn't know whether or not to take it as a compliment or an insult, since it could imply that she looked and acted soft and was a punk or something. On the flip side, she knew it could also mean the energy she resonated was actually good, and because church folks tended to have a heightened sense of awareness when it came to detecting good energy, she went with this conclusion.

* * * *

Big Daddy Blue and Preacher immediately activated their damage-control program, upon hearing that people in the streets were throwing around rumors that John Boy went down because Big Daddy's people were violating the rules, and had dropped a dime on John Boy. The first thing they did was send Silverback, Starr, and Hakim out on the streets to let folks know that if they got caught flinging around those lies, there would be severe consequences. Twice, Silverback, Starr, and Hakim had to put the blows on a few dope fiends for repeating the rumor while saying it in such a way that indicated they had animosity toward Big Daddy. After a few beat downs, most people were mums, and as expected, the rumor stopped spiraling out of control.

John Boy's people, on the other hand, weren't trying to hear anything. The young, wild heads were calling for war, and didn't care who it was against, so long as bullets were flying and blood was being spilled. But the good thing was that John Boy's second in command, Hen-Dog, was smart enough not to re-act impulsively to the rumors. Plus, Hen-Dog had heard of Big Daddy's past exploits, had mad respect for Big Daddy Blue, and knew if he gave the order to transgress against him, it wouldn't be an easy tussle, and consequences would be certain. On the first day of the arrest, Hen-Dog had to shut down all his enforcers, because they were about to respond to the rumors, and wanted to spray up all of Big Daddy's establishments, even the clothing stores, and any and all innocent workers. Hen-Dog had decided that he was going to cut their enforcer mob loose if John Boy had gave the green light, and during a Rikers Island visit, John Boy laughed at Hen-Dog when Hen-Dog told him that the word on the street was that one of Big Daddy's people had snitched on him.

John Boy toned his laughter down, and said, "Motherfucker, it wasn't Big Daddy that did this shit!" He beamed at Hen-Dog sitting across from him. "This is some real counter-intelligence bullshit. The lawyer said it was a police informant." He closely observed Hen-Dog's response, since now everybody was suspect. "He thinks it's an insider that did it, somebody right amongst us." He was glad he didn't see any signs of distrust coming from Hen-Dog; it didn't matter anyway because he had his ways of finding out, but it was going to cost. "The oldest police trick in the mufuckin' book is to make it look like a stand-up dude is snitching while the real snitch goes undetected. But it ain't going down like that. Them niggas ain't playing us out like that and you better make sure of it, Hen-Dog."

Two months later, John Boy and Hen-Dog found out who the snitch was, and instead of killing him on the spot, they simply watched, followed and carefully monitored him to see if he had any sidekicks working along with him. If there was one snitch, there was often a network of them working in cahoots with each other. Sure enough, within a week, it was discovered that Walter was working with Allen. In a carefully coordinated hit, they both were conveniently caught in the crossfire of a hit on two of John Boy's important enforcers, allegedly done by the Dominican mafia. John Boy and Hen-Dog had to sacrifice one of their best enforcers in order to kill the snitches without attracting any police attention to the fact their informants had been exposed. They both agreed it was worth it, even though the enforcer was Hen-Dog's first cousin.

* * * *

Two days before Baby Doll's graduation, Big Daddy stood staring out the window of his Evergreen Street club with a huge smile as he saw the permanent padlocks being placed on John Boy's club. After John Boy's arrest, he started closing down all of his extra-curricular business enterprises, since they were either experiments or were done to facilitate a personal agenda. In any event, now that John Boy was fighting to avoid a life bid (if convicted he would be a three-time loser), there was no time to tie up money in things that didn't absolutely bring in outlandish loads of money. Clubs were a lucrative business, but it couldn't compete with drug dealing on any scale.

* * * *

Baby Doll strutted down the aisle in her black cap and gown wearing a smile that could outshine the sun.

In the audience, along with the hundreds of other supporters, Jeanette, Edna, Tera, Karl, Wilma, and Big Daddy Blue were clapping their hands as the graduates entered the stage, received their diplomas, and sat lined up in the first several rows of seats in the auditorium.

Baby Doll sat beaming with pride and a strong sense of accomplishment. She turned and waved to Big Daddy and others, and as she faced forward, she realized that her hatred for her real family grew tremendously in that moment. Although she was grateful that she did have someone here to support her, it didn't feel right without her real family holding her down, and especially her mother. She had given her mother an invitation to the graduation, and Mildred took it, ripped it up in her face and threw it to the floor. Baby Doll had even tried to apologize to her mother, but Mildred turned her back while waiting for the elevator, and Baby Doll walked away with her head held up high.

As Baby Doll sat listening to the valor Victoria speaker, wondering if she should continue her schooling or start working full-time, she vowed that she was going to make it. Whatever she chose to do, she was going to make it; she was going to be successful, and most of all, she was going do everything in her power to mash it in her family's face and prove to them that she was somebody special, and that they weren't shit! Her bitterness had developed in such a manner that she welcomed it because it made her determined.

The energy that flowed from her hatred for her family was very inspiring and within a month and a half after graduating, Baby Doll decided to get herself a nice used car. After milking Karl for some paper, and playing on Big Daddy's benevolent heart, while digging deep into her own stash, she was able to get herself a Lexus.

She felt like the Queen Bee of all Bees as she rolled out of the car lot with her cream colored two-door Lexus that had matching velvet-like seats and drove so smoothly, it felt like the car was floating on a cushion of air. Dressed in a matching cream-colored outfit with leather Prada boots, she popped in the Biggie Small's

CD, and his rap song, "I'm Going back to Cali," thundered through the car speakers with bass so deep and powerful, it felt like a club on wheels. She cruised through the neighborhood, not caring who didn't like all the noise. Knowing how grimy the hood was, she immediately got herself one of those low-jack car thief protection systems along with a steering wheel lock to prevent car thieves from raining on her raise to greatness.

Baby Doll was so eager to show off her new ride, the first place she went was to Tilden projects. She cruised through the hood showboating a mile a minute, feeling good as the onlookers' jealous eyes were rolling all over the place once they realized it was Baby Doll behind the wheel. Baby Doll snatched up Jeanette and Edna, and all they did was drive all over Brownville, driving and drinking as if they were adolescent joy riders with a brand-new toy.

That evening Baby Doll pulled up in front of her mother's building as Tracy and Mildred were looking out the window. Baby Doll got out of her car along with Jeanette and Edna, and headed toward the building. Baby Doll looked up and saw someone in her mother's apartment window. *Yeah, you bitches, I know y'all looking! And I know y'all wish y'all could do it up like this*, Baby Doll said to herself with a gorgeous smile, feeling good because she could feel all eyes were on her. She even sensed the group of thugs sitting on the bench a few yards away next to the adjacent building was checking her out, probably fiending to get a banging chick such as herself.

That group of up-and-rising thugs was searching for someone to stickup. The leader of the crew was Nate, who lived in Brownville Houses and made it his business to do his dirt in projects other than his own, so tonight he and his peoples were on the prowl inside Tilden.

Nate spoke to the others at normal volume. "Yo' son, I'm telling you, we can get this bitch. When she comes back out, I'll get the drop on this bitch, get the keys, make her let loose the dough, and if she gets crazy, I'll put a slug in this bitch with the quickness."

A droopy-eyed teen said, "Word up, Nate, let's do it. That's her! That's the one I was telling you about! She got a sister name Tracy, who ain't feelin' her. Check it, she's holdin' crazy paper too, son. Her sister was telling me she be rollin' with mad money on her, son."

On a nearby bench, about twenty feet away, Ka-Born was lying down. He was drunk, washed up, and could past for a bum. His mother kicked him out of the crib, and he decided to spend the night on the bench. Tomorrow he knew she'd get over the fact he stole her silverware and traded it for some heroin and Night Train. He had heard Nate and his peoples from Brownsville Houses talking about robbing somebody, and when he sat up and saw them gesturing toward Baby Doll as she, Jeanette and Edna entered the building, he was on a wave of mixed emotions. His first response was a true happiness, but after his drunken mind started remembering what Big Daddy and Preacher had told him what would happen to him if anything happened to Baby Doll while she was out there in Tilden, his emotions shifted.

Nate pulled a 9mm as he said to his peoples, "Yo' check it, son. Me and Randy'll post up near the bench over there." He pointed at the bench that wasn't too far from where the Lexus was parked. "You and Johnny Ray can post up across the street. When she comes out, we'll bag her ass right up."

They all released a collective chant of agreement, as if they were a basketball team gearing up for another quarter.

CHAPTER 17

Big Daddy Blue and Preacher were sitting in the VIP section of the Cleveland Street club, talking. Big Daddy and Preacher were dressed casually, with drinks in front of them. In the background, Dorothy Moore's "Misty Blue" was playing in the background, and Big Daddy was feeling this music, since it was from his time. A time when there was such a thing as "good music." Tonight was old-timers' night and the only music played was tunes from the late sixties, the seventies, and the early eighties, primarily R & B songs along with ballads and classic slow songs. The place was filled almost to capacity, and it was clear that the oldies but goodies had a way of bringing folks out of retirement.

"After this thing with the Evergreen club," Big Daddy said, "I'm seriously thinking about throwing the towel in with these clubs. Things over at the Lincoln Place club are even getting crazy. I was talking to—"

"And give up our biggest source of income?" Preacher said, sensing Big Daddy was serious this time. He'd hinted at pulling out of the club game before, but this time he sounded serious. "This thing with John Boy was one of those rare situations where egos, attitudes, and hidden agendas started clashing."

"So what you saying, I caused this problem? Egos, attitudes, and hidden agendas clashing?"

"Easy, Big Papa, all I'm saying is that John Boy did what we did because he felt you violated when he helped you, but you didn't help him. Now, I'm not judging nobody here, or taking his side. I'm just trying to put myself in both of your shoes. In all fairness, from his perception, he felt you were obliged to help him. I don't agree with John Boy's views, but there are some people out there that would side with John Boy and would say that since he helped you, you should've helped him, regardless to what it was."

Peacher paused for a moment to place emphasis on his previous comment. "In my opinion, John Boy played himself all across the board when he couldn't respect the fact that you're against drugs and won't have no parts of them. Since we paid him what we borrowed in full along with interest, he should've wiped that slap to his ego on his chest and kept it moving."

Big Daddy looked around the club and saw the old-timers on the dance floor were doing moves that caused a flashback. Times had changed so drastically that he often felt like an antique relic sitting next to a futuristic device, and it was a relief when he was confronted with moments such as these. "Yeah, you got a point there, Preacher. John Boy had a right to feel the way he did, being that he's still stuck on stupid and can't get beyond that whole criminal element. I guess I'm feeling bad because I was about to let that chump drag me back into that world I left years ago." The thought of him having to hire Sweet Charlie in order to knock off John Boy to prevent this fool from destroying one of his clubs was ripping his conscience to pieces. "If these clubs are gonna force me back into that mentality, I gotta let this shit go, Preacher. I'll be better off investing my time in businesses that don't bring all that baggage along with it." For the past several days he'd been analyzing what he was about to do to John Boy and came to terms with the fact he couldn't change who he was. Deep down, he knew he could've simply ignored what John Boy did, and could have responded by becoming more creative in the way he handled the Evergreen club, but something inside of him made it impossible not to step to the issue in a gangster-like manner. With the type of competition John Boy was stirring up, it would have forced him to tighten up his game, and the experience could have been a good thing. Instead, he reacted in the same way he would've responded years ago. This whole incident was making him do a serious observation of what was going on inside of him, and unfortunately, he didn't like what he was seeing.

Preacher took a long swig of his drink. "I see this thing got you beating yourself up, man." He knew how hard Big Daddy was fighting not to become the man he used to be, and he commended him on the energy he asserted in keeping himself on track. Preacher had long since come to grips with the fact he was who he was meant to be, and that's just the way it would always be. "Before you go throwing the baby out with the bath water, sit on it for a month or two. This ain't the kind of decision you shot from the hip. These clubs just recently got into the profit zone, and with some minor tweaking and a few new ideas, we can turn them into a source of income that will boost your youth employment program tremendously." He knew if he started talking about the youth program, it would get him to reevaluate his actions.

There was a moment of silence as the two bobbed their heads to the Joe Simon tune where he repeatedly proclaimed he was having the best time of his life.

Preacher continued, "Not to rudely jump to another topic, but if this club thing is getting under your skin, how are we gonna put into activation the plan, where we start stepping to these stores in certain Black communities and start convincing them to contribute to this youth program of ours?" He saw he had Big Daddy's undivided attention. "A plan like that, you and I both know we might have to apply some pressure to some of them, to get them to understand that the only way for such a program to work is to get universal support and participation from all people in the community, including other ethnic groups."

Big Daddy nodded his head to that because he had just hit the nail on the head. "You're right about that, but the first phase of that plan is to work with only those who are willing to donate either money or guarantee some of the kids jobs. Let's worry about that first, and when the time comes, we'll deal with other approaches later."

Preacher sighed and said, "Well, I'll say it again. Think hard and long before you decide to drop these clubs, Big Daddy. With the cash starting to come in the way it is, we'll be able to take our whole operation to another level in six months."

Big Daddy knew what Preacher was saying was the honest-to-God truth. He'd been closely monitoring the books, and things were about ready to take off. He sighed and gulped down the last of his drink. He also knew this would not be any ordinary decision if he decided to take it. Big Daddy looked up, and a beautiful woman caught his eye. Her curly hairstyle brought out the elegant contorts of her face, her skin was utterly flawless, and heads were turning as she walked by. She looked very familiar, and the more Big Daddy examined her shapely body, the more he realized he knew her. She looked to be in her mid-forties, but was very well preserved, and it was obvious she did a lot of working out. The woman's name was on the tip of his tongue, and as he struggled to recall her name, he noticed she noticed he was staring at her. She examined Big Daddy and suddenly lit up with a smile of indisputable recognition and glided over toward him.

The woman stopped in front of the table and said with the most lovely voice, "Big Daddy Blue, my God, it's really you!"

Big Daddy was stumped; he knew this woman but couldn't remember her name to save his life. He looked over at Preacher as if to ask for help.

The woman saw he didn't remember her and wasn't the least offended. "It's me, Sabrina." He didn't catch it yet, "Sabrina Lamb. My brother is Eddie. He used to work for you—"

"Oh, yeah, Eddie." An avalanche of memories assaulted his memory bank. "You're his baby sister! They used to call you Candy. Come on, have a seat."

He waved her over and she slid next to him. "So, what you been up to Candy—I mean Sabrina? I see you still taking care of ourselves."

"Look who's talking," Sabrina had a vicious crush on Big Daddy back in the day, and she instantly noticed it was even stronger. "I heard you were out, and I've been dying to catch up with you. I'm up here on vacation, so I figured I come on down and check you out. I love this club of yours, Big Daddy."

Big Daddy was surprised he felt his nature rising. Sabrina's perfume was no joke, and it was apparent the scent had those nature chemicals in it that got men horny, because he was getting a rise for a change. He remembered the chemicals were called pheromones

"Sabrina, this is my partner, Preacher. Preacher this is Sabrina."

Preacher and Sabrina shook hands.

Preacher saw the smile on Big Daddy's grill and knew he was really feeling this broad. Checking her out, he saw Sabrina was definitely a good looker, and if Big Daddy didn't snatch her up, he had full intentions of stepping to her. By the look of their smiles, Preacher knew sparks were about to fly, and that told him it was time to break out.

"Hey, listen Big Daddy and Sabrina, I gotta run." He rose to his feet. "It's nice to meet you, Sabrina." He headed for the bar for a refill.

Big Daddy yelled to Preacher over The Temptations' song, "Papa Was a Rrolling Stone," "Hey, Preacher, tell Kenny to send me over some champagne and two glasses."

Preacher nodded his head with that grin that said, "Go for it."

Sabrina was looking around the club admiringly. "I will say you are absolutely a man who is about his business. I'm impressed with this place. If Eddie could see this, he'd be proud of you, Big Daddy."

"If Eddie was with us, he'd be more than proud; he'd be side by side with me making it happen." As Big Daddy's mind wandered into a daydream, he felt the ache in his heart at the fact Eddie died almost fifteen years ago in an automobile collision while Big Daddy was at Comstock Prison.

At the time, Eddie was the only one who was keeping it real, sending him periodic letters and money. Back when Big Daddy was deep into the game, Eddie was what might be called a henchman. He was big, black, ugly, and very intimidating, and didn't do a lot of talking. In fact, upon first meeting Eddie, most people thought he was a deaf mute. He didn't talk about it, because he was about it.

This reverie also reminded him of the fact that the very same year Eddie died, so did his younger brother, Gary J. Williams, AKA G-Gunner, who was killed in New Jersey's infamous State Prison, Rahway. G-Gunner was serving a twelve-year sentence for Bank Robbery and had clashed with one of his old co-defendants from a previous Bank Robbery where G-Gunner had stolen all the money after a successful caper.

According to the rumor, Apache rocked G-Gunner to sleep and had him shanked to death as he was on his way from the prison yard. On the tail end of this memory, Big Daddy was also reminded of what happened to his older brother, Glenn J. Williams, AKA Jazz (Tera's father), who died three years after G-Gunner. Jazz died of a massive heart attack in a Federal Prison in Indiana while serving a fifty-to-life prison sentence for conspiracy to commit murder and drug trafficking under the Federal Drug Kingpin Statute.

Big Daddy sighed stressfully at how much his entire life was surrounded by so much death, destruction, and misery. He wondered for the umpteenth time how was he and his brothers so far gone on the criminal side of life, when his mother and father were hard-working, upstanding citizens. His mother, Wanda

Williams, was a postal worker for twenty-five years until retirement, while his father, Glenn, Sr., was the lifetime owner of an auto-mechanic shop. About four years ago his father died, and shortly afterwards, so did his mother. They both were in their eighties upon expiration.

"Yeah, you two were like the dynamic duo." Sabrina smiled at Big Daddy, realizing she had pulled him out of a momentary daydream. "So this is the new you, I see. It fits you very well. So who's the lucky lady in your life?"

Big Daddy saw she was fishing, trying to see if he would take the bait, or better yet the hint. "If you hinting at marriage. . ." He showed her both of his ringless hands. "I'm not the one. However, I do have a lady friend I'm seeing. And yourself?"

"The same thing. I'm seeing this individual, but it's nothing serious." She felt herself becoming moist down below. He was giving her some signals that this might be going some place. She could still remember the dreams she used to have of Big Daddy sexing her out. Those dreams were almost twenty-seven years old, but she could still remember them; not in detail, of course, but it was clear that they were always sexual in nature. Back then she wanted him so bad, but she knew Eddie would not permit it. Big Daddy had her by almost fifteen years, and even though she was a teen at the time, she would always flirt, tease, and even touch Big Daddy in places she wasn't supposed to, practically doing everything to get him to make love to her. But he never took the bait. She was hoping she could entice him now.

They were both adults, and he still looked good as hell. It was almost as if he didn't age very much. Yeah, there was some gray hair, and a little weight around the mid-section, but he was still the infamous Big Daddy Blue and she could still visualize him inside of her. The thought of finally fulfilling a lifelong dream was making her very bold.

Big Daddy noticed her pause and said, "So what you been up to? What you do for a living? Where you moved to?"

"I'm a paralegal with a firm in Baltimore. I'm single and live alone." She lied about living alone, but he would never know. "I was married, but I'm divorced now. I won't make that mistake again. I got two adult children. My daughter, the youngest, she's twenty-one and in college, and my son, the oldest, he's twenty-five, and in prison for bank robbery." She didn't feel uncomfortable sharing her son's circumstances, being that Big Daddy had done some heavy time for murder and drug dealing, and obviously wouldn't judge like most others.

Kenny approached and sat the ice-cold bottle of champagne and the two glasses on the table and went back to the bar.

As Big Daddy poured champagne into the glasses, he said, "You can imagine where I been and what I been up to." He handed Sabrina a glass as he slid closer to her until his hip touched hers. "You probably heard what happened to my daughter Amber." The mere thought that his baby girl had OD'd on cocaine was a vicious reminder that them drugs had to go. "I got a daughter, Rachel. She's a schoolteacher; don't see much of her though." He wanted to add that the only time he ever heard from her was when she needed money, but it would display his pain. "Once I got out of prison, I snatched up my stash money and started a bunch of legit businesses. While in prison I put all that fast-lane crap in a bag and flushed it away. I got four clothing stores, three clubs, and a shitload of headaches and heartaches."

"I heard. You know I stay in contact with Regina Nelson, and she would always keep me abreast about you, talking about how you doing the right thing. She said you doing a lot of stuff for the kids, and everything."

"What brings you to New York?"

"Just visiting. You know my aunt Linda still lives in Fort Greene, and my cousin Rodney is still living in Canarsie. And they both live in the same apartments, from way back before you went to prison, you believe that!? The minute I got here I've been coming to your clubs looking for you. The one over on Evergreen is a nice place. But I must say I like this one better, I like this atmosphere; the older crowd thing, you know." She sipped on her drink. After a moment she said, "Big Daddy, you know I used to have a vicious crush on you, you know that."

Big Daddy smiled and said, "For me to miss that fact I had to have been brain-dead."

They both laughed loudly, drawing attention from the nearby table. The Temptations song was ending, and on its heels came Marvin Gaye and Tammy Terrell, singing the song, "Your Precious Love."

The music had set the prefect mood, and Sabrina decided it was time to lay it out, no holds barred. "You feel like going somewhere where I can started acting up like I used to do?" She massaged Big Daddy's leg, only inches from his groin. "I'm a big girl now, so don't you go playing that big brother bit with me."

Big Daddy couldn't pretend he wasn't interested and had no intentions of doing so. He reached his hand over, massaged Sabrina's leg, and then allowed his hand to slide up to her crouch area. He'd always had a saying, and that was, "The best way to answer sexual innuendos was to let actions speak louder than words." As he noticed Sabrina's eye rolling up in her head, he saw the saying was indeed a good one.

* * * *

At about the moment Big Daddy was massaging Sabrina's crouch area while making plans to go to the hotel about a mile away, Baby Doll decided it was time to call it a night. She was on the phone with Karl, and he was popping mad shit about her being out too late accusing her of hanging out with another dude.

"Listen Karl!" Baby Doll shouted into the cell phone. "You gonna have to slow down with all this jealous shit. You know damn well I'm here at Jeanette's house. And what the fuck you think I need a motherfucker out here in Tilden for!? These niggas out here ain't got shit I want." She sighed as Karl kept beefin'. She sucked her teeth and said with attitude, "Yeah, yeah, whatever, I'm on my way." She hung up the phone.

"Girl, you better tighten up your leash on that fool." Jeanette said.

"Well, girl, you know how it is when that pussy get 'em all whipped out. The thought of somebody else up in that thang, gets 'em all stupid and silly." Baby Doll gathered her belongings. "Let me get going." She headed for the door. "I'll give you a call in the morning. Later Jeanette, Eddie."

Edna muttered the words, "Good night," as Baby Doll exited the apartment.

As Baby Doll was waiting for the elevator, she looked out the hallway window at her car, saw her shiny Lexus standing out amongst all the hoopties surrounding it, and beamed with pride. Then, she saw two shadowy figures in the dark. Upon closer scrutiny, she saw it was two dudes sitting on the bench, and she felt a nervous ping in her gut.

The elevator had arrived, and she got on it. She hit the first-floor button and the door slid close. The piss odor was heavy in the air as usual, and for the thousandth time she wondered why motherfuckers in the projects just had to piss in the elevator. She often wished she could catch one of those sons of bitches, so she could spit his wig open to the white meat. Her head was still buzzing with liquor and weed, which made her even more sensitive to the urine smell, as well as made her want to fight somebody. Then, for some odd reason she felt nervous and sensed it was because of those dudes sitting on the bench. It was almost one o'clock in the morning and folks sitting on benches, especially thug looking dudes, weren't the norm. After going back and forth with whether she should hang tight or go back upstairs to get Jeanette and Edna to walk her to her car, she pushed her fear to the back of her mind, concluding that everybody out here in Tilden knew who the fuck she was. Everybody out here knew she was rolling with Big Daddy Blue, and if they played themselves, there would be consequences. Her false sense of security was now engrained in her mind-altered reality as the liquor merged with weed was warping her sense of logic.

The elevator reached the ground floor, and she exited the building with her head high in the air, while the liquor in her bloodstream locked her into a state of fearlessness. The late summer night air was humid and made breathing difficult, she noticed.

As Baby Doll strutted toward her car, she noticed there were two other thugs standing across the street, and when they saw her they responded as if they were getting ready to step to her. Then she saw the two thugs sitting on the bench were now standing. Something inside her was telling her this was a set-up, but her belief that everybody out here knew she was down with Big Daddy, and that they would not play their-self, kept her from reacting to her intuition. She trotted forward, sweeping her fear aside.

Nate inconspicuously pulled the gun and hid it behind his leg. He was going to wait until Baby Doll opened the door of her Lexus and then bum-rush her. As she approached, he was surprised she was alone, and actually expected her to have one of these lames from out here to walk her to the car. That would've made the night more interesting, since there would've been more people to rob, which would mean more money.

Baby Doll walked past the two thugs and gave them the grill face. She saw one of them had his hand behind the back of his leg as if he was hiding something, and her heart flashed with a rush of adrenaline. That stance was a common pose when someone had a burner and was about to pull it out. She frantically pulled her car key from her pocket, cutting her eyes nervously at the two thugs, while she hysterically opened the car door.

Nate pointed the gun at Baby Doll's back while shouting. "Hold up, little dime piece!" He eased toward her as his homie was next to him. He saw his other homies across the street moving in. "Just be easy, ma. All we want is the car and yo' money, and we won't—"

BLOOM! BLOOM! BLOOM! BLOOM!

Four shots rang out, and instinctually, everyone scrambled for cover, except for Baby Doll, who scrambled inside of her Lexus, trembling out of control. She slammed the key into the ignition and started her car with one swift turn of the key.

BLOOM! BLOOM!

Two more shots rang out when Nate aimed at the car. This time a bullet struck him in the stomach, and he literally screamed like a little girl in pain; his voice hit such a high note that even his homies were shocked.

Baby Doll started the car and raced away, tires screaming, and her heart about to beat itself clean out of her chest. Through the rear-view mirror, she saw the thugs scrambling about. Then two more shots rang out.

When the first shot rang out, various residents of 265 Livonia were racing out of their beds, and to their windows. One of the first people to get to the window was Kevin, and he saw Baby Doll's Lexus screech away. As Kevin watched the young, baggy-pants-wearing thugs scoop up one of their wounded comrades and limp away, a vicious idea came to his mind. In that very moment he saw the perfect way to get back at Baby Doll's conceited little ass for trying to get Ka-Born to kill him, and for apparently telling somebody else who was now sending him anonymous letters, trying to scare the shit out of him.

As the plan percolated inside his mind, Kevin smiled as he said to Mildred, who was about to get out of bed to see what was going on, "It's nothing, Mildred. It ain't nothing but these crazy-ass kids out here shooting and carrying on. Go on back to sleep, Mildred." Kevin watched Mildred get back under the covers, and a moment after he laid back down next to her, realizing that this time Baby Doll was going to find out firsthand why it was never wise to fuck with a real live baller. He just hoped he could get his man, Stan, to step up and do him this one major favor.

CHAPTER 8

Big Daddy Blue sat behind his desk, trying to concentrate on the financial report he received from the company accountant. Paul Grossman, a world-class public accountant, had promised him he was in store for "some pleasant surprises." As Big Daddy smiled while scrolling down the financial entries, another topic bum-rushed his mind. He couldn't seem to get his sexcapade with Sabrina out of his head. Sabrina was a scrumptious treat if ever he'd been blessed with one. After the first night he'd had sex with her three weeks ago, he'd had three more sexual affairs after that. But, for some odd reason, that first night stayed in his mind as if it was some kind of mystical event in his life. He didn't know why it was so special, but the reality was that the sex was so good, it forced him to come back three more times.

That night re-enacted itself for the twentieth time inside his mind and Big Daddy felt his wood pulsing to life. They had both stepped inside the hotel room, lust surging through their systems, and to Big Daddy's surprise, there was some strong foreplay that consisted of gentle kissing, caressing, fondling on both parts, and a slow peeling off of their clothing. By the time Sabrina was down to her undergarments, she pushed away from Big Daddy, forced him to sit down on the bed and then went into an exotic dance routine. It was clear she wanted him to savor the sight of her perfectly sculptured body. She came out of her panties and bra, flung them into Big Daddy's face, causing his mouth to literally water, drooling with the thought of tasting her juices. There was no doubt Big Daddy was into the pussy-eating business; he came correct and had a dental dam in his pocket and knew it would be well utilized before the night was over. Sabrina was buck-naked, and Big Daddy's wood was pulsating as it stood at attention.

After Sabrina did her dance she eased into Big Daddy's embrace, and they resumed kissing. Big Daddy stopped after only a minute of kissing, and upon noticing she wanted him to enter her raw, he retrieved the condom and the dental dam while operating on Sabrina with his fingers, and she was surprised he was handling his business better than most of the younger cats she tussled in bed with. He knew where her buttons were and was hitting the marks like a sure-nuff sharpshooter.

Big Daddy had slid the condom on, but before he went up in her, he put the dental dam on Sabrina's vagina and commenced to laying on her womanhood the best French kiss she'd ever experienced. The aroma that resonated from Sabrina's vagina was as sweet as paradise and Big Daddy was so catch up in the lusciousness of the scent, he stayed downtown working his tongue in ways even he didn't know was possible; almost twenty straight minutes flew by without one drop of his energy wavering. It was self-evident she had apparently sprayed some of those horny chemicals down there because it had Big Daddy going crazy, while Sabrina was hollering; when Big Daddy hit the marks, she had no shame letting him know that was it. She would make sounds that only serve to incite Big Daddy to keep it coming. He'd even caught a cramp in his jaw and was able to ignore it, in view of how much enjoyment he was receiving from eating Sabrina. He'd even contemplated removing the dental dam and tasting her actual juices, but he killed that thought with an easy struggle. He'd decided many years ago that no pussy was worth dying for, and only until he saw actual medical reports on a woman's health status, there would absolutely be no unprotected sex, no matter how fine, clean, sweet, and picture perfect she was. He'd learned about HIV/AIDS while in prison and knew that people walked around with that virus for years, didn't even know they were infected, were unknowingly (and knowingly) infecting others, and most of all, there was no way anyone could look at a person and tell if they were infected with HIV.

When Big Daddy came up from downtown, he got on top of her and allowed his condom-covered wood to snake its way into Sabrina's hot juice-dripping tunnel. Big Daddy saw that the moment he inserted himself inside of her she was already blasting off with intense convulsions of delight. Watching and feeling her ejaculate excited him immensely. Sabrina was slamming her hips at Big Daddy, literally throwing the pussy at him like there was no tomorrow. As Sabrina's explosive release died down, Big Daddy felt reassured because he'd always known that the initial pussy-eating procedure was guaranteed to provoke this sort of immediate discharge upon entering a woman, and by the look of Sabrina's reaction it was obvious it had worked on her.

About ten minutes later, and after putting Sabrina in a series of sexual positions, Big Daddy saw it was his turn now. He loved to blast off in doggy style, and the moment he felt he couldn't hold back the nut any longer, he pulled out of Sabrina, and instructed her to get on her knees, and she quickly obeyed. The sight of Sabrina's gorgeous ass staring up at Big Daddy was enough to excite him into ecstasy. He entered her womanhood and got off no more than seven strokes before his pounding increased by tenfold, and the fire erupted in his testicles.

He wasn't a hollerer, but he became one that night as the liquids in his body started shooting out of him with hard, viciously pleasing sprays. The nut was so fantastic, it felt like the nut would go on for five minutes. When the muscles in his mid-section completed its spasmodic response to this sexual release, Big Daddy couldn't help but to lay down. It felt like all the energy in his body was zapped from him, and now he suddenly felt his age of sixty-two years. He knew it was time for small talk, but his body was broadcasting to him that it wasn't going to happen. His eyelids instantly became very heavy, and as Sabrina talked, he did exactly what he didn't want to do, and that was fall to sleep.

Big Daddy was pulled out of his daydream when Preacher entered the office. Big Daddy jumped into attention as if he were doing something he had no business doing, and Preacher detected it.

"What's happening, Big D?" Preacher eyes were squinted. "That report got you excited like that, huh?" Preacher started smiling, which was something he didn't do very often. He was thrilled by the fact Big Daddy decided to stay in the club game and knew once he saw this financial report he would be pleased.

Big Daddy was flushed with embarrassment. His wood was hard as blue steel, and he was hoping and praying he didn't have to stand up.

"Pardon me for barging in," Preacher said as Mike Tyson-style voice became low-pitched. "But there's something I think you ought to come out here and see for yourself."

Big Daddy looked at Preacher with a shocked expression; he looked at him as if he was crazy. "Naw, man, I'm busy, right now."

"This is an emergency, Big Daddy, and I think you should come on out here and check it out. Come on, hurry up!"

"I'll be there in a few minutes. I need to finish reading this report." He felt the blood pulsing out of his shaft and in a few more seconds he would be back to himself.

Preacher shrugged his shoulders and said, "In a few more minutes the news report'll be over. It's John Boy. This fool done fucked around and got re-arrested by the Feds—"

Big Daddy jetted out of his seat and out of the office. A moment later, he stood in front of the TV in the lounge room, listening to the last of the news report that stated Jonathan Benson AKA John Boy was accused of masterminding the killing an undercover DEA agent and a confidential informant.

Big Daddy was able to catch most of the story, and it was alleged that one of the shooters involved in the killing of Walter Reid and Allen Carson confessed to committing the shooting in exchange for immunity. The unnamed shooter alleged that John Boy and his first lieutenant Hen-Dog had orchestrated the hit on Raymond Griffin as a way to actually kill Walter and Allen. The shooter further claimed that the hit was designed to make it appear as though the two informants were merely caught in the crossfire. Although John Boy knew Walter and Allen were informants, he didn't know that Allen Carson was much more than a mere snitch. He was, in fact, a deep-cover DEA agent.

When the news report ended, Big Daddy returned to his office, and his phone rang. He picked it up. "Hello." He sighed angrily. "How the fuck did you get my number!?"

On the other end of the line, Ka-Born said, "Come on, big papa, you know you in the telephone book." He slurred drunkenly. "I just opened the yellow pages and let my fingers do the walking, and now I'm on the jack doing the talking." He laughed, and then suddenly started coughing. "Check it, man. I need to know when you gonna hit me off. I need that break-off real bad, man."

Big Daddy wanted to curse this fool out for calling him at his job, and now he regretted that he promised to hit him off with a few dollars for what he did to protect Baby Doll. Reflecting on that situation, he was glad the police didn't believe some guy named Stanley Anderson who came forth and told them that Baby Doll was at the scene and was involved in the shooting. Thanks to the thug that got shot, they were forced to drop that particular line of investigation because the shooting victim (who was laid up in a Brookdale hospital bed) along with a friend had both insisted that there was no female with a cream-colored Lexus at the scene that night.

They both claimed that some unknown assailant in a mask came out of nowhere and started shooting at them for no reason. When asked what they were doing outside that time of night, they claimed they were walking through Tilden to get to their projects, Brownsville Houses, and were attacked without provocation.

Big Daddy said calmly, "I told you I got you, Ka-Born. I'll drive through there tonight around nine o'clock. Be over on Rockaway and Livonia. I'll see you then." He hung up, sat down, and resumed examining the report. He smiled when he got to the part that showed their profits had doubled since their May financial status. As he enjoyed the thought of knowing that his businesses were finally starting to pick up momentum, he felt even happier by the fact he'd convinced this brother named Chris Duffy who had three stores to join his Youth Employment Program. In another year, he imagined that there could be at least a dozen new businesses in his network, and the thought of how much damage they could do to the problems in the hood made him feel almost as good as he felt when he was in between Sabrina's legs.

* * * *

Around the time Big Daddy was talking to Ka-Born on the phone, Baby Doll was at the Downtown Brooklyn store in Albee Square Mall, reminiscing about the shooting that occurred several days ago. That event was an eye-opener for her, and she decided to cut down on all that drinking and weed smoking. It was obvious it was clouding her judgment in such a way that she was putting herself in danger. In other words, while under the influence she was slipping, and she knew exactly what happened to those caught slipping in the hood. She had mentioned the incident only to Karl and talked about it to Jeanette and Edna, who informed her that one of the guys who tried to rob her was shot.

The first thing she thought was going to happen was the police was going to come looking for her, and she'd been waiting for them to come knocking on her door but thank goodness they never did. She also was driving herself silly trying to figure who shot one of the guys trying to rob her and ended up assuming it had to be the work of Big Daddy. It didn't make sense, but it was the only explanation her mind could grasp. She vowed that from then on she was tightening up her game and was going to reach her goal, which was to become one of the richest bitches to ever come out of Tilden projects, and that was it.

Now that she knew what she had to do, she decided to put college on standby, only for a moment, of course. The plan was to work full-time; keep banking, saving, and milking anybody naïve enough to let her get into their pockets. Images of her owning her own businesses, a huge mansion, and having access to millions (or maybe even billions) were mental motivators that would always brighten up her days whenever she felt she was becoming unfocussed. She kept plenty of *Ebony, Vibe, Jet, Essence,* and even *Feds* magazine around her, which acted as a constant subliminal reminder that she had a mission to accomplish.

By the end of the summer, Baby Doll was so caught up in her quest to acquire money, she had refused to attend the end of the summer activities Big Daddy sponsored for all of his youth employment workers. Bear Mountain and Six Flags Great Adventures were once again on his agenda, but Baby Doll felt she was too old for that stuff now. Just last year she saw attending those places and the activities that went along with going there as a wonderful thing, but now, it simply didn't even nudge her sense of excitement.

When she told Big Daddy she wasn't going to attend this year, she saw he was shattered. She tried hard to stick to her guns, but his pain was just too much for her. By the way Big Daddy was hurt it was obvious she was about to mess things up for all her future plans, so she bowed down and went along merely for the sake of not undermining her ultimate plans.

When October rolled in, Baby Doll's relationship with Karl was just about ready to enter its Swan Song mode. She sensed he was cheating on her, but she wasn't able to catch him in the act. She was monitoring his phone calls, and even smelling his clothing for someone else's perfume, but these endeavors weren't producing any results. Since they were next-door neighbors (he maintained his crib, while she maintained hers), it was virtually impossible for either one of them to do any serious cheating at home base unless the other was led to believe the other party wasn't home. As she constructed a trap to catch Karl's ass cheating, she wondered if it mattered whether he was unfaithful, especially since she had cheated on him a few times.

One of the memorable cheats occurred when she met a dude named Panama who entered the store looking for something to buy his girl and started flirting with Baby Doll like crazy. She ended up making a thousand dollars off Panama and didn't even give him a hit of the skins. In essence, Baby Doll didn't mind giving a dude some airplay as long as he made it clear he was about splurging money on her; if he confirmed this fact she would give him some rhythm. Once she got a few serious dollars out of the cat, she would cut him loose and keep it moving.

Finally, Karl had slipped up. On night he thought Baby Doll had gone out for the weekend to hang out in Tilden with Jeanette and Edna and tried to slide one of his chicken heads into his crib.

Baby Doll had parked her car a couple blocks away, cut out all of her apartment lights, and watched Karl do his thing. As Karl and the chick entered Karl's apartment, Baby Doll stood peering out her peephole. Since she had a key to his crib (he also had one to hers), she decided to lay low until she was certain the two were deadlocked into the business, and then she would rush in, catching them in the act. About a half hour later, Baby Doll quietly slid into the apartment, and could hear the bed squeaking and the chick moaning as she tiptoed to the bedroom. Baby Doll stood quietly peeking into the room, through the slightly jarred bedroom door, watching Karl digging out the back of this real dark-skinned woman with a humongous ass, a super small waist, and a homely face. Baby Doll had to breathe lightly because it was apparent the chick didn't take care of business downstairs, and certainly didn't believe in because, boy, did her pussy have the room lit up.

Just when Baby Doll saw Karl as about to nut off, she rushed into the room screaming like a crazy woman, causing the two to damn near have a heart attack as they bolted out of the bed in sheer terror. Not surprisingly, Karl tried to lie his way out of the situation, and had even flipped the script on the woman, claiming she forced him to have sex with her, and that she was blackmailing him. When the woman he called Bambi attempt to protest, Karl tried to make it look good by mushing her in the face and the drama was on. Baby Doll slid out of the apartment leaving the two fighting, and instead of getting mad, Baby Doll saw this situation as the perfect opportunity to get deeper into Karl's pockets. The plan was simple; if Karl wanted her back, he would have to pay dearly for it.

When the first wave of snow dropped in December, Karl had grown weary with giving Baby Doll all of his money without their relationship returning back to its previous status.

Baby Doll would let him eat the pussy, but she stopped him dead in his tracks when he tried to enter her. Even though he used a condom when he fucked Bambi, she knew this was a sufficient enough excuse to keep throwing in Karl's face, and to keep something daggling in front of him. She wasn't a psychologist, but she was sharp enough to know that as long as she had something that Karl really wanted and couldn't get, she could manipulate the cash flow from his pockets and into hers.

By the time the snow was settled on the ground, Karl's frustration escalated into aggression. After eating the pussy, he tried to manhandle her, and got the shock of his life. When the fists stopped swinging, and the kicks ceased being unleashed, Karl had a black eye and a busted lip, while Baby Doll had a few minor bruises. The bump on Baby Doll's forehead was nothing to her, but she used it to her full advantage. When Big Daddy and Preacher stepped to Karl, Baby Doll was raining in Karl's money. Baby Doll strategically got back with him, knowing that now she definitely had the upper hand in the relationship, since Karl would do anything in his powers not to get Big Daddy involved again. By the time they were into the new year, Karl had wised up and finally accepted defeat. He eventually got himself another apartment, and that was the last time Baby Doll saw of him. When she did a universal count of what she got out of this trick in the pass two and half years, the amount came up to about twenty-five grand. It wasn't much, but the whole experience was something she loved, and since she had acquired free money in the process, it was all good.

Time seemed to be picking up speed for Baby Doll, and she wasn't beefing, since she was growing with the time, and was taking full advantage of everything around her. She had practically stopped hanging out with Jeanette and Edna, and therefore didn't see much of Tilden.

Baby Doll had stopped getting high, and since get high was all Jeanette and Edna did, there wasn't much to do when she did go out there to visit, so she just stopped going out there all together. Baby Doll started hanging out with a woman named Pauline

Anthony from Kingsborough Houses, who was attending Medgar Evers College for business management. Baby Doll had met Pauline at the neighborhood hair salon over on Ralph Avenue and they hit it off well. They started hanging out, going to clubs, and meeting at the hair salon, but the main reason Baby Doll got with Pauline was because she had a lot to offer. Pauline had a lot of knowledge about businesses, and Baby Doll knew one day she was going to come in handy. She had learned many years ago that networking was everything when it came to businesses. Also, because of Pauline's freehearted nature, Baby Doll was already counting how much she could squeeze out of Pauline.

When the summer returned, Baby Doll got word that Jasmine was pregnant, that Tracy had finally took her ass to a rehab center, and that Ka-Born had just got arrested for armed robbery and was on Rikers Island. Baby Doll let Jeanette talk her into going out there to Tilden, and when she was leaving, she ran into her mother. Baby Doll was enjoying every minute of their encounter because Mildred had the audacity to ask her for some money. She'd apparently got laid off, Kevin was acting funny with the money, and nobody else was helping out with the bills. Baby Doll did exactly what Mildred did to her three years earlier; she turned her back, ignored her, and walked away. She felt rejuvenated by the fact she was finally able to shit on her mother in the same way she shitted on her. The look on Mildred's twisted face when Baby Doll ignored her was engrained on Baby Doll's mind, and it was more than a pleasure to finally be able to give her a taste of her own medicine.

By the end of the summer Baby Doll had sat down and calculated her money to see where she was at financially. She had a bank account with about thirty gees in it, and cash on hand she had about five thousand dollars that she kept hidden in her crib in a safe bolted to the floor inside her closet. She had been doing some research into how much it would cost to start up a small business, and although according to Pauline she had enough to get one started, it was evident it would be a vicious grid. She wanted her own business but didn't want to start a business with just enough money that she would have to literally bust her ass and break her back trying to make it work. She wanted to start a business with more than enough financial capitol, so that its success would be more guaranteed, and she wouldn't have to work so hard. At the rate she was saving and hustling, she knew she could have enough money to make a move in another two years. A two-year wait seemed like an eternity to her, but she was eager to do this and forced herself to endure and to have patience. The thought of getting Big Daddy to back her financially crossed her mind, but because she vowed that this particular accomplishment would be done by her pulling herself up by her own bootstraps, she was able to fight back the temptation.

A week after she solidified her plan, havoc struck. On night she and probably the whole neighborhood were snatched out of their sleep when screaming car tires followed by a huge crashing sound was heard. As Baby Doll jetted out of bed, stumbling to the window, she was hoping and praying it wasn't her car that was struck. She pulled the curtains aside and saw through sleep-blurred eyes that her Lexus was totaled. The entire driver side was caved in, and she saw the van that struck her car was backing up, apparently about to flee the scene. She frantically opened her window. "Hey! Hey, wait motherfucker! Wait! That's my car—"

The van screeched away.

Baby Doll tried to catch the license plate, but it was futile. As she stared at her crash-ridden Lexus, a car she had for almost three years and had become totally attached to, a tear crawled from her left eye. She wasn't crying because she was going to miss her ride, and would now have to use public transportation, but she was shattered because this meant she would eventually have to buy another ride, and therefore, slow down her efforts to getting her own business.

CHAPTER 19

The years flew by, and when Baby Doll hit twenty-one, she had moved up to the head sales clerk, surpassing Wilma by a landslide even though Wilma was there before her. Thanks to the company policy that said the head clerk position would be obtained based on the number of sales, and overall achievements of the employee, Baby Doll didn't have to worry much about any dangerous animosity coming from Wilma and the two new workers because with this policy they only had themselves to blame for not winning the position. She been employed at this Boutique store since she was seventeen, and the four years on the job had resulted in two pay raises. The money was decent, but for what she was shooting for, Baby Doll knew she had to find a way to boost up her income.

After paying rent, the car note (she got a brand-new Toyota Camara about six months after losing the Lexus), gas bill, light bill, phone bill, cable bill, credit card bill, and a series of other miscellaneous bills, she barely had money left over to do any major saving. If it weren't for her hustling and conning endeavors, consisting primarily of utilizing her breathtaking beauty to convince dudes with money to splurge on her, she might not have had a rapidly growing stash.

Baby Doll stood behind the counter talking to the cashier, Jennifer, when she looked up and saw her old archenemy, Nicole entered the store carrying a shopping bag. She had aged considerably, and had picked up some pounds, but it was old trouble-making ass Nicole through and through. She even still had that wickedly evil look to her that broadcast meanness and foulness. The last fight they had in tenth grade twinkled inside of her mind, and it was a day she would never forget because it was the same day she met Big Daddy Blue and Tera.

In fact, it suddenly dawned on her that the fight was the actual reason she had met them in the first place. As she watched Nicole scanned the racks, she noticed it felt like the fight occurred only yesterday, but Baby Doll also noticed her animosity was still at full charge.

Nicole looked around the store and her eyes landed on Baby Doll. She instantly remembered Baby Doll since she had a one-of-a-kind type of beauty.

As Baby Doll locked eyes with Nicole, she realized she never got Nicole back for all the hell she had put her through prior to her discovery that she was affiliated with Big Daddy Blue. Back then she was so caught up with trying to get her life in order, she didn't have time to waste on revenge.

"Hey, Nicole," Baby Doll beamed with a good-natured, friendly smile. "How you doing, girl?"

Nicole approached with a smile as friendly as Baby Doll's and said, "Baby Doll. Damn, girl, I knew that was you."

Baby Doll rushed happily from behind the counter and gave Nicole one of those long-time-no-see, and glad-to-see-you hugs. "So what you been up to Nicole? How's life treating you, girl?"

"Just working too hard and trying to keep my head above water. I got two bad-ass Bebe kids that's driving me mad." She looked Baby Doll up and down enviously. *This heifer didn't age a day*, she thought with a fake smile, and then said, "Baby Doll, you still the same old beauty queen." She hated giving another female woman such compliments, but in some cases there was no getting around it. "You need to share your secrets with me, child. How do you keep your weight down like that, girl?"

Baby Doll saw the hate in her eyes. Even though she had a smile, it was like her blood was pulsing with jealousy. She was really eager to put it on Nicole now. "I go to the gym every now and then, I go easy on the junk food, you know. So what's up, can I help you?

As you can see, I work here." She grabbed Nicole's arm excitedly while talking and eased toward a rack of shirts. "Girl, we got the latest gear up in here; stuff that even Saks Fifth Avenue don't even got yet. Come on over and let me show you."

As Baby Doll showed Nicole around the store, she was trying to come up with a nice way to get Nicole's envious ass back. Twice he told herself she was being petty, but the temptation for revenge was just too irresistible. When she remembered how Nicole and her crew used to bully damn near everybody at the High, jumping people for all kind of silly shit, she knew her conscious wasn't going to talk her out of giving Nicole just what she deserved. When her eyes landed on the white security tag attached to the pink shirt Nicole was holding up in the air admiring, and then she saw the store security guard, Joseph Booker, standing by the entrance looking bored out of his mind, Baby Doll came up with an excellent way to make it happen. She smiled deviously as she encouraged Nicole to buy the shirt.

Ten minutes later, Baby Doll saw Nicole looking the other way while her bag was sitting unattended. Baby Doll inconspicuously balled up a shirt along with a security tag attached and casually dropped it into Nicole shopping bag. Moments later, Baby Doll escorted Nicole to the cashier to ring up a violet-colored shirt and two pair of dress slacks.

Baby Doll watched Nicole with a smile as Jennifer rang up her items. Nicole looked over and smiled back at Baby Doll, wishing she could have a shape and beauty like hers. Nicole then gave Jennifer a hundred-dollar bill, retrieved her change and said to Baby Doll, "I'll see you around, girl. And thanks for the service."

"You take care of yourself, Nicole, and don't let them BeBe kids of your stress you out too much." Baby Doll waved as she turned and headed for the back of the store, waiting for the sparks to fly.

BABY DOLL

Nicole walked pass the shoplifting prevention device and it rang.

Joe was right on her, blocking Nicole's from leaving. He politely confiscated her bag, swung it through the scanner, and it rang again. He looked inside and found the garment with the tag attached.

Baby Doll was hiding behind a rack of clothing giggling almost childishly as she listened to Nicole arguing and cursing at Joe. "I didn't steal shit! I ain't gotta steal, nigga! I got money, mu'fucka! You can check my wallet, I got money!" Nicole shouted, making an all out scene.

When Nicole turned and saw Baby Doll had disappeared, she suddenly started putting the pieces together, and under her breath she called Baby Doll every foul name under the sun.

Joe escorted her to the back of the store to a holding room to do his job, which was to contact the police.

For the next week, Baby Doll felt as though she had purged herself of a litany of emotional toxins, and then two weeks after the Nicole incident she saw Nicole on the street while she was entering the store. Baby Doll nervously wondered if she played herself, and if her little get-back attack was worth it, because Nicole was standing across the street looking at her with a vicious screw face. It was clear she was stalking her. Just before entering the store Baby Doll hesitated and was about to step to Nicole and give her another ass-whipping like back in the day, but the thought of making a scene so close to her job, in the midst of people who saw her as a nice, respectable young lady, forced her to ignore the apparent act of aggression.

As she entered the store, Baby Doll vowed if Nicole came back again, she would step to her. In the weeks that followed, she kept looking for her, but Nicole didn't return.

On other fronts Baby Doll was also making enemies and really didn't care, primarily because her pockets were getting fatter, and she was getting closer to fulfilling her life-long dream. She often rationalized that all super rich people had to take chances, and when chances were taken there were always risks involved, and obviously she was no exception to the rule. Since she had Big Daddy Blue holding her down, she decided to start really putting that kind of backing to good use. With this attitude in mind, Baby Doll started a hunt for a real bad boy with crazy-long cash. One day in the month of September while at work a dude with long, well-kept dreadlocks, a rugged face, and a Herculean body entered the store.

On first glance, and from the way he moved, this brother had drug dealer written all over him. Baby Doll saw that he kept staring at her with sheer lust in his eyes, and so she made the first move. She basically pushed up on him and found out he was from Clinton House. From the first word that came out of his mouth, she detected that Samson was literally infactuated with her remarkable beauty, and since he had plenty money and gave clear hints that he had no problem with splurging it on her, he and Baby Doll hit it off very well.

Baby Doll started dating Samson and found out that he had eight drug houses scattered all throughout Brooklyn. Baby Doll strategically made it her busines to introduce Samson to Big Daddy, and she was thrilled to see that even Samson knew of Big Daddy Blue and had mad respect for him. However, Baby Doll saw that Big Daddy didn't like Samson because he was a drug dealer and reminded him so much of what he used to be.

Big Daddy Blue told Samson point blank that he loved Baby Doll very dearly and that he had better not break her heart or he was coming to see him. Samson promised Big Daddy that he wasn't going to disappoint him, and immediately began showering

Baby Doll with gifts and other expensive things like a trip to the Bahamas to prove his point. During the trip to the Bahamas, Baby Doll gave Samson a hit of the skins, and just like she expected, he was wide open afterwards, and was ready to get had.

Eventually, Baby Doll started spending nights with Samson. One Winter night in the month of November, she was snooping around Samson's apartment while he was asleep and stumbled on to a huge stash. It looked like thousands of dollars and she just had to steal some of it. Afterwards, Baby Doll started slowly pulling back, because she could sense Samson knew she stole some of his money.

Unbeknownst to Baby Doll, Samson had found out his money was missing a couple days after she stole the money, and was about to approach Baby Doll on some real murder-one shit, thinking about breaking her legs and fucking up that pretty little face of hers, but when he realized that Big Daddy was holding her down, he changed his mind. He decided to wait until the time was right and lay it on Baby Doll some kind of crazy.

Samson tried to pretend nothing was wrong, but Baby Doll wasn't stupid; she was good at reading people's vibes, and since Samson wasn't very good at pretending, she cut him off, because she could see as clear as day that he knew that she stole the twenty-five thousand dollars from him.

By the devious look on Samson's face, and based on his mannerism, it was apparent he was going to doing something real foul to her; probably set her up and make it look like it wasn't him.

Just to make sure he didn't get crazy, Baby Doll told Big Daddy about their breakup, and insinuated that he was about to get on some bullshit, and without another word being uttered, Big Daddy Blue and Preacher immediately stepped to Samson, and he quickly wiped the money on his chest, at least for the moment.

As Samson watched Big Daddy and Preacher drive away, he vowed that he was not going to let Baby Doll get away with stealing his money. He'd killed two motherfuckers for far less, and there was no way he was going to let that bitch tarnish his track record for never letting anyone, not even family, steal, rob and fuck him over without there being severe consequences.

Realizing that Samson was scheming on her, Baby Doll immediately got herself another apartment. She moved into a two-bedroom apartment on Montrose Avenue and Leonard Street in the Williamsburg section of Brooklyn.

By the time she was knocking on the door of turning twenty-two years of age, Baby Doll was riding high on victory. Her stash was almost in the range of a hundred grand, and no one could tell her that she wasn't doing her thing. She felt like she was all that and much more. Baby Doll was on top of her game in all departments, and now it was just a matter of time before she would shock everybody, even Big Daddy. Her plan was to get her own busienss without the help of anybody, and she knew Big Daddy was going to be so proud of her if she could just pull it off. As much as he talked about Black folks learning to do for self by getting off their asses and putting that work in, she knew he was going to be blown away when he saw what she'd accomplished.

* * * *

Meanwhile, Big Daddy was making reasonably satisfying strides with his agendas. The biggest accomplishment by far was his opening up two new clothing stores (one on Broadway and Myrtle Avenue and the other on Flatlands Avenue and Rockaway Parkway), and a club in Manhattan, which was by most standards was the money (and party) capitol of the world. This new club was located on fifty-sixth Street and Ninth Avenue.

His Youth Employment Program, on the other hand, was growing at a snail's pace, but Big Daddy couldn't complain. The old saying, slow motion is better than no motion, was an appreciated understatement with this issue. Big Daddy hated to get bogged down with a bunch of complaining, but during the last few years he couldn't help burning out Preacher's ear with his constant brooding over the fact that he couldn't understand why most Black folks with businesses fought so hard not to help young folk. Subconsciously, he knew why, but he refused to believe there were so much self-destructive hate, fear and indifference in his people. Also, because there was something inherent inside him, possibly in his genes, that compelled him to strive to help others, and especially the youth, he was now coming to terms with the fact that he had no control over his compulsion to reach out and help others. It was a compulsion he could never understand.

Even when he was a vicious gangster, he'd go out his way to help others, and was what people in the game might call a "gentlemen thug." When he saw other Black folk refusing to help solve a problem that affected them all, it drove him insane with frustration, rage, and even hopelessness. When he saw other ethnic groups helping each other and coming inside the Black community with the sole intentions of facilitating an economic conquest, it motivated him to push even harder. It was even more heart-shattering when Black folks would go out of their way to patronize a foreigner before they would patronize a Black-owned business.

However, he did succeed in convincing a few churches to back his Youth Employment Programs, but as time progressed he saw their efforts to push the project was quite lukewarm and halfhearted. Even the church personnel weren't too enthusiastic about taking control of the problems plaguing the Black community by pushing a potential solution. Not to disrespect the house of the Lord, but Big Daddy had long since concluded that most church folks seemed happy with just talking about the problems and waiting around for God to come down from the sky and wash all their troubles away, instead of rolling up their sleeves, getting their hands dirty, and fixing the problem themselves with good old-fashion back-breaking work accompanied by blood, sweat and tears. Often Big Daddy felt like an alien from another galaxy when he noticed he couldn't incite folks to support his Youth Employment Program, even though it was obvious that the project was solution-based, and his track record of success was evidence of the program's ability to work. It was as if he was the only one who truly understood the great benefits that could be gained by putting their young folk to work at a very young age.

Nevertheless, Preacher would always bring him back to the world of reality when he reminded Big Daddy that there were so many con men, cutthroats, and criminal-minded individuals who would sting at a moment's notice, and any sane person with eyes really couldn't blame other folks for using extreme caution when dealing with others, especially when people were being asked to make heavy sacrifices.

Preacher would say, "Hell, look at some of the reverends in some of the churches. They're probably some of the biggest con men to touch our community. I used to be a man of the clothe, as you know, and I can tell you one thing for sure. Not even the house of the Lord is safe from hustlers, thieves, tricksters, and some churches are the worse places to seek refuge from that type of behavior."

Peacher made firm eye contact with Big Daddy before he spoke. "When that collection tray starts dripping with money, ministers don't got no gripes about doing some dipping and dabbing. I confess, even I dipped and dabbed a few times myself."

Big Daddy stood behind the bar of his Manhattan club, named "Big Daddy's Place," thinking about his next move. Baby Doll was his pride and joy and the superstar employee of the year. She was the epitome of what his Youth Employment Program could produce, and he wanted to reward her for staying the course. She had turned twenty-two years old last month, and she was of that age where she could now work in a club. He wondered, was she ready to handle a management position. He looked around the club. The maple oak polished wood floors, the two glass chandeliers and the huge dance floor in the back of the establishment made this place the most elegant club of all the others he owned. Not to mention, there was also a miniature casino room downstairs in the basement for specially selected customers who felt a club simply was not a club unless it provided its customers with the opportunity to quench their gambling thirst.

Big Daddy's Place also had a strippers' section for those that felt modern-day clubs couldn't exist without such service. He had opened up for business just two weeks ago, and already he was making more money than any of his Brooklyn clubs had ever made in two weeks put together.

Preacher came from the back along with the four barmaids, the three waitresses; and the six bouncers. He was instructing them on tonight's activities.

Big Daddy waited until Preacher was finished briefing the employees, and then waved him over to the bar. Big Daddy took a seat on his stool, and Preacher parked himself next to Big Daddy.

Big Daddy folded his arms across his chest. "I been thinking about making a big move, and basically I want your feedback. I know I don't gotta tell you I want the straight, raw, uncut, ghettoized version of your opinion."

Preacher was always flattered by the fact Big Daddy came to him for feedback on most delicate issues, but it seemed like a waste of time, since he didn't always take his advice. "When have I ever pulled punches when it comes to keeping it real?"

Big Daddy didn't have to answer that because it was a rhetorical question. "I'm thinking about giving Baby Doll the assistant manager spot here. If she holds it down correctly, she'll move up to manager before the year is out. What you think?"

Ah shit, Preacher thought, and knew this was going to be a hot topic if he answered incorrectly. Baby Doll was his pride and joy, and she could do no wrong in his eyes. He sighed, and said, "She's definitely got potential."

This was the truth, he realized, but Baby Doll had other issues as far as he was concerned, and those issues he sensed could pose a series of problems at a club like this one. Preacher struggled with the decision of whether or not he should let Big Daddy know that he didn't feel Baby Doll was ready for such a responsibility; sure she was faithful, trustworthy, a hard worker, loyal, but the fact remained that she had too much game. He'd noticed years ago how Baby Doll was playing on Big Daddy, using him to manipulate other people, and Preacher didn't like the way she was moving, especially when it came to how she was gold digging and conning some real live dudes. He saw a catastrophe hovering on the horizons, and had seen this same scenario before, and it had always ended bad, really bad, oftentimes.

He had given Big Daddy a clear hint that Baby Doll had issues, and his response told him to tread real lightly when dealing with any issue regarding Baby Doll. Preacher decided to bite his tongue, tuck his pride, ego, conscious, integrity, moral, honor, and even his honesty into his pocket, and tell Big Daddy exactly what he wanted to hear. "Yeah, Big Daddy, I think hiring her as an assistant, then to manager would be a damn good move. She's ready."

As Preacher listened to Big Daddy shift the topic of discussion, now explaining what he wanted him to do tonight, he hoped he didn't help lay the groundwork to the beginning of the end of their raise to greatness. Since Baby Doll was bound to start conning, scheming, and manipulating men with money once she got here, he just hoped that Baby Doll understood that some of the men who will be attending this club weren't the average two-bit project thug who was, in reality, as powerless as a gnat locked in a fight with an eight-hundred-pound gorilla. These men would do anything to punish folks that transgressed against them in any fashion, especially when people were trying to steal money from them.

CHAPTER 20

Baby Doll sat on the moving A-Train, reading an urban street novel by Don V. *Project Predators* was a fast-moving story at times, but at other times it got bogged down with a lot of useless description and other irrelevant information. Baby Doll kept looking up at the rude blond-haired White woman that kept stepping on her feet without saying excuse me or sorry. The woman had either stepped on her toes or kicked her feet five times since the woman got on the train at Hoyt-Schermerhorn Street in Downtown Brooklyn; they were now nearing the Chambers Street station, and her assaults didn't hint at stopping.

The only thing that kept Baby Doll from spazzing on the woman was the good news she was savoring. Big Daddy wanted to talk to her. He didn't know that she knew he was going to offer her an assistant manager position at his Fifty-sixth Street club. Tera had pulled her coat the other day and made her promise not to let Big Daddy or Preacher know that she had told her. *An assistant manager job!?* Baby Doll stopped reading to again ask herself was she ready for that level of responsibility? She would have mad people working under her. She would be giving them directions and instructions, while monitoring their work. In other words, she was going to be a supervisor; someone people would look to for guidance. She pushed the pessimistic thoughts aside and concluded with resounding mental force that she was ready for this job, and that was that. She was also elated by the fact this was a big-time club where big-time people with big-time money would roam. Her mouth was already watering at the thought of all the big wigs she would have at her disposal, and with her being in a manger position, she just knew she could get her hooks into the super big-time money men.

The minute Baby Doll resumed reading, the blond woman started looking out the train window in a head ducking motion, and this time she stepped full-footed on Baby Doll's foot. What made this particular assault the most irritating was that the woman had the gall to step on her foot and allowed her stance to rest there for several long seconds. It was clear now that this woman was deliberately being disrespectful. But, before jumping the gun, Baby Doll decided to wait patiently to see if the woman would say those magic words, while locking eyes with the woman. When those magic words didn't come, Baby Doll decided it was time to step to her business.

Baby Doll closed her book, cleared her throat, stood up, making sure her face was but a mere few inches from the woman's face. She could even smell her garlic breath and noticed the woman had her by at least four inches. Baby Doll said, "Excuse me, miss, what the fuck is your problem?" The venom inside her voice was unmistakable.

The blond-haired chick acted as if she was surprised. "You're talking to me, ma'am?" Her preppy voice was saturated with nerdiness.

"No, bitch, I'm talking to the motherfuckin' conductor!" Baby Doll felt she was now being sarcastic, and the urge to slap her was rapidly growing. "Don't play no fuckin' mind games with me, bitch! Ever since you stepped foot on his train you been steppin' on my motherfuckin' toes, and you haven't once said excuse me. Now, I'm gonna say this one time, and that's it. You step on my feet again, and I'ma fuck your ass up." Baby Doll's heart was pounding, her palms had suddenly become sweaty, and her adrenaline was raging through her system as she sat back down. She saw the woman was visibly shaken up by the exchange, and she wisely slid away, weaving pass straphangers.

When Baby Doll noticed several other passengers looking at her as if she was in the wrong, she gave each of them a screw face that said, "Y'all can get some too, don't get it twisted," and they all looked away. Baby Doll resumed reading her book.

About fifteen minutes later Baby Doll got off the train at the Fifty-ninth Street and Columbus Circle stop and exited the station. It was a beautiful day in the month of May, and Baby Doll walked briskly down the Manhattan streets.

Ten minutes later, she approached the club and saw the huge sign that read BIG DADDY'S PLACE, and she was literally in awe. This joint looked like something right out of Hollywood and reminded her of all the extravagant things she read in the *Jet*, *Essence*, *Ebony*, and *Vibe* magazines, periodicals she loved to read during her free time. *Oh, yeah!* She shouted inwardly, because this was the big time! She entered the club and was even more thrilled by what she saw. This place looked like a palace. She was speechless as she saw Big Daddy approach with his extended arms. She rushed into his embrace.

"So how's my Baby Doll? You like?" Big Daddy was smiling proudly.

"Do I like it? You mean do I love it? Big Daddy you out did yourself with this joint here, man." Baby Doll looked him up and down and noticed he'd lost weight.

Big Daddy escorted Baby Doll to his plush office in the back of the club, next to several dressing rooms. Baby Doll took a seat in front of the polish maple oak wood desk, while Big Daddy took a seat in the captain's chair behind the desk.

Big Daddy said, "So how's the family?"

"You know how it is, same old project drama. Me and mom's are still not speaking. My sister Jasmine just had a little boy last week; I'm an aunt now. Tracy got a job working on Rikers Island as a Corrections officer." She wanted to also say that she didn't know how in the hell Tracy pulled that off but kept it to herself. "My cousin T-Bone in Canarsie got shot the other day. They say he's gonna be alright. Other than that, I guess everything is everything." Big Daddy nodded his head. "You and your moms have got to find a way to bury that hatchet. And if you're the one who's not bending, I'm asking you personally Baby Doll to put your pride in your pocket and talk to her. You know how I'm on it about family, and your moms will always be your mom. No matter what happens she'll be the one who's truly on her side when push comes to shove."

Baby Doll wanted to refresh his memory of the fact that Mildred didn't see her as a daughter and had been treating her like shit her entire life. If there was some truth to the saying that a mother would always be on her child's side, than someone should have told Mildred what time it was, because she apparently missed that fact. Baby Doll could now honestly say she was living in paradise, now that she was out of that house of hell, and leaving was the best thing that happened to her. In fact, sad to say, she wanted to thank Mildred for kicking her out. "Yeah, you right, Big Daddy, but it ain't me who's messin' it up. I can't make her love me."

Big Daddy understood her pain, because his mom never truly appreciated him when he was about Baby Doll's age. It suddenly dawned on him that no matter how much he tried to take care of business with his mom, she would always find a way to shot him down. He shifted his thoughts back to the issue at hand, since all this reminiscing was stirring up emotions, he rather leave buried.

He leaned back in the seat and said, "I know you're wondering why I called you here?" The question wasn't meant to provoke an answer, and so he continued, "How long you been riding with me, Baby Doll?"

She hesitated to see if more was coming, and then said, "Over six years, Big Daddy."

"That's right, almost seven years, and I must say you have turned out to be the most focused person to come out of my Youth Employment Program. Out of all the participants, you're the only one who hasn't been arrested even once, graduated high school with honors, never betrayed me, never stole from me, never showed any ungratefulness, and most of all, have told me every chance you got, how much you appreciated what I've done for you . . ."

As Big Daddy went on and on, Baby Doll wanted to hit the fast-forward button; it was starting to get too sentimental, and Baby Doll wanted to let him know she recognized that he recognized how focused she was. Since he was about to make a big point, she went along, nodding her head when such gestures were expected. She'd figured out what pleased Big Daddy the first time she met him, and now was the time to show him that she was paying close attention.

". . . To make a long story short, Baby Doll . . ." Big Daddy sighed as he stared at her, feeling his stomach acting up again. For the pass couple of months his persistent diarrhea and abdominal pain were flaring up much more frequently. "I called you here because I want to know, would you be interested in working here with me?"

Baby Doll's eyes grew wide with genuine surprise merged with delight. She was a natural with acting and even faked a speechless stutter. "Y—You want me to work here with you!?" She bounced excitedly in her seat. "Yes! Yes, I wanna work here, Big Daddy. What you want me to do? Be a barmaid, a cook or something?"

Big Daddy smiled, "I want you to be an assistant manager. You'll be working under Preacher. If you do the right thing, which I'm confident you will, you'll move up to manager."

Baby Doll rushed out of her seat and hugged Big Daddy. She knew he was used to her responding like this when she was utterly elated with happiness, so there wasn't any need to alter her usual behavior. "I'll take it!" She kissed him on the cheek and sat back down. It was her turn to express what Big Daddy meant to her. "Big Daddy, you're the best that ever did it. You got all this faith in me, you always see when I'm doing what I'm supposed to do, and you always give me big ups. I'll take this job, and will not disappoint you, and that's my word is bond."

"I know you will, Baby Doll, and I know you're gonna do your best." Big Daddy went into a silent cocoon to let his next comment have its intended impact. "There's one thing I want to let you know, Baby Doll. And don't take what I'm about to say the wrong way. You're a grown woman now, Baby Doll, and technically I can't tell you how to live your life." He allowed the silence to return.

Oh no, Baby Doll thought, because this sounded like one of his drama speeches, and a speech of this nature and caliber only came when there was a serious issue brewing.

Big Daddy continued, "In the last few years I noticed you been going out with these guys that live in the fast lane. I see you like a man that got his paper right, and there ain't nothing wrong with that. But, you need to keep in mind that men who make fast money are often on the wrong side of the law, and when folks are on the wrong side of the law, they can do things and take issues to places that can get real ugly."

He paused for a few seconds. "The issue with Samson in particular was a close one, Baby Doll. Now, I don't know what caused you two to break up, and I don't really care, but all I'm saying to you right now is that there are going to be some serious people coming to this club, so be very selective in who you step to." He wanted to go deeper, and come straight out and tell her that some of the folks she's going to come in contact with were bigger and more influential than him and if she got herself into some serious hot water, she might find out that he couldn't come to her rescue as easy as all the other times, but he was certain she was sharp enough to read between the lines.

* * * *

Immediately after talking to Baby Doll, Big Daddy rushed into the bathroom to make a serious dump. The recurring diarrhea was driving him crazy, and since he didn't like using medications, he struggled with the problem as best he could.

Big Daddy sat on the toilet and the liquid shot out of him. He was also getting nervous because he started detecting blood in his feces a couple days ago. The first time he saw the blood it shocked him, and he was going to go to the doctor if he saw it again. He used the bathroom several more times without seeing any blood and sweep the issue to the side. But this morning the blood had returned. Since he had so much business on his plate, he couldn't take off to go to the doctor. He promised that if he saw the blood again, he would have no choice, but to go to the hospital.

Two minutes later, after he wiped himself, he stood and examined his feces. His heart fluttered when he not only saw blood, but a whole lot of it.

* * * *

Baby Doll came on the job like a tornado from East bubble fuck. She strutted her stuff and was hawking every rich man that entered the club without a woman on his arm. She was surprised that the dress code was very loose; some folks wore suits; other wore casual attire; but there was a strict policy of no sneakers, and the clothing had to be of a casual nature. She was also pleased to see that the club attracted a lot of heavyweights. The famous boxer, Tommy "The terror" Henson, dropped by, and so did the world-class rapper,

King Hidus. There were record company producers, corporate lawyers, high-class accountants, movie agents, and a few movie stars. And even more surprising, Tommy Nacerino, a very well-known mobster from the Mazaratti crime family was in the house. Baby Doll was like a kid in a candy store, but she was wise enough to listen to Big Daddy's advice. As she scrutinized the customers, she now understood what he was trying to say. These weren't the kind of folks that could be stepped to in the wrong way. Although she respected Big Daddy's word of advice, she had full intentions of herbing somebody.

Baby Doll took her time and scoped the atmosphere so thoroughly that she allowed two weeks to go by before she even thought about making a move. There was also a toss-up between three individuals who were pressing her for some rhythm. In the end, she decided to go with Todd Houston, a big-time record producer, who apparently was making six digit figures semiannually. This brother was always sharp and so smooth with the way he handled himself, but Baby Doll instantly saw something in him that she could use to her advantage. She also noticed he was definitely not from the hood and would be known as a cornball nigga by the people she grew up around, and would probably be abused and battered on the regular. Todd was soft and didn't know very much about the streets. She was able to make these assessments by talking to him for only twenty minutes.

Baby Doll stood near the bar with her arms folded across her chest as she watched the customers enjoying themselves with huge smiles, drinks in their hands, chatting vibrantly, and having an all-out good time. DMX was barking through the club speakers, asking where his dogs were at. The deep bass clearly had the place jumping, and when the customers moved about, they all seem to be in stride with the beat.

Suddenly, Baby Doll saw Todd Houston enter the club alone. As usual, he was suited down, clean-shaven, his short Afro was meticulously neat. He was drop-dead handsome. He slid right toward Baby Doll. As he approached, Baby Doll was wondering how much she could squeeze him for, especially in light of the fact she just found out his little secret, and she was sure that he would do anything to prevent such a damaging secret to get into the hands of anyone in the public.

* * * *

Big Daddy sat behind his desk. The distant beat of the hard-hitting bass from the music was seeping into the room from underneath the crack at the bottom of the door. Big Daddy loved DMX rap tunes, but tonight he had a whole lot of shit on his mind, and the music had no effect on him. Beside the fact he was chronically depressed, he was also scared. He'd never been scared of many things in his life, and the one only thing that he was scared of, was now on his ass once again. That thing that terrified him and stood out among any other frightening force was none other than death.

According to the doctor, he was going to die, and real soon at that. Doctor Tompkins estimated that in about another year Big Daddy would be in the grave. But, in realty, right now, Big Daddy was angrier than he was scared; there was no reason for him to be suffering from colon cancer, especially in view of the fact he took a colon examine while in prison and the prison doctors had assured him that he was just fine.

The more he struggled to figure out what happened, the more it became clear that the prison officials knew he had two potentially malignant tumors in his colon and the sons of a bitches, ignored them, knowing he would end up where he now stood. They had killed him by refusing to treat him, and this should have come as no big surprise since prison health care was grossly inadequate, and Big Daddy knew this. He asked himself for the hundredth time since receiving the bad news; why didn't he get a universal, head-to-toe check-up the minute he got out!? Why did he believe those evil, vile and vicious motherfuckers would not lie about his health status!? Why!? Why!? Why! He fought not to allow his tears to begin to flow because he knew the act of crying would transform him into a very dangerous man.

But the question that really got him on edge was, what was he going to do to the motherfuckers that did this to him.

CHAPTER 21

Baby Doll sat at the table with a French dish in front of her that she couldn't even pronounce. Todd Houston sat across from her eating his dinner with a knife and folk and a napkin tucked in the collar of his shirt like in the movies. Baby Doll was dressed in a sleek, elegant silk Versace gown that left her back bare, and had her hair neatly balled up into a bun. She looked like a million dollars. From the moment she stepped foot in this restaurant, she'd been fronting a mile a minute, and kept cutting her eyes at the other customers, mimicking the women to make sure she was acting appropriately for the environment. This was the first time Baby Doll had ever been in a restaurant as expensive and elegant as this one, but the average person wouldn't know this, since Baby Doll had watched enough soap operas, movies and TV shows to know how to act in such a place. There were people of all ethnic persuasions, old and young, all dressed in suits and gowns, and even the waiters and waitresses were dressed in matching black outfits with red collars on their suit jackets. Baby Doll was struggling not to talk with food in her mouth as Todd made inquiries.

Todd swallowed his food, took a sip of his white wine, and said, "Breana, I'm very serious about us taking our relationship to the next level."

Baby Doll sat her folk down, swallowed, and said, "I would prefer you call me Baby Doll. My government name sounds so foreign to my ears." She tried to sound proper, but saw she was doing a terrible job at it.

"I'm sorry, Baby Doll." Todd realized he would have to work a little harder on this issue. "You told me this twice already, and I keep forgetting. I'm so used to formal aspects of communication that any informalities have a difficult time sticking." He smiled sincerely and said, "So what do you say? You're gonna love my condominium."

Baby Doll was thrilled by this revelation but didn't display her emotions. "I'm flattered by your offer, Todd, but I have my own apartment. I mean, I wouldn't mine spending time at your condo, but as far as moving in . . . Well, I—I can't right now. I'm going back to school this September, and I need to have my mind focused. And I do think we need a little more time to get to know each other. I mean—I do know you well enough, but we've been seeing each other regularly for a little over a month. Moving in with someone is a big step. Why don't we take it slow? I'll spend a few nights first, and we'll go from there, okay?" Her proper expression was getting worse with each spoken word. "I hope you understand where I'm coming from, Todd."

"Of course, I understand, Brea—I mean—Baby Doll. I'm just the kind of person that goes for what I want. From the moment we met I knew you were the one for me, and I just want to let you know where my heart lies." Todd picked up his knife and folk and continued eating.

Baby Doll couldn't believe her luck could be this good. Here it was Todd, inviting her to move in with him and she hadn't even let him hit the skins. Reflecting, she was glad she had put on her easygoing, always soft-spoken, and obedient bit for Todd, because he apparently was in search for this type of woman. Baby Doll was gazing at Todd as she ate and wondered if what the Private Investigator, Michael Rafter, had told her was true. He didn't look like the type of brother that would go there, but then again it was obvious that folks with a lot of money did all type of weird and crazy shit. Whether or not it was true was actually irrelevant, she realized as she took a sip of her wine and blessed Todd with a beautiful smile. But her instincts were telling her not to rush in too fast, and to find a way to bolster her agenda. The more the merrier was always a rule of thumb when tens of thousands of dollars were about to be relinquished from someone's possession.

* * * *

Big Daddy was behind the wheel of his black Escalade, moving down the Long Island Expressway. For the pass week he'd been walking around catatonically in his own world, driving everyone around him crazy with his refusal to tell them what was wrong with him. There was no doubt everyone could see that something was terribly wrong with him, and whatever was on his mind was very serious. Big Daddy was sixty-five years old, but now felt like he was eighty; it was amazing what a little stress could do to person's whole persona. Preacher knew him better than anyone, so he simply asked once, didn't get a response, and that was it. Baby Doll gave him his space, but tried very diligently to cheer him up, while Pam was on him constantly. His views toward Pam were now changing, since she was acting strange now that he was blocking everyone out of his life. She was nervous, kept a guilty expression on her face, and was becoming extremely offensive about the littlest things, obviously due to a guilty conscious, he surmised. Big Daddy didn't want to admit it, but her response was telling him that she might be creeping on him, and apparently thought he was giving her the cold shoulder because he somehow found out what she was doing. In the end, Big Daddy decided to give her the benefit of the doubt, since he could be wrong and might even be making more out of her reactions.

But deep-down Big Daddy didn't care, because he had bigger problems on his back. Doctor Tompkins and him talked about the cancer treatment he would begin. He'd been doing some heavy reading about cancer treatments the last few days, and it was evident he couldn't avoid the surgery to remove the two cancerous tumors. After that, the plan was to start chemotherapy along with radiation. Doctor Tompkins had also suggested that he start a combination of high-dose radiation and chemotherapy prior to surgery in order to make it possible to avoid a permanent colostomy for elimination of waste, and Big Daddy agree to start the treatment next week.

Since the cancer had spread from the colorectal area to the upper area of the large intestine, and to the lower section of his small intestine, Doctor Tompkins suggested the use of three other drugs—Flourouracil, Leucovorin, and Irinotecan.

Big Daddy Blue glanced through the rearview mirror at the huge truck tailgating him. He then glanced at the side view mirror, saw the coast was clear, and eased the Escalade over to the right lane. The truck slid on by. Staring at the car littered road up ahead, Big Daddy realized time was running out. Death was on his ass once again, and this time he sensed he wasn't going to outrun it like he'd done on countless occasions. That innate voice told him this was it; he was nearing the home stretch, and the only good thing was that he was being afforded one last opportunity to solidify his legacy.

Before leaving this world, he vowed that he was going to leave a mark that said Gregory J. Williams, AKA Big Daddy Blue, was a man that helped his people, and although he made big mistakes in his life, he made up for them by turning his life around and helping others not to make the same mistakes he'd made. He was a man that had love in his heart, body and soul. If he could have those words written on his tombstone, he'd be all right. He knew his legacy would come nowhere near the one Martin Luther King Jr. or Malcolm X left behind, but he would be content if he could be remembered as someone who left behind something positive.

When he thought about this legacy in the past, he always equated it with the creation of an institution that helped others. His Youth Employment Program was what he wanted to be remembered by, but right now it wasn't big enough or stable enough to leave such a mark. If only he had five more years! And, sad to say, he feared that all these years he'd worked tirelessly building this program from the ground up would crumble into nothing, with him out of the picture. He felt a wave of tears erupting, and he had to fight not to give into the deep-set pain.

As he sighed out loud, he reminded himself again that it wasn't over. He was still alive, he was still breathing, didn't feel too bad physically, and that meant there was still a way to fulfill his legacy. He would have to find someone to take the torch and keep running with it. But who was serious enough to keep his Youth Employment Program alive? Preacher wasn't the one, that's for sure. Pam definitely didn't give a flying fuck about what he was trying to accomplish, neither was Tera or any of his other nieces, nephews, daughter, grandchildren or any other family member built for a responsibility such as this one. He knew that there was only one person who had some potential, had the incentive to want to do something great, loved him dearly, and wanted to see him happy, and that was none other than Baby Doll. She had issues like everybody else, and was dangerously fascinated with money, but she was probably the most discipline, responsible, and committed of all the other people currently in his midst. He'd been contemplating how he could get her to do his bidding, and knew that he would convince her, since his life, or what he wanted others to perceive of his life, depended on it.

Big Daddy had decided that today was the day he would let Pam know what was going on. Why he chose her to be the first to share the bad news was beyond him, but he figured it had something to do with the fact she was the person he came home to and slept in bed next to each night. Since they were like husband and wife it seemed only right that he dealt with this the same way a married couple would handle it. Preacher was next in line, and his family would be informed afterwards. Since Baby Doll was the key to fulfilling his dream, he was saving her for last.

As he pulled the SUV off the expressway, Big Daddy realized that Baby Doll had told him she was going back to school for business management. This was why he loved her so dearly; when she got involved in something, she gave it her all and took care of business on all levels.

He was so mentally devastated that he didn't even shower Baby Doll in compliments and encouragements, and hoped she didn't take it the wrong way when he didn't display his usual rejoiced outburst. He was planning to sit her down and talk to her in the next few days, and he was sure Baby Doll would understand.

As Big Daddy pulled the Jeep to a stop at the red light, he was still contemplating contacting Sweet Charlie. He was bitter; the hatred was surging very strongly through his veins, and his need for revenge was almost blinding. Those prison doctors knew exactly what they were doing, and when Doctor Tompkins made it perfectly clear that his tumors should have been detected years ago, he received the confirmation he needed to make his decision.

The light turned green and Big Daddy applied pressure to the gas pedal. He realized that finding the two creeps would be easy as flipping through the yellow pages. Since years had elapsed, it would be highly unlikely that he would be connected to their untimely demise. In any event, since he was basically dead and sinking, it didn't matter anyway since they couldn't touch him once he was in the grave. As he pulled into his driveway, he realized he needed more time to make his decision.

Five minutes later, Big Daddy was sitting in his comfortable armchair with his feet kicked up on his pillowed cover hassock while Pam sat across from him looking anxious. Big Daddy had told her he needed to talk to her, and now he decided to mess with her by saying nothing for as long as she could stand it.

Pam sighed in frustration, "What is it Big Daddy? Do you have to torture me like this?"

"I'm dying from cancer."

Pam wasn't sure if she heard him correctly. "Cancer!?" With terror in her expression, she gazed into Big Daddy's eyes and she could now understand why she felt so much pain resonating from him. Her mixed emotions had instantly subsided, now that she knew what was eating at him, and was replaced with another crippling emotion. "My God, Big Daddy, when did you find this out? Where is the cancer located!? How—How bad is it?" She shot her questions at him in rapid fire; her frantic gestures were growing, because she sensed doom was rapidly approaching. "Did you talk to a doctor?"

"Calm down, Pam," Big Daddy was somewhat disappointed, because he expected her to embrace him with a reassuring hug that indicated she was there for him every step of the way. "It's colon cancer. I found out last week. And yes, Doctor Tompkins is on it. I'm supposed to get a surgery and start treatment next week." Big Daddy got up to go to get something to drink, and as he was walking past Pam, she reached up and hugged him with all her might. He hugged her back. He saw she was crying, and Big Daddy wondered if it was because he was dying or was it because soon she would no longer have a sugar daddy to take care of her.

* * * *

Baby Doll stood on the corner of East Twenty-third Street and Eighth Avenue, waiting for the Private Investigator, Michael Rafter.

It was almost ten o'clock at night, so the traffic from both cars and people weren't heavy, which was a good thing because she didn't want anyone seeing her talking to Michael. He called her on the cell phone and told her to meet him here. She tried to tell him that it was a very inconvenient moment since she was at work, but he insisted that it was very important and that it would be well worth her time. Baby Doll got Tiffany to cover for her, then she jetted out of the club and caught a cab.

Suddenly, she saw Michael approaching. His scruffy look was still the same; his beard was unkempt as usual, his blue eyes were diluted and droopy-looking, and his clothing appeared in disarray. He wasn't a Colombo when it came to clothing, but he was apparently good at what he did.

"Baby Doll," Michael said, as she tugged at her arm for her to walk along side of him, and she obeyed as they moved down the street. "Hope I didn't have you waiting too long."

"Come on, Michael, tell me what you gotta tell me so I can get back to work."

"Okay, this is what I just recently found out. Oh, and by the way, certain types of information I never discuss over the phone. Pardon me for not warning you earlier, but to be honest with you, I didn't think this guy Todd Houston was this interesting."

Baby Doll's heart jumped; she was hoping and praying that Todd wasn't well protected by some big-time gangsters or something. From the way Michael was acting, she sensed that's exactly what it was. "Yeah, yeah, that makes sense, Michael. What's up? What you found?"

"One more thing; this is gonna cost you extra. It's not gonna cost that much over my standard rates since, as I told you before, my prices are quite reasonable—"

"Okay, okay, Michael, so it's gonna cost me extra. I'll pay you what you want. Now, let's hear it."

"Well, I don't know if it's good or bad, but this guy is related to the Cuffy family."

Baby Doll looked at Michael as if he was crazy. "Cuffy family!?" She saw by Michael's gestures this name was supposed to provoke some kind of eye-opening, hit-yourself-on-the-head response. She thought hard about the name, but nothing clicked inside of her head. "Who the hell is the Cuffy family!?"

"Put it this way. They got their hands in just about everything under the sun, including, how may I say, illicit dealings. Now, you asked me to dig deep and to let you know who this guy is, and whether or not he's connected to any important people. The Cuffy Family is very important people." As he scrutinized her disturbed response, Michael wondered what Baby Doll was up to, and for some strange reason he sensed it was something illegal. But his vow of confidentiality forbade him from going to the police; however, it didn't forbid him from going to the other side, especially when they had very long money.

CHAPTER 22

Baby Doll entered Todd's condominium, and it was just like she expected. This place was beyond fabulous; it was amazing tens over! The shining wood floors glistened as if they were wet with water; the white walls were spotlessly clean; and the black velvet-covered living room furniture looked soft and succulent enough to fuck on all night long.

"Let me take your jacket." Todd peeled off Baby Doll's jacket and hung it up on the nearby coat hanger by the closet. "Make yourself comfortable."

Baby Doll went and sat on the velvet sofa while Todd went to the bar to fix two drinks.

Baby Doll ran her fingers across the soft material and noticed it wasn't exactly velvet. It was some kind of high-tech fabric. Whatever it was, it was remarkable.

Todd approached and handed her a drink. He then went to his state-of-the-art music console, activated the Teddy Pendergrass CD, and his song "Turn off the Lights" came on.

Baby Doll instantly noticed there apparently were speakers surrounding the entire living room; the crisp, clear sounds made it feel like Teddy was right there in the room with them.

Todd went to Baby Doll and sat next to her. He saw Baby Doll caressing the fabric. "This material is refined Black Panther's skin. It's been nurtured with some kind of special chemical that prevents it from staining. It's some state-of-the-art stuff."

"Stain-proof, huh?" Baby Doll took a sip of the champagne. The tangy tasted of the drink woke up her taste buds as the bubbly slid down her throat. "So, you're saying if I spill some of this champagne on this sofa it won't stain?"

"That's right. Not only that; it won't even soak up the liquid. Let me show you." He titled his glass until a large drop of champagne dripped on to the sofa. Sure enough, the liquid drop just stood there, and eventually rolled about as if it was encased in some kind of outer covering. After a moment Todd pulled his handkerchief and wiped it. "Go ahead, touch the sofa where the champagne was."

Baby Doll obeyed and smiled when she saw it felt as dry as any other area of the sofa that didn't come in contact with the liquid. "Wow, that's some real fly shi—excuse me, I mean that's really amazing."

Todd laughed good-naturedly. He loved when Baby Doll tried to conceal her street vocabulary. "You can be yourself around me, Baby Doll. I love it when you talk that hood stuff. It makes you real. Not in the sense in which the rappers say it, but real in its true sense. You know what I mean?"

"Yeah, I know what you mean. Basically, you like for people to be who they are, not what they're trying or pretending to be." She saw him nod his head. "I just thought that with all this formal, ah, ah, you know, all this formal upbringing of yours that you would want a woman to be real classy."

"Yeah, I like the classy thing, but I would take sincerity and realness over acting any day."

Baby Doll wanted to tell him to be careful what he ask for, because she could get real ghetto if she so chose to, and once she went there she was sure he wasn't going to like it. She had told him she grew up in Brownsville, but apparently he didn't know just how grimy folks from her hood could get. He'd evidently never saw that level of realness in its unadulterated form.

She sipped her champagne again and said, "Well, you don't have to worry about me, Todd, because I believe in truthfulness. A relationship without realness is bound to fall."

Their conversation went back and forth for fifteen minutes, while consuming five glasses of champagne each in the process.

When the song "Secret Garden" came on, Todd eased over to Baby Doll and threw his arm around her shoulder, giving her the signal that he was ready to take it there.

Baby Doll wanted to crack up laughing in his face because that type of move was what little kids did when they were courting. She eased over toward him to let him know she was also ready. Baby Doll had come prepared and had her own condoms. There weren't going to be any mistakes like what Kevin had done to her. Todd's breathing increased. She had a plan and had full intentions of putting it into activation, while also getting a little sexual enjoyment in the process. She'd been checking him out since she met him, and saw he was well equipped downtown. He also looked like he had a strong back. There was no doubt he worked out on the regular, and his stamina had to be some kind of right. Baby Doll hadn't had any sex in a couple of weeks, and her hormones were roaring for some release.

Baby Doll decided that she was going to fuck this chump's brains out and stop playing games. There was no need in prolonging this thing any longer, and with that thought in mind, Baby Doll took charge. She started kissing Todd, and he greedily gobbled up the kiss with the urgency of a striving man on a deserted Island.

Todd suddenly turned into a beast she noticed as he ripped off his clothing, flinging his shirt buttons everywhere. He tossed the shirt, flipped out of his shoes, and slid out of his pants. When he started removing Baby Doll's clothing, he transformed into a delicate artisan. With the grace of painter's brush, Todd took off Baby Doll's shirt.

Baby Doll was impressed with his ultra-gentle style of lovemaking. She got nervous by the way he locked eyes with her, never once looking away as he slowly took her garments off as if he was savoring every second. When he got to her panties, she could see his dick was damn near ripping through his silk briefs. Her stomach bubbled with delight as she imagined his ten inches of his pulsating manhood easing into her. When her panties were off and she was now in her birthday suit, she stopped Todd when he was about to eat her pussy in the raw, she said, breathing hard, "Where's the protection, Todd? I got some condoms in my bag."

Todd sprung to his feet, races toward the back of the condo and returned with a dental damn.

Baby Doll saw he wasn't going to let anything rain on his pussy-eating parade. She braced herself and now realized she played herself by not bring her own dental dam. She knew she was taking a risk because if what Michael Rafter said was true, then she was messing with an individual who was a high risk for HIV.

According to Michael, Todd was a well-known swinger, a closet pervert, and Michael was able to obtain pictures of him coming out of a few gay bars. Baby Doll had the pictures but wasn't certain if the pictures were strong enough to make Todd cough up some money. Of course, the pictures didn't necessarily prove he was gay, but she had full intentions of using them in such a way as to pressure him for some dough. The only reason she didn't bust the shot was because she figured if she was going to do this thing, she should make sure she checked all avenues for any other incriminating evidence, and if it existed it would surely be here in his crib. If it existed, she intended to find it.

Now that Todd wanted to eat her out with his own dental dam, she felt a nervous tension formulating in her mid-section; she was hoping the device didn't have any holes in it and was defective. If Todd was a pervert or a homo, there was no telling what he could be infected with. She told herself that this was a risk that came with getting paid, and when she thought about all the money she was about to squeeze out of Todd, she forced her mind to get into the mode. After a moment, she went with the sexual energy, and trusted her instincts that everything was going to be just fine.

Baby Doll felt Todd place the device on her vagina in a slow and delicate manner and saw he didn't hesitate.

As Todd's lips and tongue danced inside of Baby Doll's pleasure factory, he smelled the sweet caramel-like aroma, and he wanted to encourage her to continue using this particular body perfume. He went in quick, hard and heavy.

Baby Doll instantly saw he had a vicious tongue game. After working her over for two minutes, his tongue slid down too far and wiggled its way almost into her ass hole. She wondered what that was all about until it happened again. She wanted to say something, but she realized it felt good. Then he made her get on her knees and he continued eating her pussy. This time his tongue was really all over the place. Each time it slid across her ass hole, she felt sexual electricity fire through her body, and she sighed in ecstasy. It felt so good, she felt it was making her come, so she activated her butt cheeks, making them jump like the lap dance girls, to signal to Todd that what he just did was a good spot, and he obeyed by wiggling his tongue in there some more. Baby Doll experienced an ejaculation from this sexual act, and it surprised her that it could go down like that. Although it felt remarkably good, she made a mental note to dead all tongue-kissing with Todd from here on.

After about five more minutes of this sexual extravaganza, Todd came up and was now ready to enter her.

"I got my own condoms." Baby Doll said through her heavy breathing. She slid over and retrieved a condom from her handbag. She ripped the wrapper open and rolled the condom on to Todd's wood, which was standing at full attention. She laid down, vowing that she was going to rock this nigga's world.

Todd tried to kiss her, but Baby Doll maneuvered her face away from his lips and locked him in a bear hug; he was sighing in her ear in ecstasy with each thrust of his hips.

Baby Doll's mind was swirling with utter delight. She couldn't believe she was throwing her hips back, urging Todd to slam that thing up in her and stop playing games! When he picked up speed, she felt another nut about to erupt, and she let herself go, skeeting with pleasure and delight. Screaming as her bodily juice squirted from her, Baby Doll was convulsing with earth-shattering tremors and noticed the nut was going on for longer than usual. Then she noticed the never-ending nut was happening because Todd was making sure his dick was hitting the top part of her clitoris. *Damn this nigga got his dick game down to an art*, she shouted inwardly as she trembled from delight.

Right on the heels of Baby Doll's ejaculation, Todd started coming, and he tried to hold it, but Baby Doll wasn't having it. She went wild, pumping feverishly while clamping both her hands on his ass cheeks to make sure he couldn't pull away. She threw up her legs to make sure she excited him to the point of no return. Sure enough, her aggressiveness was too much for Todd, and he came hard and heavy, hollering with a sexual delight that told Baby Doll she was almost there.

Afterwards they showered, prepared a meal, ate while laughing about small-talk issues, and had another round of sex. This time they took their sexual intercourse to the bedroom.

Baby Doll turned into a beast in the bed; she rode him like a rodeo queen, and every time he tried to make his nut last, trying to slow ride her, she went buck wild, forcing him to come. Her mission was to make sure Todd didn't out last her, and since her beauty and her sexual forcefulness mesmerized Todd, he was like putty in Baby Doll's hands. She was, however, surprised he was able to keep getting it up only after a twenty-minute wait in between each ejaculation. By the time Baby Doll drained, pulled and suctioned four nuts out of Todd, she just knew she had Todd where she wanted him by his speech slurring, and drained-out gestures.

Then, twenty-five minutes later, to Baby Doll's surprise, Todd was ready for another round; he started playing with her breasts, which was a sure sign that he was gearing up for another hit. She sighed inwardly and decided to implement her backup plan.

Todd mounted her and inserted the tip of his condom-covered penis inside of her.

"Hold up, wait," Baby Doll gently pushed him off of her. "I'm thirsty." She slid out of bed. "I'll fix us something to drink—"

"Let me do it, Baby Doll," Todd slid out of bed.

"Come on, Todd," Baby Doll pouted. "You said you wanted me to come stay with you soon. Let me get the feel of how it could be—"

"Yeah, you're right. I just feel it's my duty to treat you like the queen you are, give you the red-carpet treatment, and serve you hand and foot." He laid back down and cupped his hands behind his head. "I'll be waiting." He said with his dick standing fully erect.

Baby Doll zipped out of the room and went straight to work. She hastily snatched up her handbag and continued to the kitchen. She filled the two glasses with champagne, retrieved the perfume bottle, unscrewed the top, and poured the sedative substance into one of the glasses. She was surprised Todd had that much energy and was hoping she could simply fuck him into a comatose-like sleep, but she apparently either underestimated Todd, or put too much faith in her fucking abilities.

Baby Doll shot out of the kitchen, put her handbag back, eased back inside the bedroom, and handed Todd the spiked drink.

After they drank their drinks, they went another round of sexual intercourse. Baby Doll didn't give Todd a chance to even think he was going drag the nut out and she turned into a sexual maniac, forcing the nut out of him. She saw when Todd busted this fifth nut he rolled over and was in the third phase of sleep within ten minutes of closing his eyes.

Baby Doll saw the sedative was definitely high-powered. She waited a few minutes, and tried to awake Todd, to make sure the stuff was working. "Todd," she said while shaking him. He mumbled and rolled over. She now realized that she did use a lot of the sedative, believing it would speed up the sleep process. As she scrutinized Todd sleeping, she suddenly remembered what the dude, Cameron had told her. He had said, "Make sure you don't use too much of this shit. It can be deadly." She cursed at herself for being overanxious.

As Todd slept like a dead log, Baby Doll nervously ransacked Todd's condo, while checking on Todd periodically to make sure he didn't go into cardiac arrest or display any other signs that he was in trouble.

* * * *

Big Daddy Blue sat on the barstool with Preacher sitting next to him. They were the only ones inside the club located on Lincoln Place right off Brooklyn Avenue. Although outside the July humidity was ravaging the city, the temperature inside the club was just right in light of the air conditioners that blew cool air. The jukebox was turned down low, and an old Johnnie Taylor tune oozed through the speakers. Johnnie was singing about a cat named Jody stealing someone's girl. It was a Monday morning, and today was the day Big Daddy and Preacher checked the books, which was a standard routine for the past ten years.

"So, what is it you want to talk about, Big Daddy?" Preacher said, looking at himself and Big Daddy in the huge wall mirror across from them. In the mirror he saw Big Daddy was looking at his hands, cupped on the bar, appearing to be somewhere else mentally.

Big Daddy looked up, turned around on the stool, and put his back to the bar. He felt like a man trapped in a maze. He was still wishing there was a way to convince Preacher to carry on his legacy, but deep down he knew Preacher wasn't emotionally built for the task. Preacher had been fucked around too many times, and in the worse kind of ways by other Black folks, including young folk, to even ask him to sacrifice his life trying to help a bunch of folks that he firmly believed were bound to hurt him. Big Daddy always thought that Preacher would eventually come around, since they were focusing on the children, who were still redeemable in every sense of the word, but even this fact didn't change his position and views on life. He was who he was, and the years of pain and suffering had guaranteed that his eyes would always see things the way he currently saw them. Despite Preacher's pessimistic views, Big Daddy was certain that he loved him, or he wouldn't have stood side by side with him all these years.

After a moment, Big Daddy realized that there was no need to try to convince Preacher to carry on his legacy. However, he had something else that he knew Preacher would go for, if he made Preacher give him his word. He wasn't going to hit him with it right this minute, but he would lay it down soon.

With a loud sigh, Big Daddy said, "You ain't gonna believe this shit, Preacher."

The silence returned.

Preacher turned around and also put his back to the bar.

Big Daddy sighed loudly. "I'm dying, bro."

Preacher was not only shocked, but also confused. He wasn't sure he heard him correctly, or at least he hoped he didn't hear him correctly. "You're dying?! What the fuck happened?" He realized that at their age, it was common to be battling against all type of ailments and diseases, and it shouldn't come as a big surprise if someone their age came down with some type of life-threatening disease. The first thing he thought was it had something to do with the high blood pressure Big Daddy was living with. "Don't tell me your blood pressure problem's getting worse—"

"It's cancer." He held the silence for a moment, and then continued. "Motherfuckin' colon cancer!"

"Colon cancer!? But—but I thought you said he got a colon exam, and you were straight? You said you were good to go."

Big Daddy felt the rage boiling again. The mere thought of those prison doctors lying to him, and as a result causing him to be in this predicament, was making it very difficult to talk. "Well, apparently I wasn't good to go, because now the two tumors that I apparently had back when I did get that checkup while I was at Comstock are now going crazy inside of me and has even started eating up my small intestine."

Preacher felt like he was hit with a punch to the face. He knew without being explicitly told that those sons of bitches knew he had those tumors and did nothing to remove them when they were harmless. He nervously realized he'd better go get himself checked out again because he too had gotten a colon exam while in prison, and although they said they removed a tumor from him, he was going to make it his business to find out if they left any other tumors inside of him. He decided right that moment that he was going to get an immediate checkup first thing tomorrow. "So how much time they're giving you?" He massaged his lifelong partner's shoulder to let him know he was with him.

Big Daddy Blue noticed he couldn't get the words out due to the overpowering rage that had a stranglehold on him. After a moment, he sighed and said, "The doc is saying I got about a year; maybe two if the surgery is successful."

"Surgery?" Preacher shook his head in pain as the rapidly growing anger began to cause the tension to surge through his whole body. He also knew what was coming next, and so he felt it was time to lay the cards on the table to let him know he was going to back him one hundred percent. "I guess we'll be having another sit-down with Sweet Charlie. What those motherfuckers did to you calls for justice to be laid down the good old-fashion way."

CHAPTER 23

Baby Doll sat on the Central Park bench, watching the two squirrels playing with each other. It was a nice September afternoon, and she was feeling almost in tune with the weather. She was dressed in a forest green sweat suit, black Nike sneakers, her hair was pulled back into a neat bun, and she even wore a set of weightlifting black leather gloves with the fingers cut out.

As she watched the squirrels run away and up a tree, she wondered if Todd was actually going to pay for the videotapes of him doing a series of perverted and sadistic acts. She thought back to the night she found the three VHS videotapes inside of a safe hidden in Todd's closet. It took her ten minutes to find the key to the safe, and when she opened it she was in for a huge surprise. Besides videotapes there were pictures of him having sex with little Asian boys—little boys who couldn't be no more than seven or eight years old. Although it was evident the pictures were taken in a foreign country, she knew if the media, or anyone for that matter, got hold of these types of pictures it would completely destroy Todd. She was elated with a happiness mixed with disgust, but upon seeing the videotapes she knew she had this perverted son of a bitch by the balls. On the tape he was engaging in homosexual acts with men, little boys, and even a dog. When she saw Todd was fucking a huge Great Dane in the ass she nearly threw up, realizing that she had fucked this nasty, disgusting, perverted manic. The more she looked at the videotapes, the more she realized she was going to try to completely destroy this freak-ass motherfucker.

Suddenly, Baby Doll was pulled out of her reverie when she saw an old White couple jog by. They smiled at her, and she smiled back. She loved how old White folks in this area of the city were so friendly, and she could never understand why Black folks in her hood never smiled at each other like that.

She knew if they could start activating that kind of positive energy it could make for a positive environment for all. But getting folks to smile at each other just to be smiling was clearly wishful thinking. With all the pain and suffering going on in the hood, there was no reason for anyone to be smiling. In any event, because it was a dog-eat-dog world in her hood, she was sitting there waiting for Todd. It was plain to see that she was a classical product of that wretched environment and had no beef with that fact, since in a minute she was about to get paid.

Baby Doll turned her head the other way, and her heart fluttered with anxiety. Todd was walking toward her; he was dressed in a tan sweat suit and matching running shoes. She saw he looked embarrassed, nervous, and was acting strange. The way he was cutting his eyes, looking around shamefully, the first thing crossed her mind was that he was looking for someone. She was about to flee, assuming he called the police, but her instinct told her that Todd was acting that way because he probably thought she had someone holding her down.

Baby Doll stood and approached him.

When they were upon each other Baby Doll stepped off the walkway and onto the grass, and said, "So I guess you got my message?"

"Why are you doing this to me Breana?" Todd's voice was soft and kind. "I was growing to love you, and I treated like a queen. Why are you doing this? You're doing it for money? Is that what it is, money?"

"Yeah, you can say that it's all about the money. Lil Kim said it best; it's all about the Benjamins, baby."

"So how much are you asking for?"

Baby Doll knew she had him and decided to jack up the price from her original number. "Give me seventy-five thousand dollars, and I'll go away."

"seventy-five grand?" Todd repeated softly. "And how do I know you'll return my property, and how do I know you didn't make copies, and how do—"

"I guess you'll have to trust me."

"Trust you!? How the fuck am I supposed to trust someone that comes into my home, drugs me, and then steals from me!? Especially when all I've done for you is treat you right!? How the fuck can I trust a low life, hood rat bitch that—"

"Don't call me a bitch! You of all people shouldn't be calling people names when you're running around here molesting little boys and fucking dogs in the ass—"

CLAPAAH!

Todd damn near slapped Baby Doll's head clean off of her shoulders.

Baby Doll stumbled to her left and fought to avoid tripping to the grass. Although the blow caught her completely off guard, she pivoted her body from the force of the blow, swung her right fist and caught Todd right on the jaw with a firm overhand right.

Todd stumbled almost in the same fashion as Baby Doll did, but before he could regroup, she was all over him like a Tasmania Devil, slugging and pounding his grill with a viciousness that had him stumbling about drunkenly while waving his arms to ward her off, without any luck.

Baby Doll was furious. Her face was on fire, but she noticed her fists were even more inflamed as a result of the beating she was laying on Todd. He apparently didn't know chicks from Brownsville were notorious for whipping dudes' asses, and now he was definitely going to find out. She blessed him with a wicked uppercut that came way from California and landed in Todd's midsection.

Todd buckled over.

Baby Doll wound up her fist like she was twirling a Louisville Slugger and unleashed another uppercut to Todd's nose as he was hunched over, clutching his stomach. The knuckle-cracking blow forced him into a standing position, and this time she followed up with a field-goal kick to Todd's nuts that lifted him two inches off his toes.

The searing pain was truly blinding as Todd felt his nuts instantly swell up and throbbed with sheer agony. The pain was so intense that he couldn't even scream if he wanted to. Holding his nuts with both hands, while his mouth hung open as the scream was stuck in his throat Todd fell to the grass, moaning and groaning, his mind was silly with excruciating pain.

Baby Doll was about to lay another field-goal kick to Todd's fully exposed face, but she saw they had attracted a small audience. Breathing hard from exhaustion, Baby Doll kneeled next to him and said, "Since you want to play little bitch games, the price just went up to one hundred and twenty-five thousand. Now, this is how it's going down." She reached into her pocket and pulled out a piece of paper with a computer typed note. "Put the money into this bank account. This is the number." She tossed the paper, and it landed a few inches from Todd's face, lying comfortable on the grass. "When the money appears in the account, I'll contact you and give you your freak-ass tapes back. If you go to the police, then I'm quite sure they'll probably be far more interested in you raping little boys than me trying to squeeze a perverted, freak-ass, pedophile for a few fuckin' dollars. If the money ain't there by next week, then you will be famous before the month is out, because I'm going to send copies of all this shit to every radio station, newspaper, and any other media outlet on the planet. Whatever you decide to do, Todd, just know that the ball is in your hands."

Baby Doll glared at him. "Don't forget, I'm from the hood, and truthfully speaking, I been so broke so long, I got nothing to lose, and everything to gain." She inched her face closer to his and said with clenched teeth, "If I don't get that money, I'm going all out to destroy your sick ass!"

As Baby Doll walked away, Todd picked up the note and eased up on to his feet. His nuts were still throbbing. He now realized broodingly that he should have listened to his cousin, George, who told him to be careful with Baby Doll because he had gotten word that she was up to something. He honestly thought George was experiencing another one of his conspiracy-theory delusions. With venom coursing through his heart, mind, and soul, Todd vowed that he was going to get Baby Doll back. He didn't know how, but he was certain that he would find a way, even if he had to spend every dime he had left after he paid her. If he had to give up every single cent to see this bitch die a miserable death, he would do it without a second thought.

As he limped away, Todd wondered could his cousin George help him find a contract killer willing to do the job.

* * * *

The following day, Baby Doll got off the A-Train and exited the Columbus Circle station, wondering why Big Daddy wanted to talk to her. She could still remember how her heart instantly started pounding the minute she heard Big Daddy say over the phone, "I need you to come in about an hour earlier tomorrow. We need to talk, Baby Doll." Since he also made it clear that what he had to talk about involved something that couldn't be discussed over the phone, she knew the shit was about to sure-nuff hit the fan.

There was no doubt in her mind that this talk had something to do with Todd. How that perverted freak convinced Big Daddy to step up for him when he was raping little boys and fucking dogs was beyond her, but she was definitely certain he couldn't have mentioned that to Big Daddy Blue.

That fool must be insane for trying this, because he had to know that Big Daddy is bound to find out about his perverted, freak-ass life.

She wanted to immediately start sending copies of those perverted tapes to various media companies but figured it couldn't hurt to hear Big Daddy lecture her about her controversial ways of getting paid before taking action.

As she turned the corner of Fifty-sixth Street, nearing the club with every long, hard stride, Baby Doll just hoped Big Daddy didn't try to make her return those tapes or stop her from doing what she was doing to Todd, because she was going to break his poor heart. The bottom line was that she wasn't going to let Todd wiggle out from paying her that money, even if she had to disappoint Big Daddy.

Baby Doll entered the club and saw two of the bouncers, AJ and Ebo. She greeted them and continued on to Big Daddy's office. She knocked on the door.

"Come on in," Big Daddy said from behind the door. He was sitting comfortably behind his desk, leaning back in his executive style chair.

She couldn't help but notice he looked like he was losing weight real fast. His face even looked shrunken in a little. Baby Doll smiled and rushed over to him. "Big Daddy." She leaned over and gave him a huge kiss on the cheek while hugging him lovingly. She knew he loved to be treated like he was truly a daddy; she knew this always made his day, and every chance she got she blessed him with whatever it was that made him happy.

In her eyes he deserved it, because if Big Daddy hadn't come into her life, she would probably be roaming the hood, living like a bum on welfare, with a million fatherless kids, in jail, prostituting, drugged-out, dead, and the list could literally go on and on. She sat in the interrogation chair that was park in front of his desk. "So what's up, Big Daddy? What have I done did now?" She smiled, hoping the joke hit its mark, but she saw it didn't.

Big Daddy sighed as he massaged the temple regions of his head with his fingers, wondering if he should alter his approach. He wanted to first lay groundwork, plant seeds, and then hit her with the news. Now he was thinking about just coming right out with the bad news and then go back and lay the groundwork. After a moment, he decided to go with his first thought, since the rule of thumb says to always go with your first instinct. "Baby Doll, how you feel about the state of affairs of the Black community? What'd you think we as a people should be doing right now?"

Baby Doll was totally lost. She didn't see how this had anything to do with what she did to Todd. She thought hard about both of the compound questions and said, "Well, I think us Black folks need to find a way to come together. And . . . .ah . . . ah, I guess we gotta find a way to come together so we can start making some changes." She remembered this was a reoccurring theme in most of the speeches Big Daddy gave, and she guessed this was the perfect time to regurgitate it back to him, especially since this seemed like some kind of quiz or something to see if she was listening, she guessed.

"Have you ever wondered why I do what I do? Why I go out of my way with the Youth Employment Program, even though I oftentimes lose money keeping that program in place? I know you asked, and I already told you why, but have you really looked at it, Baby Doll?"

She nodded her head. These set-up questions had no connection whatsoever to such a situation. She sensed Big Daddy was softening her up for something that apparently had nothing to do with the Todd issue. "Well, yes, I thought about it, Big Daddy. And I told you, I think it's the best thing you ever did for the community. If we had more folks like you in the community, we could start making those changes we need so badly." Baby Doll was surprised her memory was good enough to remember some of Big Daddy's specific comments.

Big Daddy smiled. "That's right, Baby Doll. You are so right." He paused for a moment. "Listen, Baby Doll, you know I love you like you were my very own child. You know that, I'm certain. In fact, I love you more than my own flesh-and-blood children. It may sound crazy to say this, but the reality is, Baby Doll, you are my only child, and I'm proud to say I helped raised you to be what you are." He started feeling all choked up, and struggled to stay focused. "I know I'm not making much sense right now, but I'm about to ask you to do something for me. But don't feel you have to do it, unless you feel it's in your heart and soul that you can live up to the task. Now, I know you Baby Doll. I probably know you better than yourself. I know you're destined for greatness. You are the oldest soul I've ever seen in my life. From the first day I saw you, I instantly detected that you were this old, adult woman, trapped inside this little, beautiful, girl's body, and was struggling to get out because nobody understood you, or they were jealous of you because you could do so many things that they just couldn't do. You gave off this vibe that told me you were someone I should keep by me, because at some point we would both become vehicles of some sort." Big Daddy sighed, realizing he was going in much deeper than he wanted and saw he was about to lose her. "Listen, Baby Doll, I want to know, would you be willing to keep my Youth Employment Program going if something should happen to me?"

She impulsively answered the question. "Big Daddy, I would be more than honored to keep your program going. But—But, why are you asking me this?" It suddenly dawned on her. Her mind started making the connections: His losing weight, his sickly facial expression, and most of all, he was getting old. Terror started gradually forming; something in her mind shouted that he was old and old folks were the closest ones to meeting their maker.

Oh God no, don't tell me he's dying.

"Big Daddy, what's the matter?" Her voice started crackling. "Is everything all right?"

Big Daddy saw she was about to cry and figured he might as well stop prolonging it. "Baby Doll, I'm dying of cancer."

Baby Doll felt like her whole world stopped turning. She was shattered in every imaginable way. Her tears exploded as she bolted to Big Daddy and hugged him. Big Daddy struggled to his feet as he embraced her as she cried.

As Baby Doll cried, she realized Big Daddy was the only person on this planet that she truly loved, and now he was about to leave her. She felt her world crumbling. She couldn't imagine living without him around.

Big Daddy whispered into Baby Doll's ear, "Don't worry, it's gonna be all right. If you love me and want to make me happy, please keep my Youth Employment Program alive."

She whispered back, "Don't worry, Big Daddy. I won't let you down." She said it, but at heart she didn't know if she could really keep this promise. At the moment, it was the only appropriate response she could give.

As Baby Doll sat back down in the interrogation chair, wiping her eyes and listened to Big Daddy schooling her on the things she would have to prepare for in order to make her involvement with the Youth Employment Program work, she'd already felt a subconscious doubt twinkling to life. She also noticed that the more she tried to push this reservation aside, the more the thought reminded her that such a mission would prevent her from reaching her goal, and that was to become rich.

CHAPTER 24

Baby Doll paced the length of the waiting room outside the operating room, her arms wrapped around herself as if she was cold. Her eyes were tear-ridden, red, puffy, and she made no effort to conceal her severe emotional pain from all the others in the waiting room. Preacher sat reading a newspaper, one leg crossed over the other. Tera and Pamela sat on the lounge chair with distressful expressions. They had stopped crying about an hour after the doctors informed them that there were some serious complications during the surgery. The doctors weren't certain whether Big Daddy would make it, and everything at the moment was touch and go. The surgery had been going on for almost two straight hours, and Baby Doll felt chronically depressed, dehydrated, and unable to sit still.

She was thinking about all types of issues as she paced, while staring off into the oblivion. The only good thing she could savor at the moment was that Todd Houston came through with every single dime she asked for. A clean one $125,000 became a part of her bank account two days ago, and if it weren't for Big Daddy's blotched surgery, she would have been locked into a celebration. She was now worth $240,000, but she knew after she found a way to get the money cleaned up and then she paid taxes, she would be worth far less. She'd learn many moons ago that the biggest and the silliest mistake that up-and-coming rich people made was not paying their taxes, and she had no intention of following in the footsteps of Mike Tyson, MC Hammer, Red Foxx, Sammy Davis Jr., and countless others that thought they could out-smart Uncle Sam. When she got some time to breathe, she planned to talk to Big Daddy's company taxman to make sure she was in compliance with her taxes.

She had mailed Todd all of his property yesterday, but made copies of everything, including the pictures. She figured if he got stupid in any way, she would cut him down with the unleashing of those materials. She knew Todd was hurting financially, emotionally, and especially physically, and that kind of multiple pain made him very dangerous. This instantly brought on an onslaught of fear because she knew that without Big Daddy holding her down, she might be in a vulnerable situation. There was no doubt in her mind that all the people she herbed, conned, robbed, and clearly took advantage of knew if they laid a finger on her Big Daddy Blue would turn this whole city upside down. She overheard Big Daddy tell those exact words to Preacher that time when they had stepped to Samson. It went without saying that if Big Daddy died, her guardian angel would be gone, and the thought of what all her enemies might do to her brought a chill down her spine.

About twenty minutes later, Doctor Tompkins, Big Daddy's personal physician, came through the operating room door, and everyone in the waiting room stood up almost at the same time, each of them wearing grim expressions. Baby Doll stopped pacing on a dime. Preacher came up beside of Baby Doll; he towered over her, like a Mack Truck parked next to a Volkswagen. Baby Doll's attention hung on every word Doctor Tompkins uttered.

"The worst is over," Doctor Tompkins said. "Mr. Williams made it through the surgery."

There was a loud collective sigh of relief.

Doctor Tompkins continued, "Unfortunately, his cancer had proliferated in such a tremendous fashion that he's far from out of the woods. It's a miracle he didn't have any severe symptoms much earlier."

Baby Doll spoke with hopeful eyes, "Can we see him?"

"I'm sorry. Mr. Williams is in the Intensive Care Unit and won't be allowed any visitors for at least the next seventy-two hours."

With the biggest of the scare out the way, everyone left the hospital to take care of his or her personal business, planning to return once the seventy-two hours were up. Baby Doll went to school and to work, and struggled to stay focused, without much luck. Her depression was at an all-time high, since she knew Big Daddy wasn't going to be with us for very much longer. Twice she had to force herself to eat when she noticed she had gone a whole twenty-four hours without eating. She needed to talk to Big Daddy real bad, and once the seventy-two hours were up, she was the first one at the hospital. In fact, she was waiting in the hospital lobby an hour before the hospital permitted visitors to enter.

As she approached Big Daddy's room, she was hoping and praying that he would be able to talk. She entered the room and was surprised. Big Daddy was sitting up in bed watching TV with a remote control in his hand. He was watching *The Jerry Springer Show* and appeared to be into the program.

When Big Daddy noticed someone had entered the room, he turned his head and saw Baby Doll. He smiled so hard, he almost ripped the skin on his dry lips. He spoke weakly, "Baby Doll."

Baby Doll was in tears as she rushed to Big Daddy and hugged him ever so gently. She was almost scared to touch him, fearing she might handle him in the wrong way. He had lost an amazing amount of weight and looked extremely fragile. This realization made her cry even harder.

Big Daddy patted her on the back as he embraced her and whispered into her ear, "It's gonna be all right, Baby Doll. I know you're hurting, but you gotta be strong, girl. For me, for yourself, and especially for them young folks out there who needs us both."

Baby Doll pulled away from the embrace, found herself a chair, slid it over to the bed, and sat down. She wiped her eyes with the back of her hands. She noticed she'd been doing a hell of a lot of crying lately. In fact, this was the most she had ever cried in her entire life, and for the first time, this fact registered. Even when she got ass-whipping from Mildred, she didn't cry this much. "I'm sorry I'm being weak Big Daddy, but—" she swallowed back another wave of tears. "But I ain't used to losing people real close to me like this."

"Well, you better get used to it because death is a part of living. We are all born to die. That's why you gotta remember, Baby Doll, that when you're here you gotta make it count because you only get one shot to get it right. Life is short." He thought about that quote. "Actually, life is way too short. I'm sitting here on my last leg, and I can still remember when I was about your age, Baby Doll. I was just like you. I thought money was going to make me the happiest man alive; I thought money could heal all my woes and worries; everything I did evolved around money, money, and mo' money. But I also had a big heart. Yeah, I was an old mean-ass nig—" he caught himself, realizing he was flashing back a little too far. He had eradicated the *nigger* word from his vocabulary years ago.

Now that he was reminiscing, he noticed it almost slipped out. "I was as mean as hell, didn't take no shit, and had a vicious knuckle game. Boy, I was whipping ass like Jack Johnson, Joe Louis, and Mike Tyson combined, but there was one thing everybody could say about me, and that was I would lend a helping hand. I was foul when I wanted to be, but I had no problem helping other folks if they were worthy of it. I'm saying this, Baby Doll, because I see you in me, and me in you. Where my heart is right now is where your heart will soon be. We are the type of people that were put here to help others."

Baby Doll knew where he was going with this discussion and was eating it up. She agreed with Big Daddy's analogy on some points, but she had to beg to differ on his belief that she was put here to help others. Nobody ever helped her, besides Big Daddy and Jeanette, and in fact, most people she came in contact with had, at some point, fucked her around. However, she did have to admit that she was always willing to help others when she thought they were worthy of that help. She had just recently sent her newborn nephew Rashawn a huge bag of baby clothing. Although Jasmine was acting like she was still tight with her for not giving Mildred money, she could see Jazz was grateful and showed it by thanking her with her eyes. Baby Doll started recounting all the times she had helped others and had to admit that she subliminally got a thrill out of helping others when she thought they were deserving of her help. Actually, come to think of it, she realized she would get a natural high when she saw the response on people's faces when they were confronted with a gift of charity she had given them. Maybe Big Daddy did see something in her that she didn't notice, she concluded inwardly.

Big Daddy continued, "I've seen you in action, Baby Doll, and that's why I know you can take the Youth Employment Program to a place I could never take it. That time you gave that woman five dollars when she came up short when she was trying to buy some shirts or something. She was a total stranger, and you looked out for her. Yeah, at the Pitkin Avenue store."

Baby Doll was surprised because Big Daddy wasn't in the store when that happened. "How you know about that!?" She smiled, and instantly realized Helen apparently told him. "Oh, I see what time it is; don't tell me you had Helen spying on me."

"It wasn't spying; she was just evaluating your job performance. There's a bunch of other examples, but the point is . . ."

As Big Daddy went on about her finer points of helping others, she homed in on his statement—" There's a bunch of other examples"—of her having a good heart. This implied that he'd been watching her very closely for some time. As Big Daddy rattled on, she was eating it all up. But contrary to Big Daddy's belief, she felt she was put here to take care of herself, not to run around bending over backward for a bunch of ungrateful people.

About a minute later, Big Daddy said, "There's a quote in the Bible that you must remember. I'm even asking you to memorize it." He saw he had her attention, but wanted to make sure she understood that this was very important to him. "Will you give me your word that you'll memorize this Bible quote?"

"Yes, I give you my word, Big Daddy. I'll memorize it."

He stared at her without saying a word. This was his way of placing serious emphasis on what he was about to say. He knew the best way to establish to Baby Doll that what he was about to say was very important was to say nothing while staring at her. When he saw her becoming uncomfortable, he said, "This is the quote, it's from 1 Corinthians, Chapter 13, verses 1-13, and it goes like this:

"Though I speak with the tongues of men and of angels, and have not charity, I am become as sounding brass, or a tinkling cymbal.

And though I have the gift of prophecy, and understand all mysteries, and all knowledge; and though I have all faith, so that I could remove mountains, and have not charity, I am nothing.

And though I bestow all my goods to feed the poor, and though I give my body to be burned, and have not charity, it profiteth me nothing.

Charity suffereth long and is kind; charity envieth not; charity vaunteth not itself, is not puffed up.

Doth not behave itself unseemly, seeketh not her own, is not easily provoked, thinketh no evil;

Rejoiceth not in iniquity, but rejoiceth in the truth;

Bearth all things, believeth all things, hopeth all things, endureth all things.

Charity never faileth: but whether there be prophecies, they shall fail; whether there be tongues, they shall cease; whether there be knowledge, it shall vanish away.

For we know in part, and we prophesy in part.

But when that which is perfect iscome, then that which is in part shall be done away.

When I was a child, I spake as a child, I understood as a child, I thought as a child: but when I became a man, I put away childish things.

For now we see through a glass darkly; but then face to face: now I know in part; but then shall I know even as also I am known.

And now abideth faith, hope, charity, these three; but the greatest of these is charity."

There was a moment of silence as Big Daddy took a breather. Baby Doll was shocked by fact he was able to rattle off such a long quote and had even sounded like a Reverend or something. This was very serious, she concluded, and her attention was instantly turned up another notch.

Big Daddy continued, "This verse in the Bible basically explains that gifts such as wealth, wisdom, and even faith are worthless and meaningless unless they are accompanied by charity; the act of giving and helping others. Of all the tens of thousands of other verses in the Bible, it was this one that I felt spoke to my innermost being."

There was a moment of silence as Big Daddy reflected on the time he first came in contact with this verse while in prison.

Big Daddy shifted his body ever so slightly, causing a sharp pain to rip through his abdominal cavity, and said, "I'm not a religious man, as you know, Baby Doll. I don't go to church on Sundays, and I don't particularly believe there's a man up in the sky calling shots and pulling strings. But I do believe in some parts of the Bible. The parts that were put there to help us humans to become more humane to each other are what I worship. That love that flows from those verses in the Bible is the God that I have come to believe in. And what I've been doing for the last decade or so is what this God has intended me to do. It's my calling, as some would say."

He grimaced in great anguish as he felt a sharp pain erupted in the lower section of his stomach. He saw Baby Doll was about to panic, and he waved for her to be easy. "It's nothing, Baby Doll." He sucked in several deep breaths and was back to himself. "Get a pen and write that Bible verse down."

Baby Doll opened her small handbag retrieved a pen and a piece of paper.

"It's 1 Corinthians." He watched her write it back. "Chapter 13 . . . verses 1-13. The King James Version is what I quoted. Get that version; it's much more lyrical and poetic than the other versions. Plus, I'm gonna quiz you, so you gotta memorize that version."

"Quiz me?" Baby Doll said surprisingly. "You actually want me to quote it the same way you just did?"

Big Daddy looked at her as though she was crazy. "That's right. How else are you going to truly know and understand it if you don't know it word for word? Once you commit things to memory it's much easier to live them out. You can't truly live out something if it's not sufficiently inside your head."

"I'll memorize it, Big Daddy. I promised you, and I'll keep my word."

Big Daddy felt a sense of accomplishment since, if she learned this Bible verse, it would be the third test that she had passed.

* * * *

During the first two weeks after surgery, Big Daddy was receiving visits from just about all of his so-called loved ones. The word was that Big Daddy would be in the hospital for only two weeks, but when more complications developed and it was determined that his treatment might result in a six-month stay, attitudes immediately started to change.

True to her word, Baby Doll worked hard to commit the Bible quote to memory, but still hadn't gotten all the verses down pat. By the end of the second week she had three more verses to go before she completed the task. When she told Big Daddy she was contemplating dropping out of college, he talked her out of it, and they made a compromise that she would drop one class, even though she was already a part-time student with only two classes semester. With only one class, she knew there'd be no excuse for her not to stay on top of her business.

The biggest surprise visit for Big Daddy during this first two weeks came from his daughter Rachel. At first he thought it was a genuine act of concern, until he noticed her same old bad energy; she seemed to have an attitude about something she didn't want to share with him. Consistent with her usual way of dealing with Big Daddy, she only wanted to know if he could give her some money. For the first time ever, Big Daddy decided to tell her no and specifically told her, "Sorry, Rachel, but the ATM machine has officially dried up. I'm dying, and all you can think about is how much money you can get out of me? To put it to you simple and plain, my efforts to prove I love you while you can't even at least try to meet me halfway are over."

Not surprisingly, Rachel didn't see that she was acting like a foul bitch, and when she stomped out of the hospital, she was cursing, blaming and mumbling under her breath. Rachel never returned, and weeks later Baby Doll wished she had stepped to Rachel when she had the chance; she wanted to give her spoiled, spiteful, ungrateful, and nasty-attitude-having ass a nice piece of her mind. Rachel had a father who did everything in his power to please her, and all she did was shit on him and basically spit in his face every opportunity she got. People in the hood would give their right arm for a father who even gave a shit about them, and her stupid ass was fucking him around and acting the fool.

Baby Doll pondered that it was no small wonder some Black men walked out on their families, especially if they had to deal with vile, nasty, and utterly unappreciative folks of the likes of Rachel. After seeing this, she had to newfound understanding of why some good Black men would break out on their families.

By the third week after the surgery, in the month of September, Pamela started running out of gas. Instead of visiting, she was calling Big Daddy on his cell phone with a bunch of lies and lame-ass excuses. As Baby Doll sat listening to Big Daddy's phone responses, she was furious at how he was casually and unemotionally allowing Pam to beat him in the head with all those ridiculous lies. She wanted to scream on Big Daddy for allowing her to mistreat him like that. In a calm manner he had simply told Baby Doll that he wasn't unfamiliar with this sort of treatment, since this was just how they all treated him when he was in prison. Baby Doll realized she would never forget when Big Daddy told her the following: "There are two places you can go to find out who's truly on your side. Those two places are prisons and hospitals. Prisons more so than hospitals."

From beginning to end Preacher kept it real, Baby Doll noticed, and he made it his business to visit Big Daddy at least once a week. This was no small task, since Preacher was the main person running the businesses, and had limited assistance from Helen, Teddy, and a few other reliable employees. He was doing most of the work singlehandedly now that Big Daddy was out of commission.

During most of the visits, Big Daddy and Preacher talked about Baby Doll and how to make sure she was properly groomed for the task of taking over the Youth Employment Program. There were plenty of heated discussions, but Big Daddy Blue felt reassured that Preacher would hold fast to his word.

But because he knew human nature was one of the most unpredictable forces in the universe, the only thing he could do was lay groundwork, hope that their lifelong bond would always be remembered, and most of all, do everything in his powers to make sure Preacher didn't run out of steam like so many others.

The biggest surprise for Baby Doll, but the least shocking to Big Daddy, was Tera's foot-dragging and unwillingness to stay the course when it came to visiting and staying at Big Daddy's side. By the third month, Tera was making a million excuses to avoid visiting Big Daddy and had even hit Baby Doll in the head with that bullshit excuse that she hated to visit him because it was making her chronically depressed. Baby Doll had told her that even if that was true, it still didn't relieve her of making sure Big Daddy's last days were filled with total and complete support from all whose lives were better because of him

During one of Tera's visits, Baby Doll arrived after she got there, and saw the perfect way to score some major points with Big Daddy. She put Tera's ass right on the spot when she told Tera in Big Daddy's presence that she was catching a case of amnesia and was showing just how ungrateful she really was. "Big Daddy's been treating all y'all good, and the minute he needs y'all, y'all go and shit on him!" Baby Doll said to Tera, who was furious that Baby Doll had pointed out her shortcoming with Big Daddy listening. A physical fight almost broke out, and Big Daddy asked Tera to leave. As Tera left, Baby Doll saw it in Tera's eyes; she had another enemy to add to her lengthy list of haters.

By the fourth month, Baby Doll and Pam clashed. Baby Doll heard she was coming to visit, and Baby Doll strategically waited for her in the front of the hospital. She stepped straight to Pamela and damn near chewed a new ass hole on her.

Baby Doll called her a "foul, stink bitch" straight to her face and dared her to act like she wanted to do something. Pamela, like the punk she was, acted like she didn't know why Baby Doll was so upset with her disappearing for weeks when she had told Big Daddy she was busy trying to find a job. When Baby Doll discovered that the only reason Pam was coming up to visit Big Daddy in person was because she wanted to talk to Big Daddy about her credit cards being turned off, Baby Doll was so furious, she couldn't talk and just walked away.

In essence, Baby Doll, out of all the others, came to see Big Daddy three times a week, every week, and never missed a beat. Her efforts were initiated by a genuine love for Big Daddy, mixed with many other things, but the main subsidiary motivator was, she saw her ultimate goal of becoming rich growing with each visit. Big

Daddy had an empire, and it was easy for all to see that she would be the likely candidate to carry on his work. Baby Doll would get brain-locked in a daydream at work and while in her college class as she imagined how she intended to blow up beyond imagination. She had full intentions of keeping the Youth Employment Program alive, but she had her own plan that would be slightly different from Big Daddy's plan of action.

Then, about five months of visiting Big Daddy, the strangest thing happened. Baby Doll was entering the hospital when she noticed a medium-built, very handsome, Black man with a neatly trimmed goatee, a short Afro, and dressed in business attire, looking at her with a grin on his face. When the man stopped by the exit, folded his arms, and just stared at her, Baby Doll almost panicked. She nervously looked around hospital waiting room, hoping and praying the security guards were nearby; she just knew this man was here to get revenge for one of the many people she had robbed and conned. Her heart was pounding with nervousness.

The man was smiling at her, but she could see it wasn't a friendly gesture. He gave off a dangerous vibe that announced that he was someone not to be played with. When the elevator door slid opened, and as Baby Doll hastily got on to the elevator, she saw the man casually walk away as the elevator door slid close.

Staring at the elevator door, she knew in that moment that she had to do something. She wondered, should she talk to Big Daddy about this incident. After a moment she decided not to worry him. She started gassing herself into believing she could find a way to deal with it without his aide. But the more she thought about it, the more she realized that she was in a really messed-up situation.

CHAPTER 25

"I need you to take this over to Tiffany," Baby Doll said as she handed Karen, a short light-skinned, slim woman, the folder. "Tell her I need photocopies of everything in this file, and to get it back to me ASAP." As Karen rushed out of the office, Baby Doll sat back down in Big Daddy's cushiony executive-style chair, feeling like the Supreme Diva of all Divas. She still couldn't believe Big Daddy was already allowing her to test-run how it was going to feel to be in charge. Eight months after surgery, Big Daddy was still in the hospital undergoing massive radiation and chemotherapy treatments, and every time he came close to being released, another life-threatening complication developed. As Baby Doll sat looking at the clubs monthly financial reports, she sensed it must be in the cards for Big Daddy not to make it out of that hospital.

Suddenly, Preacher entered without knocking. "What's up, Baby Doll?" He took a seat in the interrogation chair. "Tonight, I'm going to see Big Daddy. I know you were planning to go see him tonight, but I need you to hang tight. Take a day off. Me and him need to talk, and it's going to take up all the visiting time."

Baby Doll didn't like it when people interfered with the quality time she spent with Big Daddy, but this issue sounded like it involved an important business matter, so she decided to bend. "I'll do that for you, Preacher. It must be something very important; it's gonna take up all the time? Is it about Pam sleeping around?"

Preacher saw Baby Doll was snooping. "Pam is the last thing on Big Daddy's mind. When Big Daddy got with her he knew she was a gold dagger and wasn't gonna last." The mention of gold dagger made him realized that he felt the same way about Baby Doll.

He knew Big Daddy saw something special in this pretty, conniving-ass broad, but whatever it was, he wasn't seeing it. He did have to admit that she wasn't like any other female from the hood he'd ever known. There was no question Baby Doll was about her business and knew how to get what she wanted. There was no doubt she was also a hard and dedicated worker. He didn't like her style on many different levels, but because he promised Big Daddy that he would hold her down, he would try his best to deal with her. "Big Daddy's used to people falling off; he ain't tripping about it, so don't let them get you unfocussed, Baby Doll."

"I'm surprised damn near everybody fell off, even Tera. I still can't understand why all these motherfuckers are turning their backs on Big Daddy when he treated all of them good, and the way Big Daddy ain't even sweatin' that shit got me cold bugging. I would dead all of them on every—"

"Most people care only about themselves, Baby Doll." Preacher knew she was about to go on a tangent. She got crazy when people did anything wrong to Big Daddy. He liked her energy in this area because he knew it was genuine. "So how did it go with Supreme?"

Baby Doll thought about the question. Supreme was the first kid she gave a job to and her first endeavor to show to Big Daddy that she could handle the head position of the Youth Employment Program. "It went real good. Shorty had a crazy attitude, but once he saw I was really trying to help, he opened up." She didn't tell Preacher that shorty had a crush on her, and she was able to cool him out by playing on that fact. "I would say in a couple of weeks, he'll be good to go."

Preacher suddenly remembered that Big Daddy instructed him to make sure Baby Doll had the Bible quote down pat, and to check to make sure every now and then, "Let me hear that Bible quote."

Baby Doll was surprised. She smiled at Preacher, realizing Big Daddy wasn't playing any games about her knowing that stuff. She wasn't sweating it because she had the verses down weeks ago and had been reciting it every time she visited Big Daddy. She recited 1 *Corinthians* 13, 1-13 with the smoothness of a Southern Baptist

Preacher, and she saw Preacher was smiling as if he was proud of her.

"Big Daddy said you had the preacher man syndrome is your blood, and I must say, he damn sure wasn't lying."

He stood as they both laughed.

As Baby Doll watched Preacher exit the office, she wondered was that a good or bad compliment.

* * * *

Big Daddy and Preacher sat talking. Big Daddy lay in bed with two huge pillows propping him up, while Preacher sat in the chair at his bedside.

"I went to the house," Preacher said. "Packed all her stuff with her standing there—"

"I told you I didn't want her there when you did that, Preacher. What happened?"

"Yo, man, the crazy bitch must've been stalking me or something. The minute I rolled up she was on me. When I told her she couldn't come inside she started going crazy, talking about she was going to call the police and that her property was in there, and that she had a right not to be locked out of a house she'd been living there for years. She went on and on, and I figured the wise thing to do was to avoid all the police drama, so I let her in and let her watch me pack her shit."

"Did you actually watch her? Did you let her roam around without watching her?"

Big Daddy had large sums of cash stashed throughout his house and knew Pam was up on a few of them. Now that she knew she was catching the boot, there was no doubt she was going to try to hit them stashes. The way he hit her with the sneak-attack lock changes, Big Daddy knew she couldn't get to the money if she hadn't already, so he'd given Preacher explicit instructions not to let her back into his house.

"I never took my eyes off the tramp," Preacher said truthfully. He didn't just not take his eyes off of her, he had actually let her talk him into giving him a raw-head blowjob. All she wanted in return was two hundred dollars, and Preacher saw this as a hell of a bargain and jumped right on it, or should we say, right in it.

"So you saying when I get home next week," Big Daddy said skeptically. "I won't find my shit missing?"

"Naw, bro, don't go there. You and I both know you just gave her ass the boot about a week ago. How you know she wasn't making moves the minute you stepped foot in this hospital? Now, if you had me on it the minute she started showing out, then you might be able to say that."

Big Daddy suddenly realized Preacher was dead on the money. Pam had months to make her moves, and nine out of ten there was no doubt she did make some moves. He could imagine that sticky-finger bitch tearing the house up looking for his stashes. After a moment, Big Daddy shoved the whole issue to the side, surmising that the little crumbs she was probably able to scrounge up wasn't worth the mental aerobics he was about to exert dealing with the issue. He concluded she could keep it, especially since right about now he was in the mood for being very extraordinarily forgiving. This vibe scared him because he sincerely felt that he could forgive anybody right now as if his soul was undergoing some kind of subliminal, uncontrollable desire to keep itself untainted with bad emotions, acts and deeds. "Well, I guess it's water under the bridge."

"If you want to, I can step to her and find out if she got crazy. If she took something she had no business taking, I can get it back."

"Forget her. Whatever she took let her keep it. I'm sorry I even brought it up. So, what's up with Baby Doll? How you think she's holding up?"

"Baby Doll is Baby Doll. She's hitting all the right marks. She's a very fast learner as we all know. I'm glad you talked to her because she's listening to me without any backtalk—"

"I didn't say nothing to her about not talking back to you. She's doing that on her own."

"Oh, pardon me." Preacher found that strange because, in the past, Baby Doll seemed to listen only to Big Daddy. "See, that's evidence that she's taking this thing serious."

"What about that kid, Supreme?" He and Preacher had agreed to reach out to this young wild kid whose real name was Henry Moore, from Brevoort Projects. His mother came to the hospital and asked Big Daddy personally to step in and try to get her son to take a job with their Youth Employment Program.

"Man, she's a natural born leader." Preacher saw Big Daddy smiling, and it made him feel extremely good to see his only true friend happy. "She was handling shorty like a magician, making miracles happen. With her in that spot, I see this Youth Program blowing up, especially when it comes to the young cats. She's so fine that they immediately start jumping through hoops to please her. Since our young brothers are the ones who need this Employment Program the most, and are the ones who are least willing to get involved, I know she's going to make this program do what it do. I just hope when she start stepping to the adults, the politicians, and the other business folks, she don't get the same results we got."

"She'll be fine," Big Daddy said with confidence, while flashing back to all those times he and Preacher had stepped to all these people and got shot down. He realized it was amazing how other Black folks would shot anything down, kill a highly productive idea or a program that could help a lot of people, solely because the person pushing the program had some issues in their past, had rectified those issues and was now trying to do the right thing. It was just as amazing how they were so busy trying to find the slightest fault or flaw in a person, while refusing to see that their very own backyard was totally fucked-up. "Baby Doll is gonna be just fine. She's got something me and you didn't have when we started this Youth Program. She got a spotless criminal record, no hidden bones in her closet or a shit load of baggage. That alone will get folks to listen to what she's got to say, and at least give her a chance to prove what she's offering is a sincere attempt to help."

Preacher had his doubts, as always, but he again kept it to himself. He knew Big Daddy always kept a case of selective amnesia when it came to issues dealing with the old crabs-in-the-barrel disease and the Willie Lynch syndrome that Black folks were suffering from. Preacher felt the strong urge to spark up another dialogue on the topic, and after a moment, he decided to let it ride. He looked at his watch, saw he had time to debate the issue for the ten thousandth time, and decided to touch on it briefly. "You might be right, Big Daddy, but don't forget how some of us can get real crazy when we see other Black folks trying to do something big and grand."

"Another one of your crabs-in-the-barrel discussions." Big Daddy shook his head with a smile, realizing Preacher would never change. "Why is it that you always hone in on the bad? My bad, I actually know why you do this, but why can't you believe that we can make it right if we *all* start believing we can make it right?"

"Because every time we try to make it right, we get a hundred other motherfuckers that don't just try to make sure we get it wrong, but always succeed in making us get it wrong. That's why. Don't get me wrong, I know if a person gets locked into negative thinking, he can create negative outcomes just by constantly thinking negative. But don't get it twisted; if you run into a situation and never looking at the negative, you can and will trip yourself up by not analyzing all angles of a situation. I'm that voice that forces us to look at it from another angle. You look at it strictly from the positive, and I look at it from the negative, and guess what? That combination, I think, is what enabled this Youth Employment Program to survive this long. Come on, Big Daddy, we talked about this a hundred times. With this Baby Doll issue, we should do the same."

Big Daddy realized Preacher just told on himself. He wasn't being totally forthcoming about Baby Doll. "I could've sworn we were talking about both the positive and the negative. So what are you saying? You've been pulling punches when we talked about Baby Doll?"

Preacher realized what he just did. He sighed. "Yeah, I admit, I did pull a few blows, but look at you man. You're sitting up in this hospital all fucked up. The last thing I want to do is put you in a stressed-out state of mind. Stress is the biggest killer on the planet. If I can make you happy, that's what a friend does for a friend."

"Bullshit! A friend don't make a friend happy at the expense of fucking up a program that can help the collective whole. You see, that's our problem; we too fuckin' busy worrying about the goddamn individual when we're supposed to be focusing on the collective whole. Now that we're clearing up the air, you might as well tell me what you really think about Baby Doll. I'm surprised at you, Preacher, because you know we can't fix a problem if we don't identify and talk about the damn thing.

He paused to give the remark its intended impact. "When we were in prison that's all we ever talked about. Identify, discuss, and then fix the problem. Fuck my feelings! This shit is bigger than my feelings, bro!" Big Daddy sighed angrily. "Let's hear it, and this time don't pull anything."

Preacher sighed and said, "First of all, Baby Doll is the most disciplined and qualified person we got. Let's get that straight. She's ready for the job, but I got two issues, and that's it. Big Daddy, you and I both know she's obsessed with money. The way she ripped off Samson, Karl, and even Ka-Born tells me she's gonna get out of hand when it comes to issues of money. I just got word she did some crazy shit to a customer named Todd Houston. That's the main issue. The second issue; she's very conniving when it comes to getting what she wants. The combination of these issues don't sit right with me. I've seen what money can make people do, and after all these years of building this program to turn it over to someone who might fuck it all up because they have an insane lust for money is crazy. But, in all fairness, the first issue is the major one that we need to be careful with; this money issue, in my opinion, is going to interfere with her taking this program to where it needs to go."

Big Daddy felt a surge of relief; he thought it was something else he was missing. He sighed and said, "If that's all it is, then, we gonna be all right. Shit, everybody knows Baby Doll is serious about making money. It's a double-edged sword, but nonetheless I don't think it's gonna pose a major problem."

Preacher was stumped. He couldn't see why Big Daddy didn't see it. "So, you mean to tell me that when she gets hold of some major money, you don't think she's gonna drop the Youth Employment Program and live her own dream?"

He saw Big Daddy staring at him with a blank expression. "You don't think a young, fine woman who's aspiration is to get rich is not gonna do what so many other rich Black folks have done once they pulled themselves out of the grit and grime, while remembering how foul, fucked-up, and vicious some Black folks can be to each other, especially those trying to help others?"

Big Daddy couldn't answer those questions, because technically Preacher was right. Most Black folks who did get lucky and pulled themselves out of the hood were either scared to reach back to help others, or just didn't give a shit. With all the jealousy, envy, and highly toxic folks plotting and scheming to pull the ones who made it out back down, it was very sensible to get out and never look back. Big Daddy sighed, feeling content that he decided to rely on the fact that he did contemplate this issue and had made some arrangements. He was certain he saw Baby Doll inside of him, and himself inside of Baby Doll. He knew what it took for him to get his sense of benevolence to where it was currently at, and he was also certain that Baby Doll would also have to experience the same trials and tribulations. As long as he had this fact on his side and knowing he made preparations, he would ride with it and trust in his heart and soul that it was going to be all right. It was time to change the topic, since there was really nothing else to discuss. "So how's Gloria? You and her figured out how to get around that mortgage issue?"

Preacher smiled and realized this type of response to his question was a clear indication that his mind was made up about Baby Doll and nothing could change it. "We're still working on it." Since he wanted to change the topic, he might as well get some answers to another issue. "So what happened at the meeting you had with Sweet Charlie? How much he's charging to bump them doctors off for destroying your life?"

Big Daddy sighed and looked down at his hands. "I'm not gonna do anything to them."

Preacher literally felt a jolt from that comment. He was certain he didn't hear him correctly. "What!?"

"I'm not gonna do anything to them."

"Hold up, wait a minute. You mean you're going let them motherfuckers go unpunished when they basically murdered you!?"

"Yeap, that's right." He locked eyes with Preacher to make it clear that he made his decision.

"Why!?" Preacher's usual cool, calm, and collective attitude and gestures had completely disappeared. "Why let them get that shit off? Why!?" He was clearly in an infuriated state.

Big Daddy thought about how to answer the question to make Preacher understand his position. After a moment, he said, "I'm dying, Preacher. There's no doubt about that. Unless they find some kind of miracle cure for cancer by next week, or sooner, my swan song is sung. You might understand this, since you used to be a Preacher. Basically, I don't want to soil my soul. Sounds crazy, but really look at it, Preacher. Back in the day, I did a whole lot of crazy shit. I shot and killed a few people. I sold drugs to people and, therefore, hurt and killed people implicitly. I went to prison for murder and drug conspiracy, and while in prison I found myself, and started cleaning myself up. Not just physically, mentally, emotionally, psychologically, but mostly spiritually. When I learned that Bible verse 1 *Corinthians*, Chapter 13, verses 1-13, I could literally feel my soul being cleansed. This shit sounds crazy, but I could feel it. I was blessed to make it out of that place alive, and I was even more blessed to do what I promised myself I would do once I cleansed myself. I wanted to get out of that place and really help people, and I did just that."

He sighed while shaking his head. "Now, for me to turn around and dirty up my soul by killing again, especially while I'm on my death bed and definitely won't get another chance to cleanse my soul after I kill those doctors, is something I can't go to my grave with. I just can't do it, Preacher."

Preacher was blown away. This was another one of the many profound statements he could add to Big Daddy's list of remarkable insights. Hearing those words roll off Big Daddy's tongue instantly made him, for the first time, really take a hard look at himself and the state of his soul. After only a two-second observation, he concluded that he had some work to do.

* * * *

Two weeks later, around the end of May, Big Daddy was released from the hospital with clear instructions to maintain his bed rest regimen. He had lost a massive amount of weight, felt chronically weak, and had lost all of his hair from the radiation treatment. For the first time in his life, his features not only showed his true age (now sixty-seven years old), but he also had to walk with a cane and had a slow moving, foot-dragging limp. Fighting desperately not to succumb to the deteriorative force of time, Big Daddy struggled to move and walk like he used to and instantly realized that he could not defeat nature, and old Father Time had finally caught up with him. He was an old man, dying of cancer, and nothing could change that, and the beautiful thing was, he wasn't bitter. At his Long Island home, he had a beautiful home attendant, a West Indian woman name Marsha Williamson, waiting for him. Marsha cared for him from sunup to sundown, and as usual, Baby Doll was with him every step of the way. Baby Doll had even moved into Big Daddy's Long Island home, just so she could be with him during his last days. Her mission was clear, and she wasn't taking no for an answer; she wanted to make Big Daddy as happy as he could be before he left this world.

Several months later, one night in the month of September, in the wee hours of the morning, Baby Doll entered Big Daddy's room as he slept, and consistent with her extreme personality, she got in the bed with him. She surmised that since Big Daddy wasn't her biological father, there would be nothing morally or ethically wrong with her giving him some sexual pleasure. She could see he was bored out of his mind, and it truly hurt her heart to see him in this state. He deserved better, and what she was about to do would give her a chance to really demonstrate her utter gratefulness. As Big Daddy slept, she pulled his pajamas pants down, and began to suck his penis without a condom. She knew his health status, since his medical records were available to Marsha, the home attendant, and she seen he had no sexual transmitted diseases.

Big Daddy was locked into a deep sleep and didn't realize that he wasn't dreaming, until he felt himself coming. He woke up as the ejaculation was convulsing his body with a much-needed sexual release and noticed he wasn't dreaming. This was the real deal and someone was giving him a blowjob. He looked down, saw Baby Doll down there and didn't know what to do. Since he'd already ejaculated, there was no taking that back. His mind was still cloudy and cluttered from all the painkillers he'd taken earlier. With all the medications he was on he was surprised he was even able to bust a nut. He struggled into a sitting position, and said softly, "Why you do that, Baby Doll?"

She held up her hand, went to the nearby bedpan, and spit the semen into it. She wiped her mouth as she returned and sat on the bed next to him, feeling a bit awkward because she was hoping he would just go with it. "I want to make you happy, Big Daddy. I want you to be happy in all ways. I know you like sex and haven't have any in a long time, so I figured I'd make sure you get that pleasure you deserve."

Big Daddy was at a loss for words. He really didn't know how to explain to her that his only true pleasure came from knowing that she would fulfill his legacy by keeping his Youth Employment Program alive, and nothing else really mattered. He definitely didn't want to hurt her feelings, when she was merely trying too hard to please him, even though it was a totally misguided display of affection. "Baby Doll, listen." He grabbed both of her soft hands.

"I understand that you love me and want to make me happy, but please understand that you are young enough to be my granddaughter, and it makes me very uncomfortable knowing I had sex with someone who is my granddaughter. I see you as my daughter, granddaughter, and that's all my mind registers. Stop worrying about my happiness so much. Just remember that if you want to make me happy, keep my youth program alive, and Big Daddy Blue will be happy no matter where I'm at, okay? Can you do that for me, Baby Doll?"

"Yes, I can, Big Daddy. And I will do it." Baby Doll reached up and hugged his frail and cancer-eaten body.

Four months later, in January, the cold was unusually severe. The temperature had plummeted to well below zero. It was a dreary day, and the clouds seem to be heavy and thick in the sky, creating the appearance that heavy rains were in the forecast. When Baby Doll entered Big Daddy's bedroom to check on him before getting ready to go to school, she instantly sensed something was wrong by the way he looked; he was in a fetal position and the covers look as if they were kicked away. As she slowly approached, she realized what made this image disturbing was that his hands looked like they were crawling at his stomach and were frozen in that position.

Baby Doll hysterically rushed to him, but she already knew he was dead the minute she laid eyes on him seconds ago. When Baby Doll touched his cold, rock-hard body, she received her confirmation. To her surprise, she didn't feel the compulsion to cry.

CHAPTER 26

Baby Doll saw that Big Daddy's funeral was one fit for a King. Dressed in a black gown, she sat next to Preacher in the second row amongst Gregory J. Williams' real family. There were so many eye-rolling assaults coming from the family that even the reverend had noticed the tension earlier when he spoke to the family. Baby Doll cried softly as the wake was in progress. The funeral home on the corner of Bergen Street and Ralph Avenues was packed to capacity. Baby Doll was surprised to see that Big Daddy knew so many people. There were even a few congressmen, city council people, the famous rapper Ja-King, and a series of other celebrities had dropped by to pay their respects. Baby Doll sat watching the assembly line of people viewing Big Daddy inside the open casket. The viewers would stop, observe, some were crying, some weren't, and would then move along.

Suddenly, Baby Doll saw the dangerous-looking man at the hospital was in line approaching Big Daddy's casket. She didn't understand why she was in awe upon seeing this man, and her eyes clearly displayed her shock. He was dressed in a very elegant light brown suit and had on some fly ostrich-skin shoes that matched his suit perfectly. It hit her like a silly stick that this man apparently knew Big Daddy and was probably visiting Big Daddy that day she saw him leaving the hospital while she was entering. The man was looking around the funeral home as though he was searching for someone. Then, his eyes landed on her and he literally stared her down. Baby Doll knew this was a clear indication that he was looking for her. He was staring so hard at her that she noticed her heart instantly started pounding in her chest.

Baby Doll nervously looked away and, a moment later, snuck a peek and saw he was still staring at her as he waited his turn to observe Big Daddy's remains.

Her mind was all over the place trying to figure out why he was staring at her like that, and the only thing she could conclude is that he was here to hurt her, and viewing Big Daddy's body was nothing more than a front. When she saw the strange man had broken that stare and nodded at Preacher sitting beside her, she wondered what that was all about. The more she thought about the exchange between the mystery man and Preacher the more she realized her eyes were probably playing tricks on her. Baby Doll watched the man leave the funeral home.

Three days after the funeral, Baby Doll, Preacher, Tera, Rachel, and about a two dozen other people Baby Doll barely knew were standing in the lounge area of a huge Park Avenue law firm, waiting to find out who would get what according to Big Daddy's Will. As Baby Doll looked around, she was surprised that any of these folks present had received notice that they were required to attend this inheritance proceeding, especially in light of the fact none of them ever did anything for Big Daddy.

Everyone present had entered a huge conference room with a huge round table that could seat two dozen people. At the head of the conference table were two attorneys. They introduced themselves as Mr. Lawrence Wilson and Mr. Richard Erkco and went right into business. When the smoke cleared, Breana "Baby Doll" Winbush basically got the top spot over all of Big Daddy's empire; she became the chief executive officer over all business and personal property of Gregory J. Williams; this included his Long Island home. Preacher got the top manager position of the Cleveland Street club with a stipulation; Tera the top manager position of the downtown Brooklyn store with a stipulation; Rachel and the others each got five thousand dollars. The stipulations for Preacher and Tera were that they could maintain management positions over the designated business property only if they stayed loyal to Baby Doll.

However, Baby Doll had the biggest stipulation of them all; she could maintain ownership over all of Gregory J. Williams' property as long as she kept the Youth Employment Program fully functioning. If, in the event she should fail to honor this clause of the will, there would be another reading of a secondary component of the will, at which time the new stipulations and clauses will be revealed.

Baby Doll didn't like that last stipulation one bit since it left her completely in the blind. She saw Big Daddy was no dummy. If she reneged, she got nothing, which was cool with her because she had full intentions of keeping her promise. She looked over and saw a smirk on both Tera and Preacher's faces; she noticed their expression gave off the imagery that they were already conspiring up ways to make sure she felt the force of that last stipulation.

* * * *

Pauline Anthony sat in the reception area of the main office of Hudson's International Realtors Group on Waters Street in lower Manhattan. Her heart was still pounding with nervousness and her palms were sweating, even though she had received a phone call from the top man of this multi-million dollar setup yesterday, requesting that she report to this location, because he wanted to present her with a business proposition. Mr. Hudson had also indicated that he had gotten her contact information from her college professor, Diana Weinstein, who said she was one of her brightest students in her business management class. Mrs. Weinstein and Mr. Hudson apparently were close and felt Pauline would be interested in such an offer. Pauline realized she was more than interested as she nervously tapped her foot on the floor. Mr. Hudson had also given her a brief heads-up on what this was about when he warned Pauline not to say anything about this meeting to her friend Breana Winbush.

About an hour after receiving the phone call, she'd stopped racking her brains, trying to figure out what a millionaire of the likes of Mr. Hudson wanted her to do in relation to Baby Doll.

Suddenly, a petite White woman with features like a model, and chestnut-colored hair opened a glass door while peeking her head inside and said, "Mr. Hudson is ready to see you, ma'am."

Pauline popped onto her feet and followed the secretary to the office down a sleek corridor. She glazed at the space age furniture and matching paints on the wall as she felt like she was walking on a cloud of air, since the brown carpeting was so thick. She entered the roomy office and saw a clean shaved White man who looked about in his mid-forties sitting behind a desk. When Pauline entered, he rose to his feet.

With a smile and his hand outreached for a handshake, Mr. Hudson said, "Ms. Pauline Anthony, I'm am so glad you could make it." After Pauline shook his hand, he said, "Please have a seat." He turned to the secretary as Pauline sat down and said, "Sarah, thank you very much."

Sarah acknowledged the comment with a nod of the head and exited the office as Ernest Hudson sat back down.

"I like to cut straight to the chase. Do you want to make some serious money, Ms. Anthony?"

With a gapped-tooth smile, Pauline was catch off guard by the point blankness of the offer, and said hesitantly, "Ah, I—yes, I would love to make some serious money, Mr. Hudson."

"How close are you and Breana Winbush?"

"Well, I would say I'm pretty close to her. We went to college together, and we lived in the same neighborhood a few years back. We hung out a lot as well. In fact, we consider ourselves best friends."

"Here's the deal. I need you to convince her to sale to me the businesses she has just inherited." He searched Pauline's facial response for any signs that the request was way over the top for her and didn't detect anything worth becoming alarmed over. "As you know, she was given control over several business establishments, and I'm very interested in purchasing those properties. She'll make a profit four times the standard price of the property. And, if you can convince her, I'll pay you . . ."

* * * *

In the weeks that followed Baby Doll took control of the four clubs and the six stores, and she let everybody know that she was the boss and wasn't taking any shorts. The February cold had set in nicely, but it was nothing in comparison to the temperature Baby Doll had unleashed on the business. At the store on Liberty Avenue and Elders Lane, Baby Doll had fired the manager, Earl Jenkins, because of an old beef she had with him that started at one of Big Daddy's annual Great Adventures trips when Earl embarrassed her in front of a group of girls by calling her "a conceited chicken head, super-duper hood rat." She replaced him by moving Sharlene Harper, the storage clerk, up to the manger position. At the Pitkin Avenue store, she removed Helen, and put her home-girl Pauline in her place.

Helen was so furious that she told Baby Doll straight to her face, "Don't let this position you got blind you to the reality that the same people you meet going up are the same ones you'll meet on the way down."

Baby Doll didn't catch it because Helen's tone was too smooth and kind. "Helen, I'm not doing this because of a personal beef with you. Pauline is college-educated in business management. She got an associate's degree in business, and I believe she can help make this store better."

"You saying I wasn't doing a good job?" Helen's anger was gradually displaying itself. "Big Daddy didn't feel I wasn't doing a good job? And I been running this store damn near for the last decade."

"Helen, please don't take it like that. What I'm going to do with you is put you to work at the store over on Knickerbocker Avenue. I think you'll be better—"

"Why don't you put Pauline in the Knickerbocker store, or the one on Broadway and Myrtle?"

Baby Doll couldn't tell her that Pauline refused those positions because they were too far from her home. "Helen, I'm sorry, but I have to make this call, and I hope and pray that you understand, and continue working for the company."

Helen rolled her eyes, sucked her teeth, and ended up accepting the job relocation. Baby Doll saw the hatred resonating from Helen and made a notation to keep an eye on her.

Baby Doll dove so deeply into the businesses' affairs that she dropped out of college in order to dedicate all of her time toward running the businesses. Although she had promised Big Daddy that she would get a college degree and that she wouldn't drop out, the fact remained that she couldn't do her best handling the businesses while being distracted with college; this excuse prevented the guilt from beating her up too badly, since it made sense, and she rationalized that it was in the name of building the Youth Employment Program.

About three weeks later, in the month of March, Baby Doll and Preacher were at the Fifty-sixth Street club, discussing matters relevant to the night's business. Baby Doll was sitting at a table next to the stage, while Preacher sat across from her.

Baby Doll decided to change the topic. She'd noticed Preacher seemed to be upset about everything; it was apparent that he was harboring some animosity toward her, and it was also obvious that if she didn't have him as a friend, there was a good chance she wasn't going to be successful. She just hoped she didn't have to give him a piece of this young pussy to keep him in line. "Hey, Preacher. Can I ask how you got that name?"

He looked at her and saw she was being nosy. "I used to be a preacher. That's kinda obvious. I grew up in a very religious family."

There was an intense silence.

Baby Doll saw she was going to have to pry a casual conversation out of him, and figured she might as well step to her business. "Why do you hate me so much, Preacher? I see the way you look at me. When I first meet you years ago, you didn't seem like you disliked me. But now, it's plain as day." She knew it may have had something to do with her conning money out of guys and he and Big Daddy having to come behind her and clean up. "I need to know what made you get on some stuff with me?"

Preacher was surprised by her straightforwardness. "Hate is a very strong word. There ain't a lot folks I can honestly say I hate, and you're definitely not one of those people I hate. I don't hate you, Baby Doll. In fact, I like you a lot. I'm just not the kind of person that show affection like Big Daddy would do. My patience levels are shot, and I don't tolerate bullshit around me."

"You think I'm bullshitting you?"

Preacher sighed, "Did I say that?"

"You implied it. I know you think I'm one of them gold-digging hood rats who's out to get paid by any means possible. Yeah, I will admit I love money. But I loved Big Daddy more. He gave me a life, and I would never betray him. I'm coming at you like this, Preacher, because I'm no dummy. I need you in order to complete Big Daddy's works."

"If this is about my telling Tiffany not to give those papers to the lawyer when you told her to give them, bear in mind, Baby Doll, that I've been running this club for a good minute. I know the ins-and-outs while you're here learning."

"No, Preacher, this has nothing to do with that one incident." Baby Doll said. "Come on, let's keep it real. You ain't feelin' me for some other reason, and you know it." She rode the silence for a moment. "It's probably hard for you to have a woman calling the shots, especially a real young woman, but I didn't ask for this, Preacher, and you know it. Big Daddy knew that it was time to pass this thing on to someone young, and since I was the only one to step up, he chose me. No disrespect, but you're way over the retirement age, so he did what any wise man would do, train somebody young to carry on. Preacher, please, try to understand that we both gave Big Daddy our word that we would keep this Youth Employment Program going. In order for us to do that, we both need to be on the same page."

"Feels like we're on the same page to me."

Baby Doll shook her head with frustration and said softly "I would like to be your friend, Preacher, kinda like the way you and Big Daddy were." She put on her sad eyes. "I'm lost without you, Preacher, and I'm asking that you hold me down. I need you to have my back. I can feel your tension, and I know I can't do this Youth Program with you working against me."

Preacher sighed. *This little conniving bitch is good*, he thought as she shifted in his seat. *She got game extraordinaire!* He wanted to put her ass through the wash, but doing that, he knew, he would be hurting Big Daddy, and that was something he couldn't live with. He felt himself being pulled in opposite directions. He would ride with her, but in the meantime, he was going to let her know what the real world was all about. "You got a deal, Baby Doll. I'll be easy, and I got your back. But you need to be forewarned that this

Youth Employment Program ain't no walk in the park. I know you probably wondering why Big Daddy didn't turn that task over to me. I'm still alive, and I damn near helped him build it up to where it is now. I know I probably should'nt be telling you this, but I believe it'll be good for you, because then you'll be able to make well-informed decisions when it's time to make them."

Baby Doll sensed he was winding up for one of those negative mudslinging temper tantrums Big Daddy thoroughly warned her would come. She buckled up and braced herself.

"I ride with this program for one reason and one reason only, because I believed in what Big Daddy was trying to do, and I gave him my word. But if it was up to me, and if I had to put up with all the hell that Big Daddy was catching day in and day out, I wouldn't do it. My whole life I can remember only one time when I wasn't betrayed and didn't get stabbed in the back. I went to prison for twenty years for a murder I didn't do, because I saved another Black man's life and he turned around and took my life. Check this, years ago, this brother I grew up with had robbed some drug dealers. They were going to murder his black ass, as sure as shit stinks. Because I knew this cat and knew he was smoking crack and made a mistake while under the influence of that shit, I stepped up and prevented the drug dealers from killing him. At the time I was in the drug game, and I had a team of some serious brothers."

He drew in a deep breath and let it out slowly. "I put my whole team in danger saving this chump and even ended up paying the five thousand dollars he stole right out of my own pocket. But the drug dealers wanted blood, they wanted the money and to break him up real bad, and again, I wouldn't let them. So, we came to a compromise. I agreed to pistol-whip him with one of their people's present and after that they would go about their business. So, I pistol-whipped him, made it look good, and I thought that was it. To my surprise, this nigga was walking around harboring animosity because I pistol-whipped him in front of a few people. The next thing I know, I'm sitting up in prison for a homicide I had nothing to do with. Months go by and I'm assuming I'm gonna be all right since I didn't kill nobody. I figured it was just a matter of time before I would be released; this was a mistake and I'll be home soon, I kept telling myself. And when the trial started, guess who comes tipping into the courtroom?" Preacher was waiting for Baby Doll to respond.

"The dude who you saved his life?"

"You goddamn right," Preacher said resoundingly. "That motherfucker got on that stand and lied on me without batting a fuckin' eye." Preacher stared off into nowhere, while shaking his head as if he still couldn't believe that brother did that to him. After a moment he came back. "Even after that, my heart still wasn't hardened enough to stop me from helping others in need. And you know what else, Baby Doll?"

Baby Doll saw he was waiting for a response and said, "What else?"

"Every single person I ever helped, with the exception of one, has stung me, stabbed me in the back, fucked me around, conned me, cut my throat, and now I'm convinced that it is a waste of time helping people, and sad to say, especially other Black people, because they have been the ones who did me the most harm."

"So why did you hang out with Big Daddy all these years, when everything he stood for was about helping?"

"Because Big Daddy was that one person who didn't cross me. And because he proved that there is such a thing as someone with true honor and integrity, I gave my word that I would roll with him. Once I give my word, it will never fail."

Baby Doll saw Preacher was all worked up now, so she decided to change the topic. "I want to share something with you. It's an idea me and my friend Pauline, the one who's handling the Pitkin

Avenue store now, have been talking about. She's an expert with this business stuff. And I was thinking, we should build a firmer foundation with all the businesses, expand as much as possible, maybe even take out a huge loan, focus all our energy on the business aspect first, and then when we have a conglomerate of stores, we can take the Youth Employment Program to a level that will make people all over the city see the value in putting our young folks to work."

Preacher saw everything he just told this broad had gone in one ear and out the other. "So, you're saying, we should put the Youth Employment Program on hold, build up the businesses, and then start back up the Youth Program after we get more businesses?"

"No, we're not going to stop the Youth Employment Program. We'll keep the kids we got, but we'll put a temporary freeze on hiring until we get a firmer foundation and more stores."

As Preacher thought about Baby Doll's plan of action, he suddenly remembered the clause in the will that said if the Youth Employment Program should cease functioning, there would be another aspect of the will that would be unveiled. In this moment he decided it was time for him to take charge. There was no doubt in his mind that Baby Doll was one of the many motherfuckers who had conned, schemed, and fucked good people over.

Ever since he'd known her, she'd been caught up in the world of chasing that dirty dollar. Now, once and for all, he was going to take action. He just hoped Big Daddy would understand. Since she was already trying to undermine the Youth Employment Program with her slick-ass suggestions about building a foundation, it was obvious he would be saving the Youth Program from imminent destruction.

CHAPTER 27

As Preacher was making plans to commence a secret strike against Baby Doll, so was her other enemies. Todd Houston was the most vigilant by far . His wounds were fresh, and he'd lost a significant piece of money. He was the vindictive type by nature and couldn't remember ever allowing anyone to get away with doing something to him. Even as a child he had secretly choreographed an alleged accident on a friend who was nearly killed when a huge piece of concrete fall on his head, because this friend had made fun of him in the presence of a bunch of girls. Just the other day Todd convinced his cousin George to approach a contract killer to do a hit on Baby Doll. The Russian man agreed to do the hit, but the only problem was, the Russian guy was asking for an amount of money that Todd didn't have at the moment. Needless to say, Todd was working diligently to straighten out that problem, and he felt he'd be ready to pay him in full in another month.

In another part of the city, Samson would clearly get the second-place award for the amount of mental and physical energy asserted toward putting Baby Doll's lights out. Once Samson heard the news of Big Daddy's death, he immediately started sending his workers out to find out as much as they could about Baby Doll. Twice they followed her to Big Daddy's old home in Long Island, so as it stood, they were merely waiting for the green light from Samson, who was merely checking everything out to make sure after he murdered Baby Doll that there would be no backlash in anyway.

Even Nicole was still simmering in a blistering hot hatred toward Baby Doll and was still plotting to get her back; she had a new boyfriend who seemed quite impressionable for a gun-toting thug, and she could see in a few more weeks and a few more tumbles in the bed, he would be ready to be sent on a serious mission.

Tera was working on another way of getting Baby Doll back that didn't involve violence. She was planning to hurt her in a way that some would say was the most painful, and that was none other than the infamous attack on the pocketbook.

On the second Saturday of the month of May, Baby Doll stood near the bar in the Fifty-sixth Street nightclub, watching the customers do what she loved to see them do—spend money like there was no tomorrow. Every time Baby Doll saw a bill spring from a wallet or purse, it brought on an instant natural high. A Jaheim song had the joint jumpin', and Baby Doll was rocking to the up-tempo beat, since she utterly loved the brother Jaheim. She'd always said if there was someone she had to marry it would be the Ja. But because marriage was the furthest thing from her mind, this was only girlish mind games. Last month, in April, she had just turned twenty-four, and as far as she was concerned, she way too young to be thinking about settling down, especially since she still hadn't accomplished her ultimate dream yet.

Baby Doll looked over at the entrance to the dance floor and saw Preacher talking to the Bouncer, AJ. She smiled because her little talk with Preacher the other day was producing results. He wasn't as locked jawed with her, and that was a beautiful thing. She was even surprised he agreed to the plan to put a freeze on hiring new kids into the Youth Program and to focus on building more stores. She wondered if Big Daddy would've approved of this move, and immediately knew he wouldn't have tolerated it.

She looked the other way and saw a short woman that could have passed for Tracy's twin. This instantly reminded her of the fact she heard Tracy lost her correction officer's job when she got caught fucking one of the inmates, while also suspected of smuggling in drugs.

Not surprisingly, Tracy was back heavy on drugs, wasn't trying to find another job, and was driving Mildred, Jasmine and Little Rashawn crazy. There was even talk that she was pregnant and was thinking about keeping the baby. Baby Doll shook her head and knew Tracy would never learn and would never change her foul, reckless, and stupid ways.

Baby Doll's glance was pulled to the main entrance when she saw the mystery man from the hospital and Big Daddy's wake entering the club. A panic sensation gripped her mind, and she had to fight to tame the frantic urge to run and hide. With a concentrated struggle, she calmly stepped behind a partition near the bar and watched him. The man was dressed in a remarkably neat black pinstripe suit, and his gestures and mannerism were very business-like, but there was something else that vibrated from this man. Baby Doll's hood senses told her that he was dangerous, and because she didn't know if he as a friend or foe, she didn't know how to respond.

When the man waved to Preacher and he waved back, Baby Doll sighed in relief. He couldn't be too dangerous to her if he knew Preacher, she concluded, as she stepped from behind the partition, catching a suspicious eye from the bartender named Rob. She noticed the man instantly saw her and he headed straight toward her. As he swaggered toward her, he stared at her with those beaming, brown, no no-nonsense eyes. Her heart leaped almost into her throat. Her eyes almost told on her and she had to blink away the terror-stricken reaction in them. When he sat at a vacant stool in front of the bar, Baby Doll sighed again. But she saw it wasn't over because he was still staring at her. She realized if he didn't look so serious she would've stepped to him and checked his ass about screwing her like that. All that reckless eyeballing shit he was assaulting her with was fucking with her nerves. She turned away hoping he would get the message. A moment later, she turned back and saw, even as he ordered a drink, he was still staring at her.

Baby Doll eased away, sneaking peeks in back of her and, sure enough, the man was still staring her down. This whole exchange was scaring her silly even though he apparently knew Preacher, and hopefully Big Daddy.

Ten minutes later Baby Doll was in the office waiting for Preacher to arrive. She had instructed Karen to tell Preacher she needed to see him in the main office, and to let him know it was an emergency. Baby Doll was pacing with her mind running wild. All the people she robbed were in her thoughts. She wondered was it worth stealing those people's money, and for some odd reason she still felt it was definitely worth it. In fact, if she could do it again, she'd robbed each and every one of them for a whole lot more.

Baby Doll was pacing nervously as Preacher entered and said, "What's happening?" His eyes were wide with deep concern. "What's up?"

"There's a man in here staring me down, and—and I think he's up to no good. I want to know who he is?" Baby Doll said excitedly. "He's wearing the black pen stripe suit; he came in about twenty minutes ago and you and him waved at each other. Who is he?"

Preacher looked at her strangely. "Why you all crazy like this? What else happened? He looked at you and that's it?"

"I saw him at the hospital when Big Daddy was there, and he was even staring me down then. He did the same thing at Big Daddy's wake. Who the fuck is he?"

Preacher sat on the edge of the desk and said, "His name is Sweet Charlie."

"Sweet Charlie? He's a pimp?"

Preacher shook as head very seriously. "Ohhh, he ain't no pimp. He's far from that."

"With a name like Sweet Charlie and the clothing he wears, it ain't hard to tell. Who is he? How you know him? Did he know Big Daddy?"

"Calm down, Baby Doll. Damn, girl, you act like the man is here to hurt you or something." He thought about that and instantly wondered if he was here to hurt her. She'd been fucking around with some high-powered folks, and Sweet Charlie was strictly about money. As Charlie would say, if a customer could pay, then he could always play. He sighed, hoping that wasn't the case. "Calm your nerves, Baby Doll. I'm sure he wouldn't be staring you down if he were here on business. That's what he does for a living, but I can assure you he ain't here for you."

"What does he do for a living?" She didn't have to really be told that he killed people because she just knew this from the dangerous persona he emitted.

"If I tell you, it stays between us." He paused and locked eyes with her. "He's a contract killer. One of the best; he's probably one of the best in the world."

Baby Doll's mind started going to work. She felt her emotions starting to simmer down. All the shit she could do with a real live professional killer was definitely reassuring. Not surprisingly, an old vendetta instantly twinkled back to life, and an onslaught of memories came back to her with the full force of an explosion. There was one person she wanted dead, and suddenly she realized her hatred had not subsided one single drop. She'd been so preoccupied with getting her money right, she almost completely forgotten about the fact that this perverted scum of the earth had to get his justice. She quickly counted in her head how much money she had to burn and knew she could hire Sweet Charlie to once and for all kill Kevin.

Baby Doll locked eyes with Preacher and wondered did he remember all the drama she had went through back in the day as far as Kevin was concerned. There was no doubt Big Daddy sensed what was going on and she knew Preacher may have also detected what was going on as well. "So he kills people for money, huh?"

"That's what contract killers do," Preacher said as he saw this broad was about to go somewhere with this. "So you called me in here because Sweet Charlie was staring you down?"

"I didn't know what this guy was up to," Baby Doll said defensively. "Now that we on the topic, how much would it cost to hire him?"

Preacher smiled, and he saw she wasn't smiling. "Are you serious, Baby Doll?"

"As serious as the cancer that killed Big Daddy." Baby Doll sat behind her desk. "You might as well take a seat, 'cause I know you want to know why."

Preacher sat in the interrogation chair. He wanted to know who this unfortunate soul was.

"I know you remember when Ka-Born came in the Pitkin Avenue store that time, and was going crazy because I broke up with him?" She saw Preacher nod his head. "You probably also remember all the shit he was saying. Remember when he told you and Big Daddy that I was trying to get him to do something to Kevin, because he was raping me?"

Preacher nodded his head. "I know and I remember it clearly." He didn't like the shit Baby Doll was doing when it came down to getting money, but he literally hated child molesters. She now had his full attention.

"I wanted to tell Big Daddy what Kevin was doing to me then, but I knew Big Daddy wasn't going to kill him, so I didn't tell him." Baby Doll sighed as she felt her anger mixed with tears struggling to take hold. "I'm keeping it real with you, Preacher. I wanted that nigga dead for all the times he was raping me. Scaring him up and that type of shit was too good for him. And since Big Daddy wasn't going to do it, I told him Kevin wasn't raping me."

Preacher knew she was dead on point. At that time Big Daddy sensed something was going on, and there was no question, Big Daddy wouldn't have killed Kevin. He probably would've talked to him, scared him half to death, but he wouldn't have laid the proper justice on him. Preacher felt the need to pry now. "So why didn't you tell her mother, or even go to the police? Not that I condone the police thing, but people in a situation like that ain't got much choice, especially when they don't got a father figure around the house."

Baby Doll felt awkward as she constructed her presentation inside of her mind. Now that she looked at the situation from her current age perspective, she realized Kevin had played her. The more the situation worked its way around her mind, the more she concluded that he was gaming her. After a year or two had gone by even if he did go to the police, they wouldn't have believed him.

When she realized she was young and totally ignorant of the law, she stopped being so hard on herself for allowing herself to be abused. "When I was about twelve years old, me and this boy named Kaleek were playing on the roof of the project building we lived in. He would always play these crazy games to try to scare me. He would climb over the railing and walk from one end to the other. He would make me come and look over the railing down at the twenty-story drop, and I would cry."

She took a deep breath and continued, "Then, one day he was walking back and forth over the railing, messing with me, and then he called me over to the railing. He told me that he was going to take his hands off the railing and that I would have to hold his hands, or he would fall. He told me to make sure I hold on tight. He grabbed both my hands with his and he leaned back, and his hand slipped from mine and he fell—" Baby Doll couldn't hold the tears back. "He told me to hold his hands, but he slipped."

Preacher gave her a piece of tissue and realized she wasn't faking these tears. He also saw this shit had the girl traumatized. He realized she was probably holding all that shit inside her for years and it was coming out in other self-destructive ways. A ping of pity started to formulate.

Baby Doll continued. "After that I ran. I was scared, and then Kevin stepped out from the stairwell, and started saying that he saw me kill Kaleek, and that he saw me push him off the roof. He told me don't worry and that he wasn't going to let the police take me to jail if I listen to him, and did what he told me to do. You can imagine what happened from that point forth. Whenever he wanted to fuck me, he simply threw that shit up in my face. I was scared to go to jail, so I did what he told me to do."

Preacher was furious. He was on fire with rage. He sat locked in state of fury. His ferocity was particularly strong because Richie Dorsey, the snitch and liar that sent him to prison for a murder he didn't commit turned out to be a child molester. Upon hearing this he felt his hatred for Richie was instantly transferred to Kevin and didn't see any difference between the two. If he could make sure Kevin got what he deserved, it would be like serving justice on Richie, who disappeared into thin air. "This guy cost a pretty piece of change. With that type of business, you definitely get what your money pay for."

"So about how much you think it'll cost?"

"I could get him down to seventy-five gees."

Baby Doll's eyebrows shot upward. That was a lot of money. But her hatred for Kevin was very strong. "No problem. But I need to be able to hear him beg and suffer. I gotta hear him in pain." She felt embarrassed saying this, since it made her appear sadistic or something. Unfortunately, right now she didn't care what Preacher thought of her, since her psyche was seriously scarred, and she felt the only way it could be healed was to at least hear this perverted son-of-a-bitch in great pain. "I'll pay extra if I got to."

Preacher nodded his head, realizing he received further proof that she was traumatized by those years of sexual abuse. He was reminded of the rumor that his daughter was being molested by one of her mother's boyfriends while he was in prison. He wondered if this was the reason his daughter Tyesha closed him completely out of her life, refusing to even recognize him as her father. It probably was he concluded, and said, "The way Charlie works, he aims to please his customers. When you want this done?"

Baby Doll thought that was a stupid question. She said with an attitude. "Shit, as soon as possible, of course."

Twenty minutes later, Preacher pulled Sweet Charlie to a seclude area in the club and explained the proposition to him. When Preacher offered to introduce him to Baby Doll, Sweet Charlie almost spazzed out on Preacher. Sweet Charlie's voice was cold and callus, as he said, "No, I don't need to meet her! You just make sure she understands that if she every talk about this after this job is complete, she will become my next job."

Preacher visibly grew nervous. He wanted to quickly tell him that he was just the messenger, and to not tear his head off. Preacher was sure there was something else going on with Sweet Charlie and Baby Doll that somebody wasn't telling him about.

By the intense and quite nasty attitude Sweet Charlie displayed, Preacher could see Charlie apparently didn't like Baby Doll.

* * * *

Two weeks later, Kevin exited a nightclub on Saratoga Avenue at about two o'clock in the morning; it was a nice comfortable Friday night in the last week of May. He was drunk and he was on his way to Mildred's apartment. As he pulled out his car keys to his old, beat-up Thunderbird, he noticed someone coming up behind him and he turned.

"Mr. Kevin Brown?" Sweet Charlie said, dressed in typical DT clothing. "I'm Detective Ellis." He showered him the fake badge.

"Yeah, what's up, officer?" Kevin stuttered, struggling to contain his drunkenness.

"There's been a serious incident. Your mother, Mrs. Margaret Brown, was shot and killed not too long ago, and we need you to look at a crime scene."

Kevin nearly collapsed. "Oh, God, no! Who killed my momma!?" He was beyond devastated. "When did it happened?" Kevin was almost hurled into a state of sobriety as his speech became frantic. "Where did—Who was—Did you find whoever did it!?"

"Not yet, but rest assured we're on, sir," Sweet Charlie sounded like the epitome of a cop. "Could you please come with me, sir, "

"But what about my car?"

"My partner will drive it for you." Sweet Charlie waved to his assistant, Tony Tee, an up-and-coming Italian kid striving to become a world-class hit man who Charlie took under the wing on the strength of Tommy Nacerino on behalf of the Mazaratti Crime Family.

He saw Kevin about to protest. "Mr. Brown, you apparently had one too many drinks, sir. There are laws against driving while under the influence as I'm sure you are aware."

Kevin shrugged and followed him to the car.

About a half hour later, Sweet Charlie was behind the wheel of the four-door Ford and Kevin was in the passenger seat crying as the car moved down a secluded back road. Sweet Charlie noticed the turnoff was coming up ahead. It was time to start the torture process. He flicked on the tape recorder. He didn't like recorders when doing hits, but the customer was always right, especially when they were paying for a particular service.

"Hey, listen, ah, Kevin," Sweet Charlie's voice was normal now. "Tell me how it feels to fuck a pretty young girl? You know, the ones when they're about twelve years old? I don't know much about that, being I'm not a child molester and all, so I was just wondering, you know?"

Kevin's heart nearly stopped beating. Sweat instantly oozed from various pores all over his body. "W—What—What are you talking about, Mr. Ellis!? I—I—I wouldn't know nothing about that?" If this was supposed to be small talk he damn sure didn't like it.

"Are you sure? Mr. Brown, I know you wouldn't lie to me, would you?"

Kevin tried to forcefully tame his nervousness as he spoke, "W—Why would I lie to you?"

For the first time, Kevin looked around at the scenery outside the car and noticed they were cruising down a dark, lightless roadway. It looked like they were somewhere upstate. He was so caught up over being told of his mother's death that he wasn't even watching where they were headed. Come to think of it, they were driving for quite some time. "What's going on!? Why you asking me crazy questions like that?"

"I'm just kicking the breeze." Charlie cut his eyes at the Warehouse up ahead. He could now hit him with the whammy. "And Baby Doll told me to let you know that pay-back is a bitch."

Kevin was jolted into a state of panic. He was about try to open the car door and make a run for it but the car came to a skidding, head-jerking halt. When he looked over at the fake DT, he saw the gun. "Please, mister, I didn't do nothing to Baby Doll. She's a liar, man. I swear to God, I didn't do nothing to her."

Suddenly, Tony Tee was standing at the passenger door.

Charlie gave him the head nod, and Tony Tee snatched the door open. He grabbed Kevin by the collar and yanked him out of the car. As Kevin saw his life flashing before his eyes, he decided that he wasn't going to the grave without a fight. Tony Tee slammed him into the side of the car, but Kevin bounced off the impact and took a swing that caught Tony Tee on the jaw.

Sweet Charlie was out the car with lightning speed, smiling with pure pleasure as he saw Kevin swinging and throwing haymakers as if his life depended on it, which it apparently did. He rushed over and stood watching how Tony Tee intended on handling this. Charlie loved the ones that put up a fight, because it made the mission much more interesting and entertaining. Plus, Tony Tee's style was too cocky at times. And for his own good, he needed a rude eye-opening lesson in not underestimating the powers of the human will to survive.

Kevin kept swinging, and pounding at Tony Tee's head, and just as he tried to run, a tremendous blow from Tony Tee dropped him to the floor. Kevin screamed a lung-shattering shriek, "Oh, please, man! Don't kill me!" He was hoping and praying someone heard him.

Tony Tee started stomping a mud hole in Kevin's ass. Charlie stood by grinning deviously as Kevin screamed and hollered.

Five minutes later, Charlie and Tony had Kevin tied down to a wooden chair inside the dilapidated warehouse and were doing things to him that would have sparked an insane jealousy in the best torturers of the Spanish Inquisition. They broke fingers, ripped fingernails from his fingers with a set of pliers and hammered his toes with a construction style sledgehammer. Tony Tee always wanted to see how it would feel to cut off a person's dick and nuts and cram them in the person's mouth. He'd heard people say that particular thing all the time and he figured this was the opportune time to see how it's done.

Kevin unleashed an ear-battering shriek when the huge lock cutter-like scissors severed his manhood. Charlie saw he screamed more out of knowing it had happened as opposed to feeling any pain. On second thought, he realized Kevin probably screamed as loud as he did because Tony dangled his severed sex organs in front of his face just before he crammed them in his mouth.

By the time they started breaking arms and legs, Kevin was no longer conscious. When they threw a bucket of water in his face, and he still refused to fully wake up, Charlie saw they had almost an hour of recording, and concluded the job was complete. He pulled his 9 mm and shot Kevin twice in the head.

About an hour later, Kevin's dead body was completely immersed in an old bathtub full of sulfuric acid. As Kevin's remains bubbled away, Sweet Charlie gave Tony Tee a B-minus grade on this particular hit and immediately pointed out where he went wrong and what areas he had to work on.

CHAPTER 28

Two days later, Baby Doll, Preacher and Tony Tee sat in the Fifty-sixth Street club office listening to Kevin's blood-curdling screams. Baby Doll's thirst for revenge was completely quenched and was being replaced with disgust and sorrow.

"This is the part where we started breaking his toes with a sledgehammer," Tony Tee said nonchalantly as though he was describing a complex component in a business proposal. "The pounding is the sledgehammer; you can hear it in between the screams if you listen closely."

Kevin was hollering with remarkable force.

Baby Doll looked over and saw Preacher was truly in enjoying this; she wanted to tell Tony Tee she heard enough. But, since she'd asked for this she had no choice but to go along. She never realized she wasn't emotional built for this level of torture; looking at Tony Tee she also realized she would be doing herself some good by pretending she was enjoying Kevin's punishment, so as to not make this crazy motherfucker uncomfortable.

When the tape was finished Tony Tee took the tape, Baby Doll paid him the last of the money ($25,000 cash), and Tony Tee disappeared out the door.

"How you feel?" Preacher said with a smile. "That's a chapter in your life you can close for good; those scars are going to finally start to heal."

"You are so right, Preacher. I feel satisfied." She lied, since this was the only logically thing to say.

Preacher stood, about to head for the door. "Don't forget you gotta go to the store on Pitkin and deal with that cat Kendu. As the chief coordinator, it's your job to deal with those kids when they act up. I would do it for you, but I gotta take Gloria to the clinic. You know how it is with us elderly people. We gotta have each other's back in these last days." He exited.

Baby Doll sighed tiredly as she leaned back in the chair. *How the hell did Big Daddy put up with all this madness?* she asked herself for the millionth time. Running the business was one thing, but also running the Youth Employment Program was crazy. These teens were literally giving her high blood pressure. Every goddamn day it was something—fights, stealing, failing to show up at work, lateness, and breaking damn near all the rules they promised to obey in order to be a part of the program. Baby Doll glanced at her watch, saw it was eleven o'clock, and decided to get moving. The ride to Brooklyn was going to be an onerous journey since she was still tired from not getting enough sleep last night. The noises she heard last night kept her up half the night, and she noticed a royal blue car with two men inside it had been following her for the last week or so. At first she brushed it off as Sweet Charlie checking to make sure she was a legitimate customer seeking his services, but the more she thought about that excuse, the more she realized that didn't make sense and started wondering if this car following her had something to do with the folks she robbed. Maybe they were about to strike.

As she exited the club, Baby Doll decided it was time to make arrangements to move out of the Long Island house.

＊ ＊ ＊ ＊

Preacher pulled his white Buick Regal into the parking space across the street from Tera's Boutique store. He got out of the car, crossed the street, and entered the store.

Two minutes later, Preacher sat comfortably in the chair with a grape soda in his hand, while Tera sat on the edge of her desk with her arms folded across her bosom.

"Can I rely on you, Preacher?" Tera said, straight to the point. "You know this bitch ain't trying to do nothing with that youth program. That bitch is a fuckin' con artist."

"Now, you know I gave Big Daddy my word that I'd watch over that girl. I agree with you that she's got her own agenda, but Big Daddy was confident that she would come through. I don't see how or why he would say that, but he was sure that Baby Doll would eventually come around. You're asking me to put a monkey wrench in the program, which is almost the same as asking me to destroy the program—"

"No, I'm not asking you to destroy the program. I'm telling you help me get rid of this bitch, and I'll take over the Youth Employment Program, that's what I'm saying. I don't know why the fuck Big Daddy didn't give the damn program to me anyway. I been with him day one he started his businesses, holding this store down—"

"Tera, you know why he didn't give you the spot. Don't even go there with me." It turned his stomach when people tried to make themselves the victim when the situation was far from it. "No person in their right mind is gonna turn over something as important as this when the job requires a certain type of discipline and dedication—"

"You saying I ain't got discipline!? I'm not dedicated!?"

Preacher was becoming extremely pissed off. He hated when folks caught a convenient case of selective amnesia. He sighed impatiently.

This exchange was bringing back memories that used to have him very bitter. "Listen, Tera, I didn't come here to talk about things that's gonna get a bunch of emotions all flared up, but the facts are the facts. You never treated Big Daddy the way he should've been treated." He saw her about to blow up, but quickly continued. "I know you don't wanna hear that, but you made the bed and now you gotta lay in it. When Big Daddy was in prison you and your whole family treated the man like he was dead. I guess in ya'll's mind he was dead since he wasn't there. The old 'out of sight, out of mind' thing, you know. Never came to see him, no letters, nothing! You didn't give a fuck about him until he was in a position where you could get something out of him."

His anger was about to reach a boil. "Even after all the abuse y'all inflicted on the man, he still treated y'all good, and then you go turn around and abandoned the man again, while he's on his death bed. Them little jive-ass visits while he was in the hospital spoke way louder than the words you talking now, Tera. When you treat good people like that, it comes back to bite you on the ass. Don't you think he should have some serious trust issues with you?"

Tera was about to blow up; she was huffing and puffing; the fury had her words stumbling around inside her head, and the words wouldn't come out, since what Preacher said was the truth.

Preacher saw he had just broken her down completely with that heavy blow; her whole world was shattered and apparently saturated with guilt. He decided to build her back up, the way Big Daddy always did when he ripped into folks with the painful truth. "Now, listen to this, Tera. I ain't judging you, and that stuff is all in the past as far as I'm concerned."

He locked eyes with her. "I understand the bad vibe you getting from Baby Doll, because I got my own doubts about her." He sighed reluctantly, since after the situation with Kevin he was going to give Baby Doll the benefit of the doubt and hold off with an attack to see if her business plan would work, and to see if she would really keep her promise to Big Daddy. Now, he was being pulled back to his initial position. He was getting too old for all this shit, he realized as he sighed real hard. "I'll get with you on this thing."

Tera smiled animatedly; her reaction had a true wickedness to it that made him realized he had better fling in a stipulation to be safe.

"I'll roll with you, but only under one condition." He saw her smiled faded like butter on a blazing hot skillet. "It's nonnegotiable, it's a take-it-or-leave-it offer . . ."

* * * *

Baby Doll stomped inside the Pitkin Avenue store furious that she had to deal with another belligerent teen that was showing out. Baby Doll approached Pauline.

Pauline tilted her head upward with a gapped-tooth smile and said, "Thank you for coming, Baby Doll." She liked being the boss, but hated when she had to discipline people, especially these young, wild teens that didn't mind playing with street sweepers and other big automatic weapons. "I've tried everything in my powers to show this kid that if he do the right thing I will be there for him."

Baby Doll was about to yell to Kendu in the back, but noticed there were several customers in the store. She stomped toward the back. When she entered the storage room she saw Kendu sitting watching TV, while the other teens, Darlene and Shaneka were pressing clothes.

"What the hell is this?" Baby Doll said with her hands on her hips.

Kendu jumped to his feet, rushed over to the table stacked with jackets, and started assembling them. "I needed a break."

Baby Doll saw this fool was a lost cause. He had literally gave a whole new definition to the word problematic, and it was clear that to keep Kendu as a worker would be to slit the store's wrist, because he was a leech, a lair, and loved to steal.

"Kendu, I need to talk to you in private." The urge to blow his foul ass up in from of the other workers was strong, but Big Daddy warned her to never do such a thing. "Come with me to the office."

A minute later, Baby Doll stood near the desk while Kendu stood near the water cooler looking at her with an attitude.

"Do you really want to work here, Kendu?" Baby Doll said. "Your attitude and your refusal to stop stealing tells me you don't."

"Yeah, I wanna work here. If I didn't I would've been broke out by now."

"So why are you still stealing from the store? I told you the last time if it happened again I would—"

"I didn't steal shit! Who told you that shit!? Pauline? She don't—"

"Pauline didn't tell me anything! I saw you with my own damn eyes," Baby Doll went to the video recorder on her desk and hit the play button. The TV that sat across from the player came to life.

When Kendu saw himself putting on a pair of pants, and shirt, and then put on his own clothes over the stolen items, he was speechless. It was evident there was a hidden camera in the storage room. "Hold up, that shit is illegal, you didn't get my permission to film me. I ain't stupid, you can't do that."

"Well, sue me, Kendu. You know what this means? This is the third time you stole from the store, and I gotta let you go. Three times you refused—"

"Fuck you, bitch!" Kendu shouted with venom. "I don't need this—"

Baby Doll shot toward him with her finger damn near touching his nose. "You better watch your mouth, motherfucker, before I break your ass the fuck up in here!" She suddenly remembered Big Daddy told her to never react like this, and it was always better to kill kids with kindness and to show them that they could get more by being respectful. But, right now, Kendu had hit a major nerve, and she wasn't about to coddle this thieving-ass, ungrateful bastard who was too stupid and ignorant to see when people were trying to help him. "You're gonna respect me, Kendu." She saw Kendu was shook to the bone. "And if you think I'm some kinda pushover, or some soft-ass nerdy motherfucker, then I'll show you what I do to motherfuckers that wanna find out the hard way."

Kendu bitched up just like Baby Doll thought he would.

Five minutes later, Baby Doll was escorting Kendu out the front door. Moments ago, she had watched him pack his belongings, to make sure he didn't steal anything else.

As Kendu exited the door, he locked eyes with Baby Doll and mumbled under his breath, *you think you one of them tough bitches, huh? I wanna see how tough you are when I step to your ass with my peoples.* He bopped down the street, already planning how he was going to rob Baby Doll at gun point the first chance he got.

After Kendu was gone, Baby Doll went and stood next to Pauline, who was lounging behind the cashier counter on a stool. Natasha, the cashier, stood a few feet away, looking nervously at Baby Doll, hoping she didn't get fired as well.

Pauline saw Baby Doll looked stressed. "You look like you need to vent, girl. Come on, let's go to the office."

A minute later, Baby Doll sat behind the desk while Pauline sat in the chair on the side. They were sipping on ice-cold ginger ale.

"I don't know why you put up with this shit, Baby Doll. Kendu's ass was supposed to been fired the first time he got caught stealing." Pauline sipped and sat the can down on the desk.

Baby Doll couldn't have agreed more, but she was working from a game plan constructed by Big Daddy Blue. "Yeah, you right, but I'm trying to do this the way Big Daddy Blue asked me to do it.

He was adamant about giving these kids out here a chance. Going above and beyond for these kids out here."

"Like I said, Baby Doll, some of them—actually a whole lot of them—you can't help, and Kendu is a prime example."

Baby Doll wanted to say amen to that comment because Pauline sure wasn't lying. "I don't know how Big Daddy did it. These are some of the foulest, most ungrateful, and treacherous folks I have ever seen. It's the dudes that are the worse, and they're the ones that need help the most. Nine out of ten of these young brothers take a job here and come in with the sole intentions of stealing everything that's not nailed down to the floor."

"Yeah, and that's why I've been telling you that if this company is going to make it we are going to have to tighten up all those loose ends. The last time I looked at the company records, Baby Doll, man, I couldn't believe how much merchandise is disappearing each month. The sad thing is that when I compared these company records with the records when Big Daddy was in charge, this problem didn't exist. Either the workers are assuming they can take advantage of you, or there is an internal conspiracy to undermine what you're doing, girl."

Baby Doll felt her angry proliferating at the speed of light. She hated when people tried to take advantage of her, especially when she was trying to be nice. "I don't know what I'm going to do, Pauline. But I will say this much, in a minute if motherfuckers don't get their shit together I'ma start firing everything moving in these stores and get a team I can trust."

"Now, you're talking like a smart businesswoman. There are people out there willing to work without stealing and fucking you around. It's sad to say you might be better off not fucking with Black folk, because they the ones that will fuck you over the minute they think you about to get a little more than them." Pauline thought about the whole scenario, and wondered why Blacks were so cruel to each other. "I can feel what Big Daddy was trying to do, but in this day and age, with all this consumerism and this me, me, me, and the I-gotta-get-mine mentality that's messing up our people's minds, I can't see it working. Not to mention, we spend more time murdering, maiming, and mistreating each other that we ain't got time to help each other. Even the Church, which used to be our strongest institution of power, has failed us miserably."

"Yeah, the church ain't what it used to be, and it has definitely fell to the waste-side," Baby Doll said, shaking her head, remembering the stuff she had read in history books about Martin Luther King Jr. and the many other Civil Rights leaders who had their roots within the church. "I approached about a dozen ministers, preachers, reverends about giving a helping hand with this Youth Employment Program, and they've been giving a whole lot of lip serve with no action behind it."

Pauline took another sip of the soda, sat the can down, covered her mouth as the silent burp escaped through her lips, and then said, "You said Big Daddy has been doing this Youth Employment thing for years, and what came out of it so far? Even you said most of the kids in the program ended up twisted."

"Not all of them; I'm not twisted. Big Daddy used to always say that if he could just save one, it would mean the program worked. That one life he saved was enough to make it all worth the fight." Baby Doll thought about all the hell she'd been going through, and realized Big Daddy was a better person than she would ever be because she didn't see the logic in going through all this just to save one person. Lately she'd been counting her money and realized she was losing ground with respect to her dream. The last time she looked at the company's gross income, she saw that if she could step up her game, she could make her dream a reality. She sighed and forced the thought to the back of her mind. Then, suddenly, she remembered the car following her. And was glad she had Pauline's ear. "Check this, Pauline, I gotta get outta that house in Long Island, and I'm gonna need you to talk to your homegirl who got that real estate spot."

"Whenever you ready, just say the word," Pauline saw her assumptions were correct—there was something else going on, and it apparently had nothing to do with firing Kendu. "Girl, what's up with the house in Long Island? Are you all right?"

Baby Doll knew she couldn't go too deep into the issue about the car following her. "Let's just say I got some beefs that tells me I should play it safe by getting away from that house." Baby Doll sipped on her soda and started daydreaming again.

Pauline sipped her drink, wondering if the time was right to present her proposal on how she and Baby Doll could literally make millions off of these businesses. Earnest Hudson was very serious about buying these six stores and four nightclubs that were now in Baby Doll's name. She was still in shock by the fact Mr. Hudson had indicated that he would give Baby Doll four million dollars for the stores and the clubs, and if she could convince Baby Doll to sell them, she would get a $150,000 commission and finder's fee for ensuring that the deal went through. For some unspecified reason, Mr. Hudson was bent on believing she had to do it in a secretive way, since he felt Big Daddy had made it to whereas she wouldn't sell the businesses for any reason; her instructions from Mr. Hudson were to use "persuasive tactics" to convince her. Pauline took another sip of the soda as she stared at Baby Doll. The more she looked at the situation, the more she realized Baby Doll wasn't stressed-out enough yet. She would have to hold off for few more weeks before she hit her with the proposal.

Reluctantly, Pauline decided to go back to the drawing board and come up with some foolproof ways to make Baby Doll see that these stores and clubs weren't worth all the headaches.

CHAPTER 29

Two weeks later, Victor Bolinsky sat behind the wheel of his souped-up black Mustang watching a very nice house about fifty yards away. He was parked on Elmhurst Street in the town of Maplewood, New Jersey. It was about nine o'clock in the evening, the sun had set some time ago, and he had been sitting here for about a half hour. The late June weather made this particular stakeout much more bearable in comparison to those during the winter months. He lit up a Marlboro cigarette and smoked as he watched and waited.

About five minutes later, Victor saw a blue Acura pull into the driveway of the house, and park, Then Baby Doll got out of the car. Victor smiled as he snuffed out the cigarette. As Baby Doll opened the door to her small one-family house, Victor pulled his silencer-equipped Glock 9 mm, checked it once again, and tucked it in his waist. Thank goodness tonight will be the night he would finally complete this hit; he could sure use the second half of that money. This particular contract hit was one he'd never forget, being that it was a serious pain in his ass. This chick Breana, Baby Doll, was like a greasy spoon (she was hard to keep hold of).

About two weeks ago, Victor recalled how he had tracked Baby Doll to a house in Long Island, and just when he was about to complete the job, she moved. After some more searching she ended up at this new place. As if things couldn't get any worse, she had purchased the home and then didn't show up here for a whole week. After he tracked her down some more and found out she was staying in a hotel, she shifted her schedule again and was now staying at this home. Because Victor was very serious about doing a professional job in accordance with the rules of the game, he didn't run up on her in a public place and start shooting.

A job of that nature was restricted to targets that couldn't be hit in their homes since they had an army of other fellow killers protecting them. A simple job like this mandated that it be done as Victor intended to do it; sneak inside the target's home and kill him or her nice and quietly.

Victor glanced at his Timex wristwatch. He would give her some time to settle down, let her get nice and comfy, and then he would put her beddy-by, permanently. He wondered what this pretty little girl did to get George's cousin, Mr. Houston, all uptight, especially mad enough to pay one hundred thousand dollars to snuff her out. In his line of work, it was considered taboo to ask, so he never did, but always wondered what made people mad enough to pay large sums of money to smoke someone.

Victor looked through his rearview mirror and thought he saw movement. After a moment of scanning the area, he brushed it off as a stray animal or something. He looked at his watch again and decided it was time to put the clincher on this deal. He opened the door of his car stepped out. Just as he was closing the door in such a way as to prevent making any noises, he heard a car door behind him, but across the street, open. He turned and saw two men walking briskly toward him. One of them had his gun drawn. Victor was about to reach.

"Easy, Victor," Sweet Charlie said. "It's family."

Victor adjusted his eyes and saw it was Sweet Charlie. His heart started pounding; his instincts told him Sweet Charlie didn't show up at times like this unless he was putting in work. He wanted to reach for his weapon so bad, but the White guy with him apparently had the drop on him. He decided to play it wisely; talk and see what's going on. Maybe he wasn't the target.

Sweet Charlie got right up on Victor and patted him on the shoulder, "Let's sit in the car. We need to talk." Sweet Charlie went to the passenger side, while Tony Tee stood screw-facing Victor, waiting for him to get in the car.

Sweet Charlie was waiting on the passenger side, "Come on, Victor." He sighed impatiently. "If you were my target, would I be here talking to you?"

Victor realized he was absolutely correct. He opened the driver side door, slid in, and opened the passenger side door. Charlie slid into the passenger seat, and Tony Tee sat behind Victor.

"Well, I'm sorry to drop in like this, Victor," Sweet Charlie said seriously. "But you gotta drop this track." He saw Victor about to protest and cut him off quickly. "The rest of your money is right here."

Tony Tee dropped a wad of money next to Victor and he picked it up.

"I'm spending all this valuable time of mine talking to you, Victor, because I now need you to do something for me." Sweet Charlie smiled. "And this is an offer I don't think you wanna refuse."

Victor looked up from counting the money and knew where this was going. "Listen, Charlie, I'm just trying to make a living as best I can; I don't step on toes. If I had known this target was off limits I would've never—"

"Relax, Victor, we all I know the rules quite well," Charlie sighed and said, "The person who put the track on Miss Winbush, I believe his name is Todd Houston. I want him to become your target. You got the money, but you haven't killed anyone for it. This'll straighten out that problem." Sweet Charlie smiled.

Victor stared at Sweet Charlie for a moment and realized if he said no, his henchman in back of him would blow his top clean off. Victor smiled broadly, because it really didn't matter which way it went, especially since he'd gotten his money. "Sweet Charlie, you got yourself a deal." He reached over and shook Charlie's hand.

* * * *

A week later, Baby Doll was exiting the Fulton Street main office, furious with all the crazy things that were suddenly happening. Everything seemed to be going wrong all at once; the delivery trucks weren't making the deliveries to the stores, whole shipments of clothing were disappearing, kids were quitting left and right, she'd gotten in two fights with store managers, and even Preacher was of no help since he said he had to take a few weeks off because his high blood pressure was acting up. Baby Doll felt steam sizzling off of her and realized if she didn't get a minute to breath she was going to short circuit, blow a fuse, and explode in any moment.

As she stomped toward her car, on her way to the Flatlands Avenue store, Baby Doll saw a group of unfamiliar thugs hanging out on the corner. Every single one of them was a complete stranger, and for some reason she felt an odd premonition, almost as if her intuition was talking to her, telling her to watch out. Suddenly, she heard the sound of running feet in the opposite direction she was looking; she turned with flinching speed and saw another unfamiliar thug with a handkerchief covering his face in train robber fashion. He had a gun in his hand.

"Don't play yourself, lady," The masked teen said. "Give me the money, and anything else you got that's worth something."

Baby Doll saw the other thugs run toward her.

"Give me the fuck money!" The masked thug shouted.

Baby Doll was so furious right about now she stared the kid in the eyes and her hatred boiled to a level that almost made her head spin. She was pulled out of the trance when one of the arriving teens snatched her purse, while another pushed her away from the car.

As they checked her handbag, confiscating everything of value, including her car keys, Baby Doll stood staring at them, imaging her tearing each of their heads off and spitting down their necks.

The teens jumped in her car, flung her a bag at her, and screeched away. Baby Doll stood watching in a trance as a few pedestrians ran over asking if she was all right. She watched her car hit the corner on two wheels and disappeared.

The next day, Baby Doll and Pauline were talking and decided it was time to take off a week and go to the Bahamas. After the robbery/carjacking Baby Doll knew if she didn't clear her mind from all the turmoil of running the businesses and the Youth Program in a very significant way she would go crazy.

After the robbery-carjacking, the police were angrier at Baby Doll than she was at the teens that robbed her because she was totally uncooperative with them. She refused to go to the police station to look at mug shots, made it clear she wasn't pressing charges, and pointed out that all the bystanders should have "mind their fuckin' business." The one thing she learned from Big Daddy, and she was going to stay the course with that particular advice, was to never put a Black man in prison when you can find a way to deal with the situation without bringing the police in. Baby Doll was going to get Preacher to look into it, since it didn't make any sense for her to get robbed when everybody knew she was basically Big Daddy Blue's daughter.

After she spoke to Preacher and his response was quite lukewarm and she instantly detected his foot-dragging response, she knew it was time to start watching her so-called associates. She sensed that robbery might have been an inside job, a setup coming from the very people who were supposed to be having her back.

In any event, Baby Doll cleared her mind and got on the jet along with Pauline on their way to the Bahamas. To pay for this vacation, Baby Doll dipped into her stash and also the company's money, and decided to do it up, because when she got back, she was going to be a whole new person. There was going to be a whole lot of house cleaning, and her new private Investigator, Tyrone Wilson, told her what she'd suspected he would, there was going to be some long faces when the smoke cleared.

Baby Doll sat comfortable in her window seat of the plane; she and Pauline had a short debate over who would get the window seat, and once Baby Doll pointed out that she was still the boss, since the company was paying for a large portion of both of their costs, Pauline quickly zipped it.

Baby Doll had also decided to stop the annual Six Flags Great Adventures trips that Big Daddy sponsored for all the kids that worked for him as a back-to-school treat. She rationalized that none of these kids deserved to be rewarded when they were sabotaging and undermining her, when all she was doing was trying to keep Big Daddy's dream alive. She didn't fully understand why she didn't even feel a ping of guilt when she took this action. The way she was able to neutralize this invading emotion with a small struggle made her realize she was becoming an expert at tucking emotions away, deep down into crevices in the far regions of her mind.

Baby Doll pulled out the paper she purchased from the newsstand. She read the first article about Congress's efforts to pass another Terrorism bill.

After reading two more articles, she saw the small article that said, RECORD PRODUCER FOUND DEAD IN PARK AVENUE CONDO. Baby Doll read further and saw the name Todd Houston, and almost passed out; her eyes nearly popped out of their sockets as she continued reading the entire article. The article said he was shot in the back of the head execution-style. The article went on to state that authorities believe Mr. Houston's death may be connected to the very large sums of money he transferred from his account to other accounts. Baby Doll was sweating bullets by the time she read the article a second time.

Pauline saw Baby Doll's disturbed state. "Damn, girl, what the fuck are you reading that got you looking all crazy like that?"

"I'm cool, girl," she turned the pages before Pauline saw the article. "I was thinking about how all this shit with the stores and clubs are suddenly happening. I guess I'm still shocked by what's going on."

Later that evening, Baby Doll and Pauline were on the dance floor of an outside club that had Palm trees and exotic bushes all over the place. Baby Doll was dancing with a muscle-bound dream man named Trevor, who was an image right out of a Hollywood movie. Pauline had a similar dance companion named Ronnie, but he was nowhere near as handsome as Trevor. They were all dancing to a hard-hitting calypso tune that was heavy on the drums and congos.

Baby Doll kept cutting her eyes down to Trevor's manhood, and wondered if that huge bulge down there was really all of him. There was no question she was good and horny. She been without a man so long, she felt her body was about to forget how it felt to have a man up inside of her. Her only source of sexual gratification came from her dildo, which earned the name Big Spike, since he never missed the marks and always hit the G-spot when they supposed to be hit.

Although Baby Doll used Big Spike sparingly, she knew there was nothing like the real thing.

As the up-tempo dance song faded to a stop and a slow song took its place, and Trevor embraced her, Baby Doll felt herself becoming moist. His touch caused silent fire sparks to tumble through her body. Even his strong manly smell was firing up her juices. There was nothing more relieving to an emotional-ridden mind than sex, she reminded herself as she allowed Trevor's hands to roam down to her backside. There wasn't any sense in pretending it wasn't going down, since this was what she and Pauline came down here for. The last time she came there with Samson and saw all these super-fine men, she vowed the next time she stepped foot on this island she wouldn't be accompanied by a male companion, and she would definitely find out how old Stella got her groove back when she would follow in her footsteps.

"What are your plans for tthe rest of the evening?" Trevor whispered into Baby Doll's ear; his deep, Jamaican accent was smoother than the actor's voice in the commercials. "I'm free if you'd like to hang out more."

Baby Doll felt his voice vibrate through her body. She said promiscuously, "I was hoping we could hang out a lot more."

They both received the confirmation they both were looking for, and two hours later, Baby Doll and Trevor had entered Baby Doll's Hotel room, while Pauline and Ronnie entered Pauline's room.

Baby Doll and Trevor went straight to the business. There was no need in prolonging the inevitable. Baby Doll was fully prepared for anything Trevor wanted to do; she had condoms and dental dams, and if Trevor turned out to be one of those supersonic sexual maniac-rude-boys that could fuck for days, she had more than enough supply to handle anything he could dish out.

Since she was backed up with an overflow of sexual juices, Baby Doll took the initiative, and started kissing him.

Trevor, from that point forth, took full control.

Baby Doll savored every moment of the clothes-peeling-off ceremony that Trevor had apparently perfected as if it was a craft. Baby Doll concluded it was more like an occupation as he started massaging her body as if he was getting her ready for a very special event.

After the body massage, she saw Trevor wasn't unlike most men; he had to eat first, and she had no beef with that. Trevor put the latex covering over Baby Doll's womanhood and allowed his tongue to do a dance that made Baby Doll's toes curl up, her body thrust outward for more, and relieved her mind of all stress.

When he mounted her ten minutes later, Baby Doll's womanhood gobbled up half of Trevor's manhood with ease; when he hinted at putting it all inside of her, and Baby Doll felt him hitting internal parts that weren't normally touched, she had second thoughts of letting him do his thing. She placed the palm of her hand on his chest and he went easy. Since he had both of her legs propped on the inner crevices of his elbows, Baby Doll knew she was getting full access to all of Trevor's ten inches. As her mind swirled with pleasure, she saw Trevor was in just as much delight. Ten minutes into their sex dance, Baby Doll looked down and saw she was taking the whole ten inches; her mind was wild with ecstasy. The mere act of looking at the dick going in and out made her blast off another nut.

In accordance with his apparent professional lovemaking abilities, Trevor accelerated his pumping motion until he was certain Baby Doll finished her business.

Baby Doll wanted to scream with sheer elation when she saw Trevor was a long-distance lover, since his Johnson was still rock-hard. Right on this thought, Trevor gently navigated her onto her knees and went in doggy style. Baby Doll could feel her entire womb was blazed with a fiery sensation of rapture, and within minutes she couldn't help but to scream with joy as she came again. Then, five minutes later, she started coming again, and this time Trevor came along with her. The louder Trevor screamed, Baby Doll noticed, the more it made her nut more delightful. There was always something in knowing she could pull a moan and groan out of a man; it gave her a sense of control and power, and let her know her stuff was octane.

After both of their explosive orgasms subsided, Baby Doll and Trevor lay together, making small talk, smiles riveted on their faces.

Two days later, Baby Doll and Pauline sat in cushioned lounge chairs near the beach, talking and enjoying the beaming hot sun. They both had drinks in their hands and were dressed in bathing suits.

"Girl, tell me this ain't the life," Pauline said, staring at the bunch of people playing in the water. "This is something we need to do as often as possible." She could still feel Ronnie inside of her.

"You ain't lying," Baby Doll said. "I feel like a hundred pounds of stress has been purged from my system."

"That was all of them backed-up nuts that came outta that ass."

They both laughed.

"Whatever it was, I'm ready for another round of that child," Baby Doll sipped on the umbrella straw in her drink. "And look at you talking; you ain't gettin' dick like that to be talking."

"I get just enough to keep me content, and when my hormones get overactive, I got some heavy equipment to straighten all that out."

"Amen to that," Baby Doll said as she scoped a brother's hardware as he walked by with his lady companion. "I keep Big Spike busy when the business gets hectic. I wouldn't dare bring in the real thing when it's time to put major work in."

There was a moment as they watched the activity on the beach.

Pauline sighed. "Imagine being able to live like this all the time?" She felt it was time to start planting some more seeds. "You could easily have this life if you wanted it, Baby Doll. Girl, you the man. You the boss of six stores, and four clubs, and ain't but twenty-four years old." She couldn't add that she was insanely jealous of her, nor could she even show it in her mannerism. "If you cashed in on those businesses, you could get four times what they're worth—"

"Pauline, you know I'm nothing more than a manager. I don't technically own those businesses—"

"That's where you're wrong. That's what certain people want you to believe. According to the law of business, you have full authority over all that property, and you can do as you please with it."

Baby Doll thought hard about what Pauline said. As she sipped and watched the rolling beach waters, she could see how it all added up to the way Pauline presented it. Those businesses, all of them, were hers. That thought sounded so good, it brought a smile to her face. The will said they were hers as long as stipulations were met.

Hold up, she realized, she couldn't do as she pleased, which was why there were stipulations. "Pauline, you are unaware of the stipulations that came with me getting these businesses. Big Daddy made clear that if the Youth Program stopped functioning, all bets were off."

"What I'm gonna do is let you talk to this lawyer friend of mine, and let him break it down to you, Baby Doll. After that, we'll talk further. I got some people that would be willing to lay out some real outrageously large sums of money for them stores—"

"Naw, Pauline, I won't sale these businesses—"

"Just talk to the lawyer first," Pauline sipped her drink and sat it down. "The way things are going with the businesses, you might not have much of a choice but to bail out. If all this backstabbing don't stop soon, there might not be any businesses left."

Baby Doll felt a fury of reminders attack her mind. There was no doubt all the sudden misfortune with the businesses wasn't a coincidence. She didn't want to jump the gun, which was the reason she hoped Tyrone Wilson would produce the facts she was looking for, because subconsciously she was itching to lash out.

CHAPTER 30

Baby Doll sat in the window seat of the plane once again. As she gazed at the contours of the landscape below, she enjoyed how it looked just like a map. It was amazing how mapmakers could draw maps without having an aerial view. It was strange how all the old maps turned out to be very accurate, even though back then there was no airplanes, yet people were able to getting it right. She'd always wondered how they were able to pull that off.

Twice she caught the handsome brother sitting in the adjacent section sneaking peeks at her. He was fine, muscularly built, and most of all, he looked like he had money. He had a diamond-studded bracelet, a gold pinky ring, alligator skin sandals, and he apparently wasn't married or engaged, since there was no ring to show for it. He looked about in his early to mid-thirties, and his thin goatee gave him a baby-face flair that made her very interested in getting to know him. Baby Doll looked in his direction again and saw him glanced at her again when he noticed her looking in his direction. She pulled back and thought about how to deal this situation. After a moment, she decided that she would open the door, and at that point, it would be up to him to take it wherever else it would go.

Baby Doll whispered to Pauline, "I'm going to the bathroom; be right back." As Baby Doll slid past Pauline, she gave the brother a gorgeous smile and he instantly smiled back. She was heading for the bar but told Pauline the bathroom to prevent her from tagging along. When Baby Doll reached the end of the aisle, she turned and saw the brother's head turned in her direction. She again smiled at him and continued on her way.

Five minutes later, Baby Doll sat at the bar. She had ordered a vodka and tonic and was about to abandon her little mission until she turned her head and saw the brother moving toward her. Baby

Doll gave him another smile, and the look in his eyes told her he was definitely interested.

"Hello," the brother said. "My name is Kenny Moye." He took a seat next to Baby Doll with his hand extended for a shake.

Baby Doll shook his hand. "Breana Winbush, but everybody calls me Baby Doll."

"Baby Doll," Kenny said softly, as though he was savoring the sound of the words rolling off his tongue. "My, God, that name fits you perfectly." He shook as head as he gazed at Baby Doll's gorgeous face; her chinky eyes, her literally flawless, creamy caramel complexion was stirring up his sense of infatuation. "Baby Doll. That is a beautiful name. I hope I'm not being too straightforward here—ahh, is it Miss or Mrs.—"

"I insist you call me Baby Doll. And it's Miss." She showed him her bare finger. "I'm single, not engaged, and the only thing on my mind right now is my career. I'm an entrepreneur."

"I was hoping I could buy you a drink, but I see you're already hooked up."

"Nothing's stopping you from ordering yourself one." Baby Doll was enjoying his masculine cologne. "If you insist, I'll take another small drink."

Kenny ordered two drinks, and they talked. Five minutes later, Baby Doll was wide open. She discovered that Kenny was a self-made millionaire with a chain of catering businesses in several major cities all across the country. He was a bachelor and an Advent Christian.

When Kenny hear that Baby Doll was in charge of four nightclubs, and six retail stores, he was very impressed, and she saw his admiration and eagerness to get with her growing in leaps in bounds. If there was a man around that she would get with, she knew it would be someone just like Kenny, and she decided she was going to open all doors for him to enter when he told her that he owned four homes, six cars, and gave her clear indications that he wanted to see more of her.

Time shot by so rapidly, Baby Doll and Kenny didn't even realize they had been talking for an entire two hours. They both were pulled out of their engaging conversation when the captain of the plane said through the loudspeakers. "All passengers please report to your seats. We are nearing John F. Kenny Airport."

They exchanged their calling cards, and other contact information, and returned to their seats. Obviously, Pauline started asking questions the minute Baby Doll sat down and had apparently snuck into the bar and saw Baby Doll talking to Kenny. After Baby Doll introduced Pauline to Kenny, they said nothing else until they waved goodbye in the airport as Baby Doll and Pauline got inside a yellow cab, while Kenny got in a black stretch Limousine that was waiting for him.

The first thing Baby Doll did when her feet touched Brooklyn was get in contact with Tyrone Wilson for a status report of his investigation. She had called him and instructed him to meet her at Junior's restaurant on Flatbush Avenue in Downtown Brooklyn. As Baby Doll entered Junior's and took a seat in the back of the restaurant, waiting for Tyrone to enter, she hoped he'd come through with something. He dubbed himself the modern-day hood version of John Shaft, and she hoped he was as good as the real Shaft in the movies. Tyrone was a brown-skinned brother with strong street flair who wore a leather jacket and crazy baggy pants.

He even advertised himself as a hip-hop investigator, bragging about how he could go inside any urban center and find out anything you wanted, and would give you your money back if he couldn't produce results. That sounded too good to be true, but Baby Doll was more than willing to give the brother a try.

As she ordered two plates of cheesecake while informing the waitress that she was waiting for a friend who should be here shortly, she now realized why Michael Rafter refused to talk to her. He was cutting off all ties to anyone who had any kind of dealings with Todd Houston. She'd called Michael to get a simple referral, and he wouldn't even talk to her. This made Baby Doll very nervous, and she was now hoping and praying that the police didn't find anything that would lead them to Michael, because he would probably send them to her. Since she was positive that she covered her tracks thoroughly, the only way she would get caught up into that investigation would be through Michael Rafter. She did find some comfort in knowing that Michael was an ex-cop and wouldn't leave those kinds of tracks behind. But even then, she wondered if Michael would drag her into this thing even though she obviously had nothing to do with his murder.

She'd blackmailed him over a year ago, and her trail, if there were one, would be cold and untraceable by now. Also, since Todd was a pedophile, she was sure the police would find out what he was doing to all those little boys and would make that fact their main lead. When Baby Doll noticed this issue was consuming her whole mental process, she shifted her thoughts to something else as she waited for Tyrone.

Three minutes later, Baby Doll saw Tyrone enter the restaurant with a thugged-out walk, and he instantly spotted her before she could wave to get his attention. He strutted quickly to her and took a seat.

"Sorry I'm late, Baby Doll." Tyrone pulled out his notepad as if he didn't even notice there was a plate of cheesecake waiting for him. "I found some real good shit, ma. I'm telling you, ma, the mufuckin' streets stay talking."

"You know my style. I want the raw version," Baby Doll nibbled on a piece of the cake. "And I hope there's no talk about you couldn't complete the investigation."

"Calm your nerves, Baby Doll." Tyrone turned through the pages of his notepad, and said, "I think I've found out everything you ask me to find out." He was about to continue, but stopped when the waitress asked if they wanted anything else.

"No, we're okay, thank you," Baby Doll said, and the waitress went about her business. She dug into her cheesecake, listening carefully.

Tyrone pushed his plate to the side and continued. "Based on what I've found out, Tera was the one who made the calls to the distributors and told them to halt certain deliveries." His whole persona changed, he became remarkably business-like, sounding like a lawyer. "I was able to find out that the kids who stole your car were from Brownsville; whether someone put them up to rob you, I can't say, since my assistance said no one would talk about that with him. Your suspicions about Mr. Donald Moore, Preacher, I haven't found much, but his alleged leave of absence appears to have been a bogus excuse, since he was seen talking to several of your employees at a time when he was supposed to be away from work. Why he would tell you he's taking a break while at the same time talking to various workers is something I guess you can fill in the blanks . . ."

As Tyrone went on and on, running down incident after incident of events that demonstrated that the people who were working for her were plotting to destroy her, Baby Doll was constructing how she was going to clean house without hurting herself in the process.

Within a week, Baby Doll turned the whole situation on top of its head. She fired damn near everyone in the stores, and with the help of Pauline she had an entire workforce of people step right into their places. There was no doubt there were some people who caught a raw deal out of all of the drama, since they may not have had any involvement in the conspiracy to sabotage the businesses, but anyone who was even in the vicinity of any situation where merchandise was mishandled got the shaft. However, the clubs suffered no real consequences, since no undermining was detected. Despite the lack of action taken with those establishments, Baby Doll was certain all employees got the message. Indeed, the streets were talking, and it was clear that it was a love/hate relationship. Either way it went, Baby Doll was making it clear that any cutthroat behavior directed toward her would be met with strong repercussions.

Consistent with her strategic mind, she knew she couldn't cut off Preacher, so she confronted him with a different way of implementing justice; she intended to ask him why he betrayed her with full intentions of making him feel guilty. She would punish him in a way that would batter his conscience, and hopefully get him back on her side.

"Why you went out on me like that, Preacher?" Baby Doll said with heartbroken force. "How could you of all people put a battery in not only the kids' backs, but also the backs of other employees, gassing them up to hurt business?"

Preacher felt two inches tall. There was no excuse for what he had done other than the fact he was stupid for allowing himself to get caught doing something as appalling and foul as this. He wanted to deny it all together, but he saw Baby Doll had done her homework. But there was still a legitimate excuse, and that was the truth. "Baby Doll, I gotta admit, I fucked up, real bad at that. I allowed Tera to talk me into this shit. Why I let her do this? Well, maybe it's because I still have my doubts about you taking the Youth Employment Program to where it needs to be. You scared me when you started talking about putting the program on hold while you build up a foundation. Don't you think Big Daddy left you a foundation in place? But, either way, you right, maybe I should have at least given you more time."

"Preacher, can't you see I've been busting my ass trying to make this program work? But how am I to do what's asked of me if everybody is working against me? If Tera and all the others were conspiring just weeks ago, imagine what they were doing the minute Big Daddy died and put me in charge? I've been fighting an uphill battle with my own team fighting against me. Stop and look at that for a minute. Wouldn't you say that if shit was going wrong it was probably going wrong because of all that backstabbing, sabotage shit Tera was apparently pushing since she heard Big Daddy wasn't putting her in charge?"

Preacher sighed; his heart was truly hurting him, and his mind was locked in a vicious tug-of-war. He wanted to believe Baby Doll, but another part of his mind was telling him not to. "I'm sorry, Baby Doll." He bowed his head.

"What would Big Daddy say about this?" She knew it was time to rub it in for its full impact value. "He's probably turning in his grave knowing the people who were supposed to help me hold the program down are the ones killing it. This is the same old song with us Black folks. If we could stop fucking each other over long enough, our problems would disappear."

She remembered this last quote was one that Preacher used frequently. She decided to drill it in, but this time she planned to do it in a dramatic, tear-jerking fashion. Her voice became soft with hurt. "I remember you would always say if we Black folks could stop fucking each other over long enough, our problems would disappear." She forced a few tears to roll and wiped them away. She stared at him and saw he couldn't look her in the eyes. She had him and wasn't going to let him slide away. "Don't you think what y'all just did to me is a classic example of what you been saying all along, us Black folks fucking each other over to the point we can't go anywhere?! I can't take this shit anymore. I—I—I can't do this anymore. I got enemies everywhere; I was forced to clean house.

There's no telling who's going to take a shot at me when I'm walking out of one of those stores—"

"That ain't gonna happen!" Preacher said with a deadly seriousness that rippled across the airwaves. "I'll give you my word, it won't happen. If you stay on track with the Program, I'll make sure it won't happen."

"How about Tera? She—"

"Fuck Tera! After I check her ass, it'll end there."

Baby Doll put on her sad face; inwardly she was enthralled with joy. She was hoping this would happen, and it did. She could see Preacher was back on her side, and he had just thrown Tera to the wayside.

* * * *

The following day, Baby Doll called her home-girl Jeanette to check up on her and was devastated when she discovered Jeanette was in the hospital suffering from cirrhosis of the liver.

After finding out that Jeanette Morrison was in Brookdale Hospital, Baby Doll went and visited her immediately. They talked and laughed during the whole visit, and Baby Doll promised to return in a few weeks if Jeanette wasn't released.

During this hospital visit, she also discovered that Ka-Born's luck had finally ran out, since he was convicted of first-degree manslaughter and assault with a deadly weapon and sentenced to fifteen years. He'd shot a man and his girlfriend, killing the man, but severely wounding the woman, over an unpaid five-thousand-dollar gambling debt.

That same day Baby Doll had a meeting with the lawyer Pauline mentioned. Baby Doll and Pauline stepped into Mark Watkins' office on Livingston Street in Downtown Brooklyn just after lunch break all across the city. Baby Doll saw Mark Watkins was a short, chubby White man with premature balding, professor-style glasses, and a serious case of chronic halitosis. The minute Mark opened his mouth to introduce himself Baby Doll felt her eyebrows were scorched from Mark's gruesome breath.

While Baby Doll and Pauline were inside Mark's office, Samson and his ace enforcer Mousey sat in their old blue Oldsmobile waiting for Baby Doll and Pauline to exit the Office.

Mousey had a Newport cigarette in between his fingers. He said from behind the wheel, "You think they're going back to Fulton and Nostrand?"

"That's where the main office is. They're going back to that spot, believe me." Samson was caressing the Beretta 9 mm tucked in his waist. "I've been following this bitch for weeks; she always go back to that spot after shit like this."

"How do we know they'll take Atlantic Avenue?" Mousey's pessimistic mind refused to believe everything would go as planned.

"Didn't they take Atlantic coming? They'll take it going back. Fuck is up with all these stupid-ass questions?"

"I'm just trying to make sure when we start blazing at these bitches we don't miss because we didn't map this shit out to the smallest detail."

Inside the lawyer's office, Baby Doll sat next to Pauline while Mark was behind his desk. Baby Doll couldn't understand for the life of her how Mark didn't realize his breath was tearing up the place; he was feet away from her and she could still smell his breath. She was even more confused by the fact Pauline was able to stomach the smell like a true trooper. Despite the foul odor, she did discover that all the property was legally hers, and if she so chose to sell the property, there was nothing anyone could do to stop her.

Ten minutes later, Baby Doll and Pauline exited the office. As Baby Doll was heading across the street she felt as though someone was watching her. She looked around to see if she noticed anyone looking at her and didn't see anyone. Baby Doll got behind the wheel of the green rental car while Pauline got in the passenger seat. They talked as they headed back to the Fulton Street headquarters.

"I'm gonna tell you straight out, Baby Doll. You got a multi-million-dollar situation right in the palm of your hands, and I can help you get that money."

Baby Doll wasn't surprised because it was clear Pauline was pushing an agenda. Since she was talking what she wanted to hear she wanted to hear more. "What you trying to say? You got somebody interested in buying these businesses for millions of dollars?"

"That's right. You ever heard of Ernest Hudson?"

"He's the real estate guy. He made all that money through real estate."

"Well, he wants to buy all of your establishments for a cool four million."

Baby Doll's eyes were wide with disbelief. "Four million dollars!? Pauline, don't play with me like that."

"I'm dead serious. All six retail stores, and the four clubs for four million. That's almost three times what that property is actually worth, and he's ready to deal."

"You're saying he'll write me a check for four million dollars for these properties?"

"That's what I was told," Pauline said, watching Baby Doll closely. "All you got to do is say you're with it, and I'll set it up."

Baby Doll glanced at Pauline. She realized Pauline was apparently working on this for a good minute. Her mind flashed back to all their previous discussions, and it was obvious Pauline was pulling strings. Baby Doll didn't like to be manipulated and would've preferred that Pauline had laid the cards on the table from the jump and had avoided all the buttering-up antics. "What you get out of this?"

Pauline wasn't expecting this sort of question, and even sensed some tension in Baby Doll's voice. She thought quickly, decided to go with the partial truth, and said, "Mr. Hudson is giving me a ten-thousand-dollar commission fee." Her demeanor suddenly became bubbly and joyful. "Since we home girls, I figured if I could get you a hookup like this, I know you'll never forget me when you start making moves with all that money."

Baby Doll sighed; four million dollars would make her a rich woman. This was what she was living to accomplish. Ever since she was a child all she ever dreamed of was becoming rich one day.

The dream was literally a reach away, and she was confused by the sudden indecisiveness that was taking hold of her. She wanted to take the money and run like hell, but Big Daddy was inside of her head. His kindness and undying belief in her ability to fulfill his dream was unmistakable.

After a moment of mental debating, Baby Doll asked inwardly, *But what about my dream? Should I give up my dream to push his dream?* This was something she definitely needed time to think about. Before she even considered giving up the Youth Employment Program, she knew she needed some time to think extremely hard and long, since it was something she couldn't do so lightly. "How could I live with myself if I turned my back on a bunch of kids that could be saved with the right touch of love?"

"You think those kids give a shit about you? They'll turn on you in a heartbeat. They just flipped on you and will keep doing it." Pauline looked over at Baby Doll. "Look around you, Baby Doll. All the people that's supposed to have your back has ran out on you. For you to continue down this road it will be suicide. Now that you fired them, what makes you think they're not going to do everything in their power to destroy you, including sending a bunch of thugs to not only rob you, steal your car, but the next time they might even kill you. I know you want to do Big Daddy's bidding. But you gotta think about your life, girl. And if you go to the police, the streets will never forgive you, and since this Youth Employment Program is geared at working with the streets, your credibility will be damaged beyond repair if you do that. The safest thing to do is cash in on those businesses and go on about your business while you still got the chance."

* * * *

Earlier, about five minutes before Baby Doll and Pauline exited Mark Watkins' office, Samson and Mousey were still staring lock-jawed at the office when, suddenly, two men approached from each side of the car.

"Lemme see your hands," Tony Tee said with the 9 mm inconspicuously pointed at Mousey, who was behind the wheel.

Almost a second on the heels of Tony Tee's action, on the passenger side of the car, Sweet Charlie said, "That includes you too!" His 9 mm was concealed inside a brown paper bag with the bottom cut out, inches from Samson's dreadlocked head. "Both of you take your weapons out slowly and toss them on the back seat."

After Samson and Mousey did as they were instructed, Charlie and Tony eased into the backseat of the car.

Sweet Charlie looked around the immediate area to make sure they hadn't attracted any attention. Tony Tee was checking the vicinity as well.

When they were satisfied, Sweet Charlie said, "Samson, I thought you promised Big Daddy Blue it wasn't gonna come to this?"

Samson was further flung into a state of shock, but this time it was mixed with profound confusion, because he had thought this was a rival hit coming from Critter and his crew. He knew Big Daddy Blue was a living legend back in the day, but this was definitely over the top. He didn't know how to respond.

Tony Tee allowed his gun to touch the back of Samson's head. "I think this is the part you supposed to say somethin."

Samson sighed, "Yo, man, the bitch robbed me, man! There ain't a motherfucker walking this hood who can say they robbed Samson and lived to talk about it, man. What am I supposed to do, let this bitch think she got it like that!?"

Suddenly, Baby Doll and Pauline exited the office. Sweet Charlie and Tony Tee scooted down in the backseat. Charlie could see Baby Doll looking around as if she was looking for someone, and then she headed for a green car. She and Pauline got in and drove away.

Sweet Charlie sat up. "This is the way this is going down, Samson." Charlie pulled out an envelope from his pocket and tossed it up to the front of the car. The package landed on dashboard. "Take a look at the contents of that package, Samson, or would you prefer I call you Bryant Myers?"

Samson was jolted upon hearing his government name. He snatched up the envelope, flipped the flap back and saw it was filled with pictures. Before he even pulled out any of the pictures he knew what he was going to see. With trembling hands he saw pictures of himself, and his entire family; the time when he was talking to his two daughters on the stoop of his apartment building was there; he saw the photo where he was sitting in his car talking to his son; there were two pictures of his elderly mother returning from the store with a grocery bag cuddled in her arms; there was a picture of each of his sisters, apparently on their way to work, and one of his baby brother, and to his surprise there was even a photo of his pit bull, Chopper, whom he loved more than some of his human family members.

"Here's the deal," Sweet Charlie said. "Keep your promise to Big Daddy and leave the broad alone. If she gets a scar on her body, me and my partner will kill everyone in those pictures and save you for last." Sweet Charlie allowed the silence to become intense. He could almost feel his words sinking into Samson's mind and then said, "So, what's it gonna be, Samson?"

CHAPTER 31

Baby Doll gazed at her image in the mirror as she put on the light brown lipstick. The mascara on her eyelashes brought out the contours of her chinky eyes, and the two-hundred-dollar hairstyle made her look like she was about to receive an Academy Award. Her gown was sprinkling with gold glitter. She was dressed beyond elegant. Kenny Moye was on his way to pick her up to commence with their second date and tonight was the night she was going to meet his parents.

For the past two weeks, since discovering she had four million dollars tinkering at her fingertips, Baby Doll had been struggling with a series of internal forces. But the biggest battle, which had its root with the businesses, came from outer forces. The new workforce was indeed a handful. They were new to the business and the ways of these particular stores, and like all people confronted with new things, they seem to be mistake prone. What made matters worse was that most of the mistakes had a way of severely hurting business.

A major issue was the failure to order particular best-selling garments at the correct moment when supplies were rapidly decreasing. These missed opportunities not only pushed customers away and caused lost profits, but also created a lack of confidence and faith in the business in the public's eye.

Dead on the trail of this issue were Tera's continual so-called secret strikes upon her. Tera was disgruntled, deranged with a thirst for revenge, and very dangerous, and had no shame in letting the world know this. Although Baby Doll knew Preacher spoke to her, it was clear that Tera had no intentions of wiping the loss of a store she'd been babysitting for a substantial portion of her life on her chest just like that.

Baby Doll turned her face, examining the diamond stubbed earrings that Kenny bought her, and determined that she would have to brace herself for whatever Tera dished out at her. Twice Baby Doll had to kick the thought of hiring a hit man to knock Tera off out of her mind.

Baby Doll glided over to the nightstand and checked her purse to make sure she didn't forget anything. The headaches of the Youth Employment Program came to her mind, and she didn't think she was going to last very long dealing with the new group of kids she'd brought in. She often wondered if it was her or if it the kids were getting crazier, wilder, disrespectful, and even stupider. It seemed like the average youth growing up in the hood just didn't care about their future, was as hardheaded as ever, was content with hanging out on street corners and getting high around the clock, and just doing all type of stupid stuff that would lead them down the road to disaster.

And the most sickening aspect of it all was that when caring people came to help them, they immediately began plotting to harm them. This mess was indeed a very sad state of affairs and Baby Doll was certain it would take the work of God to even put a dent in this problem. Since Big Daddy died knowing he didn't even succeed in putting a scar on the problem, she wondered once again how he could honestly expect her to do something even he couldn't do. The steam in her engine was dribbling at rates quicker than the speed of light, and almost everything around her seemed to be shoving her toward that ultimate outcome.

Baby Doll reflected on when she was growing up, and knew she was nowhere near as twisted as the kids growing up today. She had her issues, but at least she was smart enough to take care of business. It was so bad nowadays that for every ten kids she brought into the program, only two seemed to be disciplined enough to last a month.

She stayed wondering if she was doing something wrong. After looking closely at what she was doing, she concluded it wasn't her, even though she was a no-nonsense kind of person and was way harder on the kids than Big-Daddy ever was. Her position was that she was not playing that Mr. Nice guy shit anymore, especially after what happened with her last crew that tried to pull a coup-d'etat on her.

Though she may not have detected it, the more she clashed with the people she felt she was helping, the more she was drawn toward taking the money and disappearing and would do it with her head high and her heart intact.

Suddenly, her doorbell rang.

Baby Doll lit up with glee as her heart accelerated with anticipation. Kenny was having a vicious effect on her. He had exactly what she wanted, and she couldn't help but to fantasize how she could get a piece of some of that dough he had so much of.

Baby Doll opened the door and saw Kenny was decked out in a black tuxedo. His smile was astounding enough to evoke someone to sing a love song.

Kenny savored Baby Doll's magnificent beauty and her perfume. "My God, Baby Doll, you are—are—beautiful!" He had to touch her.

Baby Doll gently went with his embrace and the brief kiss. His cologne ignited her senses, and she saw he was paying attention, because she had told him that she enjoyed this particular cologne called Mirari.

Two minutes later, Baby Doll was sitting wrapped in Kenny's arms. They were in the back compartment of the moving limousine, talking.

"So how's the job stress holding up?" Kenny said, with a deep baritone voice.

"Everything that could go wrong went wrong." Baby Doll took this as an invitation to facilitate her agenda; make him want to come to her aide financially. "The new employees are costing the company a fortune. I'm so lost with what I should do, I'm almost at a complete loss for words."

"I have an excellent business advisor I can let you borrow free of charge."

"I have one already, and she's insanely sensitive and territorial. But it's really not her; she's doing all she can do. It's the other issue I mentioned—"

"The one dealing with the woman relative who feels she should be in charge of the company?"

"Yeah, her." Baby Doll said as if it was a struggle getting the words out. "This chick is still going out of her way to destroy this company, and me along with it."

"Well," Kenny sighed as though the issue was even painful to him. "That's a very difficult dilemma, being that she's actually related to Mr. Williams. Family often feel they're entitled to things solely because of a blood connection, even when that person knows they're the worse person for a particular project or an enterprise. I've had my fair share of that sort of stress. In fact, my younger brother, Keith, whom you might meet one day, is a case in point. He's been on drugs, been involved in every criminal activity you can think of, did hard prison time, and yet, he feels my parents and I are obtained to support his reckless and anti-Christian way of life. He wants us to give him another business so that he can run it into the ground like he's done with several other businesses we gave him. Me personally, I've made it clear to him that I will not give him a red cent until he changes his evil ways. My parents are on the same wavelength, but they bend quite frequently and cater to his foolishness. We're a very religious family, so they believe charity is not necessarily considered an enabling display of affection."

A half hour later, Baby Doll, Kenny and his mother Felicia, and his father Kenneth sat at a table in a restaurant in Westchester County, eating and talking. Baby Doll was sitting next to Kenny while Felicia and Kenneth sat across from them.

"So, Miss Winbush," Felicia said with a snobby voice that rang of bourgeoisie. "I hear you're a woman entrepreneur?" This was a major plus as far as she was concerned, since she didn't approve of Kenny dating low-class, money-chasing women.

"Yes, I'm into the retail business and social entertainment." She remembered this was how Big Daddy schooled her to present the businesses to uppity rich folks.

Kenneth sat his drink down and said, "That's very interesting, but what do you mean by social entertainment?" He was hoping this didn't mean a striptease establishment. "If you don't mind me asking?"

"Oh, not at all. I'm the chief executive officer of four nightclubs. They're more like dance halls." She threw the dance hall issue in with hopes that it would neutralize any hostile backlash, since they were Christians.

Kenneth nodded his head. "That's an honest living. And I assume the retail business deals with garments?"

"Yes, clothing of all kinds."

As the night progressed, Baby Doll saw that meeting Kenny's parents really wasn't a good idea. They were outrageously nosy and seemed to meddle endlessly into Kenny's personally affairs. She tried to give Kenny hints that his parents were going too far with some of the issues, and he never once picked up on it. By the time the night was over, Baby Doll was glad it was time to depart.

As they all stood in front of the restaurant, Felicia said, "This Sunday we would love to see you at our church. I'm sure we will see you?" She was clearly waiting for an affirmative response.

Baby Doll saw everyone was looking at her with smiles, and she was forced to say, "I would love to go to church with y'all."

Ten minutes later, as Baby Doll and Kenny was cruising away in the limousine, she had to fight not to charge Kenny up for not taking charge of the situation. His parents were bullies and seemed to be obsessed with controlling his life. She was totally disappointed with Kenny, because he didn't turn out to be the kind of strong man she expected him to be.

As Kenny embraced her, talking about how he was so proud of his mother and father, bragging and boasting about all the great things they had done to help him get to where he is today, Baby Doll suddenly realized that this was actually a good thing. He was strong as a proactive businessman, but when it came to certain types of emotional issues, he was apparently weak. Because weak people could easily be manipulated, she instantly concluded that this little flaw on his part could be used to her advantage. The money-seeking component in her mind began plotting a way to use Kenny's weaknesses to help her get to where she needed to be.

* * * *

When Sunday rolled in, Baby Doll was sitting in church with the Moye family, who had specially reserved front-row seats. She met Denise, the only girl in the family, and Baby Doll saw she had another enemy to deal with. Denise was clearly jealous of Baby Doll's looks, and the eye-rolling assaults began instantly. Baby Doll saw the Moye family was in ecstasy as they greeted fellow churchgoers, while introducing her as Kenny's new girlfriend.

Baby Doll almost spoke out when she saw each of the Moye family members put a fifty-dollar bill in the collect plate. When she put a five-dollar bill in the plate, and they looked at her as if she had just slapped Jesus Christ or something, Baby Doll was seconds from losing her composure. She felt very uncomfortable by the way they attacked her with their eyes, but she stuck to her guns; she wasn't giving up one penny more of her hard-earned money to a bunch of pimps, hustlers, and conmen. Game recognized game. Ever since she was a child she was all too familiar with the conning antics of the church, and made it her business not to allow people using God's name to have their hands in her pockets.

Reverend Carter approached the pulpit and began his sermon; he was in rare form today as far as Baby Doll could detect, since his words were quite moving at times. The theme of his sermon was friendship and charity. Kenny sat next to Baby Doll, and she could see he was really into all this Bible talk, shouting and responding when Reverend Carter asked the congregation to do so with "Amen" and "Praise the Lord."

Suddenly, Reverend Carter said, "And my brothers and sister, the best illustration the Bible gave of God's gift of Charity is 1 *Corinthians*, Chapter 13, verses 1-13 . . ."

Baby Doll jumped at attention. That was the only verse in the Bible that she knew. She instantly wondered if she still remembered those verses.

Reverend Carter continued, "I want each and every one of one to reach for your bible and turn to 1 *Corinthians*, Chapter 13, verses 1-13, because I want you all to read along with me."

Kenneth reached for the bibles stashed on the side of the bench and handed one to everyone sitting on the bench. They all began flipping open their bibles to the bible verse.

Baby Doll didn't open her bible because she was sure she still remembered the verses.

Reverend Carter said with his hands waving dramatically, "I want this entire congregation to read along. Though I speak with the tongues of men and of angels, and have not charity, I am become as sounding brass, or a tinkling cymbal. And though I have the gift of prophecy, and understand all mysteries, and all knowledge; and though I have all faith, so that I could remove mountains, and have not charity, I am nothing. . ."

Baby Doll spoke along with the Reverend, while staring straight at ahead.

Kenny glanced over and was shocked when he noticed Baby Doll rattling off the verse as if she knew it as efficiently as knowing her own name.

Baby Doll continued, "And though I bestow all my goods to feed the poor, and though I give my body to be burned, and have not charity, it profiteth me nothing. Charity suffereth long, and is kind; charity envieth not; charity vaunteth not itself, is not puffed up . . ."

When the other Moye family members noticed Baby Doll was reciting the verse with her Bible closed, they became so distracted by her memorization that they lost track of their places as they read along with Reverend Carter.

"Doth not behave itself unseemly, seeketh not her own, is not easily provoked . . . And now abideth faith, hope, charity, these three; but the greatest of these is charity."

As Reverend Carter continued his sermon, Baby Doll saw the huge smiles beaming from the entire Moye family, including Denise. For the first time, she realized with this Bible stuff she could score major points with the Moye family and decided to do some more research into the Bible, maybe even learn a few more specially selected verses.

Two days later, Baby Doll was sitting on the sofa in Kenny's two-million-dollar mansion with a glass of champagne in her hand while a Luther Vandoross song was humming lightly from the speakers hidden in areas of the living room she couldn't begin to identify. She wondered if this was the night Kenny would crack for some pussy. Since he was insane with all that Christian stuff, she knew sex wasn't a major factor in getting him to do what she wanted him to do, which was fine with her. She was in need of the physical touch of a man, but knew it was not wise to give him any sex hints so as not to make him think she was loose. However, she was feeling very good, since her Bible-quoting deed the other day had compelled Kenny to offer her assistance with her financial crisis. To prevent him from thinking she was after his money, Baby Doll had conditionally declined the offer, insisting that she couldn't give him a decision on what she wanted to do until she had a chance to thoroughly look at her company's total financial status and its ability to repay the loan.

Kenny entered the living room, pulling Baby Doll out of her reverie and said, "I had to really dig for these photos." He sat next to her and started flipping through his family photo album.

Baby Doll almost yawned twice as Kenny animatedly identified all the people in the photos. "This right here is my Aunt Sharon," Kenny said with a proud smile. "You would love to meet her; she's the coolest of all my aunts. I remember the time she would . . ."

When this photo presentation was over Baby Doll sighed in relief. She took control and decided to get it over with. "Kenny, I looked at all my records, and I'm going to have to take you up on your offer regarding that loan."

Kenny was all smiles. "So how much you need?"

Baby Doll sighed, while doing her best to make it appear as though she was ashamed to ask for the money. "Well—I—I could use about two hundred and fifty grand."

"That's all? Let's say we do this. Since I'm really impressed with the Youth Employment Program, let's take it a step further. I love what you're doing with those urban kids. It's something that exemplifies the principles of the Kingdom of God, and I've wanted to become a part of that program the moment I heard you explain what it was all about. I'll loan you the two hundred and fifty thousand dollars, but I'll invest five hundred thousand dollars."

Baby Doll almost shouted in sheer jubilee. She felt like she had just hit the lotto. The excited response almost slipped out, but she quickly held it in deep check, realizing such an energetic reaction could shatter her business image. This wasn't supposed to appear personal, even though it was.

With a smile Baby Doll said, "I would love to have you involved in this program, Kenny. The talent, the love, and the positive energy you'll bring to the table will finally transform this program into a force that will finally make true changes." She reached out and gave him a loving hug accompanied by a kiss. To her surprise, Kenny turned the kiss into an answer to her earlier question. The answer said as clear as day that he was really ready to take their relationship to the sexual level.

* * * *

Meanwhile, as Baby Doll and Kenny were engaged in their first sexual act, Tera was talking to Lawrence Wilson and Richard Erkco, the Park Avenue lawyers in charge of overseeing the enforcement of Big Daddy's will. The issues she presented to them were serious enough to have both their undivided attention.

It was indeed an after-hours visit, and under normal circumstances they would have made Tera wait until tomorrow to consider her claims, but because the evidence Tera presented to them was very clear and convincing, they instantly knew there was a need for the implementation of the secondary component of the will.

CHAPTER 32

Baby Doll sat in the Fulton Street main office staring at the letter from Big Daddy's Park Avenue lawyers that handled his will. Pauline sat across from her with a constrained smile.

Pauline saw this was the moment she'd been waiting for, "I don't want to say I told you so, but they're gonna keep coming at you until they tear you down or snatch these businesses from your control. I know you got a good heart, Baby Doll, and you gave your word to Big Daddy, but right now you would be doing justice to his dream by protecting it from Tera. If she gets control, she's gonna rape this company until its bone-dry."

"She won't get it." Baby Doll saw Pauline was working hard for that commission fee. "Big Daddy knew she wasn't fit to hold it down." She stared at the letter again, and honed in on a certain part. "These lawyers want me to appear at their office tomorrow with." She read the exact words. "Documentary proof that the Youth Employment Program is fully operable in accordance with Mr. Gregory J. Williams explicit wishes."

She sighed, knowing she was about to find out about that secondary component of the will. She was very nervous because she felt the proof that the program was operable was very weak. The number of kids she had working was way less than half the number Big Daddy normally had, and she still hadn't developed enough trust with the kids who worked for her. After the last attack Tera choreographed, she knew it was suicide to assume Tera wouldn't hit her from that same angle, but this time, bring the lawyers into the matter.

"This shit got me bugging, Pauline, because I know that bitch Tera is behind this shit. She's trying to get the lawyers to get that secondary component of the will activated. I guess she thinks that component of the will is gonna knock me out of the picture, and I guess it probably will."

"Let's bring in Mr. Hudson. His lawyers are the best around. If you say you want to sell, I can guarantee you that he'll shut Tera's ass down. This is probably your last opportunity to get access to that money straight-up."

"Naw, I'm going to deal with this head-up on my own. I didn't do nothing wrong, at least not that I know of, that will cause that secondary component to be forced on me."

Pauline sighed almost angrily. "I can tell you this much, Baby Doll. Mr. Hudson is not gonna sit by waiting for you to chase around these cat-and-mouse issues. A four-million-dollar transaction is not the type of issue you drag your feet with. The way Mr. Hudson sounded the last time I spoke to him, he's about to start looking elsewhere, so if I were you I would make a serious decision very soon."

After the meeting with Pauline was over, Baby Doll made a series of phone calls in an attempt to ascertain what was going on. She called Preacher and he was just as lost as she was and had also received a letter from the lawyers instructing him to appear at the Park Avenue office. When she called Rachel and other relatives of Big Daddy, they also informed her that they also received letters from the lawyers instructing them to appear. They all claimed they had no idea what was going on. Baby Doll then calmed her mind for a moment and took a hard look at how the youth program was going. She scrambled through various documents, and concluded again that the Youth Employment Program wasn't the best it could be, but it also wasn't twisted enough to call for sanctions to be enforced on her. She asked herself for the hundredth time, *What the hell was this foul ass Tera up to?*

* * * *

BABY DOLL

Nicole sat on the 6 train staring at a poster of a pretty White woman in a bathing suit, modeling for a company advertising a sunscreen lotion, and suddenly, Baby Doll popped into her head. Her blood boiled at the mere thought of Baby Doll. Tera was about to start huffing and puffing; that conceited bitch had cost her ninety days on Rikers Island and another boosting charge on her already tarnished record. She even caused her sister, Shirley to have to watch over her kids while she was in jail. What made it so hard for Nicole to wipe this issue on her chest was, she had stopped boosting two years ago, had found a decent secretary job, and because of Baby Doll she lost it all. There was nothing that could alter her belief that Baby Doll had put that blouse in her bag all because of a high school beef. She still couldn't understand why Baby Doll took it there, after all these years.

Nicole was seething with fury as she gave the fat White man staring at her a snare that could have instantly set a fire. The fat man quickly looked the other way. Nicole noticed just laying eyes on this fat bastard was enough to remind her of the time when Kaseim said he would step to Baby Doll and ended up breaking his promise. It wouldn't have been so bad just breaking his promise, but Kaseim ended up milking her for crazy money. He even gave her syphilis. Nicole could still recall sitting in the Public Health clinic at the Department of Health over on Flatbush Extension in Downtown Brooklyn, scared to death that Kasiem had given her the Big Monster (HIV). When she got her results back and was informed that she was HIV-negative, she took the penicillin shot in her ass cheek for the syphilis with a grateful heart, rationalizing that at least it wasn't the infamous death sentence. She vowed she would never engaged in unprotected sex again as she exited the clinic, but just two days later, she took another shot at the raw head when she had unprotected sex with this super-fine, muscle-bound brother named Positive.

Her rationale was that no man as handsome and clean as Positive could possibly be infected with a virus as destructive as HIV. Not surprisingly, Positive did a major hit-and-run on Nicole, and left her with shattered heart. When the smoke cleared, she found a way to convince herself that all of her misfortune was Baby Doll's fault. Eventually, her obsession with getting Baby Doll back for what she did to her, transformed any and everything that caused her any discomfort into a Baby Doll-initiated matter.

Luckily, she found another job as a mail clerk in an accounting firm on West Fourteenth Street. Had she not done so, she was seriously planning to walk into the Fulton Street office she saw Baby Doll enter and exit several times and go postal on her ass. She even had the gun she planned to use on Baby Doll and had been holding it for the time when she was ready to reactivate her plan. Now that she had the new job, her next move would be to try to save up enough money to pay a dope fiend to shoot Baby Doll as she came tiptoeing out of that little office of hers. Since Nicole already had the gun, it was simply a matter of few more paychecks.

* * * *

Baby Doll entered the Park Avenue lawyers' huge conference room and saw almost everybody who was present during the first reading of the will had beat her there. The only one missing was Rachel. The sight was truly appalling in view of the fact everyone sat grilling each other as though they were archenemies. She could understand everyone being pissed off with her since she wasn't blood related to Big Daddy and ended up getting the lion's cut of his worldly possessions, but the visible hostility between the blood relatives didn't make any sense to her.

As Baby Doll took a seat she concluded, who was she to judge when she didn't communicate with blood relatives, and they also, just like Big Daddy's family, practically hated each other's guts? She made eye contact with Preacher, waved at him, and saw him screw up his face with noticeable anger. Ah, shit, she thought as a nervous energy started to form.

"So glad you could make it, Miss Winbush," Lawrence said as he sat a folder in front of Baby Doll. "If Mrs. Rachel Williams isn't here in five minutes we'll begin this proceeding without her."

Baby Doll flipped open the folder in front of her and began reading the first document. It was a content sheet, itemizing the agenda at this proceeding, and a list of the other documents inside the folder. When she noticed there would be live testimony from various Youth employees, her heart fluttered. She couldn't believe Tera would actual go to this extreme. When she saw there was a document called an inter-office communication from Baby Doll to Pauline, she suddenly realized why Preacher was mad at her. *How the fuck did this bitch clip this memo?* Her mind was running wild now, because if someone had clipped that memo where she had warned Pauline that she could not fully trust Preacher since he had conspired against her in the past, and would likely do it again, it was obvious that other documents could have also been intercepted in a similar fashion. But the issue that really had her mind working overtime was the question, who had intercepted the document and given it to Tera?

Suddenly, Rachel barged into the office, didn't say a word to anyone, and sat down rolling her eyes at everyone that dared to look at her.

Both the lawyers, Lawrence Wilson and Richard Erkco, rose to their feet.

Lawrence spoke as Richard was shuffling through the folder in front of him.

"We've called you all back here because there has been a petition filed." Lawrence gestured toward Tera. "Mrs. Tera Smalls, as a blood relative of Mr. Williams, feels there has been a breach of the will and has presented clear evidence that the Youth Employment Program is not functioning in accordance with Mr. Williams' wishes. As you all are aware, Mr. Williams had a secondary clause instituted in his will, which could only be unveiled in the event it is established that the Youth Program is not in compliance. Mrs. Smalls will present her case. Miss Winbush will then be afforded the opportunity to rebut the evidence. Afterwards, a decision will be rendered. At that point, if it is deemed that the Youth Program is not as it is supposed be, the secondary clause will be enforced. Mrs. Tera Smalls, the floor is yours." Lawrence took a seat as Tera rose to hers.

Tera gave Baby Doll the look of death. "I think y'all should all know that Baby Doll—Miss Winbush—is not fit to be in charge of Big Daddy's Youth program."

There was a mutter of agreement from most of the people present.

"Even the kids don't want her there," Tera continued. "And we know if this Program is for the kids, and the kids don't want her there, then it should go without saying that this program is not fully functioning as Big Daddy would want it."

The collective mutters of agreement returned.

Baby Doll saw the bullshit coming as visible as a Mack truck barreling toward her. She even saw the family was siding with her even though they knew all this was straight-out bullshit. She sighed and scolded herself for not listening to Pauline. She should've taken the money and ran.

Tera continued, "I'm gonna let the kids tell y'all what time it is. Not just one of them, but all of them."

Baby Doll was shocked. *All of them!?* She flipped open the folder to make sure she had read the documents correctly. She scanned through all the documents, and sure enough, this crazy bitch was planning to call all these kids in here. Baby Doll looked around, wondering where they had all twelve of the kids waiting, and for the first time she noticed the twelve unoccupied seats in the corner. Before she got her bearings together, she saw Richard approach the door, open it, and whisper something to someone outside the conference room.

Seconds later, little Tameeka stepped through the door. Baby Doll stared at Tameeka in partial disbelief and saw that look on her face that said, now it's my turn to get my shit off. There was no doubt whatsoever that Tameeka was going to seriously blow the spot up. Baby Doll had been riding Tameeka in a very hard fashion from the moment she got involved in the youth program, and honestly felt she was helping to bring out the best of Tameeka's strong qualities. Tameeka was a very good and intelligent girl but could be very lazy and unambitious at times. Baby Doll knew with the right type of push, Tameeka could be well on her way to being a very productive member of society, especially since her brushes with the law were very minuet and trivial.

Tera and Tameeka lashed out, talked about every and any flaw of Baby Doll's and painted her as this utter tyrant, insane with power and authority. There was plenty of exaggerations, and way too many flagrant lies. Baby Doll wanted to lash out, but she held her tongue, waiting to hear all the so-called witnesses. The next witness was Jalil, who gave a similar account as Tameeka's testimony. Then there was Shaniqua, and again they went in on Baby Doll as if she was Satan's spawn. To Baby Doll's surprise, all twelve of the kids portrayed her as unfit to be in charge of the program.

Baby Doll was amazed by the fact Tera was able to get these kids to come in here and do what they did when snitching was deemed the ultimate street violation. Whatever Tera was paying them, Baby Doll knew she couldn't compete with her, and realized that Tera had plants even inside the new work force.

When Tera sat down, Lawrence stood up and said, "Miss Winbush it is your turn. The floor is yours." He sat back down.

The room resonated with an ear-ringing silence.

Baby Doll had no defense planned. She was caught off guard by the fact Tera had apparently manipulated the very kids she was supposed to be helping and convinced them to say she wasn't helping. It wasn't hard to conclude that this fight was over. She had clearly lost this battle, and the only thing she could do was let the lawyers and everyone else know her position and that she never meant to hurt any of these kids when she was being hard on them, which was the unmitigated truth.

Baby Doll rose to her feet. "I'm not going to call any witnesses or anything like that. I just want to say that most of the things you heard were outright lies, while a small portion was the truth. I don't think anyone in here can honestly say I did not love Big Daddy Blue. He was my father; maybe not physically, but definitely spiritually, emotional, and psychologically. Nonetheless, I gave him my word I would keep his youth program together. He chose me to carry on his legacy because I showed and proved to him that I was the one who could do it. When each and everyone in this room had the chance to prove to him that they could keep this program alive, they chose to basically give the man their backs. I'm trying to do my best, and it would be a whole lot easier to do that if I had people helping me instead of trying to hurt me."

She allowed her words to linger for a few seconds. "What is happening now is a clear example of people trying to hurt instead of help. Now, for y'all that know Tera, know she wasn't going to let me get away with removing her when she got caught sabotaging these businesses. She was fired because she violated the rules of her job responsibilities. Now, really ask yourselves, who is the real threat here, a person who would deliberately attempt to destroy Big Daddy's creation, or someone who is pushing the people around them to do better and will not accept nothing less than their absolute best."

There was a moment of heavy silence

Baby Doll allowed the silence to become uncomfortable, and then said, "And I'm willing to bet my life that every one of these kids were offered something to come in here—"

"That's bullshit, bitch!" Tera sprung from her seat. "You gotta prove that shit!"

"Please, Mrs. Smalls," Richard raced over to block Tera from getting to Baby Doll. "Please have a seat."

Tera sat back down.

"With that said," Baby Doll said as she sat in her chair. "I ask that you lawyers bear all this in mind. And if the secondary clause says I'm out, then I will honor his wishes." She was at the emotional point where she was starting not to care what they did. After all these years of backbreaking work and unwavering dedication, this was what she got in return. She had even fought not to take all the money and run because she wanted to honor Big Daddy's wishes. She was boiling with rage inwardly but maintained her emotionless facial expression. She truly loved Big Daddy and wanted to do the right thing, but with all the toxic and poisonous people all around her, there was no way she would survive as long as she continued trying to keep her heart pure.

There were a few aces still up her sleeve, and whatever happened she vowed that she would find a way to get Mr. Hudson to help her get that money.

Lawrence said, "This envelope"—He raised the manila envelope up in the air for all to see—"contains the instructions of what should follow once it has been determined that the Youth Employment is not functional. Since my colleague and I are the arbitrators of that decision as the will indicates, we are forced to rule in Mrs. Tera Smalls' favor."

Tera was all smiles; she wanted to jump up and shout, "Yes!" but was able to curtail the ghettoized response that was struggling to get out.

Lawrence continued, "Since Mrs. Winbush has not presented any evidence to refute the testimony in support of the fact the program is not functional, other than her own self-serving remarks, we are compelled to rule that the Youth Employment Program is not in compliance with Mr. Williams' explicit wishes and that the circumstances require the implementation of the secondary clause of the will."

There was a moment of silence to see if an outburst would follow. When none followed Lawrence continued, "I shall now open the envelope. We'll first assess the legal ramifications, and then share the instructions with you all."

Lawrence tore open the sealed manila envelope, pulled out a few sheets of paper, and began reading them. Richard came to his side and also began reading the documents along with him. As they both read the documents, their eyes would suddenly grow wide with surprise and then abruptly become squinted in confusion. This went back and forth until they both finishing reading the four documents.

Richard got up and went to the door. Everyone's eyes were wide with anticipation. Tera was about to throw a temper tantrum, since the lawyers' responses indicated something was terribly wrong.

Richard whispered excitedly to someone right outside the conference room, and then moments later, four security guards entered the room and took their places in various locations in the room, as though what was coming was going to evoke a violent reaction. Richard returned back to his original location next to Lawrence.

Lawrence sighed, rose to his feet, paused for a moment, and said, "Please, everyone, I would like to remind you that at this lawyer firm, we are not—"

"Just tell us what the fuck it is!?" Tera shouted as she sprung to her feet.

Two security guards rushed toward Tera, and she quickly sat back down.

Lawrence sighed again, realizing none of this made any sense. He looked at the documents again, shook his head, and decided the best thing to do was to do some further investigation to determine if it was even remotely possible to do what Mr. Williams was asking them to do.

CHAPTER 33

Ernest Hudson sat behind his desk smiling at Pauline sitting across from him. He felt victorious and wanted to pat himself on the back for a job well done. Even though Pauline did most of the work, he was the one pulling the strings and pushing the appropriate buttons, so it went without saying that this was his victory more so than anyone else's.

Four days ago, Breana "Baby Doll" Winbush sold him all of the property that had once belonged to Gregory "Big Daddy Blue" Williams, and he had promised Big Daddy this would happen.

"Pauline, you did an excellent job." Ernest pulled out his checkbook from the top draw of the desk. "I'm certain you'll take payment in the form of a check?"

With a smile Pauline said, "Whatever's convenient for you is fine with me, Mr. Hudson." She wanted to ask him a question but was hesitant. Matters from henceforth were in his hands, and if he was content with the results, then it shouldn't matter how it went. But she was curious and if she didn't scratch the itch that was driving her crazy her mind would never give her a break. She decided to ask the question, since it couldn't hurt anything. As Ernest wrote out the check, she said, "Can I ask you something, Mr. Hudson? I'm a little confused."

"Being confused is not a good thing." Ernest ripped the check from its pad, handed it to her, and she took it. "Of course you can ask a question, Pauline. Fire away." He leaned back in his chair with his hands cupped across his full-figured belly.

"I was trying to figure out how is it possible for you to take all these business properties when Big Daddy's will says Baby Doll will lose ownership of the property if the Youth Employment Program should cease functioning. If she sells the property and runs, wouldn't that deem the Youth Employment Program inoperable, and therefore she will lose ownership?"

With a smile Ernest said, "A simple answer to that inquiry would be, I have no intentions of terminating the Youth Employment Program, and therefore no breach of the will. Unfortunately, the program will function up to the level that will satisfy the requirements of the will. No more, no less. From what I can see, a simple hand full of kids will suffice. "

Pauline instantly caught on. "Oh, okay. I think I get it. As long as the Youth Employment Program is still in existence, she can sell the property?"

"Yes," Ernest nodded his head. "But I would be rather disingenuous if I failed to mention I have an excellent team of lawyers who just happen to know Big Daddy's lawyers quite well. And I would be even further untruthful if I didn't mention that money can make almost anything happen."

"You are absolutely right about that, Mr. Hudson." Pauline held up her check, savoring the sight of all those digits. "Money can make a whole lot of things happen." She decided since he wasn't offended by her asking questions, she could ask another one. "One more thing, the way you're talking, it seems you knew Mr. Williams quite well. Was this personal or was it business?"

"Those properties weren't worth four million, and you know that, Pauline. I hate to say this, but Mr. Williams, Big Daddy, made the fatal mistake of assuming I could not get what I wanted when it came to him. I've had a few encounters with Big Daddy Blue, and each time he was quite cocky when he rejected my offers. His position was that I could never, and I repeat, he said I could never get possession of his property, with him living or dead. I have never loss a wager in this area of business, and I never will." He smiled proudly.

Pauline smiled back, but inside her heart she sensed she had been prostituted and had helped to unjustly destroy something that was good for the Black community. That little voice inside her head was marinating with guilt, regret and shame, and it told her that her actions had perpetuated the concept that the greatest danger to other Black people, especially in this day and age, is often other Black people.

* * * *

Baby Doll moved through her New Jersey home barking instructions to the moving men. "Be easy with that vase! It's worth a whole day's work, my man."

The missing-tooth, medium-built brother smiled and said, "I gotcha, Miss Winbush. I been doing this for years, and I ain't got greasy fingers either."

"If you break it, you pay for it," Baby Doll said, and headed toward her bedroom to make sure the other moving men weren't mishandling any more of her property. Baby Doll was dressed for the occasion. She had on faded blue jeans that made her ass look like an upper side down heart and an old light blue sweatshirt. Her hair was tied up into a ponytail that dropped down just below her shoulder blades. She was happy, feeling good, and it was because she was finally rich.

When she added up her worth after tallying up the four million she got for the stores and clubs, this New Jersey house that she was selling for $250,000 (she made a profit of seventy-five gees), her own personal stash (seventy-five gees), and the additional two-hundred thousand Big Daddy gave her as the secondary component of the will, she was certain that she was rich enough to finally say she had fulfilled her lifelong dream. Her total worth was $4,525,000.00, and she felt every bit of it.

Baby Doll giggled inwardly at the thought of what she planned on doing for the rest of her life. She looked in the room, saw the two movers were doing what they were supposed to be doing, and she headed for the kitchen to get something cold to drink. She reflected on that day of the secondary will reading and shook her head elatedly. The look on everybody's faces when the lawyers explained that Big Daddy had hidden money in a safe deposit box in the amount of two hundred grand, which was to be given to Baby Doll, was priceless. The notarized statement signed by Big Daddy himself said that if the Youth Employment Program had increased to be functional, it was apparently due to financial turmoil, and this money was a backup so as to give Baby Doll another shot to get it right. Reflecting back on that day at the lawyers' office, she saw that the lawyers used very good judgment when they brought in the security guards before revealing Big Daddy's wishes, because Tera literally tried to get at her with an insane rage surging through her body. She had nearly climbed across the conference table to get at Baby Doll, but the security guards quickly constrained her.

Baby Doll opened the refrigerator, retrieved a can of ginger ale, saw there were three sodas left, closed the door, cracked the can open, leaned up against the nearby counter, and sipped the soda as she daydreamed of her new home down in Richmond Virginia. She bought this nice two-family house for $150,000. The place was a steal in every sense of the word, and if she had bought a similar house in New York or New Jersey, it would have easily gone for a half million dollars. She had plenty of plans, and decided to finally settle down, find her a good man with big money, and merge their money together to make even more money by investing in or opening businesses.

She would have loved to get with Kenny Moye, but he was too weak for her; plus, she couldn't imagine having his family as in-laws. She had even returned the $750,000 gees that Kenny gave her as a loan and investment in the Youth Employment Program. Initially, she was planning to take his money and running, but she knew his parents would wig out and force him to have her tracked down and possibly even arrested. She had contemplated doing what she did to Todd on Kenny, but after looking at all the money she had and the amount of time it would take to find some dirt on Kenny, she realized it wasn't worth all the headaches. She was now worth four and a half million dollars, and with that amount of money, it was apparent she had accomplished what she'd been striving for all of her life. The greed factor repeatedly tried to convince her that the more money she had, the safer it would be for her to stay rich, but the logical part of her mind wouldn't let her get reckless. She had way too many bad examples of greed taken to the extreme that worked continuously on her mind and they wouldn't let her start overreaching.

Another component of her mind started toying with her heart. An image of Big Daddy's face flashed across her mind as the sweet, acidy taste of the ginger ale caressed her taste buds, and the guilt tried to inch its way into her mind.

Again, she pushed that vibe out of her mind when she reminded herself that Tera, Preacher, and all the workers at the stores and clubs had all flipped out on her for no justifiable reason. If someone was to be blamed for the death of Big Daddy's dream, it damn sure wasn't her. She allowed her rage to boil, since it made her feel much better knowing she wasn't the reason for what just happened. They had attacked her, robbed her, lied on her, sabotaged everything she was trying to build. She did nothing to deserve any of this mistreatment, and most of all, they were jealous of her and demonstrated that they would do anything to prevent her from being successful, even at the cost of killing Big Daddy's dream. For her to stay on this course it would be suicide, and everybody knew this. She told herself constantly that with all the pressure on her back, she was wise for doing what she'd done.

Then, suddenly, she smiled when the image of Tera, Preacher, and all the other backstabbers' faces crossed her mind. When they found out she sold the property, their reaction would be a sight she would love to see. She could see the wide-eyed shock on their faces once they were informed that there was a new owner and that they no longer worked there. The thought caused her to laugh out loud. She was especially glad Mr. Hudson promised to hold off with the transition until she was long gone, so at least she didn't have to deal with their bullshit once they found out. She laughed again.

Baby Doll downed the last of the soda, tossed the can in the nearby garbage bin, and headed toward the living room. She had to do something to keep her mind busy, because the more she brooded and blamed, the more that sensation in her heart was telling her that she was wrong. But the steel-plated covering that protected her decision to take the money and run made it impossible for her to hear what that voice was trying to say.

* * * *

Kenny Moye was in the back of his limousine wondering why Roger was moving this damn vehicle so slowly. He hit the button to the electric window divider, and the window slid down with a humming sound.

"Roger, can you move this thing any faster?" Kenny said calmly; he really wanted to shout, but had vowed to never again allow his emotions to control his reactions to stressful situations. He could feel the stress management classes he had taken last year were still working and he was proud to say he still hadn't relapsed. "I told you this was an emergency, and I need to get to this destination in a hurry."

"I'm sorry, Mr. Moye," Roger said. "I'm not used to driving at accelerated speeds beyond the speed limit, but if you really insist, I'll get much heavier on the gas, sir."

"Yes, I do insist." Kenny buzzed the window back up and sat back comfortably in the seat. He was very disappointed to hear that Baby Doll was about to slip out of town. His friend George Dunn had told him he was driving past Baby Doll's house and saw moving trucks loading up all of her belongings. He knew she was dealing with a lot of problems at her job, and she had even returned the money he had tried to loan her as well as the investment money, but he didn't think her issues were extreme enough to call for moving from the area. He had to talk to her and find out what was she about to do. His mind was running wild, trying to figure out why she was moving and hadn't mentioned this to him. He hoped she wasn't in any serious trouble or planning to simply disappear out of his life, since he had really come to enjoy being with her and desperately wanted to see more of her.

* * * *

Baby Doll stood outside on the battered lawn of her Maplewood home, looking at the house for the last time. Since she only been in this house for about a year, there weren't many memories tied up with this particular place of residence, so her heart wasn't heavy with too many emotions. The two moving trucks were filled to capacity, and her Acura was packed with her closest possessions. She turned and headed toward her car. As she opened the car door, she saw Kenny's black limousine hit the corner with screaming tires. She released frustrated sigh and wanted to rush inside her car and try to race away, but that was a dead issue in light of how fast the limo was moving.

The limo came to a smooth halt and Kenny got out of the Limo as thought it was truly an emergency. Baby Doll met Kenny halfway.

Kevin's eyes were wide with concern as he said, "Baby Doll what's going on? Are you okay?"

"Yeah, I'm all right." She said impatiently.

"You never told me you were planning to move."

"I told you I'm having some major issues with the job. Some people are trying to hurt me, physically."

"What did the police say!?" Kenny caressed Baby Doll's shoulder, feeling the urge to comfort her.

"No, Kenny, I didn't get the police involved. I felt it was best that I simply move to avoid all the drama."

"Where are you moving to?"

This was the part she didn't like. It was obvious Kenny wasn't going to let her go just that easy. She suddenly felt self-conscious about lying to him. Since she had no intentions of seeing him again, she let it ride. "I'm moving to Baltimore."

"Baltimore!?" Kenny felt a blow to his heart; it was obvious she had no intentions of coming back and was basically going to just up and disappear without even telling him anything, nor even leaving a forwarding address. "Why so far away? How are you going to commute to the stores and clubs? That's such a long distance away, you'll spend—" He saw it in her eyes. She had no intentions of dealing with the stores and clubs. He sighed and said. "Listen, Baby Doll, all that drama you've been going through is not worth throwing in the towel. Disappearing like this is not going to solve the problem. How about the Youth Employment Program? Those kids need you and going about it—"

"Those kids don't give a fuck about me, Kenny!" Baby Doll decided it was time to give Kenny the real side of who she was with hopes that it would push him away. She stopped and thought about that for a moment and slowed herself down. Since he wasn't a bad guy, she didn't want to break his heart, and agreed to bring it down a notch. "I had to make a decision. I made it and I'm sticking with it. I'm no longer a part of the Youth Employment Program."

"No longer a part of it!?" Kenny's eyes were wide. "What'd you mean no longer a part of it? I thought you were the chief coordinator?"

"I gave it all up, Kenny. I can't take it anymore, so I sold the businesses. Now I'm leaving this place for good—"

"Baby Doll, no!" Kenny shouted as if he was injured by what she had just said.

The response literally surprised Baby Doll, because it was as if he was genuinely shattered.

Kenny's voice was saturated with a deep pain as he spoke, "I thought you gave your word to Big Daddy that you would make sure the youth program would live, it would stay alive!? And—and you sold the businesses!?" His hand shot to his forehead as though it was the end of the world. "Baby Doll, I can't believe you sold—"

"Kenny, I think you need an eye-opener. You don't know what time it is out there in the streets! You know nothing about the hood, and the version you get is the watered-own one." She sighed, because she wanted to go in real hard, but again decided not to. "Do you realize I've been robbed by the very kids I was out here trying to help!? They pulled guns on me, carjacked me, robbed me at gunpoint, and every day they're plotting to do something to me. I've received death threats, and all the people who are supposed to have my back are trying to destroy me. What the fuck do you expect me to do!? Sit by and wait for these snakes to sting me, pull me down, and possibly even kill me!? I'm supposed to continue trying to help a bunch of ungrateful kids that hate my fuckin' guts!? I'm doing what any sane person would do—Salvage what I can, get out of all this, and keep it moving."

Kenny was dumbfounded. He knew her plight was hard, but he didn't know the kids were trying to kill her!? How could he convince her to stay in an environment that could result in her death or serious physical injury? If it were him, he would leave as well. He was a Christian who believed in the gift of charity and helping his fellow man, but he personally would not engage in benevolence at the expense of sacrificing his own life or physical well-being when he could simply move on to other people who might be more receptive to what he had to offer.

It was a universal reality that some people just couldn't be helped; an excellent analogy was that saying, you can bring the horse to the water, but you can't make him drink. It was the same with people; you could try to extend a helping hand, but it was up to them to accept the help. Kenny realized what Baby Doll was experiencing might be an example of these unfortunate facts, and his heart went out to her. He sighed and said, "I'm sorry, Baby Doll. I honestly didn't know you were going through so much." He tried to embrace her but she held him back. "What's the matter, Baby Doll?"

"I'm sorry, Kenny, but—I—I—gotta let you go." She turned to head for the car, but Kenny gently grabbed her hand, stopping her in her tracks. She turned and stared at him. She didn't snatch her hand away, although she really wanted to. "Kenny, please try to understand that I never meant to break your heart. I'm sorry, but I'm not the one for you."

"But we need to give our relationship a meaningful chance to grow before you—"

"No, Kenny, I'm sorry, but I can't do that." She pulled her hand away and saw the devastated hurt in Kenny's eyes and bodily gestures. She turned and eased toward the car and pulled the door open.

"Baby Doll," he said, stopping her from entering the car. He waited until she looked him in the eyes. "There's something in you that tells the world you were put here to help others." He knew it wasn't just because she quoted the most famous biblical verse on the gift of charity. Her very persona literally vibrated an inner goodness of character. "I don't know why I feel this, but something tells me this. I feel it in my heart, Baby Doll, and my heart don't lie. Me. I'm probably in the middle of both extremes, which is the reason why I can tell you that you have a good heart. Look inside yourself, Baby Doll, and listen to that voice. I know it talks to you."

He paused for a moment, making sure she was with him. "It tells you things. But you gotta slow down long enough to hear what it's saying. If you can stop chasing all these distracting things that cloud and obscure the voice, maybe you could hear it." He stared at her for a moment, wishing their relationship could have developed into a serious one. By the look of all the circumstances, there was no altering her position, so he rapidly accepted the reality that it was over. "If you ever need me, I'm only a phone call away." He turned and headed for the Limo.

Baby Doll stood watching Kenny as he slid inside the Limo and drove away. She was in a trance as she watched the Limo cruise away but didn't fully understand why. Of course, she knew she was partially mesmerized because what Kenny had just said was the exact same thing Big Daddy had told her just before he died—that she was put here to help other people—but she simply did not see why or how they came to this conclusion. If they all only knew that she was simply trying to get paid, she wondered would they all feel the same way.

BABY DOLL

As she got inside the car and started the engine, Baby Doll wondered should she consider getting involved in the field of acting because she sure must be a genuine natural.

CHAPTER 34

Baby Doll saw being rich was all what she expected it to be and much more. The new house in Richmond was worth every dime she spent purchasing it, and with the expert touch of an interior decorator it became something fit for a millionaire to live in. Besides getting her house in tip-top shape, one of the first things on her list of priorities was coming up with ways to guarantee that she stayed a millionaire.

On many late nights Baby Doll surfed the internet to find out what were the up-and-coming money-making businesses. She was surprised to discover that urban hood books were making noise as far as money was concerned, and she immediately started looking for a way to get her foot into that door. Her money was definitely long enough to get in that game, but she knew nothing about publishing. She also discovered that the rap industry was a vicious money-making market, but like all lucrative markets, it was hard breaking into that business. Looking at her situation it became clear she had to reach out to someone who was influential in the business world on multiple fronts, and the only person she could think of who wasn't an enemy was Ernest Hudson. She called in a favor, and Mr. Hudson came through like a true-blue trooper. She explained that she wasn't interested in starting her own business, in the sense of doing all that heavy front-line work, but wanted to be a silent partner. She would invest money, help the company grow, and receive an ongoing percentage of the profits, sort of like what the stock market does, but more on a direct, one-on-one basis.

The first thing Mr. Hudson did was introduce Baby Doll to a good entertainment lawyer she could trust. Doug Harris was a Black lawyer who worked for various well-known R&B singers, professional sports celebrities, and even a few world-renowned Hollywood actors.

Baby Doll noticed upon meeting Doug that he was very serious about his work, meticulous, and expensive. In view of the wealth of experience and clientele he brought to the table, she sensed he was worth the inevitable headaches of dealing with a professional that was obsessed with his craft.

Within months, Baby Doll was introduced to Tina Davis, an aspiring urban book writer who had an upstart publishing company in Oakley Landing and was in need of financial assistance.

"My dream is to become the quintessential publisher of all publishers," Baby Doll remembered Tina said to her during their first visit, and when she added, "I am so hungry, I'm literally starving to pull this off. If you invest in Supremetech Publications, I swear you won't regret it, Baby Doll," she knew it was a go. They draw up a contract that indicated Baby Doll would invest $150,000 in the company and would receive an ongoing fifteen percent of all profits after the entire loan was paid in full. Tina had a stable of writers lined up, ready to start spitting out novels.

Supremetech came on the literary scene like a shock-and-awe campaign. They dropped seven books from seven different authors (three of which were incarcerated) and caused an earthquake within the urban book industry. The money came in so rapidly, Baby Doll's one hundred and fifty gees was paid back within months of the first books hitting the bookstores, and she was collecting semi-annual royalty checks that were on time like Uncle Sam's tax collection machine.

Meanwhile, Baby Doll also took advantage of the rap craze and invested in a small recording studio and record label in Farnham, a backwoods town in Virginia. With the assistance of Doug Harris, Baby Doll met a brother named David Singleton, who was a talented and very ambitious record producer with four rap acts but felt the only thing holding him back was a lack of money for quality promotion.

After a two-hour talk, Baby Doll agreed to loan David Singleton a half million dollars with stipulations that she receive an ongoing royalty percentage of ten percent of all future profits, after she received reimbursement of the initial loan money. Within months, Baby Doll was receiving returns on her rap producer investment and could see that in no time she would be rolling in dough from this investment.

Then, the strangest thing occurred on one evening in the month of May when Baby Doll returned home from the health spa and found an envelope on her floor as she entered her home. The envelope was apparently slid under the door; she reached down, picked it up, opened it, pulled out the letter inside, and saw a typed written note that said,

BABY DOLL, DON'T FORGET 1 CORINTHIAN 13, VERSES 1-13.
TIME IS RUNNING OUT. ALL DEBTS
MUST BE PAID IN FULL

Baby Doll was catapulted into a state of fear, confusion, and panic as she tried to decipher what this letter meant, and most of all, who wrote it and slid it under her door. There was no name, address, or any identifying information on the envelope or the letter. Whoever wrote it apparently knew her and that she knew this Bible verse. But what the hell did they mean by "time is running out" and "all debts must be paid in full!?" Baby Doll's mind was literally saturated with dread as she sat on her bed trying to think this thing through.

After going back and forth, almost driving herself crazy with a trillion mental questions, she pulled herself together and assumed it was either Kenny or one of his family members, or possibly even Preacher who was messing with her.

They were the only ones who knew she knew the 1 Corinthians Bible verse, so it had to be one of them. She concluded that they were trying to give her a hint that she should give more money to charity or was trying to lash out at her because she sold the businesses. Although she was able to brush the letter aside on these grounds, that voice was telling her to look closer at the other parts of the letter, since those parts had all semblances of a warning that had a strong touch of aggressiveness. Unfortunately, Baby Doll was too into herself to see beyond what she wanted to see, believe and hear. However, to be on the safe side, she did move. Two days later, she purchased another home in Warsaw County, kept her old house in Richmond, but moved into the new one as a diversion.

* * * *

About a month after Baby Doll's twenty-fifth birthday, a Latino man named Alex Gonzalez approached her with a business proposition while she and her new home-girl Rakeya were eating at a restaurant. Alex wanted her to invest in a real estate project Cobham Park County. Initially, everything seemed to be going well, until Baby Doll indicated she would have to allow her attorney to look over the written proposal. When Baby Doll saw Alex's sudden hesitation, a reaction that happened within a fraction of a second, she was convinced there was something wrong with this deal. She followed her gut instinct, and thankfully she did, because six months later, Alex Gonzalez and several other cohorts were on the evening news when the Virginia State Police dismantled the scheme that was designed to trick investors to invest in all sorts of bogus projects, and then disappearing with the money. At the time of Gonzalez's arrest, he and his five co-defendants had swindled over three million dollars from people all across Virginia and a few areas in Delaware and Maryland.

In December of that year, Baby Doll went off on her fifth date and finally felt she had a catch worth investing some significant time in. Talib Muhammad was a thirty-year-old pediatric physician, a bachelor, very rich, drop-dead handsome, a member of the Nation of Islam, and had plenty backbone when it came to dealing with his family. Not only that, but for the first time since dating, she was honestly able to put Big Spike in the closet and keep it there. Talib was also a renaissance man, since he seemed to be knowledgeable in damn near everything, even including business investing.

But Talib's most favorable attribute of them all, as far as Baby Doll was concerned, was that his chemistry on all levels was fully intact with hers. They seemed to be meant for each other, and although they had their fair share of ups and downs like all couples, they never stayed mad at each other very long, and both knew the right things to say to each other at the perfect time. Baby Doll could even see herself bearing Talib's child, and once she doubled her initial financial worth, she had full intentions of taking it there with him. He had already given her strong hints that he wanted to marry her and start a family, but she let him know explicitly that she would be ready to give him an answer very soon.

* * * *

By the time Baby Doll's twenty-sixth birthday slid by, she'd been doing a lot of introspection. She noticed she was developing an entirely different understanding of happiness. She didn't understand it, but the more the bank account grew in leaps and bounds (she now had seven million dollars), and the more she did all the things she dreamed of doing, she felt a profound sense of emptiness growing with each fulfilled desire. She had traveled the United States, visiting all major cities worth touring.

The overseas vacations were limited only to those areas that kindled her curiosity, and unfortunately that wasn't very many. But what frightened her most was that what she thought she loved most was now evolving into something she no longer found pleasure in pursuing.

At one time in her not-so-distant past, the mere thought of money brought on an overflow of excitement that would make her head spin with wooziness, her knees weak with wanting, and the pit of her stomach bubbling with an adrenaline rush. Now that she had money these mental, emotional, physical, and psychological reactions ceased, and it even caused some degree of discomfort and mental anguish when she realized she wasn't responding like she used to. It was almost like eating so much of a particular food to the point that the food started to make the person sick to the stomach upon seeing that food again. The sudden change of heart almost scared her, because she felt she was literally losing her mind.

Then, on a late September evening when Baby Doll entered her home, she stopped in her tracks when she saw another envelope on her floor. She stood staring at the letter as if it were crawling with spiders. For some odd reason she felt as if she was being watched, and instantly began looking around her immediate area. She hastily locked the door and held her breath to hear if someone was inside her home. After a moment, she noticed there were no sounds inside her house. She stared at the envelope, knowing what she was going to find. She forced herself to pick up the envelope. Sure enough, there was no return address, and no writing of any kind on the outer envelope. She sat her purse down on the small table and slowly entered her living room and sat on the sofa.

Baby Doll took a deep breath and opened the letter with trembling hands. She hated to confess it, but the truth of the matter was that the guilt involved in not keeping her promise to Big Daddy was literally eating her alive.

Just when the lid of the envelope was ripped open, Baby Doll was hurled into a trance as she reflected on the emotional roller coaster she'd been riding for the last two months or so. She knew it was the guilt but attributed it to other things like stress due to her business activities, and boredom from no longer having the same thrill she used to have for the pursuit of money. But that voice had assured her that it was guilt that was making her feel this way. She felt the urge to do something to make amends, but her fear of being judged and looked down upon was shoving her away from admitting she was dead wrong, and away from doing something to undo that transgression.

Baby Doll shook loose of the daydream and pulled out the letter. Just like before there was a typewritten noted that simply said,

"BABY DOLL, DON'T FORGET 1 CORINTHIAN 13,
VERSES 1-13.
TIME HAS RAN OUT. ALL DEBTS WILL
BE PAID IN FULL."

Baby Doll instantly detected the slight difference from the last letter. The content of the previous letter was so deeply engrained on her mind that she had remembered the words verbatim and now noticed the subtle changes in the last two sentences. In the previous letter time "was running out", while in this one, time has "run out." *Oh, my God, time has ran out, what does this mean!?* She digested the second change; the previous letter said the debt "must be paid," while this one said the debt "will be paid." Once again, the terror gripped her because these warning were clear. Baby Doll's mind was bouncing all over the place trying to figure out what she should do.

Suddenly, a noise came from behind the curtain.

Before Baby Doll had completely turned her head in the direction of the noise, she saw a huge figure stepped from behind the curtain. Baby Doll was literally frozen in utter terror because it was definitely a man dressed in black clothing, was wearing a mask, and was brandishing a gun.

He slowly approached Baby Doll with the gun held to his side.

With eyes as wide as baseballs, Baby Doll slowly rose to her feet. "W—What are you doing in my house!?"

The masked man stopped next to the armchair and just stared at Baby Doll.

Baby Doll frantically looked around for an escape route, but she instantly realized it was useless to attempt to run because the man had a gun. If she ran, he could easily gun her down. "W—What the fuck do you want!?"

"Quote 1 *Corinthians* 13, 1-13." the man said with a deep, handsome radio-host type of voice.

Baby Doll was stuck literally on stupid. She looked down at the letter in her hand. "Y—You wrote this letter!?"

There was no response.

Baby Doll struggled to calm her mind down. She had to relax. She drew in several deep breaths, and said, "Who sent you here? Is this some kind of joke to scare the living shit out of me!? Who sent you!? Kenny!? Preacher!?"

There was no response.

Baby Doll saw the masked man just stood there looking at her; she was literally trembling with fear. "Please, what is it you want!? I—I—"

"Quote 1 *Corinthians* 13, 1-13!!" the man said, but this time it was obviously not a request, but an unmistakable demand. The hate even resonated through the air.

Baby Doll felt the vibration of his tone, and it caused her heart to pound a lot faster; she swallowed hard, hoping she remembered the Bible verse because, from the way it looked, her life depended on her quoting this verse. She drew in several deep breaths, and began to recite the verse, hoping and praying she didn't forget it, "T—Though I—I speak with the tongues of men and of angels, and have not charity."

Baby Doll paused, fighting to remember. After a moment, she was able to continue. "I—I am become as sounding brass, or a tinkling cymbal. And though I have the gift of prophecy, and understand all mysteries, and all knowledge; and—and—and though I have all faith, so that I could remove mountains, and have not charity, I am nothing—"

She started sweating profusely. She forced herself to calm down and remember and in that instance she felt it had all came back to her as if a light switch was turned on. "And though I bestow all my goods to feed the poor, and though I give my body to be burned . . .And now abideth faith, hope, charity, these three; but the greatest of these is charity."

There was an intense moment of silence.

"Baby Doll, there is one more thing you should remember," The masked man said, as the gun slowly rose. "Keeping your promise is being one with the Lord." He took aim and fired the silencer-equipped weapon.

Baby Doll felt an extremely hard blow hit her in the stomach; the impact was so powerful it shoved her backwards as if she was violently pushed by an eight-hundred-pound gorilla. She had never been shot before, but automatically knew what had struck her in the gut was a bullet; the burning sensation that instantly erupted reminded her of the street slang teens used to describe shooting someone when they would say, "I'm about to put some 'hot ones' up in that ass!" She saw, indeed, a bullet was definitely a hot one.

Her hand had shot down to her stomach wound almost as fast as the bullet hit her, and she instantly felt her warm bodily fluid seeping from her gut as she collapsed to the floor, already feeling dizzy. She knew she was dying; that voice was telling her so and she knew exactly why. The man told her this when he asked her to recite the Bible verse. It was because of what she did to Big Daddy. She betrayed him, conned him, fucked him with no grease, cut-throated him, and played him like a flute when all he was trying to do was help his people. She had destroyed his lifelong dream without the slightest blink of hesitation. But, now, that voice told her she was getting her justice.

She started crying because deep down she wanted to do the right thing, but she was weak. She wanted to keep her word but all the other forces were stronger than her. She pleaded inwardly, wishing she had another chance to get it right. *Please, God, give me another chance to get it right! If I had another chance, I swear I will get it right!* These inner cries confused her because she never prayed to God before, but all of a sudden, these pleas were rolling through her mind as if they had a mind of their own. She heard that inner voice in her head yelling, "Please give me another chance," as she sensed the man moving toward her.

The man walked over to her, stood staring down at Baby Doll clutching her stomach while breathing very hard and said, "When you get to the other side, remember, all debts will be paid . . ."

Baby Doll then felt a blow to her head that literally flung her instantly into a state of triple darkness.

". . . in full," He added as he inspected his handiwork.

CHAPTER 35

Reverend Rose stood at the altar preaching the eulogy. His energy was the typical fire and brimstone kind of sermon, and the entire church was with him every step of the way. There were sporadic cries and even a few down-south-style hollering. Screams of "Oh god!" "Jesus Christ is protecting her now!" "She's with the Lord now" could be heard throughout the church, accompanied by heavy crying.

The open casket stood in front of Reverend Rose's altar and was surrounded by colorful flowers of various denominations.

Reverend Rose waved his arms in church-theatrical fashion as he said, "Our beloved sister is with the Lord, now, walking about the Holy Kingdom of God. She's in very good hands, my brothers and sisters."

"Amen," A cacophony of voices said.

"She's with our Lord and Savior Jesus Christ.

"Praise the Lord," Another cacophony of voices said.

Reverend Rose said, "For those who knew her can bear testimony that she was a gentle woman."

"Amen," The cacophony said again.

"She had a big heart," Reverend Rose continued. "A heart that God blessed her with in order to do his work, and God's work was what she did. She may not have been a regular churchgoer and may have used self-style methods to fight the evil powers that be, but nonetheless, she was one of God's children and she tried to do her best with what she had, despite the evils of human frailties. She was, indeed, an advocate for the downtrodden in her past, and maintained a willingness to help others when there was a need."

He paused. "But the Lord felt it was her time, my brothers and sisters. As we all know, the Lord works in very mysterious ways, and what He has done was most certainly for very good reasons.

The Lord chooses those to do His will in ways we will never fully understand."

"Praise the Lord," A heavyset woman in the front row shouted.

Reverend Rose continued, "But the one thing we all can say about our beloved sister Jeanette Morrison, who lay in rest before our eyes, is that she is now resting in peace in the good and graceful hands of the Lord . . ."

* * * *

Baby Doll swirled up from a region in her mind that was buried deep beyond layers of sub-consciousness that even she didn't know existed. She slowly opened her eyes, and thought she was going to see fire leaping up all around her, or she was going to be hovering on a cloud. The images of hell and heaven jumped in her mind the minute her mind clicked into its consciousness mode. Once her eyes were opened, she noticed her vision was blurred, and it felt like an arduous task just to open her eyes and to keep them open. She sighed in relief because she was sure she wasn't in hell or heaven; she was in an earthly place for sure. Then, the soft beeping sound of a nearby machine registered, then the smell of antiseptics activated her nose; her physical senses were foreign, and she realized she couldn't feel parts of her body.

As Baby Doll's vision came into focus as if someone had adjusted the lenses on her eyes like a camera, her surroundings became comprehensible. She was in a hospital. The fluorescent light overhead was beaming brightly and illuminated a heavenly aura. But, now, as all her senses kicked into action, she knew she wasn't dead.

She tried to move her body to make sure she didn't jump the gun and savored the agonizing pain that ripped through her body, in particular her stomach and her head. In fact, the pain in her stomach was so overwhelming, it gave her an instant headache.

She moved her head ever so slightly and saw she had wires and tubes attached to various parts of her body. There were tubes up her nose. After a moment, she sensed they even had plastic tubes inserted in places she would rather not imagine, and it felt very intrusive. There was no doubt she was in bad shape, but she felt grateful that she was alive.

Then, it all came back to her as though an avalanche of memories came crashing down on top of her head. The man in the mask had shot her after he made her recite the Corinthians Bible verse. Then, she remembered he stood over her, and punched her in the head, and then everything went black. He knocked her out with that one colossal blow to her temple, she realized and could now feel the pain in that area of her head just by remembering it had happened.

Suddenly, she felt a blow to her heart. This was Big Daddy's way of talking to her from the grave, and he was punishing her for breaching her promise. She didn't merely break her promise, and violated Big Daddy's dream, but she did it in the worse kind of way. She didn't just abandon the Youth Employment Program but went all out and sold everything Big Daddy built with his own blood, sweat and tears, all in the name of fulfilling her dream of becoming rich.

Her tears of shame, disgrace, and regret exploded from her eyes, and poured down the side of her face. The pain in her heart made her wish for death.

As the tears rolled from her eyes, she remembered pleading to God to give her another chance. She couldn't help believing God had answered her cries for forgiveness and for another chance to make amends when something made that man punch her instead of shooting her again. Then, something else hit her. How did she get to this hospital!?

Directly on the heels of this thought Baby Doll heard someone enter the room, and she shot her eyes in the direction of the door. She saw a fat Black woman dressed in a white nurse's uniform had entered. She had a pretty, fat face surrounded by chubby cheeks and seemed to have a smile permanently plastered on her face.

"Hey, I see our pretty little Princess has finally awaken," Geraldine Joseph said as she came over to Baby Doll's bedside to check her vials and IV equipment. "Child, how you feeling?" She began checking the tubes and other wires attached to Baby Doll and noticed Baby Doll had been doing some crying. "You in pain or something, child?"

"Not really." Baby Doll noticed it was a struggle just to speak. "I'm thirsty."

Geraldine laughed. "I bet you is, Miss. Winbush. You were in surgery for a whole hour. Them doctors took a big ol' bullet outtas yo' belly, baby. But doctor's order is you can't drink or eat anything for at least twenty-four hours. You see, that's what this intravenous hook up is for." She gestured to the clear plastic bag containing a clear liquid.

Baby Doll smiled, "What's your name?"

"Oh, I'm sorry, Miss Winbush," Geraldine said. "How rude of me. My name is Geraldine Joseph. Please excuse me for not introducing myself earlier. I tell ya, child, I'm just all over the place."

"That's all right," Baby Doll said, looking at the intravenous bag Geraldine referred to and noticed the tubing was attached to a needle inserted in her arm that was taped down. "How did I get here?"

Geraldine smiled. "The ambulance brought you here. I wasn't here when you came in, but that's what your chart said. Your chart also says the police'll be here soon to talk to you. Not to be nosy, but who shot you, Miss Winbush?"

Baby Doll hated hearing her government name. It sounded so odd to her ears. "Geraldine, please call me Baby Doll."

"Baby Doll?" Geraldine smiled. "Child, that name sure fits you. You sure are pretty as a Baby Doll even with all this Frankenstein stuff hooked up to you, child." She smiled.

Baby Doll tried to laugh, but the pain shot through her tummy. "You asked who shot me? It was a man in a mask. He entered my house and shot me."

"Was it a burglar that did it? Was he trying to rob you?"

"Actually, he just entered my house and shot me." She wasn't about to tell her or the police about the Bible recitation, because it would make her appear crazy, and it would definitely incite more questions. But she felt the urge to do something that she'd never done before, and looking at Geraldine's mannerisms, she sensed she was a religious woman. And even if she wasn't, Baby Doll was certain she could help her with this request. "Geraldine, I need a big favor."

Geraldine was all smiles. "If I can help you, Baby Doll, I would be more than happy to do that, child."

"I need a Bible," Baby Doll said; she didn't know why she felt odd making such a harmless request, but she suspected it was because this act made her look like she was seeking refuge from something, and when Baby Doll thought about it, she actually was in a sense.

"That's all, child?" Geraldine was glad she wasn't asking her to do something that could get her in any trouble. She was all too familiar with people wanting all sorts of crazy things. She remembered one patient had the audacity to ask her to buy some marijuana, and another had wanted her to sneak her boyfriend in during none visit hours so she could get her groove on. "Baby Doll,

I can do a whole lot more than get you a Bible. I can teach you a few things about the Good Book, being that I teach Sunday School at my church. I'm also working on becoming an ordain minister." She smiled triumphantly.

In the days that followed, as Baby Doll's body healed, so did her wounded spirit. From the very moment she opened her eyes and saw she was still on his planet, there was no doubt in her mind that she was going to keep her word that if she was given another chance she would fulfill Big Daddy's dream. She vowed she would keep her promise even if she had to die doing it. Her eagerness to read the Bible was provoked by the mere fact that everyone she knew who went to church saw the Bible as one of the most powerful sources of inspiration ever created, and since she knew she was going to need a whole lot of inspiration to keep her on the path of the mission she was about to embark upon, she decided to read the Holy Book from cover to cover. If the Bible was an instrument of inspiration, she figured it would be prudent to ingest the full force of everything it had to offer.

Several days later, Baby Doll was sitting up in bed reading the Bible. She was about halfway through and suddenly laid the book down as a profound realization struck her mind like a wet glove to the face.

She noticed that most of the materials in this book were stories of the Hebrews, depicting their trials and tribulations. What amazed her most was that she could see the same flaws, infallibilities, and problems had existed back then as they do today. Of course, there were obvious differences, like the lack of technology back then. But all and all, she saw human beings were basically the same then as they are today. It was amazing to her how human beings never really changed much in thousands of years and were still engaging in the sort of things that undermined the human spirit. People lied, they stole, cheated, murdered, maimed each other, violated laws, and the list could go on and on. No wonder there was a need for religion, she thought. Because if people didn't have the word of a higher force, people would go above and beyond the realm of balance and would perceive themselves as God and then would really get crazy with all those extreme human emotions.

She looked at her misdeeds and saw just how fast people could get caught up in egotistical and selfish ways of life that could invariably become destructive to others. She saw the Bible acted as a constant reminder that human beings needed to be kept on a very short leash so that their emotions, ambitions, and aspirations did not become dangerous to other human beings. She smiled at the level of deep and profound observation she was able to comprehend just by reading only half of the Bible.

As she picked the Bible back up to resume her reading, she wasn't certain whether or not she was on the right track, but her gut instinct told her that she was. When she got a little further into the Bible she decided to present this particular observation to Geraldine for confirmation.

By the time Baby Doll was three quarters through the Holy Book, Geraldine entered the room with intentions of testing Baby Doll to see just how well she comprehended the Good Book.

Baby Doll stayed smiling at Geraldine because every time she laid eyes on Geraldine, she was instantly reminded of all the church ladies from her past. The only difference between Mrs. Kirkland, Ruth Wallace, and Geraldine Joseph was that Geraldine wasn't as fanatical with Christian doctrine as Mrs. Kirkland and Ruth were. But, what really stirred up Baby Doll's mind was the fact that Geraldine had also told her what both Mrs. Kirkland and Ruth had told her; she had a pure soul, and was put here to go God's work.

When Baby Doll shared with Geraldine her profound observation regarding what the Bible was really meant to do, she had received an A grade on her analogy. Geraldine was impressed with Baby Doll's remarkable enthusiasm with learning the Bible and did everything in her power to encourage more of what she was doing.

It was no mystery that near-death experiences had this effect on some people, and Geraldine also knew there were usually specific issues in that person's life that was either haunting them or lingering around unresolved. She wanted to know what Baby Doll's story was and had tried to pull it out twice already, but she was doing it in a roundabout fashion. It was time to become more direct.

"Baby Doll, you would be my best student if you was to come on down to my Sunday school classes, child. The way you're tackling at those jewels in the Good Book tells me you're dealing with a dark past." She let that hang in the air for a moment and continued. "What's on your agenda when you get out of here, Baby Doll? From what I can tell, you're going to do the work of the Lord, and I sure would love to help you get it right."

Baby Doll saw this as a sign from above, because she obviously needed someone to help her "get it right," as well as someone to critique her plan of action, even though it was relatively simple and straightforward. "I'm going to pick up where I left off about two years ago. I used to be the chief coordinator of a Youth Employment Program in Brooklyn. My father—well not my biological father, but my spiritual father—had left me in charge of the program before he died, and I went way off track. When I get out of this hospital, I'm going to finish what I started, and what I promised my father I would do. I'm going to start a Youth Employment Program in his name, and this time I'm gonna do it up real big," She said dreamingly with anticipation and a deadly seriousness in her eyes. "And any feedback you can give me, I'm all ears."

After a moment, Geraldine asked, "What was your father's name?"

Beaming with joy, Baby Doll said, "Gregory J. Williams, AKA Big Daddy Blue."

"Well, child, you got a lot of work on your hands." Geraldine got up from the chair and checked the heart machine. "'Cause these youngun' growing up nowadays are sure gonna need a miracle from God to get some of them interested in working. Now, don't get me wrong, I know there's a lot of good kids that's on the right path. But the Lord's work always focuses on those who really need the help, and those that actually need the help are very hard to reach most of the time."

Geraldine sat back down; she wanted to share what she knew about starting up such a program but didn't want to discourage her with negative stories. Her church had started such a program a few years back, and it ended in disaster. Most of the kids caused more problems for the church than she dared to believe.

"Looking at you, Baby Doll, I know you gonna be fine, because I feel you got an old soul, child, and success is twinkling in your eyes. Just look at cha. You beaming with the eye of the tiger, child, and is as hungry as you wanna be. "

Baby Doll felt like she could save the world after hearing those words.

As the days transformed into weeks, Baby Doll got her first true experience with abandonment, and thanks to her contact with certain verses on the issue of imprisonment (Matthew 25: 36; Proverbs 22: 6; and Luke 13: 24-30), she was fully prepared not to allow herself to become bitter, even though it was the most natural human response.

Reflecting on how this abandonment felt, Baby Doll developed a tremendous amount of respect for Big Daddy and all other folks who had spent decades behind bars while their families and so-called friends turned their backs on them at the darkest moment of their lives. They still came out of such a place willing to help people, even those who had abandoned them.

Baby Doll was at the darkest moment of her life as she laid in this hospital bed, and the only one who felt compelled to visit her was Talib. Since Baby Doll had decided to dedicate her entire life keeping her word to Big Daddy, she told Talib it was over and asked him not to return to see her again. Talib was devastated and deeply confused, but when Baby Doll said, "Talib, please understand that this decision has nothing to do with you. You're probably the sincerest and prefect man I have ever met. I have a lot of ghosts from my past that I have to deal with, and I gotta face these problems alone. I would never allow my problems to become someone else's problem, so please respect my decision," he was able to put the pieces together and agreed to honor her wishes.

* * * *

Three weeks later, Baby Doll's stomach wound was healed enough for the doctors to release her. With a cane and colostomy bag tucked under her clothing, she limped out of the Warsaw County Hospital with clear instructions to take it light for another month or so, and to not miss any of her weekly checkups. As Baby Doll headed for the yellow taxicab, for the first time she wondered, Would the mask man return to finish the job he had started, but apparently didn't complete?

CHAPTER 36

Baby Doll started her mission with a bang. She sold both of her houses and purchased a simple, inexpensive home in Richmond County that was obtained solely to serve its purpose (a decent place to live). Her theory was that she was going to need every penny she had access to in order to get her plan rolling, and all that high living was a definite no-no.

The first couple of weeks were by far a living hell; the mere fact of not knowing whether or not she would return home and find the mask man waiting to finish her off was the greatest challenge she'd ever confronted in her life. If not for one particular Bible verse that was probably deemed one of the most popular of all other verses when it came to confronting seeming insurmountable and highly life-threatening ordeals, she would have never made it through this hurdle. *Psalm 23*, which she committed to memory, said, "The Lord is my Shepard; I shall not want. He maketh me to lie down in green pastures: he leadeth me beside the still waters. He restoreth my soul: he leadeth me in the paths of righteousness for his name's sake. Yea, though I walk through the valley of the shadow of death, I will fear no evil: for thou art with me; thy rod and thy staff they comfort me. Thou preparest a table before me in the presence of mine enemies; thou anointest my head with oil; my cup runneth over. Surely goodness and mercy shall follow me all the days of my life: and I will dwell in the house of the Lord forever."

Whenever she entered her home or felt threatened by a situation that made her feel she was being pushed away from her mission due to fear, she mumbled Psalm 23, and instantly her apprehension disappeared, and she was able to continue forward at full speed.

Another thing she did upon leaving Warsaw County Hospital was immediately pay all her debts. The letters she received from the mask man had made it very clear that all debts must be paid in full. While reading the Bible she came to the conclusion that she had a series of outstanding debts. What she had done to Samson, Nicole, Helen and even Karl constituted a debt. What she'd done to them was wrong, and it was done for her own personal gain, which made it unequivocally wrong under any aspect of reasoning, and therefore, these were debts that had to be paid.

Baby Doll hired an investigator, found out where each of them was living, and sent them checks in a reasonable amount to cover their losses, and a letter of apology. She had even sent her family a few dollars and shocked them immensely, because it came at a time they dearly needed it and least expected it. There were others that she'd done wrong in some way, but upon balancing other factors like what they had did to her to cause her to react, while also weighing the fact that they were inherently foul people who were out to destroy and hurt Big Daddy's dream anyway, she was able to exclude them and feel confident enough to believe those issues were debts that did not have to be paid.

Baby Doll had also visited Jeanette's gravesite over in the Evergreen Cemetery in Bushwick, Brooklyn. She propped a huge bouquet of colorful flowers on the headstone and talked to Jeanette for about twenty minutes about old times. Baby Doll felt bad she wasn't able to attend the funeral, but she sure had a very good excuse, since she was laid up in a Virginia hospital at the time of Jeanette Morrison's expiration. As she walked away from the headstone, Baby Doll noticed she felt like a fifty-pound weight had been taken off her shoulders; although she didn't make the funeral, she had at least visited her lifelong friend, who was one of the few people who had showed her love when she was growing up.

With her conscience partially cleared, she dove headlong into her main mission. She spent hours upon hours reading about programs, foundations, non-for-profit groups, community-based programs, clearinghouse grants, government loans programs. After weeks of research, she was ready to facilitate her plan. Since she wanted to do this thing the right way, and to do it as big as she could possibly take it, she decided to start her own non-for-profit group named after Big Daddy.

The Gregory J. Williams Youth Employment Organization (GJWYEO) had humble beginnings, but literally grew into a national organization overnight. The main objective of this organization was to promote, assist, and facilitate the creation of youth employment all across the country. The organization campaigned for youth employment by sending representatives to various places of business to convince them to hire youths, and even in some instances help foot the payroll bills. Also, the organization kept full contact with junior high schools, high schools, parole agencies, the courts, and any after school centers in poverty-stricken communities. The organization's creed was that any youth interested in finding employment was guaranteed help from the GJWYEOin fulfilling that aspiration. "No youth should be without employment if they truly wanted to work" was a statement that made up the foundation of the organization.

Because Baby Doll had the money, and still had a steady source coming in (her publishing and recording royalties were booming quite well), she was able to hire the best non-for-profit advisors money could buy, as well as quality workers who were very efficient. Not to mention, the government loans, donations from celebrities, and non-for-profit grants were surprisingly substantial, considering the fact Baby Doll was willing to lay her own money on the line. When these agencies and prestige people saw Baby Doll utilizing millions of her own money, they had no problem giving her a portion of what she was giving toward the organization.

The executive team Baby Doll had put together was no doubt a dream team, and once they saw Baby Doll's sincere and heartfelt desire to turn her dream into a reality, her attitude became contagious. The first year they opened up with branches in New York and Virginia. The following year, four branches sprung up in three other major cities, New Jersey, Baltimore, Detroit, and DC. By the third year, in total, there were twenty-five chapters all across the country, virtually in all major cities. Most of all, the track record for putting youths to work was truly phenomenal. Tens of thousands of youths were able to say the Gregory J. Williams Youth Employment Organization opened employment opportunities for them that they would have never had.

Baby Doll had even formulated a lobbyist group that fought to get legislation passed that gave companies that hired Youths huge tax breaks. The Gregory J. Williams bill was currently on the Senate floor, and Baby Doll was elated with something far more powerful than joy and a sense of success.

In just three years after being shot, she had transformed Big Daddy's name into a nationally known name, and she was certain he never dreamed he would one day be the root of supplying so many jobs to kids beyond the streets of Brooklyn.

The success of the organization was big news all across the country. It was so big that Baby Doll received offers to appear on television and radio talk shows. Some she appeared on, others she respectfully declined. When she received an offer to appear on *The Oprah Winfrey Show*, she was dazed with shock. *The Oprah Winfrey Show*, everybody knew, was the big of the big time. Baby Doll suddenly realized she was a celebrity, as she accepted the offer, planning to use this opportunity to springboard the Organization onto an even greater platform. This was an opportunity she couldn't pass up, even if she wanted to.

As Baby Doll sat in the make-up chair in the Harpo studios in Chicago about to go on the air to talk to the most popular talk show host in the country, she reflected back on her journey, and started crying. The road she had traveled was rocky, rough, ruthless, and unrelenting. Her tears sprung from a mixture of joy, relief, and most of all indecisiveness.

The last night before, she'd received another letter. It was in the exact same format as the previous two letters and was slid under her door, but this time it said,

BABY DOLL, 1 CORINTHIAN 13,
VERSES 1-13 IS GOOD.
TIME IS ON YOUR SIDE. ALL DEBTS
ALMOST PAID IN FULL.

As Baby Doll wiped her eyes, struggling to pull herself together, Karen, her personal make-up assistant, was very patient and was helping her soak up the tears as if she had done this a million times. The letter was on her mind because it was saying she still had other debts to pay. She cried even harder when she realized she didn't know what else she could do to pay these alleged unresolved debts. Without being told, she sensed a dark cloud of doom rapidly approaching, because she was certain there was no further higher level she could take Big Daddy's dream.

CHAPTER 37

The huge, almost movie-sized screen TV illuminated Baby Doll's and Oprah's faces with remarkable clarity. Baby Doll was explaining to millions of viewers what had inspired her to do what she accomplished. About several feet away two men sat watching the TV inside a million-dollar palace-style living room that reeked of incalculable amounts of money. Scattered about the living room was gold-trimmed furniture, expensive paintings covered the walls, and beyond the walls of this mansion that could hold ten large-size families and still have plenty of room for another seven families was a golf field, a track field, a swimming pool, and a garage that held seven elegant cars and other vehicles of various makers.

Quameek picked up the remote control on the coffee table and increased the volume to a level that was almost too much for the average delicate ear. Quameek was a bulky built Black man, with shifty eyes, a male model's facial structure, a thin goatee, a Caesar-style haircut, and huge biceps. He could pass for a human tank. Quameek sat watching and listening intently while sipping on a glass of champagne. He hated to drink alone, but there was nothing he could go about that since Charles G. Bedford, AKA Sweet Charlie, didn't drink, even on a special occasion as this one.

Sweet Charlie pulled his eyes from the TV screen, glanced at his watch, sighed loudly, and wondered, Where the hell was Kenny!? He'd made it clear that he wanted them all here, so they could collectively watch this memorable moment. "Did Kenny say he was going to be late?"

"He didn't say nothing to me," Quameek said without taking his eyes off the screen.

A moment later, Oprah announced to the TV audience that she would be right back after a brief commercial, and the audience applauded on cue.

Quameek reached over to the bottle of champagne, poured himself another glass and said, "I'm tired of you keeping me in dark with all this, Charlie. You can tell me now, fuck waiting until after we watch this program. What you did to that girl to cause all this?" He leaned back in on the sofa. "I know those envelopes you had me sliding under her door had something to do with it."

Sweet Charlie continued looking at the cleaning detergent commercial as though he didn't even hear Quameek.

"What she did is nothing short of amazing," Quameek said as he sat his glass on the table. "In three years this broad fucked around and turned Big Daddy into a sure enough urban legend. Man, you must've either put the fear of God in her ass, or hit her ass up with some serious mind control shit."

Sweet Charlie laughed. "I'll say this for now; all she needed was a little helping hand to help her see the light."

"Well, whatever it is, you need to put that shit in a pill, 'cause all these foot-dragging, no-promise-keeping-ass motherfuckers all over the place need that kind of fire put under their asses."

"Let's don't start that negative stuff, all right?" Sweet Charlie knew he had to shut Quameek down quickly. "I see why you gave up trying to be a facilitator, you got too much imbalance in your life."

Quameek was waiting for more, since he didn't catch where Charlie was going with that last remark. "What are you talking about, imbalance? I gave up trying to be a hitman, 'cause I got bodyguarding in my blood. And what imbalance I got?"

"That negative attitude of yours; that's an imbalance with any kind of occupation, whether facilitating or bodyguarding. Here's a lesson you need to put in your pocket—Not every situation is inundated with negativity. There's some good in everything. It's just a matter of finding it, exploiting it, and never letting it slip from your grasp once you get hold of it. Shit, look at Baby Doll." He smiled proudly.

Just as the commercial ended and the show came back on, Kenny Moye entered and Sweet Charlie gave him the evil eye. No one said anything as Kenny took a seat at the sofa, and smiled when he saw Baby Doll. The smiled stayed on Kenny's face until the next commercial appeared on the TV screen.

"I thought I said I wanted everyone here to watch this?" Sweet Charlie said smoothly.

"It was beyond my control, Charlie." Kenny said defensively. "The meeting I had with those Japanese investors went into overdrive. Believe me, I was fighting tooth and nail trying to get out of there. The show is being recorded anyway."

"That's not the point. I thought y'all wanted to know how I did it? And I'm collecting on the bet you lost, so don't think I forgot."

Suddenly, the Show came back on, and everyone in the living room was mums as Baby Doll went in. She talked about how 1 *Corinthians* 13 was the main Bible verse she learned from Big Daddy and how she used it to motivate her at times when things got rough. She also talked about *Psalm 23*, and by the end of the show Baby Doll had the audience almost in tears when she explained how she laid in a hospital bed suffering from a bullet wound to the stomach, realizing she would give her life to complete her mission, and how she got out of the Warsaw County Hospital and hadn't looked back since. Oprah made her final remarks, and the show ended.

When the credits stopped rolling, Quameek hit the off button on the remote control as Sweet Charlie leaned back on the sofa smiling broadly.

Kenny was in shock, "Sweet Charlie, don't tell me you shot her!" His eyes were filled with utter bewilderment.

"Don't judge until you understand why," Sweet Charlie said smoothly. "Look at the results it produced."

"What if you would've killed her!?" Kenny's rage was growing by the seconds. "Bullets are not known to act the way you want them to once they leave the barrel of a gun. Imagine if she would've died!?"

"The bullet I fired into her was doctored; I reduced the amount of gun powder in the bullet; made the head a little bigger, so when the bullet hit her, it wouldn't penetrate much, while it got tangled up in her gut. I've done this overseas several times with several diplomats who rigged up fictitious assassination attempts. I'm an expert marksman, remember. Believe me, she was in good hands. I made sure she got to the hospital before a drop of blood touched her living room floor."

Quameek was shaking his head with a smile and said, "Damn, boss, you got some serious issues here, man. You shot this pretty little girl—"

"Listen, Quameek, your job is to watch my back, guard my body, do various errands for me, not to try to psychoanalyze my methods of getting the job down."

"My bad," Quameek said with both hands held up in surrender. "But, I will say, I'm feelin' the results."

"This is madness, Charlie," Kenny was still shaking his head. Baby Doll still had his heart and even he didn't fully know why. "Couldn't you have just sat her down, talked to her, and convinced her to keep her promise, instead of—"

"You know damn well the average person chasing the American dream won't respond to that type of talk. Anybody could see Baby Doll was a good woman at heart, but was caught up in the materialistic world of today. But Big Daddy saw something in her and knew she had the potential to do really great things, and even he knew she had to first get all that poison out of her system before her true inner goodness could shine forth. From what we just saw on that television, he was right.

"The last time I saw Big Daddy at the hospital he told he that he saw himself in her and she in him. In other words, I took it as, he and Baby Doll had similar qualities, and would make their transition from the negative to the positive in similar ways. Then he told me that before he recognized and started utilizing his true inner goodness, he had to hit rock bottom. He specifically said he would have never done the things he did unless he had hit that sho'nuff rock bottom. He put so much emphasis on the fact that he had to hit rock bottom and had even used examples by pointing out some of the famous folks like Barry White, Chuck Barry, Don King, Charles Dutton, and countless others who had to damn near look death square in the eyes before their greatness was able to spring forth. I took it as he was telling me that Baby Doll would change her foul ways only after she hit rock bottom."

"So you felt shooting her would help her get to her rock bottom?" Kenny said sarcastically, refusing to see the rationale in it all, even though he knew there was a lot of truth to what Sweet Charlie was saying.

"Didn't it work?" Sweet Charlie said. "She took Big Daddy's dream to a place where even he couldn't imagine or dream of. Before he died he begged me to look after her, watch her back, and to help her get to that place in her development where her goodness could come out."

"I know he didn't ask you to shoot her," Kenny said and instantly saw Charlie had given him that "of-course-not" look. "If Big Daddy had known you was going to shoot her, he would've stopped you with—"

"If you really want to point the finger, point it at yourself." Charlie saw Kenny's squinted his eyes as if he was confused. "When you had the chance to convince her to stay on track while using all that soft-ass, kill-'em-with-kindness bullshit, you let her slip through your fingers. If you had come through like you were supposed to, I wouldn't have had to result to my humanitarian hitman tactics." He saw Kenny lowered his eyes and decided to mess with his head with his next comment. "At the rate this dialogue is going I might have to ask for a refund, since I reaped nothing from that task you were hired to do."

Kenny was instantly quieted down. Although he was rich, he knew losing money was a sure way to end up broke and back in the poor house if he developed a pattern of losing money. He'd just recently lost two multi-million-dollar investment deals; there was no need to make waves that could interfere with his flow of income, especially considering the fact Sweet Charlie constantly hired him for all sorts of odd jobs. He felt the need to change the topic all together. "How was Big Daddy able to convince a guy like you, with all this money and invaluable skills you got, to get bogged down with an issue like this? I'm sure you could be overseas somewhere getting six-digit paychecks for a few hours of work. I know Big Daddy didn't have enough money to purchase your services."

Sweet Charlie looked at Kenny for a long moment, wondering should he let him know what time it really was. He looked over and saw Quameek was waiting for a response as well. After he realized it couldn't do him any harm now that Big Daddy was dead and his dream was fulfilled, he decided to go with it. "Big Daddy Blue was my father."

Kenny was shocked; his eyes squinted in confusion. "Your biological father?"

"Yeah," Sweet Charlie nodded his head, reflecting back into his past. "I was one of his kids nobody knew about. Most people would've never made the connection, since I favored my mother and had her last name since birth. He and my mother had a falling-out when I was about ten years old, and he stopped coming to the house when she was there; but I will give it to him, he'd always keep in touch. When he went to prison, he used to write me even when I was in the military and had even sent me money from time to time. When I got with the agency, I broke ties with him. I guess those letters and those few dollars he sent meant so much to me that I developed a strong love for him. When I started my new career, we got back together on the super down-low, and he was able to teach me so much." Sweet Charlie stared off into nowhere.

"What's up with those envelopes you had me slipping under her door?" Quameek said, "I been busting brain cells trying to figure out what was in those letters. A few times I was tempted to bust one of them bad boys open and sneak a peek."

Sweet Charlie was instantly reminded of the fact that it was time to let Baby Doll off the hook. "You know something, I'm glad you mentioned that. I got one more drop-off I need you to do." He rose to his feet, went to his desk several yards away, retrieved an envelope, and returned to the sofa. "In each of those letters I had sent her a subtle warning. The letters were also designed to saturate her mind with messages so that when the rock-bottom hit came, she would do the right thing. I used the Bible verse Big Daddy was so fond of and had made her memorize. That way she would know what was happening to her was connected with the promise she made to Big Daddy."

Quameek laughed, "So basically you was fucking with her head to get her to do the right thing." He shook his head at the reality that it worked like a charm. "What did you say in those letters?"

Sweet Charlie pulled the letter out of the envelope. "I need you to deliver this to her house as soon as possible. This'll put her mind at ease and let her know she completed her mission." He handed it to Quameek. "All of the previous letters were an offshoot of these remarks."

Quameek took the letter and read the type-written note that said,

BABY DOLL, CONGRATULATIONS! 1 CORINTHIAN 13,
VERSES 1-13 IS A
SUCCESS! TIME HAS LED YOU TO VICTORY!
ALL DEBTS ARE PAID IN FULL.

THE END

About the Author

Divine G is the real person Colman Domingo portrays in the movie Sing Sing. He was also an executive producer, co-writer, and made a cameo appearance in this Hollywood feature film. John "Divine G" Whitfield is the founder and owner of Divine G Entertainment and a founding member of Rehabilitation Through the Arts (RTA). He is a four-time PEN American Center award winning writer and the winner of the 2008 Tacenda Literary award for best play. Divine G has written over a dozen novels and screenplays, performed in countless plays, appeared in a Hollywood feature film as an extra (Analyze This), hosted his own internet radio show (The Divine G Show), produced, directed and starred in his debut short film (Enigma of Love), worked with Lil Wayne as a supervisory carpenter on his 2013 America's Most Wanted (AMW) tour, and has been quoted by the United Nations in its UN Report of the Special Rapporteur on the right of education of persons in detention (A/HRC/11/8 - 2 April 2009).

Upcoming Novels from Divine G
THE TRIALS AND TRIBULATIONS OF BISHME CARLSON

Under the pseudonym John Whitfield (In bookstores Fall 202?)

The story of Bishme Carlson is one that epitomizes a tale of a man on a noble mission. After accidentally killing his family, Bishme vows to save as many lives as he can, especially young lives from the ravaging onslaught of HIV/AIDS. He pledges to start his own AIDS Prevention Organization, but there are many unresolved matters still haunting and hindering him; the most serious of them all is he's being followed by a stalker, a mysterious man who makes clear that his intentions are malevolent. Receiving his drive, energy and iron will to succeed from a statement his four-year-old daughter bestowed upon him before dying, Bishme confronts the life-threatening trials and tribulations while a tantalizing question looms omnipotently; will he survive and accomplish his mission, or will he lose his life to a heartless foe?

FOLLOW THE SIGNS...

The Sequel To TGONG (In bookstores Fall 202?)

"Follow the Signs, they are everywhere" was the recurring dream world command Rayhiem Jones had been receiving all his life. In this sequel to TGONG, Rayhiem finally discovers the reason he's been experiencing the strange, recurring dreams. He was being groomed for a divine mission to save all life on the planet from a

celestial virus lodged inside a meteorite sent to Earth by the Setphian Deities.

The Ausarian Deities (the Setphian's archrivals) reveals to Rayhiem during one of his mystifying dreams that he must find the two people on the planet who has the cure within their bodies and get them to Phoenix Arizona within 13 days to make a celestial exchange or the entire planet will perish. But, Samuel Griener, the Setphian's General on the planet, and his very powerful and wealthy subordinates have no intentions of allowing Rayhiem to succeed.

www.ingramcontent.com/pod-product-compliance
Lightning Source LLC
Chambersburg PA
CBHW060809030726
47503CB00002B/404